MN

The
Last Taxi
Ride

Also by A. X. Ahmad

The Caretaker

The Last Taxi Ride

A RANJIT SINGH NOVEL

A. X. AHMAD

MINOTAUR BOOKS ❧ NEW YORK

THE LAST TAXI RIDE. Copyright © 2014 by A. X. Ahmad. All rights reserved. Printed in the United States of America. For information, address St. Martin's Press, 175 Fifth Avenue, New York, N.Y. 10010.

www.minotaurbooks.com

Library of Congress Cataloging-in-Publication Data

Ahmad, A. X.
   The last taxi ride : a Ranjit Singh novel / A. X. Ahmad. — First edition.
     pages cm
  ISBN 978-1-250-01686-7 (hardcover)
  ISBN 978-1-250-01685-0 (e-book)
 1. Taxicab drivers—Fiction.   2. East Indians—New York (State)—New York—Fiction.   3. Motion picture actors and actresses—Crimes against—Fiction.
4. Women, East Indian—Crimes against—Fiction.   5. New York (N.Y.)—Fiction.   I. Title.
  PS3601.H573L37 2014
  813'.6—dc23

                                   2014008313

First Edition: June 2014

10 9 8 7 6 5 4 3 2 1

The Last Taxi Ride

Prologue

BOMBAY, 1979

Her daughters were late. They should have been home by now.

Nusrat Begum leaned against the rooftop balustrade of their small, crumbling house and squinted up at the sun: almost four o'clock.

Shabana and Ruksana should have arrived forty-five minutes ago, their shrill voices breaking the silence of the courtyard below.

Nusrat peered into the winding lane leading to the house. An auto-rickshaw went by, then a cluster of women returning from the bazaar. No sign of two twelve-year-olds in blue St. Agnes Convent uniforms, their neatly plaited hair tied into two loops with red ribbons.

Nusrat could go out into the dusty city and look for her daughters, but the thought frightened her. Though she had lived in Bombay for half her life, she only ventured out with her husband; she still obeyed the customs of her hometown, Peshawar, which now lay in Pakistan, on the wrong side of the border.

Her pretty, pale face turned hot with anger. The girls had probably gone to the movies again at the instigation of Shabana, the younger girl. She was dreamy and movie-obsessed, and often convinced Ruksana to take her to faraway cinemas to see old films.

The hot afternoon sun shone down and Nusrat felt her wet, waist-length hair beginning to dry. As was traditional, she had never cut it, and today she had rubbed it with coconut oil, then washed it with well water. She still had to perfume her hair, and the girls' late arrival was disturbing her ritual.

To calm herself, Nusrat retrieved a small charcoal brazier from the corner of the roof and lit it. When the coals became ashy, she added some drops of perfume from a small glass vial, bent her head, and fanned her long hair over the smoking brazier.

As the smoky, musky scent impregnated her hair, Nusrat imagined her husband returning home that evening. Noor Mohammad would kiss her neck, bury his face in her hair, and say, "You smell like home to me."

She knew that the musk of her hair would soothe his homesickness. Noor's family was of noble lineage, and back in Peshawar his family still owned a large *haveli,* a palace. Like many other young men in the 1940s, he had taken the Frontier Mail train to Bombay in search of stardom, and ended up, so many years later, as a badly paid extra for third-rate films.

As the perfume filled her hair, Nusrat felt a sudden rush of sadness. Just last week she had sold the last of her wedding jewelry—a necklace studded with emeralds and two bangles of eighteen-karat gold. All she had left were her small gold earrings, shaped like flowers, but she quickly banished the thought from her mind. What did earthly possessions matter? If it was important for Noor to live in a house, to throw lavish dinner parties, to send the girls to a school run by nuns, so be it.

Hearing shrill voices below, Nusrat looked down into the courtyard and saw the dark heads of her daughters. Their teachers claimed that they couldn't tell the girls apart, but Nusrat found that hard to believe. Even from up here, she could identify Ruksana by her thick hair; Shabana's was thin and lifeless.

Nusrat hurriedly doused the brazier and took the stairs down, her relief eclipsed by anger.

It was Noor's fault that Shabana was so irresponsible: he had taken her to see *Pakeezah,* the story of the doomed courtesan, at least five times. Shabana had memorized the whole film, knew all the lyrics, and could recite Meena Kumari's lines. But what use was that? Ruksana was more practical: she had learned to cook and sew; she, at least, would be able to keep a man happy.

Entering the kitchen, Nusrat saw the fright on Shabana's face, while Ruksana stood shamefaced in the doorway.

"*Aare*, where have you two been?" Nusrat poured some milk for them into a battered saucepan and put it on the stove to heat. She stepped into the center of the room, her hands on her hips. "Well, who is going to answer me?"

The girls looked at each other, but remained silent.

"Are you both deaf? Will a slap loosen your mouths?"

It was finally Shabana who spoke, just as the milk on the stove began to sputter and sizzle. "*Ammi*, it's Ruksana's fault, the nuns made her stay late at school. We missed the bus, we had to walk."

Ruksana's nostrils flared with anger. "You wanted to go to the movies, and you're blaming me? You lying witch!" She reached out and grabbed her sister's shoulder.

Shabana wriggled away and ran across the room, heading toward the stove, with Ruksana right behind her.

"Don't you two start that nonsense—"

Just then Shabana turned and pushed her sister, and Ruksana staggered backward, her elbow hitting the long handle of the saucepan. The pan jerked upward, and the scalding milk flew out, splashing the side of her face. She screamed and fell to the floor, clawing at her eyes, and the smell of seared flesh filled the air.

"*Ya khuda*, what has happened?" As Shabana cowered in the corner, Nusrat crouched over Ruksana, prying the girl's hands from her face. "Can you see? Are your eyes burned?"

Ruksana's eyes were squeezed shut, but then she opened them and looked up. Her eyes were spared, but the boiling milk had left a fist-sized burn on the left side of her face.

Nusrat saw the blistering, purple skin and knew that this would be a permanent mark. She turned her anger on Shabana, who stood stock-still, her eyes wide with horror. "You *bevkoof,* look what you have done! Run to the bazaar and get yogurt and honey. Tell Ramdas I will pay him later!"

While Nusrat waited for Shabana to return, she quickly cut a potato and pressed a thick slice onto Ruksana's cheek; it would cool and soothe the wound.

"Meere jaan," Nusrat said, stroking her daughter's hair, "you will be all right, don't worry. This is all your wicked sister's fault. Oh, how I'm going to punish her."

Ruksana whimpered with pain, but seemed too dazed to complain.

When Shabana came back, sweating and breathless, Nusrat quickly made a poultice out of honey, yogurt, and turmeric and applied it to Ruksana's face. The rest was out of Nusrat's hands; only time would reveal the full extent of the damage.

Seeing the terrified look on Shabana's face only increased Nusrat's venom. "Who will want to marry your sister now? What chance does a scarred girl have, when there are so many pretty ones? If your sister does not get married, I will make sure that you take care of her for the rest of your life!"

Shabana fled into the living room, and Nusrat screamed after her, "And you will not go to the movies anymore! You are punished!"

In the ensuing silence, Ruksana sobbed as the pain set in. Nusrat held her older daughter and looked blindly out at the small courtyard with its flaking plaster walls. She felt a sharp headache coming on, and all her hopes for the night faded away. No doubt Noor would take Shabana's side and say it was an accident. Like most men, Noor was charmed by the girl; all she had to do was pout and furrow her pretty eyebrows, and he did her bidding.

Twelve years old, and Shabana, on the cusp of womanhood, was already going in the wrong direction. She just lay around the house, getting by on her easy charm. Noor must drill some sense into her and put an end to all this movie watching.

Movies just caused girls like Shabana to live in their dreams.

I

THE WOMAN IN WHITE

If I had a palace made of pearls, inlaid with jewels,
Scented with musk, saffron and sandalwood, a sheer
    delight to behold
Seeing this, I might go astray and forget you,
And your name would not enter my mind.

              —Guru Granth Sahib, Siree Raag

Chapter One

August in New York City. The place is a ghost town, thirteen thousand cabs desperately roaming the streets in search of a fare.

Ranjit Singh sees the woman in the white dress waving at him from the other side of Broadway and swerves his yellow cab across a lane of traffic. Horns blare and a bicycle messenger shouts *Asshole!* as he screeches to a stop.

A bare brown arm reaches for the door handle. It clicks open and the cool air-conditioning leaks out, replaced by the smell of hot asphalt, sweat, and the faint, pungent odor of melting bubble gum.

Ranjit watches the woman get into the cab, the same way he watches all his passengers, looking for signs of trouble. Seasoned New Yorkers barely even notice Ranjit's red turban and full beard, but out-of-towners gape at him, reassured only by the hack license posted on the plexiglass partition. The crazies, of course, want to talk and talk.

This woman is different.

One long leg enters the cab, wearing a white wedge-heeled sandal, each toenail painted a perfect crimson. Her crisp white dress reveals smooth brown shoulders, her face is obscured by large oval sunglasses, and her glossy black hair cascades to her shoulders. She piles three crisp white Prada shopping bags on the seat next to her, and they crinkle against her hip.

"Seventy-second and Central Park West, please."

Her voice is low and modulated, but there are Indian undertones to it, as familiar as the voice of a long-forgotten lover.

I know this woman, he thinks, then corrects himself. *That's absurd.*

He nods in acknowledgment and pulls out onto lower Broadway, thinking of the quickest route: right onto Prince, swing over onto West Houston, cut through the Village on Sixth Avenue, and then a straight shot through Midtown to Central Park West. After two long years of driving a cab here, the city's streets are burned into his brain.

They turn and hit a red light. The taxi is caught in the seething, rumbling flow of traffic and Ranjit feels an equivalent disturbance inside himself. The woman in the white dress is looking out of the window, lost in thought, biting down on her plump lower lip.

A memory floods through him. He was still a cadet at the Military Academy in Chandigarh, and on one stifling hot Sunday he wandered into a cinema, bought a ticket, and sank down into a seat, enjoying the air-conditioning.

He'd entered in the middle of a film, a romance, apparently, because the heroine was waiting under a concrete overpass for her lover. Unlike the other Bollywood actresses, with their ample bosoms and pale complexions, she was dark-skinned and slender, with vulnerable, doelike eyes. As she waited, it began to rain, and she shrank back against the concrete, biting down into her lower lip. Transfixed, Ranjit sat through the rest of the movie, then bought another ticket and watched it again.

He was twenty-two then, and the actress on the screen was barely nineteen, the latest discovery by the megaproducer S. K. Nagpal, who had supposedly seen her getting off a bus and said, "See that girl? I will make her into a star."

The woman in his cab must be in her late thirties now: her voice is an octave lower, her slim figure filled out into womanly curves. Ranjit wishes that he could see her eyes, which are hidden behind oversized sunglasses.

The light changes to green, and the taxi nips around a bus, accelerating so hard that the woman in white is pushed back into her seat. She takes off her sunglasses and clutches them, and he can see her face clearly now. There is no mistaking her long-lashed, liquid brown eyes.

Shabana Shah catches him staring and smiles tiredly. "So you've recognized me. If you want an autograph, okay. But I cannot get you a movie role, or introduce your nephew to some producer, okay?"

He laughs. "Sorry to bother you, madam. No autograph needed. It's just that you looked familiar, and I was trying to remember—"

"It's okay. Happens all the time."

Shabana Shah leans her forehead against the window and looks out at the flower district. A man pushing a shopping cart full of purple orchids hurries past, leaving a wet trail behind him.

Ranjit finds himself still talking. "My wife, she was a big fan of yours—"

"Was? Why, what happened? She doesn't like my movies anymore?"

He feels his face flush, and remembers that Shabana's last three movies were all box-office flops. Critics have said that she is too old to play the role of the young, vulnerable lover.

"No, no, that's not what I meant. She's still a fan, I'm sure. It's just that she is in India, and I'm here. We're . . . divorced."

She looks at him with a spark of interest. "Divorced? Is that common for Sikhs?"

"No." He feels the back of his neck burn with shame.

"I'm sorry. I shouldn't have said that. It was stupid, forgive me."

"Oh, there is nothing to forgive."

Changing the topic, she gestures to the postcard he has propped on the dashboard: the Golden Temple in Amritsar, surrounded by the calm waters of the sacred lake.

"So that's where you're from? Amritsar?"

He shakes his head. "No, no . . . I'm from Chandigarh."

There is no way to explain that he used to visit the temple with his mother when he was a child. The postcard is a talisman: when he's stressed out, he concentrates on it and meditates, leaving the fray of Manhattan for the quiet, sacred space of the temple.

The taxi speeds on, slipping through the knot of Columbus Circle, the tall lonely statue of Columbus mirrored in the glass slabs of the Time Warner Center. Turning onto Central Park West, Ranjit feels a stab of sadness that the ride will soon be over.

With Shabana in his cab, he feels something that he hasn't felt in a long time: not just the quick flame of desire, but something weightier, a yearning to be recognized.

New York is full of unmoored women and a moving taxi is a refuge from the harsh reality of the city. Tired or lonely, some of these women hear Ranjit's fluent English and want to talk to him. Most of the time he humorously deflects their advances, but once he gave in.

The day he received his divorce papers, he picked up a tall blond woman at JFK airport, returning from a yoga retreat in India. They talked all the way into the city, and when she invited him up to her sleek Soho loft it seemed natural. After a drink, she simply stepped out of her clothes, and her slim, tanned body aroused him; after sex she fell deeply asleep. Gathering up his clothes to leave, Ranjit was shocked to pass an open bedroom door and see a man sleeping inside. The encounter left him feeling soiled and lonelier than before, and he swore to never pick up another woman.

But Shabana is different, and he can't help sneaking another look. Her black, lustrous hair has been artfully cut and falls in layers to her bare shoulders, almost too heavy to be supported by her slender neck. Her eyelashes have barely any mascara, and her lipstick is a modest shade of pearl, but she wears heavy makeup on her cheeks. She is older now, but he feels as though he has known her, has lain with her through a thousand and one nights, listening to her stories.

There is the sudden blare of horns on Central Park West. Ranjit hits the brake, bringing the taxi to an abrupt stop. A cop car is blocking the road, its lights flashing. Ahead, a long black limo is skewed across the road, a yellow cab with a crumpled fender stopped right behind it. No doubt the limo braked suddenly—livery car drivers drive like shit—but the cabbie always gets blamed.

He turns to face Shabana. "There's been an accident. Sorry for the delay. They'll clear it in a few minutes."

She nods, and peers out of the window.

He is conscious of staring at her. "Again, I'm sorry for the delay. I hope you're not in a hurry?"

She shakes her head. "Nope. I was just doing some shopping."

He gestures at the bags on the backseat. "Prada. Nice store. Nice design, the way that the wooden floor inside curls like a wave."

She looks sharply at him. "You shop at Prada?"

"I've been inside. Not to buy, just to look."

He doesn't say that his thirteen-year-old daughter, Shanti, will be arriving from India in three weeks, to spend a trial year with him. If she likes it, she will stay with him permanently. He needs places to take her that are free but that fit in with the glamorous ideas she has of New York.

"Now that's interesting. A taxi driver who likes Prada." She smiles, showing perfect white teeth, and he feels his heart race.

He wants to keep Shabana smiling and talking, and suddenly remembers his ex-wife returning, flushed and happy, from her shopping expeditions. She used to delight in showing him her purchases.

He gestures at the Prada bags. "So, did you get anything good?"

"You want to see what I bought? Really?"

"Really."

"Oh-kay."

She rummages through her bags and pulls out a pair of leopard-skin spike heels, holding them up for his inspection.

"Very fashionable. How do you walk in them?"

"Practice. And I got this . . ." She pulls out a slinky piece of black fabric, glittering with tiny sequins. "Well?"

"Nice. What is it?"

"It's a cocktail dress. Off the shoulder."

"Nice, but it doesn't go with the shoes."

"You're right about that." She laughs as she leans forward to look at his hack license. "You know a lot about fashion, Mr. . . . Singh."

"Ranjit, please. I don't know anything about fashion, I just notice things. Anyway, you'll look fantastic in that dress."

"You're sweet. How long have you been in America?"

"A few years. I was in Martha's Vineyard before this, working as a landscaper. But then I thought, a place like New York has more opportunities. The cab is just temporary, till I get on my feet. How about you? Are you shooting a movie here?"

She stuffs the dress back into the bag without bothering to refold it, and he realizes that her shopping hasn't given her any pleasure.

"Well, I was working on a film here, but we ran into . . . some difficulties." She smiles bravely. "So I just stayed on here for a while. Mumbai is so hot at this time of the year."

Ranjit remembers reading about the cancellation of her latest film, something to do with financing, and curses himself for asking about it. She's biting down on her lower lip again, and looking distractedly out of the window.

Up ahead, a tow truck is finally moving the damaged limo. He turns the engine back on.

"Miss Shah. Can I say something?"

She looks at him, her eyes dull now. "Of course."

"I'm sure it is a temporary setback. You are a great actress. There is no doubt about that."

"That's sweet of you," she says, but keeps staring at the flashing lights outside.

There seems to be nothing left to say. The line of cars starts moving, and the Sixties speed by. Soon he is at Seventy-second Street, slowing to make the turn at the address she has given him. He stops in front of the Dakota, a massive yellow-brick building that takes up an entire city block. With its elaborate stonework and steeply gabled roofs, it looks as though a European chalet has been dropped down onto the Upper West

Side. It even has a moat, a gap between the sidewalk and the building, surrounded by an ornate iron fence, and is so exclusive that the applications of rock stars and Wall Street moguls are routinely turned down.

"The Dakota. Very nice. You live there?" He gestures at the arched entrance on Seventy-second Street, guarded by a sentry box of tarnished copper. A doorman stands outside it, a tall, elegant figure in a peaked cap and blue blazer.

"Oh, it's a friend's apartment. I'm just borrowing it."

She begins to gather up her bags as they pull to a stop. Through the archway, he can see a dim interior courtyard with a fountain and swaying trees.

"Thank you, *Sardarji*," she says, using the honorific for a Sikh. Leaning forward, she gives him a crisp bill. "Keep the change."

He stares at it. Even with the wait, the fare is just twenty-four dollars. "This is a hundred-dollar bill, you know."

"I know. It was nice talking to you."

Before he can thank her, the doorman flings open the door and reaches for her bags. With a wave, Shabana Shah walks away, the doorman trotting behind her. As her white dress disappears into the building, Ranjit once again feels the disturbance inside himself.

He pushes the crisp bill into his pocket, his mind a jumble of thoughts.

Baarp.

A black livery car has nosed in behind the cab, and its driver is honking and gesturing at Ranjit to move. Its passenger, a short, bald white man, is standing obliviously at the Dakota's entrance, refusing to walk the twenty feet to his car.

Baarp, baarp, baarp.

There is a sharp knock on his window, and Ranjit powers it down. The doorman from the Dakota peers in.

"Move," he says, "you're blocking this entrance."

The doorman has a brown face and an Indian voice: he is a countryman, yet there is no trace of kindness in his voice. Tall and long waisted, he wears his sky-blue blazer and matching trousers like a fashion model, his cap tilted back at a jaunty angle.

"I'm moving, *bhai*," Ranjit says mildly, calling the man "brother."

"Don't *bhai* me. Get this *maderchod* cab out of here."

Motherfucker. The insult is delivered in a crude Punjabi accent.

"Who are you calling a *maderchod*?"

"You heard me. Now get out of here."

Ranjit's vision constricts. *This fucking city.* Abused by passengers, hassled by the cops, cut off by livery car drivers, and now this *chutiya* in a monkey suit, pushing him around. *Enough.*

Ranjit swings the door open and steps out. He is at least a head taller than the doorman, who scuttles backward.

"I'm trying to earn my living, just like you. Why must you disrespect me?"

"This is private property. I'm calling the cops. Got it?" The doorman whips out a cell phone and begins to dial.

Fuck it. The anger is bright red, clouding Ranjit's vision. His fists are clenched, already knowing their targets.

"A rooster can crow, but can it fight?" he mutters.

"Kya bola?" What did you say? The doorman jerks his head up.

"Tum nay mujhe suna." You heard me.

Amazingly, the fright leaves the doorman's face, and he steps forward. "Captain? Captain Singh? Is it you?"

Ranjit stops in mid-stride. The roaring in his ears fades, and once again, it is a hot afternoon and he is standing on the sidewalk outside the Dakota.

"It's me, Captain." There are tears in the man's voice as he advances with open arms. "You don't recognize me? From the Military Academy? It's me."

Who is this crazy bastard? Ranjit peers at him, seeing a chiseled face with a cleft chin. The brutal army haircut has been replaced by long, wavy hair and modish sideburns, and a neatly trimmed mustache now hides the small, effeminate mouth.

"What the hell? Mohan Kumar?"

The two men embrace.

Baarp-baarp-baarp.

The livery car is still standing behind the taxi, and Mohan whirls around, adjusting his cap. "I'll fix this *chutiya*."

He strides up to the short, balding passenger, still waiting by the entry. Saying something about a broken-down cab, Mohan walks the man to the livery car, and it swings quickly out into the street.

Mohan Kumar walks back to Ranjit, grinning and shaking his head.

"That man . . . that was Phil Smith. You know, the band Eruptions, big in the eighties. Now he's a has-been, and a has-been millionaire is the worst kind; they need me to bow and open doors. Captain, damn, it's good to see you. I'm sorry I didn't recognize you at first . . ."

"Jaane do." Forget it. Ranjit puts a hand on Mohan's shoulder. "How long has it been? Twenty years? And I see you again in this city?"

The two men stare at each other for a moment.

"What happened to you, Mohan? You just vanished from the Academy. No good-bye, nothing, you were gone. All these years, I thought you were dead . . ."

Mohan looks away. "It's a long story, Captain. And you? Why are you driving a cab here? I always thought you were going to be a general—"

A young woman with closely cropped hair and a flame-colored dress steps out of the Dakota and looks vaguely in Mohan's direction.

"Oh shit, this is an opera star, from France. Doesn't speak a word of English, and I have to get her to Lincoln Center. Do me a favor and drop her off? I get off at six, come back, and we'll have a drink and catch up, okay?"

"I have a second job, Mohan. I won't be done till late—"

"Doesn't matter, I'll be here. Just ask for me at the entrance." Mohan grasps Ranjit's hand and presses hard. "This is fate. I'll see you, Captain."

The opera star gets into Ranjit's cab, and he heads west down Seventy-second Street, his mind a whirl.

First Shabana Shah, then Mohan, both in one day. What are the chances? There are times when he's picked up the same passenger twice in one day, and what are the odds of that, with eight million people and thirteen thousand cabs?

On autopilot, he turns down West End Avenue to Lincoln Center, remembering that the entrance for artistes is on Sixty-fifth Street. When they get there, the French opera singer pays him slowly, leaving no tip.

It is almost three in the afternoon as Ranjit drives slowly down Columbus into the thickening crowd of Midtown, right on the cusp of rush hour. The hundred from Shabana is fantastic, but he still needs to make up for the slow week. Passengers think that cabbies make money sitting in traffic, but the meter actually runs slower when he's going at less than six miles an hour. The best trip is a long, traffic-free stretch, when the meter clicks every fifth of a mile.

Stopping for a light, he thinks of Mohan Kumar back at the Cadet Academy. A dandy even then, his khaki uniform immaculate. Always talking loudly and confidently, but with uncertainty in his eyes, searching to see whether he was being taken seriously. Women seemed to be drawn in by his vulnerability, which lay just below the surface, like a badly healed wound.

He was never without a girlfriend, always swearing that he'd met the woman of his dreams—until the next one came along, with ruby-red lips or a bigger bosom. The last woman he was involved with was an officer's wife, and she had begun to talk about leaving her husband. Had Mohan been frightened by the seriousness of the situation and run away?

Ranjit is so lost in his thoughts that he barely sees the fat man stepping off the curb, arm raised high.

Slamming on the brakes, Ranjit screeches to a stop. The fat man peers indignantly through the window, sweat stains marking the armpits of his cheap gray suit.

"Jeez! Were you going to run me over? JFK Airport, okay?"

Ranjit groans to himself. His wish for a long ride has been answered, but after he gets to JFK, he'll have to spend hours in the taxi queue, waiting for a fare back into the city.

"I'm sorry, sir, I was just going off duty."

"What the fuck? Your sign is lit. You *have to* take me to the airport."

"I said I'm sorry." Ranjit turns his medallion light off, then activates the OFF DUTY sign.

"Hey! I'll report you to the TLC! The mayor is cracking down on people like you."

"You do that."

Ranjit puts the cab into drive and speeds away, conscious that all it takes is one phone call, and he'll be up before the Taxi and Limousine Commission. But the man hasn't taken down his hack license number, and there are hundreds of Sikhs driving cabs in the city.

Suddenly exhausted, he decides to turn in the cab and take a breather before his second job. Driving across town to the cab depot in Long Island City, he can't help thinking about what Mohan had said. Yes, he should have been a general by now, living with his family in a cantonment bungalow in India. But here he is in America, driving double shifts in this cab and renting a one-room apartment in Jackson Heights. He thinks about the chain of events that landed him here: his attempt to start a new life on Martha's Vineyard, his affair with Anna Neals, the Senator's wife, and her unnecessary death. After that his marriage collapsed, and Preetam went back to India, taking their daughter, Shanti. He followed them back there, to persuade Preetam to stay with him, but she wouldn't listen to him, and it was too dangerous for him to remain in India, so he came here, to New York, and, like so many others, stumbled into this job. And while he punished himself, working day and night, saving every scrap of money, Preetam met a rich businessman and filed for divorce.

For the past two years, his job has been his drug, his own will subsumed by the darting needs of others, and his only company has been the other cabdrivers. Like him, these men are trying to rebuild their lives—back home they were landowners, doctors, and engineers—and, like him, they do not want to talk about the past.

Now Shabana Shah has sliced through the numb cocoon Ranjit has so carefully created. As he drives across the Queensboro Bridge, he feels again the sharp ache hidden inside himself, and, unbidden, a scrap of prayer drifts into his mind:

> *Meditate and listen to the name of the Lord, and pass it on*
> *to everyone.*
> *In this way, the filth of lifetimes shall be removed, and*
> *egotistical pride shall vanish from your mind.*
> *Sexual desire and anger shall not seduce you,*
> *And the dog of greed shall depart.*

The Uptown Cab Company is on Jackson Avenue, flanked by a graffiti-covered warehouse and a vacant lot. Its dirty white cinder-block garage is fronted by a row of antiquated gas pumps and an asphalt parking lot. The shift is changing, and the lot is packed with rows of yellow cabs, their drivers yelling greetings to each other.

Finding a parking space, Ranjit carefully puts his postcard of the Golden Temple into his battered black gym bag, which holds his cab-driver kit: a bottle of water, aspirin, a change of clothes for his night job, and a tire iron, in case a passenger tries to mug him. Shouldering the bag, he takes his trip sheet and his meter into the garage, and joins a line of men ending their shifts. Having started at three or four A.M., they all look exhausted, and the air is thick with body odor.

Ali Khan spots Ranjit and waddles over, his bulldog-like face creasing into a smile. His girth and brightly colored Hawaiian shirts hide his shrewd intelligence; a labor organizer, he is highly respected by the other cabdrivers. Ever since Ranjit helped get rid of some street hoodlums who were bothering Ali's teenage daughters, he's been a loyal friend.

"*Aare*, Ranjit, time for some food? They have *biriyani* today at Karachi Kabob. They say it's *biriyani*, but they use food coloring in the rice, not saffron, and the meat is more horse than goat. But still . . ."

Ranjit smiles. Ali always complains about the food at Karachi Kabob, the small Pakistani greasy spoon around the corner, but then eats heartily.

"Not today, *bhai*. I have to go to my other job."

"You work too much. You're a Sikh, not a Jamaican. All this driving will kill your back, destroy your knees. What you need is a wife, some nice big Punjabi woman to make sure you come home."

Ranjit inches toward the front of the line. "You're married, and I don't see you hurrying home to Naazia."

"Aare, mera bath chor do." Don't talk about me. "I have been married for thirty-three years."

Ranjit reaches the cashier's booth and hands the meter and trip sheet through the small opening in the chicken wire to old Jacobo.

"How did it go today, Taliban?" Jacobo smiles his crooked, gap-toothed smile.

He's one of the co-owners of the cab company, of indeterminate Eastern European heritage, and claims that his advanced age exempts him from all political correctness.

"Tough out there, Mr. Jacobo. I don't know where the customers have gone."

"You ever hear of the Hamptons, Taliban? Well, don't feel too bad. King Kong over there"—Jacobo gestures at a Nigerian driver—"made only twenty bucks today. But we all know that he scares customers away."

Jacobo bends his head and makes some quick calculations. After paying one hundred and ten dollars' rent on the cab and fifty-three for gas, Ranjit would have made only eighty-seven dollars if it wasn't for Shabana's generous tip. For the millionth time, Ranjit curses this job.

He heads out, waving at Ali Khan. "I'll see you later, *bhai*. Don't eat too much *biriyani*. You'll spoil your appetite for Naazia *Bhabi*'s cooking."

As he's walking away, one of the Mexican cleaners runs up to him. "Hey! I found this in your cab." The man smirks as he hands over a wad of silky fabric, covered with sequins. "Getting some action in your cab, huh?"

Shabana's dress from Prada. "One of my customers must have dropped it—"

"Yeah, right." The man makes a thrusting gesture with his hips, then runs back into the garage.

Embarrassed, Ranjit walks away quickly. Slowing down after a few blocks, he lifts the dress to his nose. Shabana must have tried it on, because he inhales her faint perfume, sandalwood and jasmine, and something muskier, the scent of her own body.

When he meets Mohan at the Dakota this evening, he'll return the dress to Shabana, and maybe she will even invite him in. He imagines himself making her laugh again, seeing her sweep away the thick fall of hair from her high forehead . . .

Stuffing the dress into his gym bag, he takes the M train into Midtown Manhattan. He finds a clean Starbucks bathroom and changes into the uniform for his next job: a black shirt with epaulettes, black cargo pants, and knee-high lace-up boots.

Looking at himself in the mirror, he sees that his shoulders are slumped over from the day's driving, and he is developing a belly—too much rice at Karachi Kabob. He stands straighter, feeling the pain shooting through his stiff back. He has to look professional; who knows, this job could even turn into a full-time gig. With Shanti coming to stay with him, he can't be driving a cab all day and night.

He emerges from the bathroom and orders a cup of Earl Grey tea. The young woman behind the counter smiles at him warmly, and he can't understand why, but then he catches a glimpse of himself in the window. In his crisp black uniform, he looks like a soldier, not a worn-out cabdriver. For a second he feels like his former self, then sees that the three gold stars on his shoulders are missing.

Don't think about all that now. He heads down the street, sipping his tea, but it tastes like dishwater, and he throws it into a trash can and hurries down the street. There is a huge shipment coming in tonight, and he can't be late.

Chapter Two

BOMBAY, 1989

Shabana began to pluck out her hair the day after her father died.

She had been in the cancer ward all morning with Noor Mohammad, but when he fell asleep, she rushed home to watch *Sasuraal,* her favorite soap opera, about a young bride going to live in her in-laws' house. At twenty-two, lacking the money to be married to a suitable boy, she worked as a salesgirl in a sari shop, and the television was her one means of escape.

Their old black-and-white had been replaced a few years ago by a Japanese color set, one of Noor Mohammad's extravagant purchases. After years of socialist austerity, middle-class people were beginning to buy things; there was even talk that the government would open up India to the outside world. The new soap operas were a harbinger of this future, colored in garish pinks and violets, full of drama and possibility.

It was Ruksana who returned from the hospital, a few hours later, with the news of their father's death. Shabana, so caught up in her fantasy world, could not comprehend what her sister was saying. Reality only sank in when she saw her father lying on a gurney in the hospital, his handsome face sunken in, his mouth reduced to a thin slash.

Shabana did not cry then, nor at the burial, the next day at dawn. As the news spread of Noor's death, the house filled with anxious creditors, and Shabana retreated to the living room and switched on the television, but even it could not drown out the harsh voices of the men. Closing her eyes, she pulled out a strand of hair, and the shock of the pain distracted her. She began to do it in secret, finally finding a way to mourn her father.

It was a few weeks before Nusrat Begum discovered the strands of hair, neatly balled up and hidden at the bottom of the garbage pail in the courtyard. She knew immediately what was going on—she herself came from a family of hair pullers, women whose sharp, hidden anxiety was expressed by their thinning hair and eyes without brows.

With the hair in her hand, she confronted Shabana. "You must stop this at once. A woman cannot catch a man if she is as bald as an egg."

"Yes, *Ammi*," Shabana said quietly, but she continued her secret practice, knowing that her mother's talk of marriage was just pure bluster. With Noor gone and large amounts of money owed, she and her sister would never find husbands.

They moved from their house into a small, cramped apartment out in Andheri. While Shabana scurried home after her day's work at the neighborhood sari shop, Ruksana worked late. She had found a position as an accountant's apprentice, halfway across the city, and spent hours commuting on the belching city buses. She returned late one night, her face red with excitement, and beckoned Shabana into the bedroom they shared. There she wordlessly pressed a business card into her sister's palm.

It was of thick ivory cardboard, and the lettering was engraved:

S. K. Nagpal
Executive Producer, SKN Films
Film City, Goregaon (East), Bombay

"I met him while waiting for a bus," Ruksana gushed, losing her usual composure. "He said that they're looking for fresh faces. He's going to give me a screen test on Friday."

"*You?*" Shabana stared at her sister. "What do *you* know about acting? I was the one who got all the leads in the school plays. You can't act to save your life."

"So what? If you can do it, how hard can it be? You'll show me how, won't you?"

"No." Shabana pouted and her lower lip quivered. "No, I will not."

"Shabbu, please. I need your help. And listen, if I get a part, I'll ask S.K. to make sure you get one, too, okay?"

"Promise?"

"I promise. Now, please help me—"

"What are you girls going *phus-phus* about?" Nusrat entered the room and took the card from Shabana's hand.

Reading it, her face darkened. Despite her years inside the house, she was no fool. She knew that the studio producers—with their flashy silk shirts, their bungalows in Bandra, and their Mercedes—preyed on young girls who wanted to break into the movie business.

"No," Nusrat said. "No daughter of mine will become a whore."

Ruksana stepped forward. "But *Ammi*, it's just a screen test. This is a chance to earn some real money. You know we're just getting by, and—"

"No."

"Our father was in the movies, and you never complained about that—"

"That was different. He was a man, and you are a woman. My decision is final, and you will obey me."

Nusrat stormed out of the room and the girls heard a clang as she threw the card into the garbage pail.

Ruksana hung her head and was quiet, but as soon as Nusrat was out of sight, she dug through the garbage and retrieved the card. Holding it in her hand, she returned to the bedroom.

"I found the card, under a huge ball of your hair. I thought you stopped doing it?"

"I . . . I try not to." Shabana's face turned red. "But sometimes I just have to."

"Well, don't." Ruksana hid the card under her pillow. "Now, will you please show me what to do for the audition?"

Shabana flicked the hair from her eyes and squared her shoulders. "The first thing is how to walk. Shoulders back, hips loose, okay?"

Ruksana strutted from one end of the room to the other, and her sister burst into laughter.

"Ruki, you want to look sexy, but not cheap, okay? Right now you look like a girl from Grant Road."

Holding her sister's hips, Shabana showed her how to walk, and after that, how to mold her face into expressions of surprise, love, and fear. The two of them were giggling and enjoying themselves, but then Ruki grew solemn.

Sitting down in front of the dressing table mirror, she examined her left cheek, the dull red scar hidden under skin-colored foundation makeup.

"How do I look? Can you see it?"

Shabana's face reddened. "Ruki, it's not even noticeable. Why do you go on and on about it?"

"Just tell me, honestly, am I hideous?"

"You look fine. You look beautiful. Besides, all movie stars wear makeup when they act. Just don't use so much foundation."

Ruksana seemed unconvinced, and continued to stare at herself in the mirror, examining her face from different angles.

That Friday, Ruksana proposed a trip to pray at the mosque at Hajji Ali, wore a faded *salwar kameez,* and took Shabana with her. As soon as they were out of their neighborhood, Ruksana unzipped her handbag and showed her sister a pink silk sari hidden within it.

"We're going to Film City. That stupid old woman doesn't know anything."

"But Ruki, you promised *Ammi* that—"

"Stop being so naive. You work for no commission in a sari shop, and that bastard accountant makes me work late and tries to feel me up. We can live our whole lives like this and never pay our father's debts back. Do you want to get married or not?"

Shabana was silent then, and they stopped by a friend's house so that Ruksana could change her clothes. One train and two buses took them to the high metal gates of Film City, where a guard stared at Ruksana's luminescent pink sari, studied S. K. Nagpal's card, then smiled wearily and let them in, telling them to go to the studios by the lake.

Ruksana walked in front, trailing perfume, and Shabana lagged behind, carrying her sister's bag. She had dressed for the grime and crowds of the shrine at Hajji Ali, and was wearing her faded blue *salwar kameez* and sandals with a torn strap; her hair was pulled back into a ponytail, her eyes hidden behind the thick black-framed glasses she wore only while at home.

They walked down gravel paths, past empty lots of scraggly brown grass, past groups of men lugging antiquated lights and metal reflectors. They saw a crowd of extras sitting under a tree, clad in the bright turbans of Rajput warriors, and then an entire village made out of mud and thatch. Shabana felt disappointed: she had expected something magical, but it all seemed old, dusty, and patently fake.

The movie studios by the lake turned out to be giant, blank sheds faced with panels of dirty concrete, and Shabana's disappointment intensified. Inside, the shed was very hot and stuffy, and a line of extras—young women dressed as scantily clad *nautch* dancers—watched enviously as S. K. Nagpal rose from his director's chair to greet them. He wore his trademark red shirt with a wide, droopy collar, tight black pants, and boots with built-up heels; without them, he would have been very short. He had small, even features and meticulously styled long hair that fell over his collar.

The screen test took place in a sweltering soundproof room at the back, and S.K. offered them ice-cold bottles of Campa Cola while the camera was set up. Shabana held both bottles while her sister turned and surreptitiously applied more foundation makeup to her scarred cheek.

"Now . . ." S.K.'s voice was low and encouraging as he put his hands on Ruksana's shoulders. "This is a small part only. You are waiting for your lover under an overpass in Bombay, okay? It is raining, it's getting later and later, and you are getting scared. Okay?"

Ruksana nodded, and walked to the center of the stage. The cameraman signaled his readiness, and Shabana watched as her sister overacted, wringing her hands and pacing back and forth, pausing to glance dramatically into the distance. S.K. did not seem to mind: he was staring intently at the patterns of light and dark on his small screen.

Watching him watching her sister, Shabana felt a strange electricity course through her body. The camera, she realized, did not simply capture the dull reality in front of it, but *transformed* it in some mysterious way.

The screen test was over very quickly, and the arc lights were turned off. While the film stock was being developed into what S.K. called "rushes," Shabana couldn't resist talking to him.

"When you look through the camera, what are you searching for?"

S.K. regarded her from under artfully shaped eyebrows. He was also wearing clear nail polish, Shabana realized.

"You see . . ." He gestured at the studio. ". . . we live in a three-dimensional world, but the camera, it flattens everything. It sees only light and shadow; it brings out patterns that you and I cannot see with our naked eyes. It loves some people, and not others. It doesn't care what they look like, or how they act. It magnifies their essence. Do you understand?"

"I do." Wanting to prolong the conversation, she changed the topic. "Isn't this the studio where Meena Kumari filmed *Pakeezah*?"

"Yes, correct. You are well informed, young lady."

"Is it true that she was very sick and did all her scenes lying down? They used a body double for all the dance scenes?"

"Yes, yes, that is true. I was just a young assistant in those days, but I was there. It was heartbreaking to see her dying as she acted her heart out."

Ruksana cast an irritated look at her sister, and Shabana shrunk back, but S.K. continued the conversation. They discussed how Meena Kumari turned into an alcoholic and had affairs with much younger men, and S. K. Nagpal smiled and said, "You are young, but you know a lot about film."

Just then the cameraman came back and said that they were all set. The trio trooped into the darkened screening room, and both sisters gasped when Ruksana's face suddenly loomed on the screen.

At first glance she looked beautiful: the camera caught the tension in her slim physique and magnified her dark eyes, but there was something wrong about the way the light caught her cheeks: they seemed flat and shiny, like plastic.

S.K. turned to Ruksana. "You are gorgeous, my dear, but perhaps a little bit too much foundation, *hanh*? Remember, in this role, you must look young, innocent. Shall we try it without makeup?"

Ruksana sat bolt upright and her voice quivered. "I . . . I don't think I fit this part. Thank you for considering me." She got up and swung her bag onto her shoulder. "Come on, Shabana."

"*Aare*. What is wrong?" S.K. looked shocked.

"Sorry, she gets like this." Shabana began following her sister out of the room. "So sorry."

"Wait." S.K. stood up. "You. Shabana. Why don't you try out for this role?"

"Me?" Shabana ran her palms over the front of her faded blue *salwar kameez*. "Wearing this?"

"Yes. Why not? Just take off your glasses."

Shabana gestured to her sister's departing back. "What about her?"

S.K. shrugged. "She is a big girl, she chose to leave. Surely you can make your own decisions? Or are the two of you bound at the hip?" He looked down at his watch. "I don't have much time. I have to start shooting in twenty minutes."

"No, we're not *bound at the hip*." Shabana hesitated. "Okay, I'll do it."

S.K. smiled. "That's more like it."

She quickly took off her glasses, slipped the rubber band off her ponytail, and shook out her hair. "What do you want me to do?"

"Hmmm." S.K. paused. "You know that scene in *Pakeezah* where Meena has finished dancing in front of the men, and she is alone? Do that one."

"Okay, I can try."

Ruksana was nowhere in sight when Shabana walked in front of the cameras. The arc lights snapped on with a dazzling glare.

Shabana panicked when she saw the camera's hungry eye staring at her, and stood frozen to the spot, breathing jerkily.

"Pretend you're Meena Kumari." S.K.'s voice came from beyond the lights. "You're exhausted. You just finished dancing in front of men who want to debase you. They threw money at you while you danced. How do you feel?"

Shabana closed her eyes. She heard music in her head, felt the thump of her heels as she danced, the silence when she stopped. She felt the hot breath of the men as they leered at her, felt their eyes boring into her.

She opened her eyes, and the camera faded away. She was Meena Kumari, in all her pain, both the actress and the character she played, but that didn't seem to have enough power, so Shabana dug deep into a well of dark emotions: she saw again the pan fly up, heard Ruksana scream as the scalding milk burned her face.

As the tears of shame gathered in Shabana's eyes, she began to move, to walk and talk and gesture.

S.K. had heard of girls like this, soft, dreamy girls who stepped in front of the camera and projected emotions so large and so pure that it was breathtaking. Like a prism, the camera took the plain white light of Shabana's essence and projected it into a rainbow.

She could not see S. K. Nagpal, standing in the darkness beside the cameraman, but his eyes never left her.

Chapter Three

It is almost six by the time Ranjit walks down West Twenty-ninth Street, and the sun is lower, throwing this block into deep shadow. Midtown is being remade with tall condos and boutique hotels, but somehow this stretch of small businesses has managed to survive: wholesalers of knockoff handbags, costume jewelry, and artificial flowers, all shuttered now, the street taking on a silent, pensive air.

He heads to the three-story yellow-brick walk-up in the middle of the block, a large tin sign hanging over the metal security door. It says NATARAJ IMPORTS in blue letters, and below it in gold is painted the classic pose of the Nataraj: the Lord Shiva dancing within a circle of flames, his left leg raised, his right foot pressed down on a fanged demon. Shiva is dancing to destroy the corrupt world, so that it can be re-created from the ruins of the old.

As a Sikh, Ranjit does not believe in the Hindu gods, but today Shiva seems to speak directly to him, and he feels a stifled excitement when he thinks of returning Shabana's dress. He presses a buzzer set beside the door and instantly the blank eye of a security camera swivels to scrutinize him.

When the door clicks open, he steps into a small tiled vestibule and waits in front of a second locked door, the cloying smell of human hair filling his nostrils. Hair is the sole business of Nataraj Imports, originally bought from China and Thailand, but now sourced exclusively from India.

Used in extensions and weaves in salons, human hair has become a multimillion-dollar business, almost as valuable as gold, and attracts the same kind of predators. At first the thieves broke into hair salons, leaving behind cash and taking only premium-quality hair; now they have begun to burgle the wholesalers, deactivating alarms and cutting through security doors. It is only a matter of time before they try to hijack a delivery, and that is where Ranjit comes in. Twice a week he stands guard as a van arrives from the airport loaded with cartons of hair. All he has is his intimidating uniform and a polycarbonate nightstick, and if the thieves have guns, there isn't much he will be able to do. Still, the job pays a lot more than driving a cab, and Ranjit is hoping that Jay Patel, the owner of Nataraj Imports, will soon hire him full time.

The second door opens, and Kikiben glances up at him, stifling a yawn with her tiny hand. She is the sole full-time employee at Nataraj, packaging and pricing the skeins of hair. Barely five feet tall, she's barefoot, and dressed as usual in a shapeless *salwar kameez*, her own graying hair wound into a long braid hanging down her back.

"Hello, Ranjit. They called to say the shipment is on its way. Can't talk now, I'm rushing a custom order to some West Coast movie star, but come and talk to me later, okay? I want to hear about your taxi adventures. Oh, and Patel Sahib is coming tonight."

"Patel's coming? Why? Something wrong?"

"Oh, you know how he is. Likes to keep an eye on things." Kikiben's voice drops to a conspiratorial whisper. "The shipment tonight is valued at two and a half million—I saw it on the invoices. Can you believe it? Well, I better get back to work . . ."

Kikiben runs up the creaking stairs to the second floor, and Ranjit heads through a door into the loading bay, his footsteps echoing on the concrete floor. One side is piled high with boxes of low-quality "comb-waste" hair for reprocessing. The rest of the space will house tonight's shipment: thirty cartons of prime Indian hair that has been acid-stripped and repigmented in Tunisia and then processed in Italy.

If its wholesale value is two and a half million, its street value could be three times that. No wonder Jay Patel is showing up tonight. He's one of the richest Indian businessmen in the city, and he keeps a close eye on the apartment buildings, yoga studios, and restaurants that he owns. Patel has a murky past—there are rumors that he started out in the Mumbai underworld—but Ranjit tries not to think about that. He needs this job too badly, and as long as he isn't asked to do anything illegal . . .

At the far end of the dock, he squats and tests the heavy rolling shutters. They are securely locked, and he feels better.

Just then there is the screech of brakes outside, and Ranjit knows that Jay Patel has arrived, driving his latest sharklike silver BMW.

Soon Patel Sahib comes through the door clutching a silver laptop, his shaved head gleaming in the dim light. Despite his years in America, Patel still moves with the characteristic slouch of the bazaar trader, stomach stuck out, dragging each foot so that his leather sandals slap against the floor. He is dressed, as always, in a simple white shirt and pants, his wrists bare except for some frayed red strings, amulets from a holy man's shrine in Rajasthan. He practices yoga for three hours each morning, and despite his ungainly walk, there is a sinewy, hard quality to his body.

"Ah, *Sardarji. Sab theek hai?*" Everything all right?

"Yes, sir. Kiki said the shipment is on its way."

"Good, good." Patel's dark, hawklike eyes rove across the loading dock. "Listen, store the boxes here, as usual. There are also five . . . special boxes. The driver knows. Bring those up to my office, okay?"

"No problem, sir."

"Good, good." Patel tries to look calm as he wipes beads of sweat from his bald pate, then climbs the stairs to his small third-floor office.

Ranjit has seen the same look of stifled anxiety on the faces of his commanding officers before a battle. Well, if the shipment is indeed worth two and a half million, Patel indeed has a reason to be stressed.

Ranjit unlocks the rolling door and pushes it upward, peering out into the narrow alley that runs to Twenty-ninth Street. A far-off street-light casts a slice of light that dies halfway down the alley, and he swings down into the darkness, gripping his nightstick tightly. He walks the length of the alley, inhaling the stench he has come to associate with New York: asphalt, impregnated with urine and old garbage.

There is no one there, not even the homeless people he has to occasionally rouse. Walking out onto Twenty-ninth Street, he feels a blast of hot air and hears the *clack-clack* of loose manhole covers as a car careens down the street, then vanishes into the distance. He looks for anyone loitering in a doorway or sitting in the rows of parked cars, but the street is empty.

Standing at the mouth of the alley, he relaxes a little and allows his mind to drift: he sees Shabana Shah in the back of his cab, smiling as she holds up the sparkling black dress for approval. What would it feel like to bury his face in her neck and inhale the scent of her thick hair?

Just then an engine growls and a van appears, white in the gloom of the street. Ranjit steps out into the street and waves his arms, indicating the alley, and the van headlights blink back an acknowledgment.

It slows to a crawl, and then backs into the narrow alley. As the driver unloads, Ranjit stands guard at the mouth of the alley, the nightstick in his hand. Used effectively, it can shatter a limb with one blow, but a handgun would make him feel a lot better.

Behind him he hears the rear doors of the van open, the grunting of the driver as he swiftly unloads the boxes. Despite the volume of cardboard cartons, the hair weighs very little, and Ranjit knows that the driver will soon be done.

Minutes later, the van doors slam shut, and it edges out of the alley. Ranjit glimpses the driver's sweaty face, and then the van is gone, gunning down the street for the West Side Highway.

Returning to the loading dock, Ranjit climbs back inside, pulls down the shutter, and locks it. He sees familiar pale cardboard boxes stacked in rows, all stamped in red with a crude Nataraj logo. Five smaller boxes are set aside, of a darker cardboard, with a different stamp that resembles a small house. They are as light as the other boxes, and he wonders if they contain a special type of hair—sometimes movie stars and celebs will have custom lengths and colors made up for them.

Gathering up two boxes, he climbs the stairs, passing the room where Kikiben works, to Jay Patel's tiny office on the third floor. Patel is sitting behind a battered metal desk, peering into the slim laptop that he takes with him wherever he goes. The room is almost bare except for three old plastic phones and a calendar hanging on the wall illustrated with a picture of the elephant god Ganesh.

"There," Patel says, pointing to a corner, and Ranjit brings the rest of the boxes up in one more trip.

When he is done, he is gasping for air, and curses himself. In the old days, he wouldn't even have broken a sweat.

Patel clicks his laptop shut and gestures to a plastic folding chair. "Sit, *Sardarji*. I've been meaning to talk to you about something."

"Yes, sir." Ranjit is eager to return to the Dakota, but maybe Patel is about to offer him a regular job.

There is a spark in Patel's eyes as he leans forward. "Tell me, *Sardarji,* how do you feel about this hair business?"

"What do you mean, sir?"

"You know that the hair comes from temples in South India, right? Women make requests of the gods, and if they are granted, they sacrifice their hair. The temples conduct hair auctions, and these days, they are making so much money that they don't know what to do with it."

Ranjit hesitates, and then decides to speak his mind. "There seems to be something wrong with that. Something immoral."

Patel chuckles. "You Sikhs are blunt, aren't you? But I do agree with you. For centuries the West has colonized us, taken our diamonds and minerals. Now they want our hair. But you know what I say?

"Let them wear our hair and pretend it is theirs. It is all part of their dream existence. They make nothing here anymore. We make the clothes on their backs. They need help, they call a number, and we answer it. All they sell is dreams, big colorful dreams, and they've been doing it for so long that they've forgotten what reality is. The West is getting weaker, and soon it will be our turn."

He stops abruptly, as though embarrassed. "*Aare,* here I go again. Just the musings of an old man. Pay no attention . . . Anyway, I wanted to tell you that we are going to be getting more shipments soon, four, five nights a week. Can you work every night? And if it goes well, maybe I can hire you full time, *hanh*? Much better than driving that *ratfatiya* taxi of yours."

"Yes, sir, of course. And full time would be very good for me. But there is one thing . . ." He hesitates, and Patel gestures impatiently. "If we do get hit, my nightstick is going to be useless. I would feel better with a sidearm."

"*Hanh.* But if I apply for a firearms license for you, they'll do a background check. You're sure there is no hanky-panky in your past?"

"No, sir." Ranjit thinks about what happened in the Vineyard, and how his client, the Senator, had arranged to have all traces of it wiped away.

"Good, good. So you come back tomorrow night." Patel opens his laptop in a gesture of dismissal.

Ranjit heads down the stairs, stopping at Kikiben's large, windowless room. Its green linoleum floor is heaped with skeins of hair neatly packaged in plastic, complete with labels that say WAVY SPANISH or PURE EUROPEAN STRAIGHT. Kiki sits cross-legged in one corner, combing out a swatch of hair by running it through a bed of nails.

"Come, Ranjit. Sit, *na*? Let's talk. I've been alone in here all day."

"I'll stay a minute. Have to go and meet a friend." Ranjit leans against the door frame.

"What, a hot date? Who is it? Tell me! Someone you met in your cab?"

"No, no, just an old classmate from India. But guess who was in my taxi today. Someone famous."

Kikiben's pinched face looks up expectantly. "Tom Cruise? George Clooney? I hear that Halle Berry is shooting in town . . ."

"No, a *desi* movie star. Shabana Shah. Remember her, in *Amerika Ke Kahanie*?"

"*Hanh, hanh,* of course. So beautiful, she was, in the old movies. But the last three, four, all flops. Did you get her autograph? What is she doing here?"

"Shooting a film, she said, but it was canceled. And no, I didn't get her autograph, she seemed preoccupied." A thought strikes him. "Is she married?"

"Shabana Shah." Kikiben closes her eyes as she thinks; Ranjit knows that she has a photographic memory and reads all the fan magazines. "No, not married. People say that S. K. Nagpal, the producer, was her lover. Seduced her when she was nineteen. But he's dead now. She never married, no kids, poor thing. She must be, what, forty? She shouldn't have continued doing those young roles, she can't compete with these young, shiny actresses."

"Shabana's still beautiful," Ranjit says stubbornly, but he knows that what Kikiben says is true. The hit films these days have sleek, fair-skinned actresses like Bipasha Basu and Karishma Kapoor, who flaunt their taut, aerobicized bodies. Shabana's dusky looks and subtle acting have no place in the new world of Indian film.

"*Aare,* looks like you have a crush on her." Kikiben giggles, her shrewd eyes lighting up with pleasure. "You're turning red, like a schoolboy."

"Got to go. And put in a good word for me, okay? With Shanti coming and all, I need a full-time job. I can't be roaming the streets all day and night in my cab."

Kikiben starts combing the hair in front of her. "Of course, of course. But listen, Ranjit. If you want to work here full time, you must know one thing . . ."

He is turning to go, but stops.

"If you work for Patel Sahib, *you work for him*. He pays well, yes, but you have to obey everything he says. And you're . . . different. You're not used to being ordered around. Think about it."

"Sure, sure. Till tomorrow, right?"

He leaves, wondering if Kikiben is alluding to Patel's past. Surely all those rumors are exaggerated: that he started out in Don Hajji Mustafa's gang, that he once stood by calmly as an informant's nose and ears were cut off. That even now, Patel's business ventures are financed through hidden channels leading deep into Mumbai's underworld.

The guy is just a shrewd businessman. He does *yoga* every day, for God's sake.

Putting all this out of his mind, Ranjit rushes to the train, the possibility of seeing Shabana again making him light-headed. As the B train rockets uptown, he takes out her dress, raises the silky fabric to his nose, and smells again the alluring mix of sandalwood and jasmine.

A Hispanic woman sitting across from Ranjit notices him, gives a barely perceptible shake of her head, then looks away. It is a New York gesture, one of disgust, followed by quick dismissal. *Weird. Whatever.*

Ranjit hurriedly puts the dress away and zips up his bag.

Chapter Four

It is past ten at night when Ranjit walks up to the arched entrance of the Dakota. A white-haired doorman peers at him suspiciously, taking in his black uniform and turban.

"I'm here to see the other doorman, the Indian guy, Mohan. Is he around?"

"Mo-han?" The man relaxes a little. "I'll call him. You better go through the archway, wait back there."

Heading through the arch, Ranjit finds himself at a locked gate leading into the courtyard, and the sounds of the street fade away, replaced by the splashing of water and the rustling of trees. Hundreds of lit windows look down into the courtyard, and someone up there is playing the piano, a slow classical piece that makes Ranjit's heart swell with emotion. What would it be like to live in a place like this, with a view of trees and sky?

Lost in his thoughts, he doesn't see Mohan cross the courtyard and unlock the gate.

"Captain, you've come. I was waiting."

The two men shake hands. Mohan wears tight-fitting jeans and a lemon-yellow shirt unbuttoned to show his chest, and Ranjit is conscious of his own sweaty uniform.

"Sorry about my clothes. I have a night job as a security guard."

"Don't worry about it. I'm just a servant here. Let's go up to my apartment before a tenant sees me and gives me an errand to run."

"You live *here?*"

"It's a shoebox, you'll see."

"Before we head up . . ." Ranjit gestures to his gym bag. "There is one thing. That actress who was in my cab, she dropped something. I'd like to return it. Do you know her?"

"Shabana?" Mohan frowns. "Yeah, I know her, but she left for the Hamptons an hour ago. Won't return for a few days. I can give it to her when she gets back."

Ranjit hesitates, and Mohan smiles broadly. "I see. You want to return it yourself. I don't blame you, she's a beautiful woman."

"*Nahi, nahi,* nothing like that. It's a new dress, she probably wants it back. But maybe later, it would be nice to meet her, get an autograph . . ."

"Sure, sure. Anything for you, Captain."

They walk to a door at the far side of the courtyard and head up a dark, winding staircase. The risers are steep, and Ranjit finds himself breathing hard again—too many goddamn greasy meals at Karachi Kabob—but Mohan climbs easily, two stairs at a time. In the bright yellow shirt, with his long, slicked-back hair, he looks more Latino than Indian.

As they ascend, the air becomes heavy with heat. There are no windows up here, only landings with arched openings in the walls, all bricked in now.

Mohan points to them. "This used to be a shaft for a dumbwaiter. Tenants would call down to the dining room for food, and it would be whisked up to each floor, delivered to each kitchen."

Ranjit nods wordlessly, and by the time they reach the top his chest is aching, and his head is light with exhaustion. They walk down a dim corridor, passing a row of pine partitions with closed doors, each labeled with a number in shaky white paint. One door is ajar, and Ranjit sees that it is a storage space, crammed with frayed rattan chairs, a huge armoire, and an overturned couch, its carved feet sticking up into the air.

"The attic is empty now, but servants used to live up here." Mohan gestures to the cubicles. "When the building went co-op in the sixties, they discovered twenty, thirty people up here. Some had been abandoned by their employers, others were just squatting." He laughs. "This place is so huge, it's been reconfigured so many times, no one really knows every nook and cranny. Except for me."

At the end of the corridor Mohan stops in front of a door and fumbles with an old-fashioned brass key. "Habit," he says. "I don't really need to lock up. No one but me lives up here now."

The door swings open, and Ranjit follows him into a small, square room, not much bigger than his own basement apartment, but with a high, pyramidal-shaped roof. There is a carved mahogany bed pushed along one wall, with a red leather armchair next to it. Most stunning are the three enormous arched windows that take up an entire wall. The view is of Central Park, its vast darkness illuminated by the globes of streetlights. A gentle breeze blows, and the tops of the trees sway, a ripple of motion that stretches away into the distance.

"You like it? Make yourself comfortable, Captain." Mohan busies himself in an alcove fitted out with a hot plate and a small refrigerator.

"It's amazing." Ranjit throws his gym bag onto the floor and studies a wall hung with faded black-and-white photographs in mismatched frames. They are portraits of stern-faced men and women in white collars, sitting stiffly with their hands on their knees.

"Hey, Mohan, who are these people?"

"Those?" Mohan appears, clutching a bottle of Johnnie Walker Red and two crystal glasses. "I don't really know. I found them in a storage area buried back there. It's full of trunks and suitcases. I think they're servants who used to work here. But look at this one."

He points at a large sepia photograph on the opposite wall: the

Dakota, taken from a distance. It looks the same as it does now, except that there is nothing around it—where Central Park should be is a muddy wasteland, and in the foreground is a row of tarpaper shacks, with goats and sheep wandering in their muddy yards.

"That's from 1884." There is a note of pride in Mohan's voice. "It was just built. They called it the Dakota as a joke, because it was so far uptown that it might as well have been in Indian territory. They even carved Indian heads over the doorways."

"You know a lot about this place. How long have you been here?"

"Almost a year. Oh, the stories I could tell you, Captain. There is a woman here who has a whole stuffed horse in her living room. Another tenant has a man come over from Tiffany's every day to wind his collection of antique clocks . . ." He sits cross-legged on the bed and pours large slugs of Scotch into the two crystal glasses. "Have a seat, Captain, relax."

Ranjit settles into the armchair, feeling the coarse horsehair within it.

"I still can't believe it's you. What the hell happened, back at the Academy? Did you leave . . . because of that officer's wife?"

"Oh, she was just the last straw. I had enough of the goddamn military, anyway . . . but for God's sake, let's have a drink first."

He hands Ranjit a glass of Scotch, the crystal tumbler hand cut and heavy.

In a flash of intuition, Ranjit realizes that all this—the tumblers, the carved bed, and the leather armchair—belong to long-dead inhabitants, and that Mohan has pilfered them from the storage area.

Mohan raises his glass. "To long-lost friends."

"I'll drink to that. To long-lost friends."

They clink glasses and swallow deeply, the alcohol burning as it goes down. Then Mohan pours them another one.

Ranjit settles back into the armchair. "So what happened? I'm waiting."

"Captain, the interregimental boxing match. You remember it?"

"Of course." Ranjit smiles. "We trained together. Those early morning runs. Sparring together. That right cross I taught you, you got pretty good at it."

"Exactly. I was a good boxer. Fast, accurate." Mohan's handsome face becomes sullen. "You didn't see me in action at the finals, you were on guard duty that night. I fought some guy from a Gurkha regiment. In the second round, I cut the guy above his eye—right cross, just like you taught me—and blood was pouring down his face, he was half blind, but the judges wouldn't stop the fight. Later on, I found out that two of them were from this guy's regiment, they wanted to punish him."

He sips his drink and smiles grimly. "So I was hitting this guy, he was covered in blood, he couldn't see a damn thing, and I couldn't take it any more. I just stopped. And do you know what the fucking judges did? They voided the fight. Told me that I was a disgrace, that I should have knocked him out." His eyes cloud over with the memory. "That night I thought to myself, I can't do this, how the hell am I going to kill people in battle? So the next night . . . I just went over the wire. I left town and kept on moving . . ."

The bottle empties as Mohan talks for the next half hour, pausing now and then to stroke his thin mustache.

He tells Ranjit about life after leaving the Military Academy: a few years of working as a waiter in Mumbai, and then a lucky break: he found a job as a steward on a merchant marine ship, and spent over a decade shuttling between Mumbai, Shanghai, Jakarta, and Tokyo.

After he worked his way up to bursar he took his first voyage across the Pacific, to Florida, and there he heard that an American cruise line was looking for stewards; tall, well-groomed, and personable, he fit their profile and was hired.

The cruise line catered to an older, wealthy American clientele, and there Mohan became aware of the widows, still blond and trim in their sixties, rich with pensions and life insurance money, and the way they looked at him as he passed by. Of course, he always had girl-friends in port—young shopgirls and nannies—but now he began to aspire to something better. On one cruise he met a large-hearted woman in her late fifties, with a quick laugh and a burning wish to relive her youth. She warmed quickly to Mohan's attention, and when the ship returned to Florida, she invited him back to New York, and he eagerly accepted. But after three months in her Upper East Side apartment he grew tired of her possessiveness, and his wandering eye noticed the firm bosom and flashing eyes of Maria, the cleaning woman. When the older woman discovered them fooling around in the stair-well, she became hysterical and Mohan found himself standing on the sidewalk with no papers, his seaman's duffel and eighty dollars in his pocket.

"So there I was, Captain." Mohan pours his third drink of the evening. "In this city, broke. I couldn't move in with Maria—she lived with her three brothers in Washington Heights—but luckily I had the phone number of a distant cousin. He let me sleep in his living room for a few months.

"Anyway, Maria was still cleaning houses, so I accompanied her. Can you imagine, me, scrubbing toilets? One day, we had a job here, at the Dakota, and it was very hot, so I took off my shirt, and when the lady of the house came back, I kept it off. There was chemistry between us, believe me, and biology too.

"To cut a long story short, Captain, she and I got along very well. So good-bye, Maria. Luckily one of the older doormen had just died, so this lady got me a job here, and this apartment. I've been here ever since. The lady and I have an arrangement, she calls me whenever she . . . needs me. Yes, it's all worked out very well."

Mohan leans back against the wall and strokes his mustache again. "Not bad, eh, Captain, for a dropout from the Academy? A regular squeeze and a place on Central Park West?"

Ranjit thinks about his soul-bruising encounter with the woman from his cab, but quickly buries the memory; Mohan seems to be comfortable with the idea of mutual use.

"Yes, of course. You've done well."

"And you, Captain? Why did you leave the army? I thought you would be a lifer, for sure."

Ranjit takes another hit of Scotch. His stomach is growling with hunger, but he needs the alcohol to get his words out.

"You didn't read about my court-martial? It was in all the papers."

"Court-martial? No, I was at sea. What could you have possibly done?"

"I was stationed up on the Siachen Glacier. Leading missions into Pakistani territory."

"Yeah, well, that makes sense . . . you were always a good climber. But the Siachen . . . I heard it was a bloodbath up there. Frostbite, altitude sickness, enemy fire. What the hell happened, Captain?"

"I made a mistake, a bad one. I was on a classified mission in the mountains. I called in an airstrike and wiped out a squad of our own men."

"A whole squad?" Mohan whistles. "But listen, it was a war, and mistakes happen in wars. That's why it's called 'friendly fire'—"

"It gets more complicated. My CO, General Handa, he wanted me to cover it up. Blame the attack on the Pakistanis, and prolong the war. I refused to, so they put me in jail for three years."

Mohan's eyes are blazing with anger. "The fucking army. They always need to scapegoat someone. But you need to fight this, Captain, you're a good man, you deserve better—"

"It's too late, Mohan. That life is over now. Anyway, I left India, moved to Martha's Vineyard with my wife and daughter, I was working as a caretaker for this black senator. And then . . ."

Ranjit's head spins with alcohol. It is too hot in this room, his shirt is soaked with sweat, and he is very dehydrated and hungry.

"It's too complicated to explain, but my wife hated it there, and a lot happened. I got involved with this senator's wife, and after that, my marriage was over."

Mohan raises his hand, palm out. "You don't have to explain to me, Captain. A senator's wife, *bahut acha*." Very nice.

"It wasn't like that. Anyway, she's dead now, and strangely, her husband and I are still in touch."

He doesn't say that Anna had betrayed both him and the Senator, and that they share this painful memory. The two men talk occasionally, mostly when Ranjit works the night shift, at two or three A.M., when the Senator cannot sleep. But recently the Senator has been gone a lot, visiting China on human-rights missions, trying to pressure the Chinese government to reform their vast, prisonlike factories.

Ranjit doesn't want to discuss all this now, and certainly not with Mohan. His stomach growls, louder now, and the small, hot room seems to close in.

"Hey, you don't have anything to eat, do you? Lunch was hours ago."

Mohan frowns. "Sorry, I mainly get takeout, there's not much space in that—" He gestures at the small fridge in the alcove.

"You like Chinese? Is there a place nearby?"

"I can do better than that." Mohan stands shakily. "How about some Indian food, and some air-conditioning? Shabana Shah had a party last night, and she's gone for the weekend. Her fridge is full of leftovers, she asked me to throw them out. Come on, Captain."

Ranjit hesitates. The last thing he needs is to be caught trespassing in some stranger's apartment. "Hey, are you sure? We can always get takeout."

"No problem, Captain, she gave me the keys to her place. And this is no crappy Indian takeout, it's from that place, Junoon, on Twenty-fourth. Tandoori shrimp, saffron *pullau* . . ."

Ranjit is very hungry, but more than that, he feels a surge of excitement at seeing Shabana's apartment. "Okay, if you think it's fine."

He staggers to his feet, and together they walk out into the long, dark corridor. They take a different set of stairs, and emerge two floors below into a wide, wood-paneled hallway. Mohan walks confidently toward the apartment door of 5C, his yellow shirt flapping around his wrists, opens it with one swift turn of his key and steps in, gesturing Ranjit to follow.

He walks ahead, turning on lights.

"Check this out." He gestures like an impresario. "A real movie star pad, *hanh?*"

Recessed halogen spots shine down from the fifteen-foot-high ceilings, illuminating the vast living room. Above the dark wooden wainscoting the walls are covered in beige suede wallpaper, and a carved fireplace takes up most of the far wall. The furniture is all low, sleek white leather, arranged around a smoked glass table, and above it, anchored in a rosette of plaster, is a chandelier in the shape of a tightly curled flower, its petals made of translucent plastic. By the tall windows are three full-grown ficus trees in clay tubs.

Ranjit breathes in deeply, smelling Shabana's scent in the air, a hint of sandalwood mixed with jasmine.

"And look at these." Mohan turns on more lights, revealing glass shelves along the wall, arrayed with statues, all variations of the plump elephant god, Ganesh, portrayed in bronze, in brass, and in sandstone.

Mohan gestures at a foot-high Ganesh carved out of white marble, hacked out of some faraway temple in India. "Check this one out."

Ranjit runs his fingers over the cool marble, thinking that Mohan seems very familiar with Shabana's apartment. "This lady you told me about? Are you . . . involved with Shabana?"

"No, no." Mohan grins mischievously. "I just do odd jobs for her, take out her dry cleaning, all that stuff. Come on, I'll give you a tour."

Without waiting for an answer, Mohan walks ahead, clicking on more lights. There is a dining room with a long, gleaming table, presided over by a painted portrait of Shabana done in the style of a film poster.

"Next is her bedroom." Mohan walks down a wide corridor, turning into a stark white room at the rear of the house. It has white carpeting, a bed with a white silk canopy, and a pale marble dresser with a huge mirror.

Ranjit is stunned when he sees the mess: the dresser is covered with dried-out bottles of mascara, used tissues, and a silver-backed hairbrush clogged with strands of long black hair. The sheets on the bed are tangled, and crumpled bath towels are strewn across the floor.

"Your idol has feet of clay. She's a real slob, Shabana. The cleaning people are in here for hours. Hey, here's her when she was a kid."

From the dresser Mohan picks up a framed color photograph and sticks it under Ranjit's nose. A pretty teenager wearing a crisp white *salwar kameez* stares shyly at the camera, and behind her are a plump, pretty woman with her head covered, and a tall, mustached man wearing the baggy *shalwar* of the northwest.

"Those are her parents. She's from a poor family. Her father came to India from Pakistan, lost everything in Partition."

Mohan is showing off now, enjoying himself, and Ranjit feels uncomfortable. "Mohan, we really shouldn't be here . . ."

"She's just a woman, not a goddess, you know. All that stuff on the screen, that's *acting*." Mohan grins. "Okay, Captain, let's eat."

They sit silently at the granite island in the kitchen, the room lit only by the undersea glow of strip lights set under the cabinets. They open takeout containers and heat their heaped plates in the stainless-steel microwave, then eat with their fingers, Indian style.

The food is unfamiliar, not the oily curries Ranjit has grown used to at Karachi Kabob: there is shrimp in coconut milk, with shreds of papaya and guava; charcoal-grilled lamb chops whose pink meat falls off the bone; rice of such fine quality that each grain holds the heady taste of saffron.

As the food hits Ranjit's stomach his buzz starts to wear off, but Mohan seems still pretty drunk, and eats with exaggerated gestures.

"Damn good, *hanh*? I told you." Mohan licks his fingers. "Relax, Captain, enjoy the food. She's not coming back tonight, she's in the Hamptons. In fact, I might just crash here, it's too hot at my place."

"Sleep here? You're not afraid of getting caught?"

"You were always a stickler for rules, Captain. You know what I've realized? Rules are for poor people, scared people." He reaches across Ranjit for a shrimp and chews as he talks. "You think the *rules* apply to the people who live here? They think they're above it all, they're better than us. The only difference is that they have"—Mohan rubs his thumb and index finger together—"and they can buy whatever they want. They buy protection, they hire lawyers and accountants. They even buy people. The things I've seen, Captain, you would not believe . . ."

This is the old Mohan, lecturing Ranjit about how the world works.

"I know about this city. Don't forget, I drive a cab now."

Mohan smiles and shakes his head. "Yeah, of course, you must see some wild stuff. Here, you take the last lamb chop—"

"No, no. I'm getting fat, you eat it—"

"You're not fat, *yaar*. Besides, you are my guest." Mohan slides the lamb chop onto Ranjit's plate and sits back. "So, what's the craziest thing you've seen in your cab?"

"The usual. Fare beaters—they always have some story about a friend who will give them the money. People making out in the back— that usually happens on Friday or Saturday night. Drunk people, who get in, but can't tell you where they want to go. It's not really interesting."

"Ah, but a handsome guy like you, you must meet a lot of women in your cab, *hanh*? Late at night, when they're drunk and horny?"

"Yes, there are women." Ranjit thinks of the pale, long-legged Russian strippers leaving work, catatonic with exhaustion. The party girls who've thrown up in his cab. Girls who have just been dumped, and cry the whole way, mascara dripping down their cheeks. "But I don't mess with that stuff."

"So you have a steady girlfriend, *hanh*? Good for you."

"No girlfriend. I live alone."

"Captain, Captain." Mohan pushes his plate away and peers at Ranjit's face. "What is it? Still hung up on the ex-wife?"

Same old Mohan. Ranjit laughs. "That was over a long time ago."

"So it's this Senator's wife you're hung up on? The dead one?"

With his strange mixture of bluster and insight, Mohan has nailed it. Ranjit closes his eyes as he feels the pain. When he first came to New York, he would see Anna's slim figure everywhere: jogging through

Central Park, drenched in sweat, or walking down Park Avenue, wearing her backless yellow cotton dress. Now he no longer sees her, and all that is left is a bundle of emotions, pain at her betrayal mixed in with sadness.

"So I was right, *hanh*? Captain, when was the last time you went out with a woman?"

Ranjit remains silent and Mohan presses on. "One year? More than that?"

"Mohan, forget about it, *yaar*—"

"No. You are too young—we are too young—to live like this. This city is packed with single women, desperate to meet a nice guy. I tell you what. I get together with a group of friends every Friday night, at this place, Izizzi, it's in the Meatpacking District. We have some drinks, some laughs. You should come."

"I'm not sure that I—"

Mohan raises a hand. "You should come. It's a few people from around here, my cousin, and some ladies. There is this Indian girl, Leela Rampersad, she'd be perfect for you: she's smart, really cute. She used to be a nanny here at the Dakota, but now she's going to night school at Hunter. Let me see if I have a pic . . ."

Wiping his greasy hands on a paper towel, Mohan pulls out his cell phone and clicks through a series of pictures, all of brown people in semidarkness, their eyes and teeth shining. The men wear untucked shirts, and the women are in short black cocktail dresses.

"Thought I had a pic, but maybe not." Frowning, Mohan puts his phone away. "Anyway, she's really cute, this girl. You have to come, *yaar.*"

"*Hanh, hanh.* I'll try—"

"This Friday. Promise. And no taxi driver clothes, no security guard clothes. Wear something nice. This Leela is a classy lady, okay?"

"Okay, okay." Ranjit can't help laughing. He washes his hands in the sink and dries them on a kitchen towel. "I should be going. I'm driving tomorrow, and it's almost one. So you're still going to sleep here tonight?"

"I have the keys to the kingdom, Captain." Mohan holds up a large bunch of keys and jangles them.

"You haven't changed at all, you're still a bullshit artist."

"And you, you're still a worrier. Here's my number."

They both laugh, and exchange phone numbers. Mohan says that Ranjit better leave through the back door, since the management is uptight about people going in and out at night.

They go down the stairs, but instead of heading into the courtyard, they walk through a musty hallway that is crowded with gardening equipment. It leads to a small door, which Mohan unlocks.

"All clear," he says, peering around the door. "Go down the alley, it will lead you to Seventy-third Street," he says. "Captain . . . can I say something?"

Ranjit waits and Mohan continues. "I can see you've taken a beating . . . but remember, the past is the past. You know what they say about New York?"

"No, but I have a feeling you're going to tell me."

"New York is a bitch goddess. She gives success to some, keeps it from others. What I say is, make your own luck. Reach out and take what you want."

"What the hell does that mean?"

Both men laugh and embrace, and Ranjit walks away down the dark alley. The last he sees of Mohan is a slim, disheveled figure in a lemon-yellow shirt, his hand raised in farewell.

Finding the nearest subway station, Ranjit takes the stairs down to the fetid, stifling platform, and just makes the southbound local. It's only when he's halfway to Queens that he groans, remembering his black gym bag, left behind on the floor in Mohan's apartment. In it is his postcard of the Golden Temple, and he doesn't like to drive without it. It's too late to go back now, and he resolves to call Mohan first thing the next morning.

As the subway rattles and screeches, Ranjit thinks about the girl Mohan is setting him up with. Leela is an old-fashioned name, and he immediately conjures up a prim and proper Indian girl with thick glasses, hair held back with one of those big plastic clips. The kind of girl who still lives at home and remains a virgin till marriage. But he's probably being ridiculous; she must be pretty cool if she goes out drinking with Mohan.

Meeting his old friend was indeed a stroke of luck. Ranjit has spent so much time in the company of dour, exhausted cabdrivers, he's forgotten that there is life out there. Instead of fantasizing about some movie star, he should buy some new clothes and go out on Friday night. What the hell, he might even have a good time. Thinking about it, he feels a surge of excitement, an emotion he hasn't felt in a long, long time.

Chapter Five

Ranjit wakes the next morning in his tiny basement apartment in Jackson Heights, hearing the rattle of trucks unloading on Thirty-seventh Avenue, not the predawn silence that he is used to. With a curse he reaches for his alarm clock: nine thirty.

He had forgotten to set an alarm. There is no hope in hell of getting a cab to drive now, and the next time he goes in, Jacobo will chew him out.

Groaning, he sits up in bed, and across the room, a shadowy figure does the same: to make this tiny room seem larger, the previous inhabitant had covered the far wall with mirrored tiles. Whatever Ranjit does, his every movement is reflected, as though he has a phantom roommate.

He rises from his bed and stares at himself: his eyes are bloodshot, his beard is streaked with gray, and worse, there is that thickening of his midriff, the muscle from his army years now overlaid with fat. Soon he'll end up like all the other cabbies, their cholesterol through the roof, their backs and knees ruined.

Well, all that is going to change. To hell with driving. He'll take the day off, relax, buy some new clothes for his date on Friday. But first, some exercise.

Falling to the floor he does fifty push-ups, his arms turning to rubber. Then a hundred sit-ups, his stomach cramping, but when he's done he feels more alive than he has in a long time.

After showering, he wears a white T-shirt, his old jeans, worn brown boots, and then ties on a bright red turban. His hangover is gone, and the figure in the mirror now looks presentable, maybe even handsome.

Walking down Seventy-fourth Street, Ranjit heads into the heart of Indian Jackson Heights. The coolness of the morning has burnt off, and the shops are coming to life, shopkeepers pulling up their shutters and washing down the pavements.

Inside the plate-glass window of Shree Krishna Jewelry Store, a pretty, dark-haired young woman is draping the mannequins in heavy gold necklaces. She waves at him as he walks past, and he waves back; everybody in the neighborhood knows the tall, unmarried Sikh.

Ranjit has never believed in luck, but today he feels as though the bitch goddess of success is smiling at him: he has found an old friend, he has a date on Friday night, and his daughter is coming in three weeks. Life is good.

Hurrying down the street, he buys a hot, milky *chai* from a Pakistani sweet shop, flavored with cinnamon, cardamom, and cloves. He stands on the sidewalk, inhaling the aroma, savoring every sip, when his cell phone rings.

Shit. It is Jacobo's number, and he doesn't answer, fearing that he'll be called in to work as a substitute. The phone immediately begins to ring again, and this time he sighs and accepts the call.

"Ranjit. Where the fuck were you this morning?" The old man's scratchy voice fills his ear.

"Sorry, Mr. Jacobo. Not feeling well. I'll be back tomorrow morning."

"Bullshit. You haven't missed a day in two years—" Jacobo pauses. "Look, we have a problem. I need you to come in. Now."

Ranjit's heart races. Has the fat guy from yesterday reported him to the Taxi and Limousine Commission? That will mean a huge fine, maybe a suspension of his license.

"Has someone complained? If so, I can assure you—"

"Just get your butt here. Hold it." Jacobo's voice fades out as he addresses someone else. "Yes, ma'am. Yes, I'm stressing the urgency of the matter." His voice gets louder. "You hear me, Ranjit? Come in, now."

"Yes, sir."

Ranjit hangs up. *Who was Jacobo talking to? Has the TLC sent an inspector?*

It is only when he's on the subway that he realizes the seriousness of the situation: Jacobo had called him by his name, instead of "Taliban." And that has never happened before.

Getting off the train at Court Square, Ranjit walks quickly toward the depot, feeling his anxiety grow. Soon the Uptown Cab Company appears in the distance, looking like an outpost of civilization among the vacant lots of Jackson Avenue, but with all the cabs out on the streets, it seems deserted. The mechanics are still to arrive, and have left a half-gutted cab elevated on the lift.

Ranjit looks for an official-looking car parked outside, but there is only Jacobo's aging white Mercedes, its license plate reading OFFDUTEE.

As long as it's not the TLC, he can handle it. Taking a deep breath, he enters the concrete block building. The cashier's cage is empty, and there is no sign of Jacobo, so he takes the stairs to the office up above. Entering it, he instantly senses the change.

Normally the air conditioner is whirring, trapping the smell of cigarette smoke, but today all the windows have been flung wide open. Jacobo is sitting behind his wooden desk, his bald head bowed in respect, and across from him are a man and a woman. All three of them swivel and their eyes focus on Ranjit.

The woman is slim, fiftyish, with stylishly cropped gray hair, dressed in a smart brown pantsuit. Next to her is a short, wavy-haired Hispanic man, wearing a rumpled tan suit. He might have shaved this morning, but a dark shadow already shows on his wide face.

The woman turns to Jacobo. "Thank you. You can go now."

The old man rises, and whispers as he passes Ranjit. "Remember what I told you about the cops." He shuts the door softly and his footsteps clatter down the stairs.

The woman gestures to Ranjit to take Jacobo's still-warm chair, then leans in. Her eyes are gray-green and shrewd, her nose as sharp as a blade.

"I'm Detective Martha Case, and this is Detective Santos Rodriguez, NYPD."

NYPD. It can't be about the fat man. Ranjit's mind flashes to his job at Nataraj Imports; it is off the books. "I'm sorry, how can I help you?"

Ignoring him, the man named Rodriguez picks up a manila folder and opens it.

"You've been driving a cab for two years now. No traffic violations. You have a green card, sponsored by a Senator Neals." He looks up. "So you have friends in high places. Before the cab, you worked as a caretaker in Martha's Vineyard, also for this Senator . . ."

Ranjit forces himself to be calm. "My green card is in order. My taxi license is brand new. I even retook the vision test."

Case turns her hawklike gaze on him. "Yes, we know all that. We also know that you moonlight as a security guard for that scumbag Jay Patel. So you're not exactly a solid citizen."

Ranjit is silent. *So it is about Nataraj Imports.*

Case twists her thin lips into a tight smile. "So where were you last night?"

"I was . . . visiting a friend."

"At the Dakota?" Rodriguez closes the file. His voice is louder now, edged with impatience.

Ranjit doesn't know whom to look at as he answers. "Yes, I visited my friend Mohan Kumar. He's a doorman there."

"And you went into Shabana Shah's apartment?"

Damn it, has Mohan been arrested for trespassing?

"Answer the question."

Suddenly Ranjit remembers what Jacobo was referring to. When he first started driving, the old man had said: *The fucking NYPD are not our friends. If you get into an accident, don't say, "Yes, I killed that man, sorry." Shut your mouth and get a lawyer.*

Ranjit forces himself to remain calm. "What is this about?"

Case continues calmly. "You gave Shabana Shah a ride in your cab yesterday. Then you returned to her apartment at night. We know that. We also know that you have one of her dresses in your bag. We found it in your friend's apartment."

"Shabana dropped the dress in my cab. I was going to return it—"

Rodriguez leans in. "What was it, some kind of sex thing?"

"What? What the hell are you saying?"

Rodriguez sighs dramatically. "Oh, come, Mr. Singh."

"I need to know exactly what you are implying here—"

"Shabana Shah is dead."

"What? It can't be—"

Both the detectives just stare at Ranjit. In the silence he can hear the mechanics laughing outside, hear the whine of the lift as they lower it.

Rodriguez leans in. "You and your friend Mohan went to her apartment and bashed her head in with a big marble statue. We have both your prints all over the statue. And now your friend has split, leaving you to face the rap. Where is he, Mr. Singh?"

Disjointed images flash through Ranjit's mind: Shabana dropping her dress in his cab, perfumed with sandalwood and jasmine; her stark white bedroom, littered with dirty clothes; eating in her kitchen, then Mohan saying that he was going to spend the night there . . .

Rodriguez raps his knuckles on the desk. "Hello? I asked you a question."

"I don't know anything about this. I barely know Mohan, we used to be friends, years ago—"

"So that's how you're going to play it. Okay."

Rodriguez stands, buttoning his crumpled suit jacket, and glances over at Case. She rises too, her mouth compressed into a thin line.

"You're coming downtown with us. We're charging you as an accessory to the murder of Shabana Shah."

"No. Wait. Please." Ranjit remains sitting, gripping the threadbare arms of Jacobo's swivel chair.

Rodriguez is taking the cuffs from his belt, walking around the desk, and Case has her hand on her holster, the blunt butt of her pistol clearly visible.

The sun shines through the window, and the laughter of the mechanics floats in.

Rodriguez jerks Ranjit upright and pulls his arms behind him.

The cuffs cut into his wrists, and Rodriguez holds him tightly under the elbow as they go down the stairs and out the back door. A police cruiser is parked behind the taxi depot. No one will have seen the cops enter, or leave.

Rodriguez clears coffee cups from the backseat and shoves Ranjit's head down as he gets into the cruiser. It is a gesture that Ranjit has seen a thousand times, on television and on the street, but what is happening now is real: he smells the stale coffee, sees the wire mesh that fences in the backseat, notices that the doors have no handles.

What in God's name has Mohan gone and done?

As they drive away, Jacobo's wan face appears in the upstairs window, and he lifts a hand in farewell.

Chapter Six

BOMBAY, 1991

Shabana and S.K. sat high up in the gloom of the Eros Cinema, waiting for the movie to begin.

The balcony was a graceful Art Deco curve that protruded into the darkness of the cavernous hall. In the old days, families would pay top prices to sit up here and watch the latest blockbuster. Now the air-conditioning barely worked, and the balcony was empty except for a few college students busy making out.

S.K. looked around and hid his anxiety with bluster. "*Aare,* don't worry, the crowds will come. The first showing is always like this."

"I'm not worried. Not when you are the director." Shabana smiled demurely at him. Her face was devoid of makeup, and she looked radiant and much younger than her twenty-four years.

Her smile masked her doubts about the film, because everyone knew that Bollywood was in trouble. The reigning superstar Amitabh Bachchan, "King B," had produced a string of flops. His violent, angry-young-man films, with their vigilantes and corrupt officials, now seemed like relics of the 1970s, when India stagnated, cut off from the outside world. The country was opening up now, and the new middle classes had cable TV and VCRs; even slum dwellers watched foreign television shows where blond women in bikinis cavorted on beaches.

With this film, Shabana's first, S.K. had added a romantic subplot to the standard story of revenge and retribution. *Maro Ek Baar, Maro Do Baar*—Hit Me Once, Hit Me Twice—was to be a test, and the critics would be harsh. Vast armies of unemployed youth still went to the movies, and when they disapproved, they ripped up the red leather seats with their switchblades.

The crowd in the cheap seats below was still talking when the music swelled and the film began. The star, Pinku Kapoor—pushing forty, with a large paunch—played a young policeman fighting against a feudal landowner. When he came onscreen the crowd tittered, but were silent during the first two scenes of village life. Then came the obligatory scene where Asha, the starlet who played Pinku's wife, was raped by the landowner, thus setting up the cycles of retribution that would drive the film.

As Asha, clad in a white sari, fled from the landowner, her bosom heaving, the crowd burst into laughter. A man shouted, *Hey, fatso, did you forget your girdle?* And someone followed up with *Go home to your children, oi!*

S.K. sank deeper into his seat. *Wait till intermission,* he told himself. This was just the beginning. He would jump to no conclusions.

The story cut to Bombay, where Pinku's young sister was living in poverty. She was waiting for her boyfriend under an overpass, but he did not show up, and it began to rain. A young man offered to share his umbrella with her, and she fell in love with him, not knowing that he was the corrupt landowner's younger brother.

S.K. was so wrapped up in his fears that it took him a few minutes to register the silence that now filled the vast cinema. Even the college students in the balcony had stopped groping each other and were transfixed by the screen.

It had been Shabana's first scene, and she was so nervous that S.K. had to shoot it a dozen times. Giant fans had simulated the monsoon

rains, blowing water at Shabana, and she had been soaked to the bone, but had never complained.

The scene deepened—raindrops shone like jewels in Shabana's eyelashes as she walked through the rain with the young man—and S.K. could hear the audience holding its breath. After the man escorted her home, Shabana broke into a heartbroken song, lamenting that she would probably never see him again.

A few people clapped when the scene ended, and it set a pattern: every time Asha appeared there were jeers and whistles, but Shabana's appearance led to pin-drop silence, followed by applause.

S.K. turned to look at Shabana, but she didn't seem to have noticed, and was gazing steadily ahead.

In all his years in the business, S.K. hadn't seen anything like this. Women in the films of the last few decades were decorative, mainly to give the audience a break from the unrelenting violence. Plus it was Bollywood lore, engraved in stone, that leading ladies came from one of the six established film families of Bombay, carrying in their DNA the big bosoms, pink cheeks, and light eyes of their mothers and grandmothers. Why was the audience responding to this elfin girl with no chest, no hips, and a quiet, subdued manner? Was it a girl-next-door phenomenon? Did the unwashed masses now want to see themselves in films?

Sitting silently next to S.K., Shabana felt a strange thrill run through her. She realized that the audience was feeling every one of her emotions: when she sobbed, they sighed, and when she wept, they too wiped their eyes. Like an alchemist, she had found a way to transmute all the guilt and sadness of her life into gold. In that moment she was hooked, and she never wanted to stop acting.

When the film ended, two and a half hours later, she was sick with anticipation. Standing by the exit, she tried to read the faces of the audience, but they were uniformly mournful—the character she played had died in the end, trying to protect her lover from her own brother's wrath.

The college students left, holding hands. The unemployed young men drifted into an alley to piss, or clustered around a street stall to purchase single cigarettes. Not one person had recognized Shabana. In a simple cotton *salwar kameez,* her hair up in a ponytail, she simply did not look like a movie star.

"So? How did we do?" Shabana blinked as she walked out into the afternoon sunlight.

"I don't know yet. Come, let's have a cup of tea."

Holding Shabana's small hand in his beringed one, S.K. crossed the road, heading to a dingy *chai* shop. Shabana looked confused, but S.K. pointed across the road: from here they had a clear view of the ticket counter at Eros Cinema.

Twenty minutes passed, and as Shabana sipped the too-sweet, milky tea, the magic of that moment slipped away. She felt like her own dull self and began to crave the communion of the darkened movie hall.

Soon it was time for the next show, but there was no one at the ticket window.

S.K. grew tense, and blew on his hot tea to hide his concern. The unemployed young men, with their greasy long hair and their grimy polyester shirts, remained clustered at the corner, talking desultorily and taking long, stylized drags at their cigarettes. Then one of them flicked his cigarette butt to the ground and walked back toward the cinema.

The man bought a ticket. His friends followed him and a short line soon formed. S.K. waited expectantly: he knew that if these men liked a film, they would see it over and over, filling their empty lives with its dialogues and fantasies.

By the time S.K. ordered a second cup of tea, the line snaked all the way to the corner. And most joyously, the ticket scalpers had appeared; they took one look at the line, and instantly began to buy blocks of tickets. Very soon they had cornered the market and stood in front of the cinema, their hands in their pockets, muttering, *Ticket, ticket, ticket,* out of the corner of their mouths. Latecomers walked up to them, grumbling, and pressed twenty-rupee notes into the scalpers' hands.

"Shabana," S.K. said, "how would you like another role? As the star this time?"

"Me?" She gasped in surprise. "I would love that, S.K. What is the story?"

"Story?" S.K. thought quickly. Clearly, the masses wanted romance and escapism, not violence. And if they liked Shabana wearing rags and standing under an overpass, they'd eat her up in a more glamorous role. "Story? Okay, there is this young village girl, she is engaged to be married, but . . . one day, returning from the fields, she gets hit by a car and loses her memory."

"I'm the girl?"

"You're the girl. So the girl loses her memory . . . and the car that knocks her down is driven by this millionaire's son. He lives in America, but has returned to India to visit his ancestral village, okay? So he knocks down the girl, and falls in love with her. She's in a coma, so he takes her back to New York, and she has surgery, and wakes up.

"He is in love with her. She travels with him all around Europe, he proposes to her in Paris, they decide to get married. Then, one day, she hits her head again and remembers who she is, and that her true love is back in the village. Does she stay, rich in America, or does she go back to India?"

"I love it. But S.K.-*ji*, how about a part for my sister? She's so disappointed not to be in the first film."

"Your sister." S.K. was tired of the mournful Ruksana, who shadowed Shabana and sat like a ghost in the corner. "Look, we can't have both of you in the film, it will be too confusing. Why don't you give her a job to do? Make her your manager." S.K. waved grandly. "You'll need someone to take care of all the details. Because this time, we'll be shooting internationally. New York, Amsterdam, Paris! Big budget, lots of locations!"

"Abroad?" Shabana's mouth fell open. "But where will you get so much money?"

"Money? Don't you worry about money! When Bollywood hears this story, the financiers will throw money at us!"

S.K. was loud and confident, but he knew that making a film was a risk-laden proposition, and that loan officers at UCO Bank and State Bank of India would just laugh at him. Most of the films in Bollywood were financed by undeclared "black money," delivered in hard-topped suitcases by men in badly cut safari suits. These "financiers" were just fronts for the Mumbai mafia, and once the mafia was involved, there was no telling what could happen. Directives could come down from mobsters to replace one star with another, or to give a key role to a niece or nephew.

There had to be some other way. S.K. thought of his friend Jayram Patel, a lanky Gujarati accountant. Jayram-*bhai* was a modest man with a quiet demeanor, but he did the books for Don Hajji Mustafa, the most powerful man in Bombay. And Don Hajji was moving into legitimate businesses like construction and import-export. Maybe the Don would like to become the producer for a film.

Yes, S.K. would talk to his friend. Jayram Patel was a clever man, and more importantly, behind his accountant's bland façade, he was a romantic, always infatuated with the latest young starlet.

S.K. smiled and squeezed Shabana's shoulder. "*Aare,* don't you worry your pretty head about money. I will take care of all that. We'll call the film *Amerika Ke Kahanie,* The Tale of America, what do you think of that?"

S.K. could see the whole movie in his head, and ten more after that. He would ensure that Shabana lived forever on the silver screen.

II

BLOODSTAINED COTTON

Make contentment your earrings, humility
   your begging bowl
Let meditation be the ashes you apply to your body
Let the remembrance of death be the patched coat you
   wear.

—Guru Granth Sahib, Jup

Chapter Seven

Ranjit is having trouble breathing.

The air in the basement cell of the Manhattan Detention Complex is stale, as though all the oxygen has been used up. He sits on a hard wooden bench, each labored breath reminding him of the three years he spent in the army prison in India, most of it in solitary confinement. He had developed very bad claustrophobia, and it is all coming back now.

How long has he been in here? It must be past midnight, but without his watch, he can't tell. They took his watch, wallet, and belt, and even made him remove his turban before marching him down a twisting stair into the basement. He wishes he had his postcard of the Golden Temple, so that he could concentrate on it and meditate, but the cops must have that too, stashed inside his gym bag.

He leans against the yellow tiled wall, the ceramic cold against his cheek. Across from him sit two stunned teenage girls arrested for smoking pot in Washington Square Park, an African man who was selling fake Louis Vuitton handbags, and a chaste-looking woman in a pink twinset who has kicked off her shoes and fallen asleep.

Ranjit has been waiting to use the wall phone, but it has been occupied by a stocky Hispanic man who has been making endless calls to his girlfriend, his baby's mama, and his own mother. Now the man smiles apologetically and flashes Ranjit the "just five more minutes" gesture.

The MDC isn't called "the Tombs" for nothing. It is stifling hot down here and there is a strong sense of being buried deep under the earth. Ranjit closes his eyes, but he can still feel the walls closing in.

He takes one deep breath, then another, forcing air into his body, and tries to imagine that he is at the Golden Temple, the marble tiles warm under his feet. But each time the temple comes into focus, it is interrupted by the images they showed him during four hours of interrogation: Shabana, sprawled on the polished parquet floor of the living room, her face smashed into a bloody pulp. Her fine high brow was gone, as was her nose, and her broken mouth was full of shattered teeth. Only her hair, lying around her in a glossy fan, still retained its luster.

It was as though the attacker had tried to erase every trace of her beauty.

Ranjit's body tenses at the memory. *Breathe.*

Rodriguez had played the tough guy and shouted into his face, while Case hung back and watched him with her gray-green eyes. Rodriguez said that the doormen across the street had remembered him dropping off Shabana earlier that day. Later that evening, he had appeared on the security camera at the entrance to the Dakota; he was seen walking across the courtyard with Mohan, but there was no record of him leaving. His prints were all over the marble statue of Ganesh, along with Mohan's, and Shabana's dress had been found in his bag in Mohan's apartment.

Breathe. Keep breathing.

Leaning over Ranjit, Rodriguez said, "You are fucked, Mr. Singh. Royally fucked. We have enough evidence to nail you." His breath was foul, a mixture of stale coffee and something rotten inside him. "Talk to us. Tell us where your friend is, and we might be able to help you."

Breathe. Remember to breathe.

They made him tell them, again, and again, what had happened that night. Strangely enough, they also wanted to know all about his job at Nataraj Imports. Case asked him many questions about Jay Patel, and though he had little to tell her, she scribbled it all down in a notebook.

None of it had made any sense. Nothing, except that Case said Mohan had been involved with Shabana for over a year. The other doormen all knew that he spent a few nights every week in her apartment.

When Ranjit heard that, he knew it was true. So that was why Mohan had taken him down to Shabana's apartment, hinting, in his own perverse way, that he knew her well. Why hadn't he come right out and told Ranjit? Was it his shame at being a kept man?

Ranjit thinks of his friend's scornful comments as they stood in Shabana's messy bedroom: *Your idol has feet of clay.* Did he resent his status as a kept man enough to kill her?

No. Mohan would never do something like that. The man that he knew was a seducer of women, yes, but he adored them, thinking that each one would save him.

One thing was for sure: Mohan wasn't supposed to be in Shabana's apartment last night. Had she perhaps returned late, with another man? He imagines her in her white dress, stepping into her living room, laughing, turning on the enormous plastic chandelier.

Maybe Mohan had awakened and come out, sleepy and disheveled. Had there been an altercation? Something so terrible that Mohan picked up the staute of Ganesh—it was heavy, at least twenty pounds—and smashed it into the face of his beloved? Then, terrified and full of remorse, he had run away, vanished into the city?

"Hey, buddy, I'm done, you want the phone?"

The Hispanic man gestures at the receiver in his hand. When he hands it over, the mouthpiece is warm and smells strongly of spittle.

Ranjit dials the number he has memorized, praying that Senator Neals is home at his town house in Georgetown. After Anna's death, the man had turned into an insomniac, nursing a Scotch and poring over his papers deep into the night.

The phone rings and rings, and a clipped voice finally answers. "Senator Neals's answering service. How can I help you?"

Ranjit stifles a groan. "I'm a personal friend of the Senator's. It's urgent I reach him. Is he back from China?"

"Sir, I cannot reveal that information. Would you care to leave a message?"

"Look, it's urgent I talk to him—"

"Would you care to leave a message?"

Ranjit pauses, and then collects himself. "Tell him that Ranjit from the Vineyard called. He has my number. Look, I need to talk to him urgently, any idea when he'll call back?"

"Sir, all I can do is convey the message. Have a good night."

Ranjit slams the receiver down and the Hispanic man glances up at him. He is long-haired, wearing granny glasses and a dirty jean jacket covered with sixties PEACE and LOVE patches.

Ignoring the man, Ranjit dials again, trying to remember the number that Jacobo had made all his drivers memorize before they went on the road.

"Al's Pizza."

Fuck. Hanging up, Ranjit reverses two numbers and redials.

"Krumholtz and Thompson. Sandy Thompson here."

"My name is Ranjit Singh. I drive for Jacobo, at Uptown Cab. He said to call this number if we ever needed a lawyer."

"Jacobo? How is the old crook? So what did they get you for? Moving violation? Please don't tell me that you hit a pedestrian."

Ranjit pauses. "No, I didn't hit anyone. This isn't about the cab. They're saying . . . accessory to murder." There is a silence. "Hello, are you there?"

"Yeah, yeah. Where are you? When did you get picked up?"

"Around noon. I'm in the Tombs. It's on—"

"I know where that is. Look, for Jacobo, we usually work on a preset fee, but this . . . this is open-ended. You sure you can afford a lawyer? Maybe a public defender is better."

"Don't worry, I can pay." Ranjit thinks of the eleven thousand dollars he has saved up for a new apartment, so that Shanti can have her own bedroom. "Can you handle this kind of thing?"

"Yeah. I've been doing this for twenty-one years. Give me your name and tell me who arrested you."

Ranjit spells out his name, and then tells the lawyer about Rodriguez and Case.

"Okay. I'll be there in an hour. And listen, do not talk to anyone. This is not TV, Mr. Singh. You get zero points for being cooperative. Just shut your mouth and sit tight."

The line goes dead and Ranjit slumps back on the bench. The Hispanic man sidles up to him. His round glasses are tinted purple, and deep lines appear at the corners of his eyes when he smiles.

"Hey. What happened to your hair?"

The man gestures to Ranjit's topknot, held in place only by a black bandanna.

"They took my turban away."

"Shit. That's an invasion of your civil liberties, man." He springs up and goes to the bars. "CO. Yo, CO."

A heavyset female corrections officer in a dark blue uniform heaves into sight.

"Why you hollering at me?"

"This man needs his turban back. And I'm hungry. When are we getting breakfast?"

"Do me a favor, Hector. Shut the fuck up."

The woman waddles away and Hector settles back onto the bench.

"See, they know me here," he chuckles. "They know me, but they can't hold me. Know what they got me for? Turnstile jumping. Can you believe that shit? Bankers on Wall Street are robbing the country blind, and they're after me. Well, at least we get breakfast. They got these small boxes of cereal, and milk. You gonna eat your breakfast?"

The thought of eating anything makes Ranjit sick. "If I'm still here, you can have it."

"Oh, you waiting for your lawyer? They always say they'll be there in an hour, but it's never an hour. If he's any good, he's gonna call around, talk to some cops, see what he can suss out."

"Well, in that case, maybe I can get some sleep." Ranjit closes his eyes, praying that this lawyer can get him out of here.

Hector tugs at his shoulder. "Buddy, don't fall asleep. If you asleep when they call your name for the judge, they ain't gonna wake you up. Then you gotta spend twelve more hours in here."

Ranjit is forced to open his eyes.

"Hey, you think they got Cocoa Puffs for breakfast? I love Cocoa Puffs."

Five hours pass, and breakfast still hasn't been served when they call Ranjit's name and escort him to a single cell on the first floor. At least this one has a small, barred window high on the wall, and Ranjit drinks in the sight of the pale dawn sky.

After Hector's nonstop monologue, Ranjit is glad to be alone. He sits, listening to the murmur of far-off traffic: outside these walls, the city is waking up.

His cell door suddenly rattles open. A corrections officer steps aside to let in a short man with uncombed, faded red hair and a patchy beard. The lawyer wears an expensive checked suit and penny loafers. Ranjit is reassured, and then notices the faint food stains on the man's lapels, the rim of dirt on the soles of his loafers.

"Mr. Singh? Sandy Thompson. Here's the deal. I bill at two-fifty an hour, but because I owe Jacobo, this consult is free, okay? After that, you pay."

"All right." Ranjit feels sick to the pit of his stomach.

Thompson sits down, clicks open a calfskin briefcase with gold-edged corners, and takes out a yellow pad.

"So. They are charging you as an accessory to the murder of this actress, Shabana Shah. The most important thing is that you make bail."

"Bail? I'm innocent. I had nothing to do with this, I—"

Thompson lifts up a finger to stop him.

"This is an arraignment, not a trial. Nobody is judging your guilt or innocence. You'll go before a grand jury in a week. They're the ones who will decide if there is enough evidence to try you. If we don't post bail, you'll spend that time on Rikers Island. You're a Sikh, right? With your turban and beard, someone will fuck with you for sure. You don't want that."

"Bail? How am I going to do that?"

"I can arrange for a bail bond. The most important thing is to establish there is no flight risk. Can an employer vouch for you? Jacobo doesn't count."

"I used to work for Senator Neals, as a caretaker. He's the one who sponsored me for my green card."

"Clayton Neals? The black senator? I can work with that. Okay, I gotta put all this together. We're going in front of the judge very soon. You just keep quiet. I'll do all the talking."

"I must get out. I can't stay in here, I have . . . claustrophobia."

"Yeah, well, let's hope the judge got out of the right side of his bed today. Lansky is a real motherfucker, but he's quick. If . . . when you get out, go across to Pham's Pho, on Baxter Street. There's a back room there, ask for me."

The arraignment takes place in a small, shabby courtroom with dirty, dark green walls. The judge sits at a battered wooden stand, looking tired and cranky. The public prosecutor is a stooped man in a shabby suit who doesn't even look at Ranjit, just speaks in a monotone directly to the judge. He and Sandy Thompson exchange a bewildering array of papers.

All Ranjit hears is the prosecutor saying that he is not a United States citizen, and thus a flight risk. Sandy Thompson buttons his jacket and stands up.

"Your honor, this man was previously employed by Massachusetts Senator Clayton Neals. In fact, it was the Senator who sponsored his green card. Mr. Singh has no prior convictions or outstanding arrests, and he is an active member of the New York Taxi Workers Alliance."

"Senator Neals?" The judge hesitates, then sets the bail at three hundred thousand dollars. Thompson looks satisfied and nods at Ranjit before leaving the courtroom.

After another two hours in a holding pen, a corrections officer gestures at Ranjit with an upward jerk of his chin. Ranjit walks down a long corridor, signs for his possessions, and heads out of the Tombs into the hot morning air of Chinatown.

They don't return his turban.

Pham's Pho is one street over on Baxter, a narrow storefront tucked between two bail-bond places. At this hour of the morning it is completely empty, and a small Vietnamese man takes Ranjit through a beaded curtain to a small, windowless room in the back. The lawyer is sitting at a round plastic table, his red hair even more disheveled, jacket off and shirtsleeves rolled up. Judging from the large bowl in front of him, he is just finishing his breakfast.

"Ah, there you are," he says brightly. "Pho? I highly recommend the brisket."

"I'm a Sikh. We don't eat beef. And I need some tea."

"Fish balls, then? Hey, Pham, one large fish ball, and a green tea." The man in the doorway nods and scurries off.

"Mr. Thompson, what are my chances here? I need to know. My daughter—"

Thompson holds his finger up. "Eat first. We'll talk after."

Pham sets a mug of tea and a large bowl of steaming broth in front of him, full of noodles and round white fish balls. Next to it is a plate piled high with bean sprouts and fresh basil leaves.

The green tea isn't *chai,* but at least it is strong and fragrant, and the soup is delicious. As the warm liquid fills his stomach, Ranjit's nausea eases, and he begins to feel very sleepy.

"Nothing like some pho to settle your stomach after a night in the Tombs. Plus, Pham keeps his mouth shut, so we can talk in here. I have twenty minutes, then I have another arraignment in Brooklyn."

"Mr. Thompson, I assure you, I had nothing to do with this—"

The lawyer holds up a finger, a habit that Ranjit is beginning to dislike.

"Here's the most important thing. I don't care what you did or didn't do. Let's get that out of the way—"

Ranjit feels a sudden rush of anger and bites into a fish ball, splitting it cleanly in two.

"As I was saying, accessory to murder is a Class Two felony, which means that you go in front of a grand jury, and they decide if there is enough evidence for a case. The cops have to prove that you knew the murder was taking place, but didn't report it. They're not naming you as a principal, or getting at you for 'aiding and abetting,' so I think they really don't know what happened. It's a pressure tactic for you to give up your friend. If you do know where he is, we should tell them. There's no reason for you to take the heat on this thing."

"I have no fucking idea where Mohan is."

"Okay. So you want to tell me what happened that night?"

Thompson takes out his yellow pad and looks up expectantly. Ranjit pushes away his bowl of half-eaten soup, wipes his mouth, and begins to talk, his voice trembling with anger.

His soup has grown cold, and the bean sprouts sit in a soggy pile at the bottom of his bowl. Thompson has been scribbling steadily for the last twenty minutes. Now he looks up, and his pale eyes are distant.

"So let's see. They can establish a link between the two of you lasting one day. You were ID'd dropping Shabana off, then returning that evening. No one saw you leave, since you went out the back way. You guys ate dinner at her apartment. You touched the statue. You forgot your bag in his apartment, with her dress in it . . ."

He taps his pencil against his pad. "This Mohan. In their minds, he did it, no doubt. He's been intimate with the actress for some time now. Real ladies' man, huh?"

Ranjit nods. "He was at the Academy with me. Always had a girl-friend. He used to meet women everywhere—in the bazaar, on the bus. He's a seducer, that's how he gets his thrills. I don't think he's capable of killing."

Thompson's gaze is piercing. "People change, Mr. Singh. This is a guy who's been living off his wits for years. He got the job at the Dakota because of her; he was at her beck and call. Anything else?"

"As I said, we were friends a long time ago. All I know is what he told me last night."

"Let's look at the facts, Mr. Singh. Mohan beat Shabana's face in with a statue. If you plan on killing someone, there are easier ways to do it. Which makes it a spontaneous act of passion. Which means you couldn't have helped plan it. That's our best argument." Thompson hands Ranjit a business card, then gets up and shrugs on his jacket. "Look, I gotta go. Call my secretary, set up a retainer. I'm going to start with ten thousand, okay?"

"Wait. Mr. Thompson—what are my chances? My daughter is coming to visit me in three weeks, and I need to know—"

"What can I tell you? There are no guarantees in this business."

Seeing Ranjit stare at him, he pauses.

"What? Do I have food in my beard?"

"No. Your shirt." Ranjit points to the brown food stain on Thompson's white shirtfront.

"Crap. I have a clean one in the car. Now, remember, you're out on bail. So you don't drive a cab, you don't talk to anyone, you just sit at home and watch TV. And one more thing. You think you could lose the beard and the turban? Juries these days, they hear about terrorism, the Taliban, all that stuff."

"I'm a Sikh. This is part of my religion."

"Yeah, yeah, but think about it, okay?"

Thompson leaves, and Ranjit stares at his bowl of cold soup. *A retainer of ten thousand dollars.* As soon as he pays the lawyer, all the money he has scraped together will be gone. What if Thompson needs more money after that?

The slim Vietnamese man appears. "You want something else? Mr. Thompson will pay."

"No thanks." Ranjit rises. "Tell me, is Thompson a good customer? Is he here a lot?"

"Oh yes, almost every day." The man gestures across the road at the Tombs. "People come from there."

Ranjit thanks the man and heads out of the door. At eight in the morning Canal Street is already bustling with traffic and people. As he walks west, he has to weave past sidewalk vegetable stands and stores selling live fish that flop about in metal tubs of water.

A familiar figure is standing on the corner, his hand held out. Hector's faded jean jacket looks even shabbier in daylight, and all his bravado seems to have evaporated.

Seeing Ranjit, he quickly smiles and extends his fist for a fist bump. "Hey, bad boy, you out? Cool, cool. They didn't have Cocoa Puffs today. I think they only have Cocoa Puffs on Sunday morning."

"Yes, I got out. Now don't go jumping any more turnstiles, okay?"

He attempts to walk past, but Hector holds out his hand, blocking Ranjit's path.

"Yo, I hate to ask, but I got to get to work. You got a buck or so for the train?" Ranjit digs into his jeans and peels off a twenty. "Here you go."

"Wow. Thanks, man, you a *prince*. Hey, you ever need any help, you need anything, you come and see me, okay? I'm in Central Park, you know Strawberry Fields?"

"The John Lennon memorial? You work for the Parks Department?"

"No, man, I work for *myself*. That's my *spot* up there. Come by, okay?"

Hector dances to the side, raises a hand in farewell, and dives into the crowd. Ranjit walks on, his head now swimming with tiredness. He needs a hot shower, and then some sleep. He has to think through this situation with a clear mind.

The R train to Queens is packed at this time. A man swaying three inches away reads a newspaper New York–style, having folded the pages vertically into thirds.

On the front page is a large headline, GARBAGEMEN TO GO ON STRIKE. In the sidebar, a smaller headline says, RATS IN THE CITY VEN- TURE OUT. Farther down the page, almost swallowed up in the fold, is the word MURDERED. Below it, the smiling, elfin face of a much younger Shabana Shah stares up at him.

Ranjit forces himself to look away, but her dark eyes seem to follow him.

Chapter Eight

An hour later, Ranjit is in his darkened apartment in Jackson Heights, hovering on the edge of sleep, when the laptop in the corner of his room begins to trill. It is Shanti, calling him on video-chat from India.

Bleary-eyed, he checks his watch: ten thirty A.M. here, eight in the evening in India. He has to talk to Shanti: the last two times they were supposed to video-chat, he had to work, and ended up canceling.

Picking up the laptop, he sits on the bed and switches on his webcam. "Hello? Hello, *Papaji*?"

A fuzz of static clears, and his daughter's face appears on the screen. For a few seconds he is too choked up to talk, taking in Shanti's face—so like her mother, with her mother's high forehead and hazel eyes. But she is already taller than Preetam, and there is something wary about her that she has inherited from him.

"*Papaji*, are you okay? You look terrible."

"Oh, I'm fine. Just worked all night, that's all. What are you up to?"

Shanti wears an old T-shirt and jeans and holds a chewed pencil. He sees the ceiling fan turning above her, and glimpses a window to one side, filled with the dark outline of a gulmohar tree. He can imagine the rest of Preetam's parents' house: high-ceilinged rooms and a wide, open veranda that looks out onto a sweep of manicured lawn.

She shrugs her thin shoulders. "Just doing my homework. There's a math test tomorrow. I hate school here. I can't wait till I come and live with you."

He knows that after returning from America, she's never really adjusted to the Indian school system. The math is hard for her, and she hates memorizing facts for exams. It doesn't help that she's the only girl in her grade with divorced parents.

"Now, remember the deal, Shanti. If you like it here, you can stay on with me. That's what your mother and I agreed."

"Of course I'll like it. And Mama won't even notice that I'm gone. All she does is go to the movies, or go out with Mr. Big."

He pauses. *Mr. Big* is code for Preetam's new boyfriend, a rich businessman with a leather export business.

"*Beti,* your mom needs . . . friends. Don't be so hard on her. You'll just end up fighting with her, and that's no use."

"Friends, okay. But this is so embarrassing. She's all lovey-dovey. I swear, if she marries this guy, I'll go crazy."

"Look." He tries to conceal his own turbulent emotions. "Just hang in there. It's just three more weeks."

Her eyes become dreamy. "New York. I can't wait. What clothes should I bring? Because I've been watching TV, and I saw that kids there wear . . ."

Shanti chatters on, and soon he feels sick with guilt. What if he's in jail three weeks from now?

". . . Oh. Mama's back now." Shanti looks over her shoulder. "And Mr. Big is with her here. I hope he hasn't brought me any presents. I hate it when he brings me presents. Like I don't know he just gave his secretary a thousand rupees and told her to go out and buy something shiny."

There is the sound of Preetam's voice, drawing closer, and Shanti looks over her shoulder again. "Okay, *Papaji.* Why don't we talk again tomorrow?"

"I might be driving, *beti,*" he lies. "But I'll call you."

"Okay."

He can't bring himself to say *I love you*, like all the American parents do, automatically, as easily as sneezing. In any case, that phrase cannot express the tortured mix of affection and loss that he feels for her.

"Take care of yourself, *beti*. And don't fight with your mother, okay?"

"Yes, okay. You take care, too. Drive carefully."

He puts his palm flat against the screen, and she reaches forward and does the same, trying to connect across the space of eight thousand miles.

Reaching out, he hits the log-off button and the screen turns black.

Sleep. He must get some sleep.

But his tiny room is stiflingly hot, and when he closes his eyes he thinks of Shabana's bloodied corpse. He breathes deeply, imagining the Golden Temple: he is a boy again, slipping off his shoes and washing his feet in a pool of water before passing through the darkness of the Eastern Gate.

Entering the vast temple compound he sees the golden dome of the Harmandir Sahib, floating in the waters of the sacred lake. He does a circuit of the lake, and the noise of the city fades away, replaced by a serene silence. Old learned men sit under the shade of the sacred trees, and as he passes each one, he hears a snatch of prayers, words that enter his brain and stay there.

His anxiety drains away, and soon he is hovering at the edge of sleep, the darkness he so desperately craves.

Bzzzt, bzzzt, bzzzzzzzt. The harsh ringing of his buzzer jolts him awake.

The darkness withdraws its promise of oblivion, and he curses.

Bzzzzzzzzzzzzt.

Getting out of bed, he presses the intercom button. "Who is it?"

"Ranjit Singh?" A man's voice, one he does not recognize. "I have a car outside. Jay Patel sent me. He wants to see you."

With a sick feeling, he remembers that he was supposed to be at Nataraj Imports last night.

"Tell Mr. Patel that I'm not well, I'll be back at work tonight."

"I said, Patel wants to *see* you. Let's go. He doesn't like to be kept waiting."

Ranjit slumps against the wall, his head fogged with exhaustion. He remembers all the questions that Case had asked him about Nataraj Imports. *How often did shipments come in? How many boxes? Who delivered them? How many people worked there?*

What the hell was that all about?

Bzzzzzzzzzzzzzzzt.

He presses the intercom button again. "Hang on, I'm coming."

"Hey. Where are we going?"

The driver, a bullet-headed white man, is cut off by a smoked glass partition. Either he does not hear, or he chooses not to answer.

The black Lincoln Town Car heads across the Triboro, connects to the Deegan, and slides across to the Cross Bronx. Soon they are heading across the George Washington Bridge to New Jersey, and Ranjit sinks back into the plush leather seat and watches the massive cables of the bridge flash by, the water far below sparkling with sunlight.

Jersey. Patel Sahib has sent a car to take him all the way there, not to the Nataraj Imports office downtown. It doesn't make sense. There is no way that Patel could have known about his arrest: getting off the train in Jackson Heights this morning, he'd stopped at a newsstand and flipped through all the newspapers—Shabana's death was told in gory detail, and Mohan was mentioned as a "person of interest," but there was no mention of his own name. Yet he feels a sick foreboding, and wishes he could think more clearly, but the desperate need for sleep clouds his brain.

The bridge ends and they hurtle down a wide highway that has been carved into the earth, with blasted brown cliffs on either side. This is a no-man's-land, lined with gas stations and cheap motels. Even the green of a few trees and the baby-blue sky overhead cannot disguise its ugliness.

The limo takes one exit amongst the tangle of signs, and drives along a road parallel to the highway. The Paradise Motel flashes by, followed by the misnamed Riverview and the Skyline, all of them offering day and night rates. One look at their parking lots—rusty Fords and Chevys mingle with new Mercedes and Beemers—tells Ranjit that the haves and the have-nots are mingling here, engaged in the only activities that cut across class lines: drugs and purchased sex.

The limo turns in toward a motel just like all the others, but cleaner, painted a saffron color, its exterior walkways devoid of loitering men. Despite the empty parking lot, the neon sign that says PATEL MOTEL has been switched off, and as if to underscore that message, a smaller lit sign says NO VACANCY.

The driver heads to the back of the lot, overshadowed by a rocky cliff face. He lowers the glass partition and points wordlessly to a door at the end of the motel.

Walking toward it, Ranjit feels the adrenaline beginning to kick in: whatever Patel throws at him, he can handle.

The door is ajar, and he enters a darkened room with soft music playing. As his eyes adjust to the darkness, he sees that this is the living room of a larger suite, with heavy silk drapes pulled across the windows, Persian rugs covering the floor, and, instead of chairs, there are large silk cushions. In one corner is the blue light of an expensive stereo system; the music playing is a *bhajan,* a chant to the elephant god Ganesh.

A pair of leather sandals lies by the door, the soles deeply eroded by the imprint of large feet—Patel Sahib's, no doubt—and Ranjit slips off his own boots before walking onto the plush silk carpet. He waits, the melodic words of the bhajan familiar to him:

"Shuklaambara dharam vishnum, shashi varnam chaturbhujam, prasanna vadanam . . ." He who is attired in white, who has the complexion of the moon, who has four arms and a smiling face, upon him we meditate to remove all obstacles . . .

Jay Patel walks through a doorway, dressed as usual in his white shirt and trousers, and clutching his slim metal laptop.

"Ranjit. You have arrived. *Aao,* come, sit with me."

He gestures to the silk cushions, and Ranjit sits awkwardly on one.

Patel sinks easily to the floor and sits cross-legged, placing the computer beside him. He does not speak, and the music swells around them. *"To the elephant-faced one, with trunk and lotus body and eyes, we pray day and night. To the one with the single tusk who grants boons to his many devotees, we pray day and night."*

Ranjit is the one who breaks the silence. "Sir, you wanted to see me? I apologize for not coming to work yesterday. I'm sorry, I was not well. I was going to check in with you today."

Patel smiles, baring his teeth. "That's not exactly true, Ranjit. You were arrested, and let out on bail a few hours ago."

Ranjit's face betrays his surprise. "How . . . how did you know?"

The Cheshire cat smile remains. "That does not matter. When one of my employees is given the hospitality of the NYPD, I make it my business to know. What matters is that you just chose to lie. That pains me."

"Sir, I assure you, the police are mistaken. I had nothing to do with the murder. This Mohan Kumar, I knew him many years ago in India, and I—"

"Ranjit, of course I believe you. You are an honorable man, you are ashamed of what happened, it is natural that you try to hide it. But from now on, you need to tell me the truth."

"Yes, sir. Of course."

"Mohan Kumar." Patel's smile is replaced by an expression of disgust. "I'm surprised that you would know a lowlife like him. What he has done is despicable. He has blackened the name of our community. The Americans will think we are animals, killing each other.

"I know—used to know—Shabana very well, she was a customer of ours. A very fine actress, and more than that, a fine, fine lady. To die like that . . . it is unthinkable." Patel's voice thickens, and he pulls a snowy white handkerchief from his pocket to wipe his eyes. "Now. Ranjit. You will tell me everything that happened. Leave nothing out."

"Sir, I already have a lawyer, he is handling this—"

"Tell me." Patel's voice hardens into a command.

For the third time in twenty-four hours, Ranjit finds himself recounting the events of that evening.

Patel leans in, listening intently, and when Ranjit finishes, he speaks, his voice low and modulated again.

"So . . . the police asked you about your job at Nataraj. And you told them?"

"They wanted to know about the shipments—how many, when they arrived, where they came from. I told them nothing that they couldn't find on a shipping manifest."

"I see."

Patel sits silently, his eyes closed. The *bhajan* plays in the background, the Sanskrit words filling the dark room. Is Patel meditating? Ranjit wishes he could see better, but in the dark all he can make out is the sheen of the man's shaved head.

"Ranjit." Patel opens his eyes and his voice is hard. "I want you to find this Mohan Kumar. Find him, and bring him to me."

"Sir?"

"You bring him to me, and I'll take care of all this. The police will hear what they need to, and you will be free of this mess."

In heaven's name, why is Patel getting involved in a murder investigation?

"Sir, I don't understand . . . you want me to bring Mohan here, to the motel? Why?"

"I have my reasons. That's all you need to know."

"I wouldn't know how to find him. This is a huge city, he could be anywhere."

"I hear you have certain skills, from your military days." The smile is back on Patel's face. "Look, my friend, you must understand the reality of the situation. This lawyer of yours—Thompson, correct?—what is he going to do for you? He's used to fixing parking tickets. He's also been brought up in front of the bar twice for disciplinary measures. You think that fool can handle a grand jury?

"And the police. You think they will find Mohan? They will go into Jackson Heights, into Curry Hill, flashing his picture, and no one is going to talk to them. They are white men, with guns, and half our people are illegal. And as you know, Mohan has connections with the shipping lines. What is to stop him from getting on a ship to Japan? Once he disappears, you are all that the cops have. They will put you in jail for a long time."

Patel's eyes bore into Ranjit. "You are going in front of a grand jury in a week. To them, you are not a citizen, you are just another brown immigrant, you are riffraff. Of course it will go to trial, which will take, what, at least a year? So all that time you sit in Rikers, and then a prison sentence—at least three years—after which they will deport you. Much better that you find Mohan. Find him and bring him to me."

Ranjit feels the fear in the pit of his stomach. He must acknowledge the truth of what Patel is saying.

A sitar strums in the background, and a plaintive voice sings over it. "*. . . Guru brahma, guru vishnu, guru devo maheshwara, guru sakshat parabrahma . . .*" The Guru is Brahma, the Guru is Vishnu, the Guru is Shiva. The true Guru is the Highest, formless god. I prostrate myself before the holy Guru . . .

Ranjit rises unsteadily from the cushion and pulls on his boots. "I have to think about this."

Patel Sahib stands up in one quick movement. "Think fast, then. You don't have much time. And here's a little additional motivation. If you find Mohan, I will give you a reward. Fifty thousand, cash."

Seeing Ranjit's stunned expression, Patel places a bony hand on his shoulder. "Don't be stupid about this. Who can you trust? Some washed-up American lawyer, or your own people? I am offering you my help, Ranjit. If you turn me down, you are at the mercy of the American people." He chuckles and shakes his head. "The American people, God help you."

He gestures to the door. "You may leave now. My car will take you back."

As Ranjit walks out of the room, Patel has opened his laptop and is staring into the screen, its blue light washing over his face. The *bhajan* is still playing in an endless loop, soft and hypnotic, the words of hope and surrender traveling through hundreds of years: "To the elephant-faced one, we pray day and night. To the one with the single tusk, we pray day and night . . ."

The same driver takes Ranjit home and the journey seems interminable.

Fifty thousand dollars to find Mohan? Patel must want him very badly—but why? What do a doorman and a multimillionaire hair importer have in common? The link is Shabana, poor dead Shabana, with her beautiful face and stalled career, living in her expensive apartment, soothing her sorrow with her shopping sprees. Patel's eyes had welled up with tears when he talked about her—does he want to avenge her death and find Mohan? But it makes no sense for a legitimate businessman to get involved in a high-profile murder investigation . . .

They cross the George Washington Bridge and speed across the northern tip of Manhattan. Skirting the Bronx, they cross back into Queens, and the storefronts begin to have Hindi names as they approach Jackson Heights.

The limo screeches to a halt by Ranjit's apartment, and he climbs out into the heat of the afternoon.

"Wait." The driver powers down his window and hands over a bulky manila envelope. "Patel Sahib said to give you this."

"What is it?"

"How the hell do I know?" The man sneers. "You want it or no? Should I take it back and say you rejected it?"

Ranjit tucks the package under his arm and watches the car drive away, noting its number plate.

When he's inside his apartment he rips open the envelope and empties the contents onto his tangled sheets. Out falls a white envelope and a gray plastic-looking handgun with three extra magazines taped to its textured grip.

Despite its lightweight polymer construction, Ranjit knows that it is a standard police-issue Glock 17. In the envelope is a firearms license authorizing him to carry the weapon, a stack of hundred-dollar bills, about three thousand dollars total, and Jay Patel's business card with a phone number scribbled on it. There is no mistake about it. He is now firmly in Patel's employ.

The panic rises in his throat. He pulls out his cell phone and dials Thompson.

"Krumholtz and Thompson. Can I help you?"

"Yes. This is Ranjit Singh. Sandy Thompson is my lawyer. I need to see him right away. Where is your office?"

"Mr. Singh, Mr. Thompson is a very busy man. He's going to be in court till late this evening. Maybe he can call back then."

"When?"

The voice takes on an edge of exasperation. "I couldn't say exactly. He has many clients. Now, please leave a message."

"Forget it."

Ranjit disconnects, picks up his laptop, and looks up Krumholtz and Thompson's Web site. It has testimonials in a cheesy Comic Sans font and a post box number, but no street address. He thinks about the lawyer's stained clothes, and then it hits him—*Thompson has no office.* He probably works out of his car, and sees clients in the back room of Pham's Pho. Maybe Patel was right: putting his life into the hands of a man like that is useless. And if Thompson bills at two-fifty an hour, what does a real lawyer cost?

Patel wants him to find Mohan. In this city of eight million people, he has a week to find one man. How is he going to do that?

What day is today? Friday. The days and nights have blurred together, but he feels an old surge of excitement when he thinks about tonight. Of course: he was supposed to get together with Mohan and his friends at the club downtown, and meet that girl, Leela.

Mohan's buddies will definitely know about the murder by now— it's all over the news—but what if some of them show up at the club? It sounded like the Friday nights at Club Izizzi were a ritual.

Thompson has told Ranjit to mind his business, to stay out of trouble, but there is no law against going to a club. It's worth a shot.

Ranjit slumps onto his unmade bed. Across the room his reflection looks back at him, haggard and exhausted. Lying on the unmade bed next to him is the crisp bundle of hundred-dollar bills and the brand-new handgun.

Almost without thinking, he reaches for the Glock. It feels light, almost like a toy, but the magazines are real enough, seventeen rounds of 9mm Luger bullets that have real stopping power. He slides one in and feels it click into place. Holding it, he feels better. Whatever he's heading into, at least he will be armed.

Putting the gun carefully on the table, he sets his old digital alarm clock, strips off his clothes, and lies down; he must get some sleep before tonight, but his mind keeps racing. He tries to imagine the Golden Temple, aching to enter its calm, sacred space, but today the memory will not resurface.

How long has it been since he has been true to his faith? There are plenty of *gurdwaras* in New York City, but never has he entered one. He has been aloof from his community, and proud and vain and sinful.

He desperately tries to pray, but the scrap of prayer that comes to his mind is like a rebuke:

> *In the fourth watch of the night, when the Grim Reaper comes*
> *   to the field,*
> *When the messenger of death seizes and takes you away,*
> *No one will know where you have gone. So think of the Lord*
> *   now!*
> *All your weeping and wailing later is false. In an instant, you*
> *   will become a stranger. You will obtain exactly what you*
> *   have deserved . . .*

Turning toward the wall, it takes him a long time to fall sleep.

Chapter Nine

SIXTY KILOMETERS OUTSIDE BOMBAY, 1992

"Are they still there?" Shabana's lips barely moved as the makeup man leaned over her, powdering her cheeks. At twenty-five years old, she needed very little makeup, but still, it took forever. "Are those people still outside?"

In a corner of the canvas tent, Ruksana put down the sketchpad that she was drawing on. It was very hot, and the portable fans only sent forth gusts of warm air. "What are you talking about?"

"You know what I mean. Go and take a look, please."

Ruksana shot her sister a dirty look, slipped on a pair of oversized sunglasses, and walked outside. The tent was pitched on top of a barren hill, looking down onto a brown, sluggish river, spanned by a wooden footbridge. It was now set up with camera crews and reflectors, and on the far side of the river, the hillside was covered with hundreds of people squatting patiently in the hot sunlight: all the inhabitants of the neighboring village had come out to see the shooting of Shabana's first high-budget film, *Amerika Ke Kahanie*. S. K. Nagpal's initial idea had been fleshed out into an elaborate script that allowed for plenty of glamorous scenes shot in New York, Amsterdam, and Paris, but it would all begin here, in this dusty village.

One of the villagers spotted Ruksana and a shout went up. The hillside erupted in waving arms and cries of *Shabana zindabad*, Shabana forever!

They had mistaken Ruksana for her sister. She stood for a minute, her red sari fluttering in the wind, savoring the attention, and waved grandly back at the villagers, who cheered even louder.

Heading back into the tent, she reported to her sister, "They're still there. Hundreds of them."

"Oh God, how am I going to act with those yokels staring at me? They all smell of sweat and smoke." Shabana's voice thickened with distress. "I heard them shouting. They thought you were me, right?"

"I don't know what you're talking about." Ruksana slumped down in her corner, her face reddening, and the scar on her left cheek began to throb. At first, Shabana had treated her fame as a lark, but lately she had begun to put on airs, showing up late on set and acting like a diva.

Outside, the voices on the hillside rose to a crescendo.

"What is it now? Has Vineet arrived? Go and see, no?"

Vineet Gokhle, Shabana's costar, was to play the American-born playboy who hit her with his car, then fell in love with her.

Before Shabana could send her sister out again, S. K. Nagpal swaggered into the tent. In the year since Shabana's first movie, S.K.'s hairline had receded, and he had put on weight, but he still strutted confidently in his high-heeled boots.

"You look like a queen." S.K. half-bowed to Shabana.

Sitting in her corner, Ruksana watched as S.K. fawned over Shabana. They had become close and often spoke in whispers when Ruksana was around. S.K. acted as though that first screen test had never happened, as though he had not chosen Shabana over her.

Ruksana touched the scar on her cheek, hidden by a thick layer of makeup. Shabana said that it wasn't noticeable, but Ruksana always felt as though people were staring at it, that they could see how ugly she was. What did it matter, anyway? Shabana was the star, and she was the invisible one.

If only the milk hadn't been so hot . . . if only she had just stepped aside . . . Ruksana shut her eyes and tried to will away the memory, but her left cheek began to redden and throb.

". . . he drove all the way from Mumbai to wish you well," S.K. was saying to Shabana, his voice light and joking. "Come and meet him, *na?*"

"If I go outside, all my makeup is going to run." Shabana pouted and her lower lip protruded, emphasizing its fullness. "Why is this old man so important, anyway?"

All the jolliness left S.K.'s voice. "This *old man,* as you call him, is the main backer of your film." He snorted. "I'll wait outside for you, five minutes. Don Hajji Mustafa expects to be kept waiting by a star, but any longer, he'll get angry. And you don't want to make him angry."

"Don Hajji?" Shabana's eyes widened. "You said you were going to get financing from the *banks.* You said—"

"Sweetie, the amount that the bank was willing to lend us wouldn't even have covered your costumes. The Don is a professional, he won't interfere with the film. I'll see you outside."

S.K. left, and Shabana stared at herself in the mirror.

"Ruki." Her voice was soft now. "Come with me, *na?* I don't want to meet these people alone."

Curiosity overcoming her anger, Ruksana slipped on her sunglasses again and covered her head with her *dupatta*. She trailed Shabana down the hillside, watching her sister's walk change, shift into a slower, seductive rhythm, as though she were listening to some faraway music. Shabana's chaste white sari and modest, plaited hair—she was supposed to be portraying a village girl—only emphasized the sexiness of her walk.

On the hillside across the river, the villagers stirred, but they did not utter a sound. The name of Don Hajji Mustafa had a dampening effect on them. Everybody in the state of Maharashtra—and many beyond—knew his name. The Don now owned a huge construction

company and a garment exporting business, but the faint odor of his past still followed him, like dog shit stuck to a shoe.

An open tent was pitched at the bottom of the hill and Don Hajji Mustafa sat within it on a red plush couch that seemed to have materialized out of nowhere, surrounded by his entourage. With his nondescript round face, paunch, and cheap aviator shades, the Don could have been one of the thousands of anonymous clerks who toiled in offices in Bombay.

Seeing the man, Shabana's shoulders stiffened, but she smiled and salaamed prettily.

"*Salaam aleikum*, Uncle," she said, using the honorific.

The Don took off his aviators and gazed at her. His dark eyes had a fierce, burning gaze, like the eyes of a dying beggar, or one of the emaciated mystics who stood on riverbanks. They were the eyes of a person who was barely there, who inhabited his own, fiery world.

Shabana gulped, and Don Hajji Mustafa slipped his sunglasses back on.

"*Waalekum as Salaam, beti.*" The Don's voice was surprisingly soft and gentle. "Ah, you are a star, but so well mannered. As well mannered as your father, Noor Mohammad. I used to know him, many years ago. A shame that he didn't live to see your success. It must be hard for your family, three women and no man. This is your sister? The resemblance is—"

Hidden by her sunglasses and *dupatta*, Ruksana felt her heart race.

"Oh, she is a simple girl. She doesn't like acting and all that." Shabana smiled again. "She is my manager."

S.K.'s boots clacked as he stepped forward eagerly. "Don, thank you for gracing our humble set—"

"Humble?" Don Hajji Mustafa gave a thin-lipped smile. "This is the most expensive film I have ever financed. But my accountant here, Jayram Patel, he convinced me that you will not fail. He is a big fan of yours." The Don turned to a tall, thin man in white trousers and a white shirt. He was painfully thin, and had thick black hair. "Jayram is my right-hand man. Without him, I am lost."

Patel slouched forward and put his hands together in a *namaste.* "Pleasure . . . you are a true artiste, madam. Anything you need, please let us know."

The Don waved at a dark-skinned, squat man with a handlebar mustache. "And this is Veenu Gopal. Our nickname for him is 'the Hammer.' He will be helping you with security for your film. Not just crowds, also these *saala-gandu* journalists. On our last film, this journalist fellow, he sneakily took some pictures of our star while she was bathing . . ."

"And he is still in the hospital." The Hammer smiled and shook Shabana's hand. His white T-shirt could barely contain arms as thick as tree trunks. "You have nothing to fear, miss. We will protect you."

"And this . . ." The Don waved his arm tiredly at a gangly youth standing beside him. "This is Lateef, my nephew, my late brother's son."

Acne covered the youth's forehead and chin, and he was wearing a silky blue tracksuit, with fancy American sneakers that would have cost one of the villagers a full year's income.

"Shabana-*ji,* what a pleasure." The youth leered at her. "I heard that there will be nudity in your film? Will it need an adult certificate?"

"Chup." Quiet. The Don cut off the youth and smiled tiredly. "Lateef is my nephew, but I treat him like a son, I spoil him. So sometimes he says stupid things. Don't you, Lateef?"

The youth scowled, thrust his hands into his pockets, and slouched away.

S.K. stepped forward and smiled ingratiatingly. "Don-Sahib, I am happy to sit and talk with you, but Shabana needs to finish her makeup . . ."

"Of course, of course. *Beti,* you should know one thing about me." Don Hajji Mustafa took off his sunglasses, and it was as though a window had been opened onto a fiery place. "This is not just a business for me. It is a family. I will be like a father to you. If you have pain, I feel that pain. If you have problems, they are my problems."

"Thank you, Uncle—"

"And because we are a family, we trust each other. We do not go outside the family. I know you understand what I am saying. You are a smart girl. Now, work hard on this film, and make us all proud."

Shabana *salaamed* again prettily, and Ruksana followed her back up the hill. As soon as they entered the tent, Shabana slumped into her chair and stared at the mirror.

"Oh God, my makeup is ruined. That man gives me the creeps. What was all that about? *Family?* They say that the Don was an *animal,* worse than an animal, a rabid *dog.*"

Ruksana felt a sudden rush of victory when she saw that her sister's composure had been disrupted, but before she could say anything, a voice came from the tent flap.

"A rabid dog? My uncle won't like hearing that. He doesn't mind being called a *chutiya,* a *gandu,* a *maderchod.* But a dog? He hates that."

Shabana jerked around. The Don's nephew, Lateef, stood smiling smugly, his hands tucked into the pockets of his blue tracksuit.

Ruksana moved forward protectively. "Listen, get out of the dressing room. You have no right to be here. I'm Shabana's manager, I'll tell S.K.—"

"And what? That faggot is down there right now, kissing my uncle's arse." Lateef moved closer, loose limbed and suddenly confident. "We just welcomed you into our family, and you call my uncle a rabid dog. *Tsk, tsk.*"

Ruksana changed her strategy, making her voice soft and placating. "Now, Lateef, she didn't mean it, she didn't mean it at all. A simple slip of the tongue—"

"You're her sister?" The youth stared at Ruksana, now without sunglasses, her head uncovered. "The two of you look—"

"Never mind me. You need to leave, please."

"What's your name again?"

"Ruksana. But everybody calls me Ruki."

"Ruki, huh? Well, Ruki, if your sister didn't mean it, we can kiss and make up. After all, we are family now. What is a kiss between a brother and a sister?" Lateef jiggled his hands in his pockets. "One kiss, and all is forgotten."

Ruksana glanced back at Shabana, who quivered with fear.

"Or I could talk to my uncle, right now. He listens to me, you know, he does."

"Okay, okay." Ruksana turned to her sister. "How about it? One kiss, and he's gone, right?" She looked at Lateef. "And don't mess her makeup."

"No." Shabana jerked backward. "I won't. I won't."

"Shut up. Just do it."

The boy stepped closer, and Shabana flinched, then offered her cheek. Lateef leaned in and pressed his lips against hers. Then he stepped back, a pleased look on his face.

"Well, sister. That wasn't so bad, was it? See, I don't bite. I'll be seeing you." He turned and sauntered out of the tent.

Shabana leaned forward and spat onto the floor. "Oh my God. I'm so humiliated. Ruki, I can't believe you let him—"

"Maybe you should have kept your big mouth shut."

"Cheee." Shabana spat violently, her whole body shaking. "I want to die. I want to die right now."

Ruksana could feel the scar on her cheek begin to throb again. "Sister, you talk too easily about dying. What do you know about death?"

"Get out of my sight." Shabana's face was red now. "Go." She reached up and pulled out a strand of hair.

"Don't start with all that pulling nonsense. We don't have time to do another weave."

"Leave me alone! Go away!"

Just then S.K. walked in and saw Shabana's reddened face, spit dripping down her chin.

"What the hell is going on? What happened?"

Ruksana shrugged. "Nothing. Shabana wants to die, that's all."

Chapter Ten

Are Mohan's friends at Club Izizzi?

Ranjit leans against the frosted glass bar, rows of backlit glass bottles shining behind him. He looks around again, sipping from the vodka and tonic he's been nursing for the past half an hour. It's almost eleven, but the large dance floor is empty, and only a few couples sit on the U-shaped white banquettes at the edges of the room. No sign of a group of Indians.

He managed to sleep for a few hours, but he's still exhausted, and the vodka isn't helping. He wants to ask the dreadlocked barman what time things get busy here, but that will involve shouting above the thumping bass music. Instead he sips his vodka and watches the flickering projections that fill one high wall. They follow the logic of some forgotten dream: the lips of a Japanese geisha nibble at a red cherry, a flight of birds rises above a ruined temple, a tiger's sinewy body is barely glimpsed, sliding through a thicket of tropical bamboo.

So this is where Mohan liked to come on his night off, to unwind and become something more than a doorman. Ranjit can imagine him here, amongst the dreamlike projections and the house music, his lemon-yellow shirt unbuttoned to his navel, his hair slicked back with gel.

Hanging out here with his friends, did Mohan pretend to be unattached and chat up other girls? The cops said that he and Shabana had been lovers for quite a while, but Ranjit has a hard time imagining it: sure, Mohan is good with waitresses and shop girls, but what would a famous actress see in this hick from small-town Haryana?

He imagines Mohan having her apartment cleaned, emptying out her refrigerator, bringing back her dry cleaning. And apparently, in return, Shabana had let him occasionally spend the night, using him to fulfill her needs. Or has Ranjit got this all wrong? Was theirs a love that transcended money and class? Did they eat and laugh together in that kitchen, re-creating some earlier, simpler world?

Whatever their relationship was, it has ended horribly: Shabana, dead, sprawled out like a rag doll, her face gone, her hair spread around her in a black, lustrous fan.

Raising his glass, Ranjit takes a swig of vodka.

The club has begun to slowly fill up with people, some heading for the bar, others sprawling on the banquettes. Ranjit sips his vodka, watching the men, some in tight T-shirts, others in untucked plaid shirts, boots and lumberjack beards, the latest downtown look. The women wear tiny dresses that show plenty of cleavage and a few coy tattoos, their shiny, long hair falling to their shoulders. He knows that in a few hours, this crowd will have lost their luster and will be out there hailing cabs. The lucky ones will snag a partner, while others will go home alone, puking all over some unlucky cabbie's backseat.

The bass music rises to an oceanic roar. Waitresses appear, silver buckets of champagne held high in one hand, lit sparklers in the other. People move onto the glass floor, dancing in stuttering, fractured gestures, jerking their necks around like parakeets.

A girl alone at the bar is pushed down toward Ranjit by the new crowd. She is very short, with an afro of curly black hair, the spaghetti straps of her tan dress revealing smooth brown shoulders. She must be twenty or twenty-one, and there is something catlike about her upturned nose, small mouth, and perfectly arched eyebrows. Most incongruously, her eyes are a deep sea green. In another few years, she could be overweight, but right now she is as perfectly rounded as a ripe peach.

Clinking an empty glass onto the bar, she orders a fresh drink. "A sidewinder, please."

Despite her height—five one, maybe—she has the small woman's gift for sexual projection, her dress stretched tight over muscular thighs, her stilettos adding at least four inches to her height.

She glances at Ranjit and smiles abstractedly, and he smiles back, both attracted to her and appalled by his attraction. He wonders for a second if this is Leela. *No, it can't be. Mohan said that she was Indian, and this girl looks Hispanic, or Brazilian.*

The dreadlocked bartender hands her a tall drink, smiling ingratiatingly. "Here you go. Have I seen you here before?"

Without answering, she sips her drink and wrinkles up her pretty nose.

"*Yo.* I asked for a sidewinder. What's this?"

"It's a sidewinder."

"No, it isn't. You need to use fresh tea."

The bartender's smile is frozen as he takes away her drink. Ranjit turns toward her. "Your drink has tea in it?"

"Supposed to have vodka, cinnamon, and *fresh*-brewed tea. Not some Lipton's crap."

"I agree. I hate tea bags."

"Most people don't know the difference, but I'm picky. No Lipton's for me, I like a good Darjeeling."

He is surprised at her humorous, matter-of-fact tone. Most good-looking girls in Manhattan are cold and distant. "I've been looking for a good cup of tea in this city, but I haven't found—"

"Hey, Lenore! What are you doing in this place? You look great."

A tall, Italian-looking man is walking up to the woman, his eyes widening in exaggerated surprise. His thinning hair is brushed straight back, and he wears a tailored seersucker suit. The girl turns toward him, and the man leans in as they start a conversation.

Ranjit feels a stab of disappointment, then shrugs. Despite his new clothes—a peaked black turban to match his new black embroidered shirt, dark trousers, and ankle-high boots—he feels like a fish out of water.

This is a waste of time. No one is coming. Finishing his drink, he heads to the restroom, and on his way out, he looks at the bar one last time.

The man in the seersucker suit is leaning into the woman, his arm around her bare, brown shoulders. He says something, and she shakes her head in disagreement. When he leans in to kiss her on the lips she jerks her head away, crushed up against the bar by his weight.

Ranjit is just drunk enough to do what he does next. He crosses over to them in a few long strides, a big, cheesy smile on his face.

"Hey," he says to the woman. "Where have you been, honey? Been looking all over for you."

The man turns, sees Ranjit's turban and beard, and seems confused, but the woman catches on immediately.

"Oh, there you are," she says, smiling, and moving away from the man. "I've been looking for you."

Ranjit ducks past the man and stands beside her. "Is this a friend of yours?"

"Business acquaintance. He was just leaving. Right, Joey?"

The man smiles uncertainly, then smooths back his thinning hair with both hands. "Yeah, well," he growls, "I'll see you at the club, baby."

He walks away to a banquette across the room where two tall Russian women instantly make a fuss over him, ruffling his hair and playfully pulling at his lapels.

"Thanks." The girl smooths down her tan dress, and Ranjit tries not to stare at her. "Usually I can handle them, but this creep was really pushy."

"Don't mention it. I'm Ranjit Singh, by the way."

The girl stares up at him, her small lips parted in surprise. Across the room, the projection on the wall changes to a sumptuous sunset, tinting her face orange.

"You're Ranjit?"

"Yes." Confusion clouds his brain. "Do I know you?"

"I'm Leela. Leela Rampersad, Mohan's friend. We were supposed to meet here."

"You're Leela? But I thought you were . . ."

"Indian? Well, I am. Half, anyway. I'm Guyanese: my mom's black, my dad's Indian." She gestures at her tight, curly black hair. "It always throws people off. Mohan didn't tell you what I looked like?"

Ranjit feels his face redden. "No. And I guess he didn't tell you that I'm a Sikh?"

"He just said that you were tall, which you are. Trust him to leave out the key details." They both laugh, and she continues, "Where are all the others, do you know? Mohan's always late, but the rest are usually at the bar . . ."

How could she not have heard? The murder has been all over the news.

Leela glances at the tall Italian man across the room, and there is a spark of fear in her eyes. *This may not be the best time to tell her about it.*

"Hey, would you like to get out of here?"

She puckers her small lips and nods. "This place isn't fun anymore. All these Wall Street creeps. I'll just freshen up and meet you outside, okay?"

He watches her walk away, head held high. The projection of the tiger is back on the wall, and she vanishes against it. The tiger slithers between the stalks of bamboo, headed for some unknown destination.

The tall Italian man had called Leela "Lenore." Ranjit registers the fact, then shrugs. People in this city lead complicated lives.

Walking outside, he passes the long, drunken line to get into Izizzi. There are clusters of single men and women, already flirting with each other and swaying to the faint thump of music.

Standing under a streetlight, he breathes in the hot night air. The Meatpacking District used to reek of congealed blood and diesel, but now smells of perfume and the rich odor of grilling steaks. A few meat wholesalers still survive here, but most of the brick warehouses have been turned into trendy bars and restaurants. On a Friday night, it will be hard to find a quiet place where he can talk to Leela.

Just then she emerges from the club, walking quickly. In the sodium vapor light from the streetlight he can see how short she is, clattering over the cobblestones in her high stilettos.

"Would you like to go for a drink?" He suddenly remembers a quiet place. "There's a good bar at the Hotel Gansevoort, a block from here."

She shakes her head. "That's very nice of you, but I think I'm going to call it a night. I'm really tired, I probably shouldn't have come out tonight." She extends a small hand with manicured pink nails. "Maybe we can do this some other time? And maybe Mohan will actually show up, too."

So she definitely hasn't heard about the murder; he has to stall her departure. "Mohan told me you're a nanny. Working with kids must be exhausting."

"*Uh-huh*. A four-year-old boy. He's sweet, but sometimes he's a handful. Well, good night. I'll just get a cab."

"Look, why don't I drop you? I'm driving." Ranjit had asked Ali Khan to sign out a cab for him.

"I live all the way in Richmond Hill. Little Guyana. Probably out of your way."

He takes a step closer and smiles. "I'm in Jackson Heights. It'll be no problem for me to swing over. Really. You look beat."

She hesitates, swaying a little in her high heels. "Are you sure?"

"Absolutely. I'm parked over there, by the West Side Highway."

She shrugs, a pretty little gesture. "Okay, I guess. Thanks."

As they walk toward the river, her heel catches suddenly in the cobblestones, and she trips. He catches her upper arm, holding her up, and for a second her soft, warm body brushes against his.

"Whoops, thanks." She smiles embarrassedly, he lets go of her arm, and she picks her way carefully down the street. When they reach the parked cab, he walks around to unlock the driver's door, but she just stares at him with her sea-green eyes.

"This is your car?"

"Yes." It is his turn to be embarrassed. "Didn't Mohan tell you? I drive a cab."

"He said you owned an import-export business."

"Close. I work as a security guard at an import place."

She chuckles. "He's such a bullshit artist. And all this while I thought you were some uptight, rich business guy."

"That I'm not. Welcome to my chariot."

Sliding into the passenger seat, she leans forward and examines his hack license.

"What a terrible picture. You look like a terrorist."

"I assure you, I'm also not a terrorist. You have nothing to worry about."

"I'll reserve judgment till I see how you drive."

She smiles at him, and there is a flash of a different, relaxed person. Turning the key in the ignition, they drive down Horatio Street. The windows are down, and he can smell the musty odor of the river, and something else. He has caught a whiff of it from time to time, when a young couple gets into his cab, starry eyed and in love.

Despite everything that has gone terribly wrong, he smells, with this girl beside him, the warm, human scent of possibility.

Chapter Eleven

They work their way across the island, and even though his medallion light is unlit, people try to flag him down. Each time this happens, he says, "Morons," and Leela laughs, but otherwise she seems content to sit in silence.

They take the Midtown Tunnel and head east on the Long Island Expressway, and Ranjit is suddenly at a loss for words.

As they pass the Calvary Cemetery she stares out of the window at the thicket of tombstones, crowding right up to the highway. The streetlights play across her composed, catlike face, lighting it and erasing it. *She's just a kid,* he tells himself again. *Find out whatever you can, drop her home, forget about it.*

They are reaching Flushing when he finally speaks.

"So, you know Mohan well? You guys get together often?"

"He's a nice guy." She shrugs her shoulders. "Not like the other guys." She points into the darkness at the tall, abandoned observation towers in Flushing Meadows. "Those are so weird. Like flying saucers."

"Yeah, I think they're from the World's Fair. From 1964."

"Oh." She lapses into silence, and he realizes that for her, the sixties are ancient history.

He tries again. "And you know Mohan from the Dakota?"

"*Hmmm.*"

"Must be a tough place to work, huh? All those super-rich people?"

That seems to work. She sits up a little straighter.

"The kids are okay," she says softly. "Kids are just kids, you know? All they need is love, but the adults . . . You know, when I first got here, I thought that people who live in those fancy buildings must have it made. But working there, you see how messed up they are."

At least she's talking. "How are they messed up?"

"Like . . ." Her sea-green eyes shine with reflected light. "This kid I take care of, Alex, he's four. The mom, she's gone all day, the dad travels a lot. They only want him to eat organic peanut butter, organic this, organic that. And you know what the kid wants? He wants to go to the park and get ice cream from the ice-cream truck. But they won't let him." She pauses. "And he hardly sees his parents. Sometimes they come back late and wake him up so they can play with him. Last time that happened, he said, *No, no, I want Leela.* His mom was really mad, but what could she say? So the next morning the bitch yelled at me for being five minutes late."

They turn south on the Van Wyck and speed past the darkness of Corona Park.

Ranjit nods. "Mohan said the same thing. He said that the tenants, they treat him like a servant."

"Oh, Mohan." She smiles tiredly. "He's really good with those kinds of people. He does things for them, little things, and they become dependent on him. He'll go out in the rain to get Swiss chocolates for this old lady . . . and the younger ones like him too."

Ranjit doesn't reply, and she hastens to explain.

"I mean, he's not my type, but the other women, doesn't matter if they're nine or ninety, he charms them all. There's this actress . . . no, I shouldn't gossip."

"Shabana Shah? He was talking about her."

"Yes. The other guys say that they have a thing going on, but Mohan, he won't talk about it. He's funny that way."

"Who are your other friends who come to Izizzi? Mohan said they're a nice crowd."

"You know Kishen? Mohan's cousin?"

Ranjit shakes his head, and makes a mental note. Leela's tiredness seems to have been erased by the darkness and the motion of the cab. He's seen it happen before with his passengers, who open up on long rides, as though he is a priest in a confessional.

"Kishen's really fun. Sometimes he brings his buddies, but they're a little rough. They dress all flashy, but you can still smell the grease on them."

He must look confused, because she explains. "Kishen works in a garage somewhere in the Bronx, he's a mechanic, fixes fancy cars. Lamborghinis, Ferraris, like that."

"And they're tight? Mohan and Kishen?"

"I guess so. They're from the same village in India or something . . ."

Maybe Mohan is holed up at this Kishen's place. How hard could it be to find an Indian mechanic in the Bronx?

An ambulance goes by in the other direction, siren wailing. She swivels her head to see its red taillights, then turns to him. "Hey, I've been talking and talking. What about you? How long have you been driving?"

He is conscious of the spaghetti straps of her dress cutting into her smooth shoulders. "About two years. The cab is just temporary. Till I get back on my feet."

She laughs, a quick exhalation of breath.

"What's so funny?"

She shakes her head in amusement. "You know, that's exactly what my dad used to say. He drove a cab here for fourteen years."

Ranjit has to smile. Ali Khan and all the other cabbies always claim that their decade-long careers are "just temporary."

"Yeah, well, nobody *wants* to drive a cab. So your dad got out? What's he doing now?"

Leela is silent, and when she speaks, he strains to hear her voice.

"He passed away. A couple of years ago." She stares off into the darkness.

Damn it, why did he have to ask that? "I'm sorry if I upset you."

"No, it's okay. Sometimes, when things were quiet, I'd ride around with him. This reminds me of him." She gestures at the dark, sleeping city. "At the end, when he was in the hospital, the other cabbies would come and visit him. They'd talk about potholes, speeding tickets, the best route from here to there. He was dying, and that was what he wanted to talk about. I couldn't understand it then, but now I can. He just wanted to feel normal. That's what people want, right? To feel normal?"

Ranjit thinks about Shanti sitting, far away, in Chandigarh, and aches to hug her.

"You're right about that. So you were close with your dad?"

"He left Guyana when I was fourteen. I only got a visa to come here when I was nineteen, so I hadn't seen him for a long time. And he was so strict, I couldn't get used to that. Plus I didn't like living in Little Guyana. Everybody is always in your business, everybody gossips . . . it's worse than a village."

"But you still live there."

"Yeah. I don't like it, but who can afford Manhattan?"

He nods.

"Hey, you're divorced, right? How long has it been?"

Her question stuns him. "Two years. It's that obvious?"

"I can always tell. Divorced men, they ask questions, they listen. They're more, what's the word . . . solicitous."

He likes this girl. He likes her laugh, and her directness, and the way she searched and found the one particular word she needed. And so far he hasn't told her about the murder.

"I think I'm just old-fashioned. Listen, Leela, I wanted to tell you something—"

"No, you're not *old-fashioned*. Indian men either want to worship women, or treat them like whores. You're not like that. You saw that creep at the club, you got me out of there. Other guys, they would have ignored it, or picked a fight."

Ranjit is silent as they turn onto Liberty Avenue. They are deep in the heart of Queens now, amongst cramped, long rows of houses, with yards the size of postage stamps. The garbagemen must still be on strike, because the curbs here are crowded with trash cans; he sees a rat the size of a small cat jump out of a can and disappear into the shadows.

As they get closer to Little Guyana, the street comes alive with people out in the warm night, strolling and shopping. They pass a shop selling gaudy chandeliers, a hundred of them blazing in the darkness, and then a shop selling gold ornaments. Stopping at a light, he watches a man with a cart full of green coconuts slash one open with a machete, pop in a straw, and hand it to a waiting couple.

They drive past a white concrete Hindu temple which sits cheek by jowl with Matty's Mini-Mart and the Famida 99 Cents store. They pass Little Guyana Bake Shop, Anjee's Sari Shop, and Spice World. Everywhere Ranjit sees India, but somehow distorted, the colors wrong, the smells unfamiliar.

Leela points into the distance. "Hey, you can drop me off across from Sonny's Roti Shop. It's that one, under the El, with the yellow awning."

"I can take you home, no problem . . . And, Leela, there is something I have to talk to you about."

She's smiling now, her face in half-shadow as they drive under the dingy iron structure of the elevated train line.

"Yes, okay," she says.

"Okay . . . okay about what?"

"You were going to ask me out, right? So, yes, okay."

Despite the confusion, he feels something swell inside his chest. "Great. But Leela—"

"I'm working tomorrow. So maybe Sunday? We can meet at Sonny's." She gestures at the large yellow awning with its red lettering. "Say, seven? They have good doubles."

"I've never had doubles. What's that?" He pulls the cab to a stop.

"Roti, filled with chickpeas, chicken, tamarind sauce, mango pickle. Well, thanks for the ride. It was sweet of you." Her hand rests on the door handle.

"Sounds good. But listen. There is something else—"

She looks expectantly at him with her sea-green eyes.

"Look, I didn't tell you the whole story about Mohan, why he wasn't at the club tonight. I thought you would know about it."

"What are you talking about?"

"It's all over the news. Mohan, he . . . they suspect that he killed Shabana Shah, the actress."

"What?"

"And the cops think I'm mixed up in it. Mohan's vanished somewhere, and I have to find him. If you have any idea where he might be, please tell me."

In the fluorescent light from the shops he sees her eyes go blank.

"Shabana's dead?"

"Yes. Last night, at the Dakota."

Her voice is a whisper. "My God. I can't believe it . . ." She covers her mouth with one hand. "I can't get involved in this. I can't."

"What do you mean? Why would you be—"

"You don't know these people."

She is out of the cab in one movement, and the door slams.

"Hey, wait—"

She moves fast, running across the road, and he jumps out of the cab and follows her.

"Leela, listen—"

She passes Sonny's and rounds the corner, running down a side street lined with tiny detached houses, overflowing trash cans lining both curbs. Two young men sit in folding chairs out on the sidewalk, drinking forties, and Leela yells something at them, wrenches off her stilettos, and keeps on running, her shoes held in her hands. Her dress flares under a streetlight, then vanishes into the garbage-smelling darkness.

"Yo, man, why you after Leela?"

The two young men saunter out into the street. They have Indian features, but they're way too muscular, with broad shoulders and thick biceps under their baggy white T-shirts, and their style is Hispanic, with shaved heads and thin beards carved onto their chins.

Ranjit is already breathless. "I just want to talk to her."

The bigger man steps into Ranjit's path and pushes a hand into his chest. The smaller, ferret-faced man giggles excitedly.

"She don' wan' to talk to you. Fuck off, turban man."

He pushes harder, and Ranjit stumbles backward.

"Just give me a minute. You don't understand—"

"You don' fuckin' understan'. You about to get hurt."

The big man's arm pulls back, forming into a fist. The smaller man moves closer.

Just as it used to in combat, a part of Ranjit's mind detaches, and he knows the movements of both men, knows exactly where the big man's fist is going to be.

He sidesteps, easily ducking the blow, then punches hard into the side of the man's thick neck. As the big man gasps and doubles over, Ranjit brings his knee up, hearing it crunch into cartilage, and the man falls moaning to the street.

The smaller man's thin face contorts in anger and he reaches under his baggy shirt. Ranjit knows that he is going for a gun, but there is no time to get out of the way. His foot finds a trash can and kicks at it.

The small man pulls a snub-nosed automatic from his waistband, but he takes a second to sidestep the rolling trash can, and in that instant Ranjit dives into the street. A bullet cracks above him, and then he is rolling and ducking behind a car parked on the other side.

Shielded by the flank of the car, he comes up in a half crouch, and the Glock appears in his fist, an automatic reflex. Peering through the car's darkened window, he sees the small man swaggering across the street, his gun hand out, a perfect target, silhouetted against the streetlight. Without thinking, Ranjit raises the Glock, ready to shoot through the car window, one bullet smack into the man's chest.

His finger is tensed on the trigger, when he catches himself. *No. No matter what, he must not fire.* Lowering the weapon, he peers into the mirror again, seeing that the small man is still advancing, a sneer on his face, the gun held sideways, gangsta style. Very stylish, but hard to shoot accurately like that.

Ranjit will have to chance it. Sticking the gun back into his waistband, he suddenly rises and runs, crouched over, using the line of parked cars as cover.

"Fuck you! Fuck you!" The small man is screaming excitedly as he fires, two shots going wild. One of them ricochets off a car, and there is the sound of shattering glass, followed by shouts. Lights are coming on all down the street as Ranjit rounds the corner.

The cab is where he left it, and he sprints across the avenue, jumps in and guns the engine, which roars into life. Thank the Guru that his cab is a retired Ford Vic police interceptor.

As he speeds away down Liberty Avenue, a shot comes hurtling out of the darkness, cracking into the cab's right-hand side mirror.

He speeds through a red light, seeing a group of boys in shiny football jerseys staring at him open-mouthed. Sirens wail through the darkness, and as Ranjit gets onto the Van Wyck, two police cars pass him, going in the other direction, lights flashing.

As soon as he's on the Van Wyck, he's just another yellow cab, lost in the stream of cabs heading in both directions. He leans back in his seat, soaked in sweat, realizing that he'd come within a split second of shooting the weasel-faced man. It is as though someone else took over, a self that he thought was long gone. So the instincts are all still there, hidden deep inside, there when he needs them.

The adrenaline high fades away, and he realizes that his right hand is throbbing from the punch he threw. Yet he feels more alive than he has in a long time, and then he realizes why: his anger is back, burning nakedly in his chest, incinerating all the stored-up fear.

As his breathing subsides, he thinks through what happened back there.

Clearly those men thought they were protecting Leela. He's seen guys like those in every outer-borough neighborhood: small-scale drug dealers mostly, self-styled neighborhood heroes. Leela probably knows

them from the neighborhood, a pretty girl who brings out their chival-
rous instincts.

He thinks of her last words, blurted out before she ran: *You don't
know these people*. Who the hell is she talking about? Damn it, if only
he'd had a few more minutes with her. *Calm down, try and figure this
out*. Shabana lived at the Dakota, and Leela and Mohan both work
there. Was Leela referring to someone from the building? Another
doorman? Her employers?

There is no way of knowing more, but at least Leela had told him
about Mohan's cousin; an Indian mechanic in the Bronx can't be that
hard to find.

When Ranjit reaches home, he parks in an alley and examines the
cab's right-side mirror: it hangs on by a few shreds of plastic, with a bullet
hole cobwebbing the glass. Grunting, he rips off the mirror and pushes it
deep into a trash can. He doesn't want Ali Khan returning a cab with a
shot-up mirror. Better to call it an accident and pay for a new one.

Half an hour later, he lies on his narrow bed, thinking of Leela running away like a frightened animal. She's the first woman with whom
he's had a real conversation in two years, and all he's done is scare
her to death. He thinks of his ex-wife, Preetam, all her beauty and self-
confidence evaporating during their marriage. He thinks of Anna Neals,
coughing blood as she died in his arms on a remote beach in the Vineyard. Maybe he should just stay away from all women.

What about his daughter, the one woman in his life that he cannot
ever abandon? Shanti is coming in three weeks, and he can't see any way
out of this mess. Will he end up losing her too?

He checks the time: three A.M., past noon in India. On an impulse
he calls her, and she picks up on the first ring.

"Hi, *beti*. What are you up to?"

"*Papaji*, you never call me this late. Are you okay? Is something
wrong?"

"I'm fine, fine, I just wanted to hear your voice." He can hear the
sound of the television. "What are you watching?"

"I was just thinking about you. This actress, Shabana Shah, she was murdered in New York, it's so sad. They're doing a program about her. Did you hear about it?"

He stiffens. "Yes, I heard something, it's terrible."

"Mama is worried about me coming to New York, she says it's a dangerous place—"

"Now, look." He closes his eyes and pinches the bridge of his nose. "We've been through all this, I'm not going to renegotiate everything with your mother. It's perfectly safe. I'm looking for a nice apartment, and we'll be fine. Let's talk about something else."

Shanti tells him about school, and her Hindi test, and Ranjit listens, but has nothing else to say.

"Are you sure you're okay, *Papaji*? You're very quiet."

"You're right, it's very late here, I'm tired. I'll call you again, soon." He pauses and then forces himself to say it. "And I love you, okay?"

There is a shocked silence. "I love you too, *Papaji*."

He hangs up, and across the room his reflection stares back at him. He lies awake for an eternity, and reminds himself that no matter how much he loves his daughter, what happens next is not in his control, has never been in his control. A scrap of prayer drifts through his mind:

Some form alliances with friends, children, and siblings.
Some form alliances with in-laws and relatives.
Some form alliances with chiefs and leaders,
But my alliance is only with the Lord, who is everywhere . . .

What happens now is in the hands of the Gurus.

Chapter Twelve

BOMBAY, 1995

Shabana was in the middle of a dance sequence, her long black hair whipping around her head. Thumping music filled the air, Hindi lyrics combined with the latest techno beat, and a row of backup dancers swirled behind her.

After the success of *Amerika Ke Kahanie,* she had no shortage of roles, and was now shooting four movies at the same time. Today, she was deep into her role as Laila, the disco-going daughter of a rich family who had fallen madly in love with a poor street boy. *Laila Aur Paul* was a Bollywood remake of *Romeo and Juliet,* supplemented with dance scenes and fantasy sequences.

Shabana's hips gyrated to the hypnotic beat, and she had just started a split when the world suddenly slowed. She became aware of her thigh muscles tensing, heard the swish of the backup dancers' dresses, could smell their sweat. Then: blackness.

She woke to warm hands stroking her cheeks. They were so tender that she wanted to fall into the darkness again, and allow the hands to keep on caressing her. People touched her all the time—wardrobe assistants, makeup men—but not like this. This touch awoke a tenderness in her that had been hidden since her father's death.

"Madam. Wake up, madam."

The hands rubbed gentle circles into her cheeks, and she reluctantly opened her eyes. She was lying on the stage with her legs splayed out, the heavy red silk of her *ghaghra* bunched around her waist. The dancers circled her with their heavily made-up faces, the concern in their eyes mixed with satisfaction: the biggest star in Bollywood, so removed from them, was human, after all.

The hands withdrew, and Shabana looked up into a young man's face. He was not conventionally handsome: his face was too long perhaps, the jaw too heavy, covered with a three-day growth. But his eyes were a deep hazel, and a lock of his badly cut, too-short hair flopped boyishly onto his forehead. He was very muscular, and wore a faded gray T-shirt and jeans torn at the knees.

"Madam, you fainted. Are you all right? Have you eaten today?"

Shabana thought back to her five A.M. start and the two other films she had worked on before coming onto this set at noon; her usual workday stretched from early in the morning till late at night.

Had she eaten? All she remembered was a cup of tea somewhere along the way. She shook her head.

"*Aare,*" the young man shouted offstage in an authoritative voice. "Get Madam a cup of tea, lots of sugar, and bring the biscuits from my locker."

The young man pulled her to her feet. There were orange starbursts in her peripheral vision, and when she staggered, he put a muscular arm around her waist.

They sat on folding chairs in a corner of the set, and she held her aching head in her hands.

"I hope you like Britannia biscuits. The orange ones with cream filling." He smiled, and she could see that his two front teeth overlapped slightly. Along with his dark, heavy eyebrows, it gave him a wolfish, hungry look.

Out of the corner of her eye, she saw the director of the film enter the set, accompanied by a thin, bespectacled man she recognized as the studio doctor.

She turned quickly to the young man. "Are you an actor?"

"No, I just graduated from the film college in Pune. I'm the third cameraman. Third *assistant* cameraman."

Cameraman. Thank God. Actors were impossible to date, with their competitive jealousy and their narcissism.

"I love orange biscuits," Shabana said, mustering a faint smile. "My father used to buy them for me."

"Nice to meet you. I'm Sanjeev."

"I'm Shabana."

"Yes, I know who you are." Sanjeev smiled his wolfish smile and Shabana felt herself blush.

Just then the director and the doctor came hurrying up, and Sanjeev walked away. He returned a few minutes later, wordlessly handed her a packet of biscuits, and vanished beyond the glare of the lights. She took a bite of a biscuit, and the citrus sweetness filled her mouth, a taste from childhood.

She inquired about Sanjeev, and the makeup woman said that all the backup dancers were in love with him. He ignored them, though, and spent all his time messing around with the Arriflex 35mm cameras and pestering the older cameramen about obscure technical issues. Hearing this, Shabana felt heartened.

At age twenty-eight, she had dated all sorts of men: young, swaggering actors; older directors; tycoons in suits who collected art. But nothing lasted, and none of them could handle her; they ended up resenting her stardom or viewed her as a trophy.

Now she relied on Ruksana to shield her from men. Like an old-time governess, Ruki would stand next to Shabana, her arms folded over her chest. As soon as a take was over, Ruki would hustle Shabana to the next set, handing her a script in the car.

"There is no time for these useless *lafangas*," Ruki would remind her. "They just want to brag that they're sleeping with a star. And if word gets out to the press, you will lose respect, the roles will dry up. We don't want to be poor again. Ever again."

"Yes, Ruki," Shabana would sigh, wishing she could meet someone who valued her for herself. Now, thinking about Sanjeev, she felt an unusual quickening of her pulse. Other men had wooed her with diamond rings, private jets, trips to Bali; never before with a packet of orange biscuits.

Three days later, after a neurologist pronounced her fit, Shabana returned to Film City to reshoot the dance scene. She was so nervous that she couldn't even tell if Sanjeev was there, hidden behind the lights and the hungry eyes of the cameras.

She danced like a demon to the thumping music, surrounded by the troupe of dancers. By the time she finished, she was slick with sweat, and a girl assistant hurried up to her with a hand towel. When she took it, she felt something heavy within its folds: it was a packet of orange biscuits. Looking up, she saw Sanjeev standing at the edge of the stage, smiling his wolfish smile. He was wearing his torn jeans again, and another faded T-shirt, red this time.

Seeing him, she blushed. She walked toward him with her undulating walk, thinking up a pretext—should she ask him if the camera angles were okay?—when Ruksana, whose radar was finely tuned, swooped down upon her.

"*Chalo*, let's go." Ruksana scowled. "We have an interview at *Filmfare* in fifteen minutes."

In front of her sister, Shabana's courage ebbed away. Smiling weakly at Sanjeev, she trailed Ruksana to the waiting car.

Later that evening, she returned to the huge flat in Bandra she'd shared with Ruksana ever since their mother died. She sat alone on its wide veranda and ate the whole packet of orange biscuits, cramming her mouth with their buttery sweetness.

The next time she returned to the set, Sanjeev slipped into her changing room. She was sitting in front of her mirror, plucking her eyebrows when his reflection just appeared in her mirror, making her jump, but he said nothing, just leaned against the wall and crossed his arms. She sat stock-still with her back to him, her tweezers halfway to her eyebrows.

"So, what? You'll eat my biscuits but you won't talk to me?" His words were teasing but his tone was serious.

She addressed his reflection. "No, no, it's not that. I'm so busy, doing four movies right now, and—"

"That was your sister. She doesn't approve of men, right?"

Shabana was stunned at his perception, and swiveled to face him.

"Yeah. I've heard about her. You know that everyone calls her *kala makra,* black widow spider? What, she won't let you even talk to any-one else?"

"She . . . she protects me. So that I can just work."

"She doesn't like you."

Sanjeev said it as though it was a fact, and Shabana knew it was true. Ruksana's resentment came through in so many ways: she packed Shabana's schedule, kept their finances vague, and conducted complex negotiations with Don Hajji Mustafa. When Shabana asked for details, Ruksana answered curtly, saying that Shabana need not worry her pretty little head. Over the years, Ruksana's very presence— her hair pulled back into a severe bun, face hidden behind huge sunglasses, her skin turning dry and ashy—had become a rebuke to Shabana's beauty.

"Look, don't worry about your sister. After you finish this scene, here's what you do." Sanjeev leaned in and whispered into Shabana's ear. Without waiting for a reply, he winked at her and slipped out of the dressing room door.

The next scene was a cocktail party, and Shabana wore a little black dress and a diamond necklace and looked the part of a rich, spoiled girl. Going out onto the set, Shabana was surrounded by a crowd of extras— the men in black tuxedos, the women in heavy brocaded gowns, all sweating under the heat of the arc lights. She found it hard to concen-trate, and kept messing up her lines, and each time the director had to restage the entire elaborate scene. During take after take the extras went through the same clockwork gestures and mouthed polite nonsense, and Shabana began to feel that she was surrounded by automatons.

Six takes later, she finally got it right. As she walked off the set, she felt as empty as an earthen pot: if someone dropped her, she would break into a thousand pieces. She saw Ruksana gesturing at her from the entrance, and knew that she would soon be whisked away, perhaps to a shoot at another studio, or another print advertisement, adding a new image of herself to the thousands already plastered on giant billboards all over the country.

Enough of being bullied by Ruki. Remembering Sanjeev's whispered instructions, Shabana turned to her sister.

"Just one minute. I forgot my script in the changing room."

"Get in the car, Shabana. I'll send a boy for it."

"I'll be right back. You go ahead."

Ruksana snorted in exasperation, but turned toward the waiting car.

Shabana walked quickly past her dressing room, then down the long corridor beyond it, passing the badly lit dressing rooms that the extras used, the mirrors clouded with talcum powder, tuxedos lying in heaps on chairs. She reached the end of the corridor, and there was Sanjeev, leaning against the wall with his arms crossed. He looked vaguely bored, like a man waiting for a bus.

"Hello."

She halted. "Were you worried that I wasn't coming?"

"No. Why would you do that? After all, I was being my most charming."

He smiled his wolfish smile, opened the back door, and helped her down the wet, slippery metal stairs to the empty parking lot below. She saw the tattered trees dripping with water and realized that she had missed the entire rainstorm.

He handed her a motorcycle helmet, slipped on another, then reached down and hand-started his motorbike, an old, heavy Royal Enfield Bullet.

"Hang on to me, okay? Lean when I lean." He had to shout above the racket of the engine.

She nodded and climbed behind him, holding tightly to his slim waist. He kicked away the stand and the bike roared away, faster and faster, the grounds of Film City giving way to the broken asphalt of the main road. She smelled the wet earth, felt the whip of air in her face, and leaned into his strong back.

It was like a scene from one of her movies, but, for once, it was real.

On that first date, she wore huge sunglasses and one of Sanjeev's baseball caps, and they walked around the Hanging Gardens. It was empty except for some old people reading newspapers. When Sanjeev pulled her behind a hedge and kissed her, she couldn't stop giggling.

Shabana put fake beauty parlor appointments and personal training sessions on her calendar, and went on surreptitious dates with Sanjeev for three months. They behaved like any other young couple in Bombay, except that she wore shabby *salwar kameez*, huge sunglasses, and always had her hair up. They walked on the beach in Juhu, kissed on a bench in the Hanging Gardens, and roared through the city on Sanjeev's motorbike, her face hidden by a motorcycle helmet.

Once they were almost caught in a Chinese restaurant on Cuff Parade, when an off-duty film photographer took a snap of them holding hands. It took all of Sanjeev's considerable charm, as well as fifty thousand rupees, to get the man to hand over the film.

After that they ate only at Azeem's, a *biriyani* place that had private "family booths," separated from the main dining room by dirty pink curtains. Other desperate young couples bribed the waiters, and used these booths to make out. Shabana and Sanjeev enjoyed the *biriyani,* but it was always accompanied by the heavy breathing and rhythmic moans of their neighbors.

Shabana giggled, and just went on eating, but Sanjeev's face became serious.

"How long can we go on like this, Shabbu?"

"What's wrong? Isn't it fun?"

"Yes, it is, but what about six months from now? Are we still going to be hiding? We'll be caught, sooner or later. This is crazy, you're a movie star, not some penniless girl living with her parents. Why are you so scared of Ruksana?"

Shabana stopped eating, and the *biriyani* in front of them grew cold.

"Well, what is it?"

"She has no one, and, well, I don't want to hurt her feelings." Thinking about Ruki made Shabana's head hurt. "And she says that being involved with a man will harm my career. The fans like to think of me as single and glamorous. She says that if I get married, I won't get these roles anymore. Don Hajji agrees, and he's the one who finances all of my films."

"So . . . we can never be a couple, because your sister and some has-been mobster have decided it?" Sanjeev leaned closer, his eyes blazing. "Shabbu, wake up, this is 1995. In case you didn't notice, the Indian economy has been liberalized. Hell, your ads for Pepsi and Gucci make more money in one *day* than the old movie stars did in a *year*. The multinationals are calling the shots now, not the mob.

"The Don's strong-arm tactics don't work anymore. If you say good-bye to him, what's he going to do? Send that guy . . . what's his name, 'the Hammer,' to break your fingers? You don't need the Don. A goddamn bank will finance any movie you want to make."

Shabana wiped her mouth. "Really, you think so?"

"One hundred percent."

"What about Ruki?"

"What *about* Ruki? You don't need the *kala makra*. Get a professional manager."

"But Sanjeev, she's my sister, how can I—"

Sanjeev sat back and smiled grimly. "Shabbu, you know I'm right. She's ruining your life—*our* life. Fire her."

Fire Ruksana? Shabana knew that Sanjeev was right, but . . . the two of them had always been together. Her sister knew her better than anyone on earth; Ruki could take one look at her and know that she was about to pull out her hair. Yes, Ruki was a pain, but what would life be like without her managing all the complicated logistics? Their lives were intertwined, impossible to unravel.

"Fire her," Sanjeev repeated. "Get a professional manager, get a lawyer, get financing from a bank."

Shabana resisted at first, but Sanjeev kept explaining to her how it could be done. He said it so many times that it began to feel like a real possibility.

Chapter Thirteen

The morning after his encounter with the two men, Ranjit wakes early, his body caught in a tangle of sweaty sheets. He is still exhausted, but cannot sleep anymore.

Getting up, he forces himself to do a hundred sit-ups. When his belly starts cramping, he turns over and begins push-ups. He has to stop at sixty-three, his arms giving way, but he has succeeded in clearing his mind.

After a cold shower, he sits with his battered laptop and types into a search engine. In ten minutes he has a list of sixteen garages in the South Bronx with Indian-sounding names. From long experience, he knows not to call; nobody will give out information over the phone.

Soon the Saturday crowds will invade Jackson Heights, but right now he has the neighborhood to himself. He strolls down the unswept streets, past stores with their shutters still pulled down. Luckily the Pakistani shop is open, and he gets a cup of *chai* to go, the sugar entering his bloodstream and giving him a sudden burst of energy.

The yellow cab he's borrowed from Ali is parked a few blocks away in an alley. He examines it again in the harsh morning light, finding no damage other than the missing mirror. Even if the cops give him a citation, a busted mirror is much easier to explain away than a bullet hole.

Ali was expecting the cab back last night, and is bound to be pissed off, but Ranjit needs it for a few more hours.

He gets into the hot, stuffy cab and drives down Broadway toward the Triboro. Bare-chested men have appeared on street corners, selling cold drinks from their large plastic coolers. The sky is cloudless and glittering with heat.

Sixteen garages. It is going to be a long, hot morning.

It is just past noon, and Ranjit's long-sleeved white shirt is soaked in sweat. He's headed down a narrow road in Hunt's Point, not really sure of where he is going.

The first twelve garages were washouts, but he's made his way through a large swathe of the South Bronx, from the larger garages on Webster Avenue to the shadier shops in Hunt's Point. Some of the garages were owned by Sikhs but employed only Hispanics; other Indian owners frowned at him when he asked questions about their employees, and wouldn't talk until he convinced them that he wasn't from U.S. Immigration. He has smiled, bullshitted, drunk cups of tea, and shaken so many hands that his fingers now stink of auto grease, but no one knows anything about Mohan's cousin, Kishen.

There are four places left: Khalsa Autoworks, Lakshmi Narayan Motors, Singh Repair, and the place he's now trying to find, Golden Temple Mechanic.

He turns onto Oak Point Avenue, passing what seems to be a colonial graveyard, complete with leaning tombstones and a chipped stone obelisk. He drives past large warehouses with barred windows and a waste processing plant, all seemingly deserted. He hasn't seen a person for the last twenty minutes, and after the clamor of the other boroughs, the echoing silence feels eerie.

He finally sees a garish blue and yellow sign that points down an unpaved street. Bumping over potholes, he hits a dead end, curses, manages a tight K-turn, and heads down another unmarked fork.

This must be the right place: he sees a corrugated metal shed with a dilapidated shack next to it, rusted car chassis littering the yard.

When he turns off the engine, the quiet is broken only by the cry of a rooster.

As he wipes the sweat from his eyes, a portly Sikh emerges from the shed. He is at least sixty, with a long white beard, and wears a saffron turban wound tightly into a tall cylinder. The man's style tells Ranjit that he is an orthodox Sikh, probably a supporter of Khalistan, a separate nation for Sikhs.

"Yes? What do you want?" The man's lips are hidden under his whiskers.

"*Sat Sri Akal.*" Ranjit uses the religious greeting.

"*Sat Sri Akal, bole so Nihal.*" The man's frown softens. "What can I do for you? Want that mirror fixed? I have a spare one, cheap."

Something tells Ranjit not to rush the man. This place is so remote, it would be a perfect spot for Mohan to hide out.

"How much for a mirror, *bhai*?"

"For you . . ." The old Sikh considers. "Twenty-five, okay?"

That's at least twenty cheaper than Manhattan. "Thanks. Could you do it now?"

The old man nods, and delves into the shed, returning with a mirror. He grunts, handling a socket wrench deftly as he unscrews the mirror attachment. Ranjit leans against the car and watches.

"So . . . how long have you had this place?"

"Since eighty-five. Good thing you found me today. Next week I'm going back to Punjab. Had enough of this bloody country. Nothing is the same since nine-eleven. Hey, you don't want to sink too much money into this piece of junk." The old man gestures with his beard at the car, his hands busy. "Those TLC *chutiyas* are going to make you all buy those new minivans, *hanh*?"

Ranjit nods. The mayor wants to replace all the Ford Vics with energy-efficient vans that will probably handle like hippos. Never mind that most garages cannot afford to replace their aging fleets.

"*Sardar*, you're right about that . . . Listen, I'm looking for a guy, Kishen. He works somewhere around here—"

"Kishen? You think I'm stupid?" The old man stops working.

"You didn't come here for a bloody mirror. I already told your people, I don't know where Kishen is."

"Hey, wait—I'm not with anyone. What people are you talking about?"

"You damn well know." The old man grabs the half-attached mirror and yanks it off, screws flying into the air. "Get out of my garage, or I'm going to beat your brains out!" He raises his socket wrench threateningly.

Ranjit takes a step back, when suddenly the old Sikh gasps and leans against the car. His face is pale and beaded with sweat.

"Hey, are you okay?" Ranjit grabs on to the man's arm, steadying him.

"My heart." The old man's voice drops to a raspy whisper. "Pills are inside, on my desk."

The interior of the garage is a nightmare of salvaged car seats, tires, and boxes of auto parts, but on the old wooden desk, amongst stacks of papers, Ranjit finds an orange plastic pillbox.

He hurries back and the old man dry-swallows two Sorbitrate tablets. Grasping Ranjit's arm, he staggers back into the garage and sinks down onto the ripped-out backseat of an old Ford. His face is pale, his breathing labored and arrhythmic.

"Shall I call an ambulance? Is there anyone else here?"

"No ambulance." The old Sikh jerks his thumb toward the back of the lot. "My wife's here, but don't call her. She can't see me like this, she gets too worried."

He sits with his eyes closed in the grease-smelling gloom, breathing deeply, and soon his normal coloring returns. *Why has talking about Kishen triggered his heart condition?*

"Feeling better?"

"I'll be fine. The pains come and go." The man opens his eyes, looking ten years older.

"I promise you, I have nothing to do with the people who came here before. Tell me what happened."

"Kishen used to work for me. He vanished from here, about a month ago, with two Mercedes engines. I told the cops, but what do they care? Then yesterday, two men showed up here, dressed all fancy, wearing blue blazers, cowboy boots. But when they opened their mouths, I could tell they were low class, they spoke Mumbai Hindi. Asked me where Kishen was, where some fool called Mohan was. I *told* them that I didn't know. They said if I was lying, they would come back and break my legs . . . I took a tire iron and chased them out. *Hanh*, they left in their fancy limo fast enough—"

The old man is getting agitated, his face reddening as he relives his memory.

"Okay, okay. Thanks. Now are you sure you're going to be okay?"

"*Hanh, hanh*. Thank you for your help, *Sardar,* you're a good man. Why is everyone suddenly looking for Kishen?"

"It's better that you don't get involved. Here's my number. Call me if they come back, please."

"Like that, *hanh*? Well, if you do find Kishen, ask him where the hell my Mercedes engines are, okay?"

Ranjit nods, and walks back to his cab. A rooster has wandered in from somewhere, and is pecking in the dirt a few feet away.

As he drives away, Ranjit's head hurts from the heat, and his mouth is thick and gluey. His one lead is a dead end: Mohan's cousin has vanished, having stolen from his former employer. But who are the two men who came here and threatened the old Sikh? Who else could be looking for Kishen?

He desperately needs to talk to Leela and find out what she knows; maybe he should go back to Little Guyana. She probably doesn't live too far from where he lost her, and he could ask around . . . but if those two thugs find him snooping around, things could get ugly. The last thing he needs is to get into another gunfight.

Just then his cell phone rings. All morning he's been letting Ali Khan's calls go to voice mail, but now he gives up and answers.

"*Aare,* Ranjit. Have you gone mad? You were supposed to give me the cab back last night. Jacobo is going to cut my balls off! You want me to go through life with no balls? *Hanh?* Is that what you want?"

Ali calls him a goat fucker, a cow fucker, and the son of an alligator. Usually Ranjit retaliates with his own invectives, and the two men escalate their abuse, using all the animals they can think of. Today Ranjit maintains his silence, speaking only when Ali pauses for breath.

"I needed the car, but I'm heading back now. See you at Karachi Kabob in half an hour. I'm sorry, okay?"

There is a sudden silence as Ali hears the defeat in Ranjit's tone.

"*Oi*, Ranjit? Are you okay? What is going on?"

The sun is in Ranjit's eyes as he passes the deserted Hunt's Point wholesale market, its chain-link fence surrounded by big loops of barbed wire, like a prison yard. Thinking of the events that have brought him to this godforsaken place makes him sick to the pit of his stomach.

"Ranjit? You okay, right?"

He takes a deep breath. "I'm fine, Ali, I'll see you in a bit."

He hangs up, and then it hits him: yes, Mohan is holed up somewhere in this enormous city, and Kishen has vanished, but he has an incredible resource at his disposal: his fellow cabbies go everywhere, see everything, and come into contact with thousands of people every day. If he puts the word out, someone is going to see something.

All the Indian and Pakistani cabbies will be eating lunch right now, a perfect time to make an appeal. Ranjit speeds on Bruckner Boulevard out of the spooky silence of the Bronx and toward the clamor and bustle of Queens.

Karachi Kabob is squeezed in between a strip club and a used car lot, a long, narrow space that barely fits a counter and a few greasy plastic-topped tables. Its walls are painted a bright orange, and the television in the corner blasts Bollywood dance videos at a deafening volume. The window at the front is so dirty that the outside world has taken on a blurry, under-sea aspect, but the cabbies don't seem to mind; they come here for the food, not the atmosphere.

Ranjit walks in, smells the aroma of roasting meat and rice, and realizes that he is very hungry. He waves to Ali, who is in his regular corner seat; today he's wearing an orange and purple Hawaiian shirt with naked women on it.

Ranjit peers into the steam trays: there is rich rice *biriyani*, chicken *korma* swimming in oil, even *paya*, cow-hoof curry. Remembering his vow, he avoids these, and orders the healthiest food there is: whole-wheat *rotis*, a dish of thick *kaali-daal* lentils, and some salad with a yogurt dressing.

As he walks toward Ali, he passes two tables, and the cabbies sitting there nod at him curtly. To an outsider, all the men—brown skinned, clad in polyester half-sleeve shirts and trousers—look the same, but Ranjit can easily spot the differences.

The Pakistanis are Punjabis from the north, taller and burlier, their plates heaped with orange *tandoori* chicken and hunks of mutton curry. The Indians are slighter, Gujaratis from the west and some South Indians, and they prefer smaller dishes of fried vegetables, scooped up with puffy *puris*. Usually the two groups eat together, but today they are sitting strangely stiff-backed at separate tables.

Pulling up a chair, Ranjit sits across from Ali and gestures at the men.

"What's going on, Ali *bhai*? They're behaving strangely. What is it, a cricket match?"

The rivalry between India and Pakistan is played out these days through cricket matches, and when one country wins, there is a rift between the two groups. It usually lasts a few days.

"Worse than that. There was a match, yes, but also a lot of drinking." Ali's bulldog face wrinkles in concentration as he sucks the marrow from a mutton bone. "Some fools started arguing, and it got out of control. One of the Pakistanis stabbed one of the Indians. You didn't hear about it?"

"Who did it?"

"Afzal Mian, the stupid hothead. The Indian guy ended up in the emergency room with a punctured lung. They don't know if he's going to make it. Now the police are all over us. Banging on doors, asking to see papers. Everyone is pissed off."

Ranjit knows Afzal. He's a young tough who favors tight T-shirts; rumors are that he's the black sheep of an important Pakistani family.

"Did they catch him?"

"No, *yaar*. Who's going to talk to the cops? You answer one question, they want to know about your wife's cousin's sister, and then the next thing you know, your whole family is deported. Afzal's hiding at his aunt's place, above the noodle shop, in Flushing. Fucking idiot."

Ranjit thinks about what Patel said: these days everyone fears the cops, immigrants most of all.

Ali sucks out the last bit of marrow and slurps it down.

"You didn't know this happened? Where have you been, anyway? You were supposed to return my cab last night."

Ranjit has to think fast. The truth is too big and complicated for Ali to handle. "Sorry, *yaar*. I went on a date with this woman last night, had a little too much to drink, whacked the mirror on your cab. When you called, I was trying to have it fixed, but I couldn't find a replacement part . . ."

"Naughty, naughty." Ali waves a beringed, chubby hand at him. "Who was it? One of those Latinas you meet in your cab? *Hanh?* I hope you didn't take her to the parking garage?"

Ali is referring to an abandoned parking garage in Midtown, well known to all the cabbies; it has a faulty barrier that can be easily lifted up. The men take women up there, or go there to nap.

"No, not the garage. This was a classy woman, she had her own place in Chelsea . . ." Ranjit smiles modestly, and Ali grins from ear to ear, his chins wobbling with mirth.

"Okay, I'll forgive you this time. Jacobo will chew my ass off for the mirror, and it'll cost a hundred at least, but I forgive you."

"There is one more thing . . ." Ranjit breaks off a strip of *roti* and scoops up some of the thick *daal*. He hates lying to his old friend, and his hunger of a few minutes ago has evaporated.

"*Kya?* Because if you want to borrow money, let me remind you that you owe me thirty from that time we went out for dinner."

Ranjit knows that Ali doesn't mean this; his friend would give him the Hawaiian shirt off his voluminous back.

"You know that Shanti is coming, and I'm moving to this new place in Astoria, right? They want a security deposit, first month's rent, last month's rent, plus I have to buy a bed for her. I'm wiped out, *yaar*. And there's this guy, he owes me five hundred bucks, and he's vanished, the *chootiya* . . ."

"Who?" Ali chews on a fresh piece of mutton. "One of the drivers? I'll take care of him, no problem."

"This guy, Kishen—he's from my village in Punjab—came over here as a mechanic, didn't have a pot to piss in. I lent him the money to get settled, he swore he'd pay me back. He used to work as a mechanic in the Bronx, but now I don't know where he is. I need that five hundred back, *yaar*."

Ali belches and pushes his plate away. It looks like a battlefield, littered with shattered mutton bones and half-eaten pieces of potato.

"This mutton is lousy. Five hundred? And this guy has done the bunk?"

"He's still somewhere in the city, at some garage. Works exclusively on fancy cars. If you put the word out with your guys, maybe something will turn up . . ."

Ali nods. "I can ask the Pakistani drivers. But that's like using one hand. If you really want to find this guy, we'll need the Indians, too. And those fools aren't talking to each other."

"I'll talk to Murgi." Ranjit gestures at the far table, where a bespectacled Indian driver sits reading a battered paperback. With his math brain, Sridhar Murugappan could have found a job at a software company, but his Marxist beliefs keep him driving a cab.

Ranjit takes his tray of cold food over to Murgi's table. The driver snaps shut a book titled *Capitalism and Its Discontents* and looks up, his pointy nose quivering. Ranjit retells his made-up story, and Murgi looks gloomy.

"Ranjit Sahib, I'd love to help you, but our people are angry at the

Pakis. It's stupid. The proletariat should be united. We need to stand together, not feud like this. As it is, this mayor is making our life hell. Maybe the next thing he'll do is outlaw turbans and beards. Maybe we'll all have to wear pastels and do a song and dance for the tourists . . ."

Ranjit takes another bite of food. "Look, Murgi. Someone should just go and tell the cops where Afzal is. That way he'll be behind bars, and everyone will feel better."

"Nobody is going to talk to the cops." Murgi looks around nervously. "A lot of these guys, they were driving on nine-eleven, but they got no compensation, no medical treatment. Instead, the cops questioned them, roughed them up. They could be shipped off to Guantanamo at any time. It's in the interest of the state to have an extra-judicial process . . ."

"Okay, okay, I get your point."

Ranjit looks around the room of sullen men. These guys have to help him find Kishen; that's his only connection to Mohan.

Grabbing Murgi's thin arm, he hoists him to his feet. "Come with me."

He whispers in Ali's ear, and the fat man slowly levers himself to his feet, his ponderous gut pushing against the table.

Flanked by Murgi and Ali, Ranjit clears his throat, and bangs on the table for silence. The conversation gradually ebbs, someone mutes the television, and the two tables of cabbies stare at Ranjit.

"Bhaiyo," he begins, addressing them as brothers. "I need a few minutes of your time. You all know me. I am a man of few words." He gestures around the room. "Look at you, sitting apart from each other. This way we are behaving towards each other—it is unnatural. We've all broken bread together. We've been to each other's houses."

He stops to gaze around the room. "Okay, Afzal Mian did a bad thing. But he is one man, he does not represent all the Pakistanis. Look, back home, the politicians do their best to fuel the hatred between India and Pakistan. It helps to always have an enemy to fight and to blame.

"But here, in America, to follow those false divisions is suicide. You think the Americans can see any difference between Indians and Pakistanis? We're just a brown face in a taxi, they treat us the same, they tip us the same. Who of us hasn't been called 'hajji' or 'towelhead'? Who of us hasn't been told to go home? *Hanh?* All we have is each other. The next time you're on the Cross Bronx and your tire blows out, you won't worry if the cabbie who stops to help you is Indian or Pakistani. We are in this *together.*"

The silence is broken only by the shuffling of feet and the clearing of throats.

"Look, I need your help right now. This guy, Kishen Singh, he owes me money, and he's disappeared. I'm not a rich man, and my daughter is coming very soon. I need my money back, and I need to find him. You all are out in the streets every day, you see everything, you hear everything. Please work together, and help me find this man.

"Please," Ranjit repeats. "I am appealing to your good sense. Help me."

One of the Pakistani cabdrivers, a stooped man with gray hair, gets up slowly. He carries his plate over to the Indian table and sits down in Murgi's vacated seat.

"*Sardar*, I will help you," he says. "I agree we are one."

There is a rumble of conversation—Ranjit can't tell if it is assent or anger—and then men are getting up. They are sitting down at each other's tables, clapping each other on the back, and soon the restaurant echoes with the sound of loud, embarrassed voices.

Ranjit waits. When the conversation has died down, he tells the men everything he knows about Kishen Singh. The cabbies listen intently, and when he is done, many of them come up to shake his hand.

Ali Khan claps Ranjit on the back. "*Wah-wah.* What a speech you made. You should consider running for union president, *yaar.* And now, some of us have to go to work. Can I have my cab back?"

After giving him a bone-crushing hug, Ali departs, and Ranjit pushes away his plate of half-eaten food. Through the filthy window, he watches the big man lumber to his cab, gingerly feel the stub where the mirror had been, then drive away. The other cabbies are already on their phones, gesturing as they walk to their cars.

The word will spread exponentially now, branching out to garages and chop shops, greasy restaurants and tea-joints, to every nook and cranny of the cabdriver universe. No doubt the story will get garbled with each retelling, but that's okay: the message will be that one of their own has been wronged, and that Kishen has to make it right.

The cabbies could take a day, or a week to find him. Meanwhile, Ranjit can't just wait as precious time ticks away. He could go back to Little Guyana and track Leela down, but that is way too dangerous . . .

Wait. He won't have to go back there. Even if Leela is hiding from him, she will have to go to work today; surely nannies at fancy places like the Dakota don't get Saturday off. And if she is looking after a four-year-old, surely she'll leave the building and take the child for a walk—Americans are very insistent that their children get fresh air.

And Central Park is right next door to the Dakota. He remembers the clusters of nannies he's seen there in the late afternoon, dark-skinned West Indian, Guyanese, and Haitian women pushing their fair-skinned charges around in six-hundred-dollar strollers. If he's lucky, he can find Leela there, far away from her hoodlum friends.

Feeling a flush of excitement, he heads toward the elevated subway station at Court Square. If he takes the train into Manhattan, he could make it to the park just as the afternoon cools down and the nannies begin to emerge. Leela should be relatively easy to spot amongst the groups of thickset, middle-aged nannies.

It is four o'clock when Ranjit walks down the wide asphalt path that curves along the west side of Central Park. On this hot weekend afternoon, the trees are reduced to dark shapes, the sun shines out of a cloudless sky, and it seems as though the whole city is seeking refuge in the park.

An obese man in a sweat-stained T-shirt jogs slowly past Ranjit, followed by a pack of long-legged girls, moving as easily as thorough-breds. Bicyclists zip by, clad in multicolored spandex, and in their wake are the Rollerbladers, twirling and showing off. On benches lining the pathway are the watchers, men mainly, their eyes caressing the taut backsides of the running girls.

Ranjit walks through it all, his eyes searching the crowds. There are nannies everywhere, pushing strollers, their faces beaded with per-spiration. Tall West Indian women, shorter Filipinas, Sri Lankans, and Haitians, all wearing bright, cheap T-shirts and baggy pants. No sign anywhere of a curvy, short girl with an afro.

The sun shines down, and sweat begins to pool in Ranjit's armpits. How stupid he was to think that he could find one single human being in this mass of humanity.

He walks north, heading toward the yellow-brick bulk of the Dakota, hoping that somehow, miraculously, he will run into Leela, but of course he doesn't. Soon he's right at the edge of the park, across from the Dakota, and remembers the lawyer telling him not to go any-where near the crime scene.

Tired now, he looks for a place to sit for a few minutes. Following the sound of a guitar, he turns back into the park, and enters a clearing. In its center is a circle of gray mosaic stone set into the ground, the word IMAG-INE inscribed into its center. This must be the John Lennon memorial, because red roses and scribbled notes are strewn across it, and a group of solemn Japanese teenagers are taking pictures with large cameras.

Ranjit walks toward the benches at the perimeter, and stops in sur-prise. Sitting on a bench, legs spread out, as though he owns the place, is Hector. He is still wearing his faded jean jacket covered in peace and love symbols, and his round granny glasses, complemented today with a red headband.

Hector's eyes widen in surprise. "Hey, bad boy. You stopped by. Sorry, I can't pay you back, man, but soon, soon. I'm working on it."

"It's okay, I didn't come for the money. You *work* here?"

"Look, I'll show you, man."

Hector walks up to some laminated pictures placed at the edge of the mosaic memorial. They are of John Lennon, as a clean-cut Beatle, and later, long-haired, with his arm around Yoko Ono.

Gesturing to the Japanese teenagers, Hector smiles and says, "Hey, you want a picture? Picture?" He mimes taking a photograph, then throws up his hands in peace signs. "Peace and love, right?"

The teenagers nod and step up. They take turns posing with Hector in front of the laminated photographs, and when they're done, they tip him with a handful of dollar bills. Stashing the money deep inside his jean jacket, Hector bends to realign the photographs.

"These kids, they come here all the way from Japan, they expect a real memorial, and this isn't much . . ." He gestures to the drab stone circle. ". . . so I add to the experience. For a couple of bucks they can take pictures of me and my pictures. They can't get enough of it."

"Very innovative."

"Hey, I'm providing a service. The Parks Department should pay me, not hassle me. Now, bad boy, what can I do for you? Wish I could pay you back, but I'm still behind on my rent . . ."

"It's okay." Ranjit sits down next to his former cellmate and wipes his face in the sleeve of his shirt. "So you're here all day? Next to the Dakota?" He gestures at the gabled roofline beyond the trees.

"Yeah, man, it's a good spot. All the tourists go over there, see where Lennon was shot, then they come here, all emotional."

"I'm looking for a friend, maybe you saw her? She's a nanny over at the Dakota, she's out with her kid here. Pretty girl: short, maybe five-one, green eyes, afro?"

Hector whistles. "Wish I had, man. Sorry."

Ranjit nods, feeling the hopelessness of the situation. "Well, good to see you. Good luck with your business—"

"A bunch of other nannies from the Dakota just went this way, though. The kids, they always come by to say hi to me."

"Did they walk that way?" Ranjit gestures to the asphalt pathway.

"Naw, man. They always go to the same place—" Before Hector can continue, an African man in a tank top walks up, and stands word-lessly in front of him. Looking apologetic, Hector digs through his army surplus satchel, and hands a small, paper-wrapped package to the African. The man slips Hector a bill and quickly walks away.

Hector catches the expression on Ranjit's face. "Naw, naw, it's not like that. No drugs. I ain't that stupid." His voice falls to a whisper. "I'm a drop box. A human drop box."

"What the hell is that?"

"See, suppose you're walking around all day with a package, and you don't want to. For a small fee, you can leave it with me, collect it later. I'm always here, seven A.M. to nine P.M., rain or shine. Better than the United States Post Office."

Ranjit nods admiringly. "You're a real businessman. Now, where did the nannies go?"

"The Sheep Meadow, man. Over there, on the far side. They'll be there till five o'clock. You know those white kids, need to be in bed by seven."

"Thanks, Hector. I'll be seeing you." Ranjit raises a hand in farewell and heads off in the direction Hector was pointing. As he leaves, a fresh group of Japanese tourists arrives, and they point their cameras at Hector, who immediately throws up his hands in a double peace sign.

It is hard work walking through the expanse of the Sheep Meadow. The lush green grass is littered with scantily clad bodies, some lying neatly on beach towels, others sprawled directly on the grass. Ranjit picks his way through them, inhaling the heady scent of sweat and suntan lotion. Some women wear bikini tops, while others have turned onto their stomachs and undone their bras, willing the hot sun to erase the white lines across their backs.

He passes a young, long-haired woman lying next to a tanned, muscular man. Their bodies are covered by a yellow sheet, their hands busy underneath it. The woman opens blind eyes as Ranjit's shadow falls over her, and he quickly looks away.

Even after two years in New York, the raw carnality of the city stuns him, the erotic energy of so many bodies packed tightly together. He thinks of the boys and girls he's seen, kissing in the back of his cab, more turned on, it seems, with being in New York than with each other. The promise of fame, of unbounded sex is always around each corner, and even he's felt it, in his drab role as a conveyer of people.

Right now, with the sun beating down on him, surrounded by bare flesh, the city becomes a bittersweet promise that sticks in his throat. Life has been so dull here, and so hard, sustained by the promise of the future: *when* he has enough money for a better apartment, *when* Shanti arrives. And now that future is about to be taken away, made worse by the days that have gone by, unlived and unspent.

He makes his way through the sunny heart of the Meadow; at the fringes the crowd is thinner, and he can walk faster. Hector said the nannies were at the northeast corner, and he sees a group of women standing around a tree, their dull clothes and sturdy bodies contrasting with their lithe, brightly clad children and their large strollers, all slick nylon mesh and huge chrome wheels.

When he gets closer, he sees a dark West Indian woman peering up into a leafy tree.

"Tyler!" she shouts upward, cupping her hands around her mouth.

Another three nannies—Guyanese, he can tell, from their Indian features and thick gold earrings—also cluster around the tree, looking terrified. One nanny wears a tiny pink halter top and jeans and is young, but the others must be in their early fifties.

Ranjit smiles his most charming smile. "Good afternoon, ladies."

"It's evening, fool," says the West Indian nanny. "And you can be on your way. We ain't buying nothing." She steps in front of him, trying to block his view.

He smiles again. "Oh, I'm not selling anything. I'm just looking for a friend. Hey . . . what's he doing up there?"

High up in the tree there is a flash of red clothing. A young boy sits astride a branch, looking terrified, his eyes closed, and holding on tightly with both hands.

"Tyler, you come down here, right now—" the West Indian nanny bellows, then moans under her breath. "Oh, Lord. I'm going to be fired, for sure."

Ranjit steps forward. "Don't shout at him. He's terrified. You're just making things worse."

"Can you help me?" The woman tugs at his sleeve. "Get the boy down? I don't want to call the police, fire department, all that, you see, I got no papers, and . . ."

"I'll get him down. Give me some room." Pulling off his shoes and socks, Ranjit rolls up his shirtsleeves and approaches the tree. As he hugs the tree, his bare feet find purchase on the rough bark, and he jackknifes upward. Reaching a low branch, he hauls himself onto it. From here, he clambers from limb to limb, staying close to the trunk; the greatest risk is that the branches won't bear his weight.

The leaves close around him, and the bark scrapes his arms as he climbs, gauging every move, moving higher and higher into the dense foliage. Soon he reaches the terrified boy, and the hardest part is persuading the child to let go of the branch. Ranjit speaks in a slow, calm voice, telling the boy what to do; he shivers, but reaches out and wraps his arms around Ranjit's neck, then climbs onto his back.

With the boy safe, Ranjit pauses for a second, tingling from the adrenaline of the climb. The park is spread out below him, green and undulating, and he feels, for a second, the way he did when he climbed high up on the Siachen Glacier: at peace, removed from the fray of everyday life. From up here, everything seems neat, organized, making perfect sense. It's on the ground that life becomes complicated and confused.

Ranjit makes his way slowly back down, bent under the boy's weight, struggling to breathe as the boy's hold tightens around his neck.

When he reaches the lowest branch there is an excited murmur from the nannies, and hands reach up and grab the child.

Swinging down to the ground, Ranjit gasps for breath. His hands are scraped, and one shirtsleeve is ripped where it snagged on a branch.

"Tyler! How many times have I told you—" The West Indian nanny holds the boy tightly, pushing his sobbing head into her ample bosom. "Oh Lord, oh Lord, this child could have fallen . . ." She turns to Ranjit. "Thank you, sir, thank you."

The other nannies are clustered around, the young one in the pink halter top with her hand clasped over her mouth.

Ranjit bends over, hands on his knees, breathing hard. Red spots dance in front of his eyes.

"Come and sit down." The West Indian nanny gestures to a bench. "You want some water?"

Ranjit sinks down onto the bench and drinks plastic-tasting water from a disposable bottle. The nanny stands in front of him holding the child, who is now blubbering quietly.

"You wearing too many clothes, man." She gestures at Ranjit's dark trousers and his long-sleeved white shirt. "You Indian? Indian people always wearing too many clothes."

The other nannies standing around the bench titter at this observation.

"Yes, I'm from India. Thank you for the water."

The young nanny in the pink halter top steps forward. "Hey, my great-grandpa, he was from India. From that part of India, where they dance with sticks, you know?"

Ranjit knows she is talking about the *daandia raas,* a harvest dance that Punjabi farmers do, twirling and rhythmically clashing short bamboo batons. "Yes, I'm from there. From Punjab. You ladies from Guyana?"

The West Indian nanny makes the introductions. "Uh-huh, they're all from Georgetown. They're Indian too, but they are Christian. This is Norma, and Ria, and Vashtee. I'm from Jamaica. I am Harriet."

"Nice to meet you ladies." Ranjit sips the warm water as he talks, conscious of the women's bright eyes fixed on him. "I'm Ranjit Singh. So you ladies work on the Upper West Side, huh?"

Harriet, clearly the leader of the group, continues the conversation. "Uh-huh. How do you know?"

"Hector told me to come here—the guy at the Lennon memorial. I'm looking for a friend of mine. She's Guyanese, works at the Dakota, I thought she might be out here today."

"Oho, you like Guyanese girls. Friend? Like a special friend?" All the ladies laugh uproariously, and the mood changes from tragic to hilarious. "She's hiding from you?"

He decides to play along. "Something like that. We had a little tiff. I want to make it up to her, take her out to dinner."

"You can take me out to dinner. Anytime. Nice tall, strong man like you."

The boy has stopped crying and looks up at Ranjit, his blue eyes full of curiosity. "What does the man have on his head?"

"That's a turban, boy. He is a coolie man from India." The laughter grows even more uproarious, and the ladies slap their thighs.

Harriet continues. "So this friend, what's her name?"

Ranjit is smiling as he speaks. "It's Leela. Leela Rampersad. She works at the Dakota—"

Harriet's face darkens, and she clutches the little boy. "Leela. Lee-la? She's that *dougla* girl?"

"I don't understand. She works at the Dakota?"

"*Dougla*. Half black and half Indian?"

"Yes, that's right."

"No. We don't know any Leela."

The laughter has gone out of the women's faces, replaced by a stony impassivity. They all shake their heads, and Ranjit feels confused.

"But you just said . . ."

"No. We don't know her. Thank you for saving the child. God bless you. Come on, girls." Harriet turns away and grips her stroller.

"Please, I need to get in touch with her. If you know—"

"I just said, we don't know nothing, okay, mister?" Harriet's voice rises.

Ranjit watches helplessly as the women buckle their children into their strollers and walk away across the Sheep Meadow. From their stiff backs and quick gait, he can see there is no point following them.

Sitting on the bench, he watches the women dwindle into the distance. They had clearly known who Leela was, so why the hell wouldn't they talk to him? They are Indian and black; surely Leela's mixed race is not an affront to them.

He picks up the water bottle and holds it to his mouth, but there is nothing left. It's baking hot and he's probably dehydrated; he should find a vendor and buy a bottle of cold water. Yet he remains sitting there, and images swim through his head: Leela saying, *I can't get involved.* Her slim legs blurring as she ran away down the dark street. And now these women, ostentatiously denying that they know her. Some kind of dark knowledge clings to Leela, he's sure of it.

He glances at his watch; five o'clock, but the warm summer day shows no sign of abating. The sun is still high, the sky is blue and cloudless, and it will be light till almost nine: one of those endless summer evenings, and he has nowhere to go and nothing to do.

On evenings like this he has always been working, and he suddenly misses it, the endless driving through the endless streets. And afterward, a meal at Karachi Kabob, talking with the other cabbies, their lewd jokes and banter a bulwark against the emptiness of America . . .

Without the safety of his cab, he's suddenly lost. He sits with his eyes open but unseeing, feeling New York City stretching endlessly around him, the green of the park edged by the walls of skyscrapers, the street grid extending beyond that. He feels a profound sense of disorientation, of complete loss and utter exhaustion.

"Hey, mister. *Pssst.*"

He jerks his head around, and there is the young nanny in the pink halter top, pushing a stroller with a toddler asleep within it. She must have jogged back from the other side of the meadow, because the front of her halter top is soaked with sweat. A scrap of dark hair has come loose from her ponytail and flops across her forehead.

"Yes? Did you leave something behind?"

"No, no. Listen, come here. I don't want the others to see me, okay?"

He walks into the shade of the path and the woman speaks breathlessly.

"You did a nice thing, okay? And those ladies, they were not nice to you, so I came back." She stops, and he nods encouragingly.

"I know her. Leela. She was working with us, one year almost. Then she left."

"Did she do something wrong? Something to upset you all?"

"No, no. She did nothing wrong, but she did something wrong in *their* eyes. She left here, she found another job."

"You know where she works? Please tell me."

"Okay. But you didn't hear this from me, mind? Leela, she fought with her employer, she left and got a job in a club." The woman's face twists in disdain. "Her *aja*—grandfather—was a respectable man in Guyana, but now she is a hostess in a club, working nights. One time she came back here, all fancy, nice dress, nice shoes, and things. The other ladies, they don't like that, they bad-eyed her. They said she looked like a *garmant* whore." The young woman nods for emphasis, sweat dripping down her neck. "So why do you look for her? Really?"

Ranjit ignores the question. "Do you know which club? Izizzi in the Meatpacking District?"

The woman shakes her head. "No, not that one. Someplace called Ghungroo. And you be careful now. Leela, she's always in trouble, always finds some man to get her out of trouble." She turns and begins to walk away, then stops. "You ever looking for a nice, nice girl, to talk to? You come back and talk to me, Vashtee, okay? I'm always here, evenings."

"I will. Thank you."

He smiles at her, and Vashtee winks back at him as she walks away, her rump swaying, heavy gold bangles tinkling on her wrists.

Ghungroo. So Leela works at a club.

He's taken club girls home in his cab before, at three or four in the morning, and they always seemed drained, kicking off their high-heeled shoes and curling up on the seat; a few have even fallen asleep. None of them want to talk, and he associates a kind of sadness with those silent rides through the sleeping city.

Maybe Leela is just a hostess, but she could also be a stripper; she'd lied to him about still working as a nanny, and clearly hides what she does for a living.

Ranjit has never heard of a club called Ghungroo. It's not one of the many in the trendy Meatpacking District, or the hipster joints in Williamsburg, or the cluster of large, garish places in Midtown. He recognizes that word, though: *ghungroos* are the ankle bells worn by classical Indian dancers and courtesans, the tinkling of bells amplifying the stamp of their dancing feet.

A strange name for a club. Still musing on the name, he gets up and walks across the Sheep Meadow.

A few clouds have floated into the sky, blocking the sun, and there is suddenly a summer drizzle, so fine that it is almost invisible. All across the vast lawn there is sudden movement as sunbathers sit up and grab for shirts, their faces dazed and swollen, the outlines of grass imprinted on their cheeks.

One woman stands abruptly, twisting her long black hair into a ponytail, and Ranjit suddenly has a vision of Shabana in his cab.

Trying not to think of her dead, smashed face, he makes his way carefully through the crush of bodies.

Chapter Fourteen

At ten thirty that night the sudden rain is just a memory and it is hot again, and humid, the temperature barely dropping after the sun goes down.

Ranjit walks slowly down West Thirty-seventh Street. Club Ghungroo should be right here, but there is no awning, no lines, and no thick-necked bouncers. All he can see is a darkened nine-story building with a brightly lit glassed-in elevator lobby at street level. Two men in dark jackets stand inside, with the alert expressions of those in the service industry.

Damn it, is this the right place? Ghungroo wasn't listed, and neither Ali nor Murgi had heard of it. All evening Ranjit called cabbies, who in turn called others. Finally, half an hour ago, a Pakistani driver remembered dropping off some well-heeled businessmen at this strangely named club on Thirty-seventh.

Ranjit walks past the address, then ducks into the wide archway of a darkened office building; from here he has a clear view of the building. West Thirty-seventh Street, south of the hubbub of Times Square, is a strange place for a nightclub. This block is lined with nineteenth-century brick office buildings, the kind with creaky elevators and small, dark offices housing importer-exporters, insurance agents, and freight expediters. During the day the street must be busy enough, but now all the buildings are dark. The only light comes from the brightly lit elevator lobby, which casts a yellow lozenge of light across the street.

If there is a club here, it must be at the top of the building, perhaps with a roof terrace that takes advantage of the Midtown views. Craning his neck, Ranjit looks up, but sees only darkness. He reaches for his phone and starts dialing the cabbie to confirm this address, but just then a black stretch limo hums down the street, and stops right by the lit elevator lobby.

Hanging up, he peers into the street: the limo's tinted windows block his sightline, but he can see the tops of three men's heads as they saunter into the lobby. They show something to the men inside, then vanish into the elevator. The limo drives away, and the street is silent again. The dark-jacketed men in the lobby stroll outside, their eyes scanning the street.

Ranjit ducks back, thinking that they have seen him, but the men stop right by the door. A flame flares in one man's fist, and they both light up cigarettes, taking quick, hungry drags. Another limo turns into the street, and both men crush their cigarettes under their heels, and hurry back into the lobby.

The second set of visitors—men this time too, in suits and ties—enter the elevator. And as soon as this limo departs, another one rolls up, and then another. It is almost as though the cars are following a premeditated plan and have staggered their arrivals. Are the men all together? It's hard to tell.

What seems to be the last limo stays motionless for a longer time, and as its passengers depart, Ranjit can hear the sound of raucous voices. At first he doesn't understand, and then catches an entire sentence, shouted from one of the passengers to the men in the lobby.

"*Baas. Khatam. Elevator bundh karo. Abbhey, suna? Jaldi, jaldi.*"

The man has spoken in Hindi: We're finished. Shut down the elevator. Did you hear me? Quick, quick. It is not the polished, Urdu-inflected Hindi of the north, but the crude dialect of Mumbai.

Hearing it, Ranjit stiffens: so the Ghungroo *is* an Indian nightclub.

The man continues talking in Hindi, telling the driver to park nearby and wait for them. Ranjit strains to glimpse the speaker, but he's hidden behind the limo, and by the time it pulls away, the lobby is empty. The limo drives by slowly, and the driver finds a space in the middle of the block, reversing in jerkily.

The limo's interior light goes on for a second, and Ranjit sees the driver, dressed in a dark livery uniform, complete with a peaked cap. The driver hauls himself out of the car, then locks the car door, tugs on the handle to check it, and walks away slowly.

Ranjit has to make a decision: stay here and watch the elevator lobby, or follow the driver and try to get some information about this club: livery drivers, like cabbies, are lonely, and happy to gossip with their fellow drivers. Glancing back at the street, Ranjit sees no more headlights, and the darkness makes the decision for him.

It is easy to follow the limo driver, who moves slowly, with the stiff, hobbling gait that affects so many longtime chauffeurs. The man turns decisively down Ninth Avenue, passes a sushi place and a deli without slowing down, then crosses the street and enters a brightly lit diner.

It has red leatherette booths along one wall, and a counter along the other, with a lone counterman in a filthy apron, busy wiping down the grill. These kinds of diners—which serve omelets, matzo ball soup, and meatloaf—are disappearing in Midtown, replaced by cheap ethnic food and chopped-salad chains.

Ranjit hesitates. All the booths are empty, as is the long counter; once he enters, he will be instantly noticed. He watches the driver hoist himself painfully onto a stool at the counter, then take off his cap and run a comb through thick, iron-gray hair. His immaculately combed hair and aristocratic profile are in sharp contrast to his shabby, too-large jacket.

Come on, Ranjit tells himself. *This guy is just another worn-out livery driver. He's probably lonely after driving all day, he'll want to talk.*

A bell above the door tinkles as Ranjit walks in, and the counter-man looks up sourly. Ranjit sits on a stool, leaving a seat between himself and the driver.

"Got any tea?" he asks. "Real tea?"

"Whaddya mean? There's Lipton's or Earl Grey."

"Never mind. Just give me a poppy-seed bagel, toasted. No butter."

The livery driver looks up from studying a laminated menu. "I'll have the lumberjack breakfast."

The counterman's face darkens. "We don't serve breakfast this late."

"Nonsense." The driver's English is clipped, almost British, the English of the Indian upper classes. "It says here on your menu: 'Breakfast served all day.' *All day*, yes?"

Muttering, the counterman moves away, and the grill goes on with a hiss.

Ranjit turns to the driver. He must be in his late sixties, but his smooth skin and well-combed hair make him look younger. The only signs of his age are the deep creases that bracket his thin, downturned mouth.

"You're from India, right? I'm Ranjit Singh, from Chandigarh. Food any good here?"

"Anil Tiwari, from Mumbai. The food is bad. But one comes to these places for bad food. So one could say it is good bad food."

Ranjit smiles, but the driver doesn't smile back. Ranjit gestures to the man's uniform. "So, you're driving, yes? Me too, my cab is outside. How is business?"

"How long have you been driving?" Anil Tiwari examines him through hooded eyes.

"Two years. But it's temporary." Ranjit thinks of Leela when he says this.

"Ah. Well, you will find out, as I have, that there is no easy answer to your question. So I will say, business in New York is always good, if you are willing to take it up the ass." The obscenity is incongruous, coming in that cultured accent. "Take me, for example. I've been eating this same shitty food four nights in a row, because my customers want to go to this club down the street."

"I hear you, Anil Sahib." Ranjit uses the honorific, wondering what misfortune happened back home to condemn this man to a life as a livery driver. "The waiting is really the worst part."

The man pushes up the cuffs of his too-long jacket. "I could be home, having dinner with my wife. But, no, I have to hang about here, like a servant. These people behave like they're still in India, they think they can kick people around."

"Yeah, I know. Those Indian bankers, they're real assholes. Sometimes they'll get into my cab and keep yammering on their cell phones, as though I should read their minds and know where they're going."

Tiwari nods vigorously in agreement. "The men who hired me call themselves businessmen . . . *tchaaa*. Businessmen, my ass. They're thugs, from Mumbai. You should hear their Hindi. Straight from the Dharavi slum. They think they're tough guys. But you know what they're scared of?"

"What?" Ranjit's mind is a whirl.

"Rats." Tiwari smiles for the first time, his teeth stained and yellow. "This guy I drive, he got out of the car, a rat ran across the street, and he turned white as a sheet. Big, tough guy, scared of a rat. Yelled at me, as though it was my fault. What can I do, with the garbage strike and all? You know there are thirty-two million rats in New York City? Four for each person?"

Just then the food arrives. Tiwari looks skeptically at his stack of pancakes, eggs, and sausages, pours syrup over everything, and begins to meticulously cut it up.

Are Tiwari's clients actually thugs from Mumbai, or is he just exaggerating? Ranjit needs to know more.

"So, Anil Sahib. You're stuck here till late at night? Let's go and get a drink after this."

"I dare not. My clients could be hours, or they could be out in a few minutes. Depends if they find any girls. Last night, my client had me pick him up fifteen minutes after I dropped him off. I went to the service entrance, at the back, and he was standing there with a girl. Took her straight back to the hotel."

"So it's a strip club, yes? The girl was a stripper?"

Tiwari chews his food slowly. "Stripper-*shipper*, I don't know. This girl was pretty, but she looked like a regular girl." He shrugs and begins to chew on a piece of sausage. "She was Indian. Can you imagine it? That girl's parents came to this country, slaved away, probably sent her to college, and this is what she does. Disgusting. *Tchaaa . . .*"

Tiwari continues to eat, rambling on about Indian-American children, and how fast they forget their values. He talks on and on, but Ranjit is no longer listening, his mind busy trying to assemble all the pieces.

Leela had said, *You don't know these people,* before running away from him. Now it turns out that she's working at a strip club that is patronized by Indian thugs. Ranjit's next question is based on a hunch.

"Anil Sahib." He interrupts Tiwari in mid-flow. "Do you know who owns this club?"

"Ghungroo? Some rich Gujarati guy, Patel. He owns a lot of places. Hair places, yoga places, beauty parlors."

Bingo. Jay Patel owns the club where Leela works. So the rumors about his connections to the Mumbai mob are true. Clearly Leela has learned something while working at the club, something that has frightened her into silence. *He must talk to her.* Maybe she will be able to tell him why Patel is so interested in finding Shabana's murderer.

And now he knows that the club has a service entrance at the rear. It makes sense—the management wouldn't want the workers taking the fancy elevator up. He'll wait there till Leela comes out, and this time she won't be able to run away.

Tiwari is still talking, though somehow most of the lumberjack breakfast has vanished into his skinny frame. ". . . ah, I'm going to quit this job next year. Maybe the year after. Go back to India, get myself a chauffeur, never drive again. Just sit back and see the world go by."

Ranjit nods in agreement. He's heard this retirement fantasy many times from his cabbie friends. Taking out a twenty-dollar bill, he beckons to the counterman.

"For me and my friend here." Leaving his bagel untouched, he slides off the stool. "Nice to meet you, Tiwari Sahib."

"*Aare?* What is this?" Tiwari looks up in astonishment.

"It is my pleasure. Good to talk to a fellow countryman."

"Wait. Wait." Tiwari pulls a crumpled card from his wallet, smoothens it out, and hands it over. "My number. You can call me if you need anything."

"Thank you, Tiwari Sahib. Drive safe, now."

Heading out of the door, Ranjit glances back. Tiwari is hunched over his food, pouring syrup over his last pancake.

Now to find the rear entrance to the Ghungroo. Walking toward the club, he thinks about Anil Tiwari, the name strangely familiar from somewhere in the past. Tiwari, Tiwari . . . wasn't that the name of the banker in Mumbai, the one convicted of fraud? Or was it one of the bureaucrats caught up in the Bofors arms-trading scandal?

Ranjit finds an alley that runs parallel to Thirty-seventh Street, allowing him to approach the back of the Ghungroo building. Back here, its ornate white terra-cotta facing gives way to a bare brick façade, and the windows on the top three floors have been bricked in. That must be where the club is, though Ranjit can't hear even the faintest trace of music.

At the base of the building, metal stairs lead up to a small loading dock and a door: this must be the service entrance. Judging from the cars jammed into the alley—a Camaro, two Beemers, and an old Jaguar XJ6—the employees of Club Ghungroo are doing well.

A fixture over the service entrance casts a dull yellow cone of light, and Ranjit stands in the shadows, next to a row of tall trash cans. As he waits, the reek of the trash seeps into his nostrils, fermented and alcoholic, and soon the smell becomes a taste at the back of his throat. And Tiwari was right about the rats: dark, furry shapes run across the alley, avoiding the light.

The stink of the garbage is making it hard to breathe and he tries to ignore it. He meditates, focusing on his breathing, and is getting somewhere when a spill of light shines through his eyelids.

Opening his eyes, he sees a car drive into the alley, two figures in the front. It is a Ford Crown Victoria, painted an unobtrusive brown, but its three tall antennas are a dead giveaway. He has seen these un-marked police cars before, parked all over Midtown, waiting for taxi drivers to make illegal turns.

The dung-colored car stops in the center of the alley, and Ranjit hears the soft *click-click* of a camera as the license plates of the parked cars are captured. The photographer is a woman with close-cropped hair, and the driver is a man with well-oiled, dark hair, his parting razor-sharp. Even from this far away, there is no mistaking Detective Case and Detective Rodriguez.

What the hell are they doing here? If the cops find him in the alley with the Glock tucked into his waistband, they'll arrest him for sure, and this time, there will be no bail.

The camera held in Case's hands moves as she clicks away, and Rodriguez sits calmly at the wheel, sipping from a tall canister of cof-fee; the detectives seem to have come prepared for a stakeout. Case lowers the camera, nods to her partner, and the Crown Vic reverses slowly down the alley.

Ranjit knows that he has to get out of there, but have the cops left, or are they waiting out on the street? There is only one way to find out. He takes a step forward, then hears the rumble of another car and ducks back behind the trash cans.

A black stretch limo trundles down the alley, something about its cautious progress telling him that the driver is Tiwari. The service en-trance door at the back of the building opens, and the sudden sound of laughter spills out into the alley. A tall man walks out onto the loading dock, laughing uproariously, half-turned to the woman behind him. Despite a face pitted with old acne scars he is slim and handsome, with short black hair, the front stylishly tufted up. In his untucked white shirt and dark pants, he could pass for a finance guy, except that his hands are covered with thick gold rings that glint in the dim light.

A much shorter woman trails behind him, and at first all Ranjit can see is the electric blue of her cocktail dress. As she walks farther out onto the loading dock, the light shines down on her short platinum-blond pageboy hairdo, one long swoop of hair almost covering her left eye.

Under the hair—either a wig or a weave, he cannot tell—Ranjit recognizes Leela's catlike features. Her blue cocktail dress is cut very low in the front, revealing deep cleavage. The tall man skips down the stairs and stands impatiently by the stopped limo. Leela picks her way carefully down, her high black heels clattering on the metal treads, a smile frozen onto her face.

The driver hops out to open the rear door—yes, Ranjit was right, it is Tiwari—and Leela hesitates at the open door. The tall man pushes her roughly into the car, and climbs in after her. The passenger door slams shut and Tiwari hurries to the driver's seat.

As the limo moves off into the darkness, Ranjit leans forward in frustration: without a car, he cannot follow them.

At least he can see if the cops follow the limo. He moves quickly, staying close to the alley wall as he runs toward the street. Pressed flat against the brick wall, he peers around the corner, just in time to see the red taillights of the limo reach the end of the block. The dung-colored cop car pulls out of a parking spot and heads after it.

So the cops are interested in the tall guy who escorted Leela out of the club. *Who was he?* Ranjit feels a surge of anger as he remembers the man's arrogant laugh, the way he had shoved Leela into the car.

Straightening up, Ranjit walks around the corner, out into the street.

There is a flash of metal in his peripheral vision. A length of pipe comes down, out of the darkness, aimed at his head, and he throws up his left arm to block the blow. He feels bone shatter, and then stunning, hot pain, but his training kicks in, and he whirls to face his dark-jacketed attacker.

He ducks the next blow, feeling the pipe whiz over his head.

He hears the footfalls behind him a second too late. The second man must have come down the alley, and there is no time to duck. This blow catches him on the back of his head and he pitches forward, the trash-scented asphalt rushing up to meet him.

Chapter Fifteen

The pain has its tendrils deep inside him. Ranjit is lying on his shattered arm, facedown, tufts of dirty carpeting pushing into his nose and mouth. He stifles his impulse to roll off his arm, to stop the unbearable pulse of pain.

"The *maderchod* has a gun. A Glock, police issue."

"Tiwari said he was asking a lot of questions about the club. What goes on with the girls, *blah blah blah*."

The two men talk on, standing right over him. They are breathing hard, and must have dragged him inside the club.

"He's got a gun, he's in the alley, he could have nailed Lateef, easy. Fuck. I've been telling Patel, we need a camera back there, we can't keep track of everything . . ."

"Lateef's gone?"

"Yeah, he took that girl, Leela."

"Shit. She's nice, that one—"

"Bullshit, they're all whores. Don't forget that. And this one will keep her mouth shut, not like the last one. One fucking peep from her, and the old woman and the kid are screwed."

"She's nice, *yaar.* I talked to her a lot, when she worked on the floor . . . What do we do with this *maderchod*? Call Lateef?"

"I say we take this fucker to the Bronx, finish him off— *Oi,* he's waking up."

The pain is white hot, and Ranjit must have twitched. Arms reach down and turn him over, and he screams.

"*Abbhey, Sardarji,* don't make so much noise." The narrow point of a cowboy boot slams into Ranjit's ribs, but this doesn't even register against the constant pulse of the larger pain.

He blinks up at the two men in blue blazers and cowboy boots. He's in a narrow room with dirty white walls: a bank of lockers fills one wall, and the other one is papered with peeling photographs of women in cocktail dresses and G-strings. He must be deep inside the club, because he can hear the *thump-thump-thump* of techno music.

His left arm lies uselessly on his chest. His right creeps over the carpeting, looking for anything he can find.

The man on his left raises his booted foot and presses down on Ranjit's broken arm.

The scream comes out of him involuntarily. Tears stream down his face.

"I said, don't make so much noise. And stop trying to be a hero."

All Ranjit wants is for the pressure on his arm to go away. He blinks his eyes in submission. Let them think he's finished.

The foot moves off his arm, and he can breathe again. The man kneels down, while the second one stands by the door. Both men are clean-shaven, with babyish faces, and both wear crisp white shirts under their dark blue blazers.

These were definitely the men who were looking for Kishen. The old Sikh in the Bronx had said they wore jackets and cowboy boots.

The kneeling man addresses Ranjit. "So. You think you can finish off Lateef, here? Who sent you, the Hammer? You guys are losing the war in Mumbai, so you want to start a war here?"

Ranjit lies still, tears still streaming down his face. "I don't know who the Hammer is. Nobody sent me. I'm—"

The kneeling man stands and raises his pointy-toed foot again. His boots are new, the soles clean, the heels sharp.

"Don't fuck with us. You moved fast out there, you have training. Talk, or we'll break your other hand. Then your legs."

"No, wait. Listen to me, please." Ranjit raises his right arm, palm up, in a gesture of supplication.

"Talk. We're listening."

The booted foot hovers over his broken arm again. There is something fearsome about these baby-faced, clean-cut Indian men. They must be, what, twenty-two, twenty-four, with the look of poor boys who have made good.

"You have this all wrong. I don't know anything about this Lateef—"

"Bullshit. You pumped his driver for information. Luckily that old fuck had the sense to call us."

"Yes, I did talk to Tiwari. But, listen, I'm working for Patel Sahib. He wants me to find someone. I'm just looking for this one guy—"

The man standing next to Ranjit dips his hand into his jacket pocket and comes up with the blue, plastic-looking gun. "You are working for Patel? That's a good one. So that's why you're in the alley, with a Glock?"

The cowboy boot slams down, and Ranjit screams again. The white-hot, electric pain shoots down his arm, jacking directly into his central nervous system.

"In . . . in my wallet." Tears are flowing from Ranjit's eyes, falling back into his throat, turning his voice into a hoarse rasp. "Look in there. I have Patel's card, with his direct number. Call it."

"Bullshit." But the man takes out Ranjit's wallet from his own jacket pocket, and rifles through it.

Ranjit lies on the floor, trying to breathe in the pain, then breathe it out of his body. The fluorescent light shines directly into his face.

"Fuck me. You do have Patel's card." The man holds up the crumpled card.

"Call the number."

"Patel won't like that. He goes to sleep at eight o'clock. You sure you want to do this?"

"Call it."

The two men look at each other, and then the man with the card shrugs. He steps past his colleague and goes through a metal door—Ranjit glimpses a long, dimly lit corridor, hears female laughter—and then the door slams shut.

The second man's eyes never leave Ranjit, but he suddenly yawns, as relaxed as a cat. Ranjit knows from his army days that there are many reactions to violence. It thrills some men, and nauseates others. The ones who kill and maim easily, almost indifferently, are the most dangerous, because they have been raised in a different moral landscape.

From outside comes the muffled sound of conversation. Ranjit lies, half conscious, praying for the pain to stop. Seconds pass like minutes, and thoughts flood his mind.

Shabana, lying dead on a parquet floor, her face destroyed. Despite everything that the cops said, Ranjit has never really believed that Mohan was capable of such violence. But these men are—they would destroy the face of a beautiful woman with very little compunction. Are Patel and the mob somehow behind Shabana's death? That would explain why Patel is searching for Mohan: to find him and silence him. But why would Patel want Shabana dead? And who exactly is Lateef? Why are his men afraid of an attack by the Hammer? Who the fuck *is* the Hammer?

All that is academic. If Patel doesn't confirm his own story right now, Ranjit is sure that these men are going to kill him within the hour. And that thought leads to Shanti, half a world away: the thought of not seeing her again is unbearable.

He closes his eyes and prays:

The one who created the day also created the night.
Those who forget their lord and master are vile and despicable.
O Nanak, without knowing the Name, they are wretched
outcasts.

O humble servant of the Lord, I offer my humble prayer to you,
I am a mere insect, a worm.
O True Guru, I seek your sanctuary. Please be merciful . . .

The door suddenly clicks open. The man walks in from the corridor, a cell phone in his hand. He bends down and jams it into Ranjit's ear.

"Hello? Are you there?" It is Patel's voice, fuzzy with sleep.

Ranjit raises his head. "Patel Sahib—"

"Why are you at my club? What have you got yourself into, Ranjit?"

If he gives Leela up, what will these two do to her? "Sir, I'm close to getting Mohan. I heard he might be here, tonight. I don't know what else is going on, I swear—"

"If you heard something, why didn't you come to me? Why wait in the alley behind my club, *hanh*? Are you trying to play some sort of double game? You think I'm a fool?"

Patel's voice is hardening, coming to a decision about what to do. *Give him something, anything.*

"I was about to call you. Sir, the police are watching your club. The same two detectives who arrested me, they were here, in the back alley. They followed a limo that left from here."

"What?" Patel's voice erupts into anger. "You're sure about this?"

"Yes, sir. Case and Rodriguez, they were taking pictures, in the alley."

There is a silence. Ranjit knows that his life rests in that silence, in a motel room in Jersey covered with rugs and pillows.

"Okay." Patel makes an effort to lower his voice. "I will take care of this. Now, you listen carefully. Your job is to find Mohan. You stay away from my club, from all my businesses. Is that clear?"

"Yes, sir."

There is another pause. "How badly did they hurt you?"

"My arm is broken, sir."

The hand pressing the phone into Ranjit's ear quivers with suppressed anger.

"Okay. We will take care of that. And I'll tell them to give you the gun back. Let me talk to them."

Ranjit looks up at the stony faces of the two men standing over him. *Lateef's men beat him up and Patel apologizes.* It makes no sense.

The phone is yanked away from Ranjit's ear, and he rests his head on the carpet, his neck muscles cramped from the effort of raising up his head.

The man with the phone goes back into the corridor. Ranjit can hear Patel's voice coming through, hard and punitive, and the man just murmurs his replies.

A few seconds later both men pull Ranjit to his feet. Biting down on his lip to stop himself from screaming, Ranjit allows himself to be half carried, half dragged down the corridor, past many closed doors, the techno music growing louder. At the end of the corridor is a thick metal door, which opens onto the service entrance.

Ranjit finds himself being hustled down the stairs and into the backseat of one of the Beemers parked there. The two men get into the front.

"Where are we going?"

"Don't fucking worry, *Sardarji.* Your boss, Patel, he said to put you together again. Like Humpty-Dumpty, *hanh?*"

The two men laugh. Ranjit slumps back into his seat, each bump and sway sending hot pain into his arm. Mercifully, he passes out as they drive away.

The doctor is a worried-looking bald man with a faint Eastern European accent. They must have hauled him out of bed, because his breath stinks, but his office, on a high floor of an uptown building, is immaculate. Ranjit sits on a metal examining table as the man feels his arm with careful fingers, murmuring apologies whenever Ranjit winces.

"Aren't you going to take an X-ray?"

"Don't have one." The doctor looks up with tired eyes. "Don't worry, I set plenty of arms in Bosnia. This is simple, your ulna is fractured."

The doctor injects anesthetic into his arm, and in a few minutes the pain fades to a dull ache. Ranjit watches as the doctor gently sets the broken bone, then slips on a tight, stockinglike sheath. He wraps it with cotton tape, then adds a layer of blue fiberglass tape, smoothing and cutting it with the concentration of a sculptor.

There is no noise except for the buzzing of the lights, and far off, the sound of a siren moving through the dark city.

"How bad is it?"

The doctor shrugs his thin shoulders. "You need to keep the cast on for six weeks. Meanwhile, no driving, no pressure on the arm whatsoever." He takes out a medicine bottle and fills it with pills. "Percocet, a painkiller. These are high dosage, space them out every six hours, and don't overdo it, they're addictive. We're done."

The two men in cowboy boots are gone, and the doctor shows Ranjit out to a deserted bank of elevators. When he emerges from the bland glass building, he makes an effort to remember the address: on the corner of Seventy-fifth and Amsterdam, a few blocks from the Dakota.

The anesthetic is wearing off, and the pain is terrible. He dry-swallows a Percocet, noticing that there is no label on the medicine bottle. Fumbling in his pockets, he finds that they have returned the Glock, and his wallet, with enough money to take a cab. Peering into the thin stream of traffic, he hails a cab, which does an illegal U-turn to pick him up.

The cabbie is Pakistani, and from the way he bobs his head, Ranjit can tell that he doesn't speak much English, so Ranjit switches over to Hindi and tells the man to take him to Jackson Heights. The man frowns, and Ranjit knows that he won't be able to find a fare back, not at this time of the night.

"Don't worry," he says. "I'll give you twenty extra, okay?" and the cabbie smiles in relief.

The cabbie drives down Central Park West, and the Dakota comes into sight, its gabled roofs and dormers silhouetted against the dark sky. The bronze sentry booth by its arched entry is lit up, and tonight it resembles nothing more than an upright coffin. Inside he glimpses a doorman's blue uniform.

What if Shabana had hailed a cab thirty seconds later? He wouldn't have met her, would never have run into Mohan. He'd be driving his cab right now, not riding in one, and his arm, his life, and his future would have been intact. He would have been ferrying home drunks and amorous couples, ending the night wiping down the backseat of his cab. He would have been still living in the future, the future of Shanti arriving, of moving to the new apartment.

What if, what if . . . The Percocet is taking hold now, making him still and dreamy. The lights on one side of him are a blur, the darkness of Central Park rushing by on the other. Like it or not, he has been plunged into the present now, and every hour is as sharp as a dagger.

Leela. Where was that man Lateef taking her? He tries to remember what they said about her: something about an old lady and a child, and keeping her mouth shut. He knows that he has to find her now, before this darkness he is in finds her too, and swallows her whole.

They are moving swiftly across the darkened city, and he recognizes the landmarks without even thinking: the latticework of the Queensboro Bridge, the long stretch of Queens Boulevard, and then a short distance on the BQE. He is almost home when his phone rings and he fumbles it to his ear. Ali's voice comes through, loud and worried.

"Ranjit? Where have you been? I've been calling and calling."

"Can't talk now, Ali. Not now . . ." He is slurring his words.

"What is going on? Are you drunk? Where are you?"

"Heading home. Arm's broken. Not drunk, it's the painkillers." He doesn't mean to say this, but somehow finds himself unable to lie.

"What? Your arm's broken? How?"

"These men. Ghungroo."

"You're not making any sense, my friend. Are you cracking up? *Hanh?* Been driving two, three shifts nonstop?"

"Tomorrow. Come by tomorrow morning. Talk then."

The cab swerves down Thirty-seventh Avenue into Jackson Heights, and he pays the cabbie, adding an extra twenty. The man looks curiously at him, having overheard the entire conversation.

"You're Ranjit Singh, right? You're looking for that guy, Kishen something?"

Ranjit rears back, alarm bells going off. Then he remembers that he had put the word out. "Yes, that fucker owes me money. You know anything about him?"

"No, *bhai*. But I'll keep my eyes and ears open. I just started driving this week. I was a computer programmer in Pakistan. This is just temporary."

Despite the pain, Ranjit manages a grim smile.

Somehow he gets himself down into his basement apartment. When he turns the light on, the man in the mirrored wall stares back at him, face pale, his trousers, white shirt torn from climbing the tree, darkened with dirt from the alley.

He pulls off the shirt, sheds his trousers, and puts the Glock on the floor next to him. He gets into bed, but something is bothering him about the gun.

Turning the lights back on, he pulls out the magazine from the gun. It is empty. Those men have returned his gun, as instructed by Patel, but they've kept all the bullets.

He sits up in bed, the empty gun in his hand. From the mirrored wall, his reflection stares back at him, hollow-eyed and bankrupt. *No bullets. Arm broken. Grand jury trial in five days. Trapped between the cops and Patel's commands.*

He's been in bad jams before, but never have the odds stacked up against him like this. When he was up on the Siachen Glacier, he'd been resigned to death: the only way to function was to assume you were already dead, and then go from there. But that was a war, with an enemy. He thinks of himself lying inside the club on that dirty carpet, seconds away from dying at the hands of two unknown men. He had prayed then, the words pouring easily out of him, begging the Gurus for help. And he had been saved.

All these years in New York, he has let himself go, both his body and his mind. His body started screaming for care, and he had heeded it, but what about his soul? How could he have lost his faith so easily, turning to it only in a moment of crisis?

He stares at his reflection in the mirrored tiles, but his phantom self has no answers, either.

Chapter Sixteen

MUMBAI, 1997

Early one October morning Shabana left her bungalow and walked the short distance to her waiting car.

The monsoons had ended, washing away the gray smog that hung over the city, and there was a nip in the air; she sipped at a travel mug of hot *chai* as she walked, lost in her thoughts. Today she would begin shooting the most daring film of her career: a remake of the classic film *Pakeezah*.

The doomed courtesan had been changed to an aging bar girl, drunken and desperate, taking on young lovers to stave off her mortality. The setting had been changed, too—Bombay had now been officially renamed Mumbai, and the film was set in this new globalized city of call centers and high-tech billionaires, its twelve million inhabitants marching to the beat of cell phone ringtones.

Ruksana had been dead against Shabana acting in the *Pakeezah* remake. Even Don Hajji Mustafa—under investigation for tax evasion, he had fled the country and found a safe haven in Dubai—called Shabana and cautioned her against taking on the role. But Sanjeev was certain she could pull it off, and Shabana gathered up her courage and defied them both.

When Ruksana screamed and yelled and threatened to quit, Shabana quietly accepted her resignation, leaving her sister stunned. Sanjeev helped Shabana to hire a professional manager, and an international bank, flush with money, had willingly stepped in to finance the film, replacing the Don.

Shabana missed her sister, not all the time, but when she was alone. It was strange to have control over her own time, and not entirely pleasant; she had grown used to Ruksana making decisions for her. She tried to telephone Ruki, to check in with her, see what she was doing, but her sister wouldn't take her calls. Shabana had heard that Ruki was devastated and deeply depressed, and didn't leave her new flat, though there were other rumors that she had taken up painting.

Well, Ruki was an adult—that was what Sanjeev said—and would have to find her own way. Anyway, Shabana had to concentrate on her own career, and the remake of *Pakeezah* would take up every bit of her creative energy.

No other actress had ever dared to reinterpret the role defined by the iconic Meena Kumari, and Shabana felt tremendous pressure. As it is, she was being excoriated in the film press as a "loose" woman, because she and Sanjeev were openly living together. He had moved into her flat after Ruksana moved out, and they had fallen into a domestic routine: he made her *chai* in the morning, and they ate dinner together every night.

As Shabana walked to her car, sipping *chai* from her travel mug, she reminded herself that the days of living under Ruksana's—and the Don's—rule were over. She was her own woman now, and to hell with what people thought. As long as she had Sanjeev's company at the end of each day, she would be fine.

When a white-bearded man appeared out of nowhere and held out his hand, Shabana was puzzled. He was too clean to be a beggar—though his white *kurta* was old, it was washed and ironed.

Just then a black Maruti van zoomed in, cutting Shabana off from her car, and four men emerged, their faces masked by checked handker-chiefs. She stood, stunned, and the old man gently took the mug of *chai* from her hands before the men grabbed her and pushed her into the black van.

It all happened so fast that Shabana only felt afraid when the van accelerated away and she smelled the brownish odor of the men pressed up against her: they smelled of poverty and slums and bathing outside under a tap.

Rough hands tied a blindfold around her eyes, and a voice said, "Keep still. The Boss wants to see you."

"Why are you doing this? Who is your boss."

"Shut up. You'll find out soon enough."

The men said no more. Plunged into darkness, Shabana felt the pressure of their bodies against hers as the car sped up and stopped, making its way through morning rush-hour traffic.

Fighting down her panic, Shabana tried to remember what she had heard about the Mumbai mob. With Don Hajji Mustafa in exile in Dubai, his lieutenants had started their own gangs in Mumbai, and were battling for control over the city. To finance their operations they were extorting money from film directors, industrialists, and the new-tech millionaires: those who wouldn't pay up died in their cars, shot at close range. One gang left a hammer behind as a trademark; others threw *laddoos,* orange sweets, onto the bodies of their victims. Shabana had heard all this, and, secure in her new love, never even thought it applied to her.

Which gang was kidnapping her? The constant jolting of the car caused the blindfold around Shabana's head to droop for an instant, and she caught a glimpse of a giant billboard outside, with her own smiling face on it advertising Sunsilk shampoo. The men quickly tight-ened the blindfold, but that glimpse told her that they were in Andheri, heading north.

She began to count the number of times that the car stopped at traffic lights. After fifteen lights, they screeched to a stop, and the men hustled her outside. They warned her that there was a wide, open drain right ahead of her, and she walked, still blindfolded, across a wooden plank. Then there were sixteen wooden stairs, old and creaky, and she climbed them slowly, one man on either side of her. As she ascended, she heard the *thwop-thwop* of clothes being beaten against stones, and knew that there was a *dhobi-ghaat,* a washerman's colony, close by. At the top of the stairs, they walked through a short corridor and entered a room where her blindfold was taken off.

She thought that the small, dark room was empty, but as her eyes adjusted, she saw a man sitting on a bed, so dark-skinned that she could see only the flash of white teeth.

When he flicked on a bare bulb, she gasped. It was Veenu Gopal, the Don's muscleman, nicknamed "the Hammer." He was bare-chested, his muscle turning to flab, his eyes bloodshot.

"What is this? You know me. What are you doing?"

"What am *I* doing? Ask yourself, what are *you* doing, *hanh? Hanh?* You have broken with the Don, you have no protection, and you have shacked up with some man. You have become a shameless whore."

"How dare you. I'll tell the Don."

The Hammer laughed. "The Don? He's just an old man in an air-conditioned villa, far away in Dubai. I rule the streets here. And you will do as I say." He slammed a huge fist into the palm of his other hand, and Shabana saw that his knuckles had been broken and reset so many times that they were hard knobs of bone.

The Hammer picked up a cell phone and handed it to her.

"Call your people. I want twenty-five lakhs, now. Think of it as a tax for the life you live. Or you can choose to die. Up to you."

With trembling hands, Shabana called Sanjeev, but he did not answer. She tried again and again, thinking that he was in the shower, or on his motorbike, but all she got was a busy signal. She tried her manager, too, but he did not pick up. Finally the Hammer snatched the phone away from her.

"You are time-wasting." His enormous hands were trembling with rage. "Call someone who can deliver. You have one more call. That's it."

Shabana paused, bewildered.

"Come on, phone. Now."

She dialed a number that she hadn't called in months. It rang for a long time before it was answered.

"Ruki?" Shabana spoke quickly. "Please don't hang up. It's me . . . I need your help."

"You." The voice was corrosive with disdain. "You need help? Why are you calling me? Where is your boyfriend, *hanh?*"

"Ruki, please. This is serious, it's a matter of life and death."

"You know, you're always talking about death. It's very boring. Maybe you should have thought a little more before getting rid of me. Good-bye."

She hung up and Shabana was left listening to the dial tone.

Across from her, the Hammer frowned and cracked his knuckles, the sound filling the room like a gunshot.

"Wait. I'll call her again. She'll listen to me, I swear." With trembling fingers she redialed Ruksana's number and listened to it ring. *Come on, pick up, come on . . .*

"Why are you calling me again? I told you, I can't help you."

"Wait." Shabana was in tears. "Ruki, I'm sorry for firing you. Deeply sorry, and I need your help. The Hammer, he's kidnapped me. I'm in this room—"

"Who are you talking about?"

"It's the Hammer. He wants twenty-five lakhs, today. Or else he will—"

Ruksana laughed. "That big lunk is now in the kidnapping business?"

Perhaps the Hammer heard the laughter on the other end, because his frown deepened. "Who are you talking to? She is laughing at me?"

Ruksana chuckled some more. "So. The Hammer has picked you up, and your boyfriend is missing, and you want me to help you? Why should I?"

"Please, Ruki, please, I need your help. If he doesn't get the money, he says he'll kill me."

"He will *what?* Put that fool on the telephone."

Shabana handed over the phone. When the call ended, the Hammer's face was flushed with rage, but he didn't say another word. He got up, pulled on a shirt, and left, locking the door behind him.

Shabana stayed in that dark room for six hours more, most of them alone, and she took comfort in the sound of the clothes being washed next door. It reminded her of childhood, when her mother washed their school uniforms, thwacking them against the stone floor of the courtyard.

Somewhere during that time the white-bearded man appeared and brought her hot tea in her own travel mug. He made a *tsk-tsk-tsk* sound when he saw how frightened she was, and said in a soothing voice that it would all be over soon.

Late that afternoon she was blindfolded again before being driven away. She was pushed out at a busy intersection near Eros Cinema, and when she made her way home, she found Ruksana waiting at the flat. She had secured Shabana's release for nine lakhs, delivered in a fake leather gym bag to a certain *bhelpuri* stall on Chowpatty Beach.

Shabana broke down and sobbed till she lapsed into an exhausted silence. Ruksana just watched her, then spoke in a businesslike voice.

"Needless to say, you will give me my job back. And this time, it will all be in writing. I will have a contract drawn up." Shabana nodded, and she continued. "And we need to make one more call."

"The police?"

"Why would we do that?" Ruksana smiled a twisted smile. "They are the most dangerous of all, because they'll sell their loyalty to anyone. No, we are calling Don Hajji Mustafa. Where do you think I got the ransom money from?"

The Don's voice, coming over a remote wireless network from the Arabian Desert, was crackly and faint, but his tone was mild and comforting, the tone an indulgent father uses with his wayward daughter.

"*Beti, beti, beti* . . ." he said. "*Aare*, I am so sorry about what happened. You tell me exactly what happened, and I will fix it."

In a small voice, Shabana told him all that she remembered: the billboard, the fifteen traffic lights, the old creaky stairs, the sound of clothes being washed.

The Don listened, and said that she had done well to remember all this.

"And Don, please, one more thing." Shabana threw all caution to the wind. Sanjeev's T-shirts and jeans were still hanging in the closet, but his motorcycle was gone. "My boyfriend, Sanjeev, he is missing. He did not go to work today. He has disappeared. Please find him. Please, for me."

"Don't worry your pretty head, *beti*. It is done. Now you rest."

Ruksana stayed over that night. Shabana took two sleeping pills and cried herself to sleep.

The next morning, she awoke late, befuddled from the medication, to find that the bag with the ransom money had been returned. And in that morning's papers, she read the headlines and saw the blurry photographs: four of the Hammer's men had been found dead in a room in Jogeshwari, shot in the head sometime during the night. The soles of their feet had been burned before they were killed. The newspapers said that it was the start of a bloody gang war; the absent Don Hajji Mustafa was asserting his muscle to get his former lieutenants back into line.

Shabana looked closely at one of the photographs and screamed: the white-bearded old man who had brought her tea lay in a pool of his own blood, both his ears cut off.

She took two more sleeping pills and went back to bed. When Don Hajji Mustafa called that evening, she spoke through a haze.

"Don, those men, they . . . they didn't do anything to me. That old man, he made me tea, he was harmless . . ." She began to cry.

The Don remained silent for a moment, then spoke. "*Beti*, there is a line with me. If you cross that line, you know what will happen to you. Those men crossed that line. Now, don't worry your pretty head about this . . . incident."

Shabana forced herself to stop crying. "Don, my friend Sanjeev, he has not returned. I can't sleep, please help me."

"*Beti.*" The Don paused. "I have some bad news for you."

"No." Shabana felt herself sinking through the floor. "He can't be dead. Not Sanjeev."

"He is not dead, don't worry." The Don paused. "But he should be. Your Sanjeev is the one who set up this kidnapping with the Hammer. They were going to share in the ransom. Now he is nowhere to be found."

"It cannot be. Sanjeev would never, ever—"

"My information is never wrong, *beti*. You should know better than to question me." His tone hardened. "Wasn't Sanjeev the one who encouraged you to fire your sister, to break with me?"

"No. He just wanted me to be independent—"

"Well, there is your answer."

Shabana slammed down the phone and looked at the triumphant expression on Ruksana's face.

"*You,*" Shabana screamed. "*You* did this. You *bitch*. You couldn't stand to see me happy with Sanjeev. Somehow you did this, you, you . . ."

A servant came running into the room, but Ruksana gestured at the man to go away. "My sister is hysterical," Ruksana explained, "she's had a very bad shock."

Shabana reached for more sleeping pills, but Ruksana stopped her.

"That's enough for now. What do you want to do, kill yourself? Stop all this melodrama."

Going into her bedroom, Shabana locked the door. She took one of Sanjeev's dirty T-shirts from the wash basket and climbed into bed, inhaling his smell trapped within the worn cloth.

Chapter Seventeen

The morning after the men beat him, Ranjit's arm hurts like hell. Sitting in Ali's yellow cab, he swallows the first Percocet of the day and waits for the pain to recede. Ali picked him up half an hour ago, and they are now parked on Liberty Avenue, in the heart of Little Guyana.

An elevated train rattles overhead, sending down a layer of fine dust, and then the avenue is quiet again. The midmorning sun shines through the metal structure of the El and casts zebra-striped shadows across the street below.

Without the velvet sheen of night, the neighborhood looks like any other in Queens, rows of small stores on either side of the elevated tracks, their blue and yellow awnings flashes of color in the gloom. Pigeons waddle in the middle of the road, and then swoop up into the cast-iron web above them, the beams and columns spattered with a century of guano.

"I can't believe those bastards broke your arm. How bad does it hurt? Is the painkiller helping?" Ali gestures to the plaster cast. Today he wears a yellow Hawaiian shirt covered with red pineapples, the colors so violent that it makes Ranjit's head hurt.

"It'll kick in soon." Ranjit looks away as he talks. "Hey, you ever heard of someone called Lateef? Or 'the Hammer'?"

Ali Khan stares at him. "What planet do you live on, *bhai*? Veenu Gopal is a huge Mumbai gangster. They call him 'the Hammer.' You don't watch Zee TV or what?"

"I don't have a TV."

"*Hmmmpf.* This Hammer, he used to be a lieutenant for Don Hajji Mustafa, but he started his own gang, took over huge parts of Mumbai. The funny part is that the Don has fled to Dubai, and this Hammer, he is now hiding in Indonesia." Ali chuckles, and his chins quiver. "So it's a remote-control gang war. Both of them sit in their mansions and calls in hits."

And clearly the Hammer doesn't seem too fond of Lateef. "Did the TV mention a man named Lateef?"

"Lateef? Half of India is called Lateef. I personally know six Lateefs."

"A gangster called Lateef?"

Ali scowls as he thinks. "There are lots of smaller hoodlums, but I don't think any of them are called Lateef. Why?"

"Just interested, that's all."

"Can you please tell me what the hell is going on? I'm tired of you sitting there silently." Ali's face turns red with irritation.

"Okay, but you're not going to like it . . . I think Patel had something to do with Shabana's death."

"What? He's a businessman. He owns apartment buildings, he sells hair."

"Look, Ali, the cops are convinced that Mohan did it, but I don't buy that. He's a seducer, not a murderer. Sure, maybe he knew something about the murder, he took off, he was frightened. Now Patel wants me to find Mohan, before the cops do. Why? Does he want to shut Mohan up?"

"Okay, that makes sense, but what's the link between Patel and Shabana Shah?"

"I don't know, but this girl, Leela, she does. She pretty much told me that someone else was involved, and she works at Patel's club. All those rumors I heard are true—Patel's definitely mixed up with the Mumbai mafia, and the cops know this, that's why they're staking out the club . . . Leela is the key here, she knows something."

"I doubt that she's going to just pour her heart out to you. She ran away once, clearly she's terrified." Ali gulps. The Mumbai mafia and nightclubs are far from his reality of driving a cab. "If there are mobsters involved, go tell the police. You can't poke around on your own, it's too damn dangerous—"

"Tell the cops what? That I saw them on a stakeout? Then I'll have to explain what I was doing there."

"If the cops can't help you, then run. Go to Canada, go to Mexico, just get the hell out of here."

"Ali, just listen to what I have to say, okay? Yes, Leela was scared that night, but if I can just talk to her quietly, I have a feeling she'll help me. But first, I have to find out where she lives. That's where you come in."

Ranjit reaches one-handed into his pocket and pulls out a lady's lilac pocketbook with a gold clasp. He found it in his cab, and should have turned it in to the central lost and found, but it's been lying in his apartment for months.

He hands the pocketbook to Ali. "The guys at Sonny's Roti Shop must know Leela. She said that she goes there all the time. Just walk in there and say she dropped this in your cab, and you want to return it. Ask them where she lives. It's somewhere very close by."

Ali looks down disbelievingly at the pocketbook. "You think this is going to work? Sounds dangerous to me—"

"It's a *roti* shop, for God's sake. Don't be such a coward." Ranjit's arm throbs with pain. "Ah, I'm sorry, I didn't mean to snap at you."

"Okay, okay, I'll do it." The big man heaves himself out of the car, pulls down the tails of his Hawaiian shirt, and waddles down the sidewalk toward Sonny's.

Ranjit sighs and settles back into his seat, seeking some position that will hurt less. He watches the old Guyanese ladies in their crumpled skirts and cheap slippers stand by a vegetable stall, squeezing eggplants and tomatoes, raising them to their noses to sniff out ripeness.

Some shopkeepers are brushing at their wares with colored feather dusters, and that gesture reminds him of India, as does the smell of incense drifting out of the small shrines in the shops.

How strange, he thinks, to transplant Indians to the Caribbean, where they lose their language, and all their memories of India. All that remain are these scattered gestures.

Another train rumbles overhead, and the whole cast-iron El shakes. A few passengers trickle down the stairs from above, and then it is quiet again.

There is the blur of Ali's yellow-and-red Hawaiian shirt as he emerges from Sonny's Roti Shop. His face is reddened—from embarrassment or exertion, Ranjit cannot tell—and he is clutching a grease-spotted brown paper bag to his chest.

The smell of hot *roti* and mango pickle fills the cab as Ali gets in.

"So?" Ranjit's eyes dart worriedly to his friend's face.

"So? I bought some chicken doubles. Three for me, two for you. Or if you don't want any . . ."

"Stop messing around—"

". . . and while I was buying these, I inquired, casually, about your friend, Leela, who dropped this purse in my cab. I said she had green eyes, and was beautiful, as you described, and the lady behind the counter laughed. She gave me this—" Ali holds up a takeout menu with something scrawled on it. "—and said that the beautiful princess lives close by, on 120th Street."

"Thank the Guru." Ranjit slumps back in his seat.

Ali reaches forward and turns the key in the ignition. "So, you want to go there? What about those local hoodlums you tangled with? What if they recognize you?"

"I don't think so. Look at me, *yaar*. I'm practically undercover."

Ranjit gestures at his own clothes: he is wearing jeans and a crumpled blue half-sleeved shirt that is misbuttoned, and flip-flops, since he couldn't tie his shoes. He couldn't tie his turban either, so his long hair is in a topknot, and covered by a baseball cap with MIKE'S TOW written on it.

"*Aare,* Ali, don't worry so much. Bad guys only come out after dark."

"Okay, okay."

Ali switches on the engine and drives away one-handed, chomping on a *roti* roll with the other.

They park a block away from the address scrawled on the takeout menu, in the scant shade of the scrawny trees that line the narrow road. Ranjit asks Ali to wait in the cab, and he grunts contentedly, chewing on his second *roti* roll.

Walking slowly down the street, Ranjit looks at the numbers on the small two-story wooden houses, feet away from each other, with tiny yards facing the street. Despite their modest size, they are all freshly painted in bright greens, pinks, and yellows. High stone balustrades have replaced many of the chain-link fences, and the more affluent homeowners have even refaced their front façades in brick.

In those details, Ranjit recognizes the Indian belief that stone and brick speak of respectability and permanence; only the poor live in wooden houses. There are other traces of India, too: the bright red of chili pepper bushes, and statues of Krishna and Lakshmi displayed in the large picture windows, some accompanied by crossed American flags.

Unlike the scrappiness of Jackson Heights—where only the poorest Indian immigrants live, departing as soon as they can for the suburbs—this street speaks of community and prosperity. These Caribbean immigrants are clearly here to stay.

These are all single-family houses, and Ranjit wonders whether Leela rents a room in one of them. But the address that Ali has obtained—on the corner of 109th Avenue—is a faded yellow single-family, with no name on the mailbox, and only one buzzer.

He stands uncertainly by the chain-link fence, half overgrown with weeds; maybe there is another entrance around the back. Turning the corner, he walks the length of the house, toward a long, grassy backyard, bordered by more chain-link fence. It is shaded by a huge, leafy tree that must have existed for a hundred years before these houses were built. In the sunny part of the yard a girl stands by a dug-up flowerbed, one foot pushing down on a spade. She is wearing cutoff jean shorts and a gray T-shirt stained with sweat. Ranjit can't tell if this is Leela: her face is masked by white plastic sunglasses, and her hair is covered with a brown kerchief knotted at the back.

The girl digs deftly, turning over the earth, and then crouches to scatter seeds from a packet. The rest of the flowerbed contains masses of yellow marigolds, blue hydrangeas, and tall sunflowers that sway in the breeze.

A screen door slams and an older woman comes out of the back of the house, carrying a tray laden with a jug of lemonade and plastic glasses. She is in her sixties, and wears a faded red pantsuit, with dyed, jet-black hair and painted-on arched eyebrows. A small black-haired boy in yellow shorts and a matching T-shirt walks behind her, and when he sees Ranjit he stops, shyly rubbing one shin against his other leg. He has plump cheeks, a round belly, and solemn brown eyes.

"Dev, I told you to bring the folding table—" The older woman jumps when she spots Ranjit standing by the fence. "Oh my Lord."

She steps backward, still holding the tray, her face contorting with fear.

The girl by the flowerbed hears this and turns around quickly. There are streaks of mud on her catlike face and dark smears on her T-shirt. It is Leela, Ranjit realizes, but without her tall stiletto heels and platinum blond hair, she looks very different from last night. And clearly, she doesn't recognize him without his turban.

"Leela, it's me, Ranjit."

"Oh." She takes a step backward, the spade still in her hand.

The only friendly one is the boy, who walks up to the fence and smiles at Ranjit.

Ranjit crouches down. "Hey, big guy. How old are you? Ten, right? You in fourth grade?"

The boy waggles his big head. "*Nooo.* I'm five. I'm in first grade."

"You're pretty tall for first grade. Can you drive?"

"Drive? *Nooo.* We don't have a car." The child looks up at Ranjit, catching on to the game. He has Leela's smile too, bright and effortless.

Leela throws her spade down and walks toward the fence.

"How long have you been standing here?" Her voice is a whisper. "Did anyone see you?"

"I just want to talk. I'm sorry I frightened you last time." He gestures at the plaster cast on his arm. "I went looking for you at the club, and Patel's men did this to me."

The old lady must have heard him, because she gasps again. "Leela, what is the man saying?"

"It's fine, Ma. I'm handling it."

Ranjit stares at Leela: her gray T-shirt, faded from many washes, has a printed pattern of brown palm trees, and her denim shorts cut into her thighs. Without her heels she is very short and looks much younger, and suddenly vulnerable. And there is something else: a dark bruise on one cheek is half hidden by her sunglasses, and there are red welts high on both her forearms.

"Who did that to you? Lateef?"

"Leela? Who is this man?" The old lady's voice quavers with anxiety. She still holds the heavy tray of lemonade, and her arms tremble from the effort.

"He's a friend, Mama. Take Dev and go back into the house for a few minutes. Please." She pauses while the old lady and the boy scuttle back into the house. "How do you know about Lateef?"

"These two men, they beat me, in the alley behind the club, and I passed out. When I came to, they were talking about you. I heard some things I shouldn't have." He points to the bruise behind her sunglasses. "Lateef did that to you, didn't he?"

She tilts her head and examines him, and then she nods slowly.

"Okay, we can talk. Not here, though. You have a car?"

"Down the street." He nods in the direction where Ali is parked. "A yellow cab, you can't miss it."

"I'll be there in five minutes. Go now."

She marches back into the house, and he can hear her raised voice issuing instructions.

•   •   •

True to her word, Leela walks down the block five minutes later. She still wears the same clothes, but has changed into high wedge-heeled sandals, and her catlike face has taken on her old, confident look. He gets out and opens the back door for her, but she pauses and peers into the cab.

"That's my friend, Ali." Ranjit holds up his cast. "I can't drive. Please, get in."

He gestures to the cab, then realizes that this is the second time in twenty-four hours that Leela is being told to get into an unknown car.

She ducks into the backseat of the cab and he shuts the door. Ali stares hard at her in the rearview mirror, and Ranjit nudges his friend's ample midriff.

Leela twists and looks through the back window. "We can't talk here. Someone will see us."

"Where do you want to go?"

She bites her lower lip. "Umm. Do you know Jamaica Bay?"

Ali clears his throat and addresses her in his best cabdriver fashion. "Where, madam? By the North Channel Bridge? Where the Guyanese ladies like to go?"

"Yeah, sure."

She leans back and crosses her arms, and Ranjit knows she isn't going to talk to him, not with Ali here. He looks over at his friend and raises his eyebrows. *Where the hell are we going?*

Ali waggles his hand, palm out, in a gesture that means *Wait. Trust me.*

They drive down Lefferts, leaving behind the crowded streets of Richmond Hill. A jet roars overhead on its approach to JFK airport, so low that Ranjit can see dark heads in the window. He remembers arriving in this country, peering out of the plane window at the strange landscape and wondering what it would be like.

Soon Ali is on Cross Bay Boulevard, heading toward Jamaica Bay. Soon, Ranjit smells salty air, and sees the bright glint of sunshine on water.

Chapter Eighteen

The cab is now a small yellow speck, far away by the North Channel Bridge.

A trail of footprints lies behind Leela and Ranjit as they walk along the wet, sandy shoreline of Jamaica Bay. She has taken off her wedge sandals and carries them in one hand, the wooden heels clacking against each other.

They pass some narrow beaches, sloping down to the water, and other parts where the tall grass fringes the shore. Leela doesn't say a word. She walks fast, her bare legs scissoring angrily, and Ranjit struggles to keep up, half dazed from the sunlight glinting on the water. In the distance, shrouded in heat, he can make out a long arm of land that must be the Rockaways; from here, it looks like some enchanted world.

The sand grows dirtier. There are curious circles of ashes, and farther in, tangled in the grass, the flash of saffron cloth.

Drawing closer, Ranjit peers at it. "Is that a sari? And those things, next to it? Coconuts?"

Leela walks on silently. He stoops to pick up a scrap of cardboard, and sees a crudely printed image of the Hindu god Vishnu, his face surrounded by a fan of snakeheads.

"Leela? What is this place? What is going on here?"

She still doesn't answer. They round a curve of beach, and see a young man and a woman, dressed in traditional Indian clothes, standing in knee-deep water. The man pours a pitcher full of orange liquid into the water, and the woman has her eyes closed, her palms pressed together tightly.

"*Shhh*. They are praying." Leela stares at the couple, as though afraid of being recognized, but they are oblivious, and she relaxes a little.

They walk quickly down the beach, and soon are alone again, the silence interrupted only by the soft lapping of the waves. As though reaching a decision, she stops and turns to him. The front of her T-shirt is black with sweat, and rivulets run down her flushed face.

"You asked about this place. It's a special place for Guyanese. That couple back there? They want a child, so they're offering saffron milk to Ma Ganga. People come here to pray, to make offerings. Ma Ganga, she takes away your pain, your sadness."

Ma Ganga? That is what Hindus in India call the Ganges, the holy river that runs through North India.

"But Leela, the Ganges is in India. This is Jamaica Bay—" He sees Leela's face darken, and stops. "Wait. Do you have a Ganges in Guyana, too?"

She nods. "Yes, we have a holy river."

"Okay." The Guyanese, it seems, are used to adopting their local rivers and treating them like the Ganges. "Do you come here to pray? To ask for help?"

"Sometimes . . . yes."

"What's wrong, Leela? Why do you need help?"

She turns her back to him and stares out at the Bay. She is so short that he can see clearly over her head to the glittering water.

"I'm not a whore, Ranjit."

The statement comes out of nowhere, and he doesn't know how to reply.

"I'm *not* a whore." Her voice is breathless. "Yes, I work at the club, but I'm a hostess."

"I'm not judging you, Leela. You do whatever you have to, to survive. I understand that. I worked for Patel for a year, and I knew he was up to something, but I just ignored it, because I needed the work. But I can't ignore what happened to Shabana."

Despite the heat, a slight shiver runs through her slim shoulders. He notices that, and decides to press his point.

"The cops showed me photographs of what happened to her: someone beat in her face with a statue of Ganesh, a big, heavy marble statue. They smashed her nose, her mouth, teeth, shattered her cheekbones—"

"Stop. I don't want to hear any more." Her lips are trembling.

He decides to press on. "What happened to *your* face?"

"I wasn't looking. The club was dark, I walked into a door."

"I saw you leave Ghungroo with that man, Lateef. You looked very frightened. He beat you, didn't he? Is that how he gets his kicks?"

She stands with her back to him, her arms crossed over her chest. Walking in front of her, he gently tugs the sunglasses from her face, and she does not try to stop him.

Her left eye is swollen and red with blood, and there is a vivid purple ring around it. There is a deep gash on her cheekbone, the kind left by a raised ring. He thinks of the many gold rings on Lateef's hands, and feels the slow burn of anger.

"Why are you letting him do this to you? Why don't you just leave the club?"

"I can't. You don't understand."

He realizes that something else is different, too: her eyes are hazel, not sea green. It's amazing how colored contact lenses, heels, and a platinum-blond wig can transform this ordinary girl into an exotic nighttime creature.

"Leela, I want to help you, but you have to talk to me."

"You can help me? How? You're a *taxi driver*." She snatches her dark glasses from his hand and puts them back on, masking the bruise.

"When the NYPD questioned me about the murder, they kept asking me about Patel. They know he's connected to the Mumbai mob." He decides to lie a little. "They have a surveillance team watching the club, twenty-four hours. They want him badly, but I don't think they have anyone inside the club. If you give me some information, I can cut a deal with the cops, they will help both of us."

She ignores his words, and sits down, throwing her wedge heels next to her. She works her toes deep into the sand, as though trying to bury herself in it. He sits down next to her and waits.

Over her shoulder he sees a wave come in, depositing a broken clay vessel and two rotting limes onto the sand; this, too, must have been some anxious, lonely person's offering to the gods. The thought of Leela coming to this desolate place to find solace fills him with sadness.

When she does speak, her voice is almost absentminded. "I'm sorry, Ranjit. I have nothing more to tell you."

"Damn it, Leela! Damn it." He scrabbles with his good hand and levers himself to his feet, towering over her. She lowers her head, her feet frantically burrowing into the sand.

"Shabana is *dead*. Patel is going to find Mohan and kill him. I'm going to jail. And you know what? You're so scared, you let Lateef beat you up. Why? Does he pay you well?"

"I told you, I'm not a whore." Her lower lip quivers.

"I've seen the rings on Lateef's hands, he's going to cut you up badly. His men were talking about him, he's a real animal—"

"Yes, he's an animal all right, he's worse than a pig. But I'm still not talking to you."

Her fists push violently into the sand on either side of her, expending the anger stored inside her. She is furious about what is happening to her, but why won't she talk to him?

He remembers the two men standing over him last night. What had they said? *This one will keep her mouth shut . . . One fucking peep from her, and the old woman and the kid are screwed . . .* At the time, it hadn't made any sense, he hadn't known about Leela's family.

"That old lady at your house, she's your mother, and the kid is your son, right? If you say anything, something bad will happen to your family?"

"You leave my family out of it—"

He remembers the fear on the old lady's face, and has a flash of intuition. "Are they illegal? Is that it? That's what Patel is holding over your head?"

Her fists pushing in the sand grow still. She says nothing, just draws her knees up to her chest and lowers her head.

"Leela, tell me what you know about Shabana's death. I can go to the cops, cut a deal, get documentation for your family. It's done all the time. What the hell is a green card to them? It's just a piece of paper." He doesn't even know if she is listening. "Think of your son. He's going to grow up here in fear, seeing his mother being beaten up. Is that what you want?"

Leela jerks her head up. "He doesn't know what's happening. I make sure he doesn't see anything."

"That's bullshit. Children are like sponges, they absorb emotions. You think he's fine, but he's being scarred. He will go through life carrying your pain, your fear. Is that what you want?"

She doesn't reply, just sits as immobile as a rock, the twin lenses of her sunglasses reflecting the glittering water. Ranjit is suddenly exhausted, and his arm throbs with pain. *Maybe Ali was right, after all. Maybe he should just run, go anywhere he can, Canada, Mexico, just get the hell out of here—*

"If you go to the cops. Can you guarantee that they will let my mother and son stay?"

"I'll do my best, Leela. I'll talk to them—"

"No. You have to *promise* me that they won't be deported." She pulls off her glasses and glares at him, one eye hazel, the other full of blood. "Who is the most precious person to you, in this world?"

"My daughter, Shanti."

"Swear on her life that nothing bad will happen. And remember, Ma Ganga is watching."

This is really infantile. "Okay, I swear on my daughter's life."

"No. You have to mean it."

He places a hand over his heart, and Shanti's heart-shaped face flashes into his mind. "I swear on Shanti's life that your son and your mother won't come to any harm. I swear."

Even as he says the words, he is conscious of passing across a threshold: he is responsible for Leela now, and for her mother and son, and he feels the weight of it.

She pats the sand next to her, and he sits down clumsily, so close that he can feel the heat from her body.

"I thought I could take it, Ranjit, I thought I could take it for their sake, but Lateef—" She shudders. "—he's awful, I'm afraid of him, and—"

"It's okay. Tell me what happened. From the beginning."

She stares out at the ocean and licks her dry lips with her pink tongue, a quick, catlike gesture.

"When I met Mohan I was working as a nanny at the Dakota," she says slowly, "looking after that little boy I told you about."

He knows then that she is going to start her tale from far out, from a place of safety, then circle in to the hard truth.

"Mohan was always nice to me, and the child I looked after. He would let the boy wear his uniform hat, and play in the sentry booth. Kids that age, you know they like that kind of thing . . ."

Her voice gathers strength as the story takes hold of her.

Chapter Nineteen

Leela says that soon after she came to live with her father in Richmond Hill she found herself alone all day, while he drove his cab. She was supposed to study for a nursing degree, but stuck in that stuffy house, she couldn't concentrate; she was used to the bustle of Guyana, and the silence here unnerved her. Besides, America was out there, far away in Manhattan. A lot of young girls from the neighborhood worked there as nannies, and she saw them walk to the train each day, wearing their tight designer jeans, their hair done up in weaves and braids.

One older girl told her that she was leaving her job at the Dakota, and that Leela could interview as her replacement. The hours were long, the girl said—the mother worked as an editor, and the banker father traveled—but the child had been potty trained, was well behaved, and even understood Creole. Leela fought with her father to let her take the job. At first he wouldn't hear of it; only when she threatened to go back to Guyana did he agree.

At first she was thrilled by her job. The Dakota, with its hushed corridors and high-ceilinged apartments, seemed like another world, filled with rich people and celebrities—she bragged to her friends about how she once took the elevator down with Connie Chung. Even the air on the Upper West Side seemed sweeter, perfumed with luxury and money. The little boy she looked after, long-lashed and blond, was adorable, and they soon fell into a good routine of playtime, naps, and trips to the park.

The child was only four, and often asleep when his parents came home at nine or ten at night. But then the mother started working even later, and the father—tall and gym fit, with Scotch on his breath—stared at Leela. One night he pushed her up against the wall and squeezed her breasts so hard that she almost passed out. This, Leela found out from the other nannies, was part of the reason for her generous hourly rate.

Having fought so hard to work here, Leela felt as though she couldn't leave, but now, the apartment—with its dark wood paneling, chandeliers, and shining parquet floors—felt like a trap. To fend off the man's advances, she kept the child up later and later, or got into bed with him and locked the door. The little boy, sensing something was wrong, became whiny and insecure, and when she went to the bathroom he stood outside and banged on the door.

It was only when Leela walked out to Central Park that she felt free. And every time she passed the young Indian doorman, Mohan, he instinctively sensed her mood, and cheered her up with a joke or a piece of gossip. He said that she reminded him of his younger sister, and, with his swagger and charm, he reminded her of the boys back home. When he was off duty he would walk over to the park and sit next to her, and she began to confide in him. Mohan didn't judge her, or seem surprised at the rich banker's behavior—as the doorman, he was used to sending young, scantily clad girls and pretty boys up to the apartments of famous people. Besides, Leela knew that Mohan lived a compromised life himself—the other nannies gossiped that he was the lover of the famous actress on the fifth floor.

Mohan never talked about Shabana, but Leela saw them together a few times a week, at ten or eleven at night, getting into a cab. He wore nice civilian clothes, and she was always dressed up, in a pink or red sari with gold embroidery, and heavy gold jewelry.

The situation with Leela's employer went on for six months. Then one night, the father, drunker than usual, pinned her to the wall in the corridor and unzipped his pants. When Leela refused to comply, he called her a cock tease. He told her that if she didn't obey him, he'd fire her, and without a reference, she would never find work as a nanny again.

Leela gathered up her things, kissed the sleeping child's sweaty brow, and left, knowing that she would never return to that apartment, even though her employers owed her two weeks' wages. Mohan was just going off duty, and seeing the tears in her eyes, he grabbed her wrist, took her to a bar, and bought her a succession of apple martinis. Holding back her tears, she told him what had happened, and he listened, his eyes becoming hard with rage.

"A squeeze here and there, okay, you can tolerate that. But this is over the line. You go home, and I'll get your money for you."

Two days later he called her, and they met on a park bench by Columbus Circle. Without a word, he pressed a roll of bills into her hand, and she gasped when she counted it: four thousand dollars, more than three times what the man owed her.

Mohan grinned, and said, "Severance pay. Don't worry about it."

She didn't ask him how he had obtained the money, and he didn't tell her. The money was fine, she said, but now she was out of a job. Even if she returned to studying for her nursing degree, it would take at least two years, and living for two years with her father would drive her insane.

Mohan hesitated, and then told her about a job opening at a night-club. It was an exclusive place, frequented by rich Indian and Pakistani businessmen, hedge fund guys and Wall Street types. These men wanted to go out, but they didn't want to deal with the American club scene of bouncers, promoters, and half-drunk bimbos from Jersey. These men wanted *samosas* and *pakoras* with their magnums of vodka and champagne, and they wanted to be waited on by pretty black and brown women. Mohan said that this club was looking for ethnic-looking bottle girls, and when Leela seemed puzzled, he explained it to her.

The club made all its money from selling massively overpriced alcohol, he said. But just a nice atmosphere would not make an investment banker buy a three-hundred-dollar magnum of Grey Goose vodka. There had to be a personal touch involved, and that is where the bottle girls came in: they acted as hostesses and sat with the businessmen as they drank, subtly urging them to buy the expensive liquor.

The bottle girls had another job, too. Along with their overpriced alcohol, their male customers wanted women. The club allowed in young, attractive women, but they were not allowed to approach the men, and instead lingered at tables, or tried to attract attention on the dance floor. It was the role of the bottle girls to know which of these women were discreet, and to bring them over to the men.

"I'm not going to sugarcoat the job," Mohan said. "It is what it is. This is New York. There is nothing clean, nothing dirty. It's all about what you want."

Leela stayed silent, and he continued. "Look, what you have to do is look good, show a little cleavage, flirt, make small talk. All you need—" He examined her like an artist inspecting an unfinished painting. "—is an exotic look. Maybe tinted contact lenses, one of those glue-on weaves." She looked blank, and he became a little impatient. "You buy the hair in a packet, you do it yourself, no need to go to a salon. That money I just gave you?"

She looked down at the bills in her hand, the most money she had held since coming to New York.

"At the club, you can make a thousand dollars *in one night*. If you're smart, you'll save it. Then study for your nursing degree, go back to Guyana, whatever. Much better than getting groped in a hallway for six hundred a week . . . and that guy, the banker, he wasn't the only one. A pretty girl like you works as a nanny, you can't win. The fathers will eye you, the mothers will hate you, and sooner or later, you'll get fired. Trust me, I've seen it happen again and again."

They sat together on the park bench. Out of the corner of her eye Leela could see Columbus Circle, a stream of red taillights swirling around the tall statue in its center. Beyond were the blue glass mono-

liths of the Time-Warner Center. She had once walked into the tall lobby lined with exclusive shops, but she couldn't even pay the price of a coffee and a pastry. Now Mohan was offering her a way to earn more money than she'd ever imagined.

Leela stops her story and stares into the glare of Jamaica Bay. A wave comes in, flecked with debris, and when it recedes, Ranjit sees a waterlogged garland of marigolds lying on the sand: another offering to Ma Ganga.

So far everything she has told Ranjit has the ring of truth to it, but now comes the tricky part. Will she be straight with him, or distort the truth?

"So you went to work at Ghungroo?" he prompts. "Then what happened?"

"It was fine, at first . . ." Leela digs her bare toes into the sand. "I was making a lot of money, just like Mohan said. It seemed incredible. All I had to do was dress up and go there. I did the blond weave, bought colored contact lenses, called myself Lenore.

"Soon it became routine. I'd go up to the whales when they came in—a whale is a banker or a hedge fund guy, with a black AmEx card—tell them they looked good, lost weight, whatever. Sit with them, let them kiss me on the cheek—but no hands on me, never any hands. And most of these guys had class, they wouldn't dare make a scene. I'd order champagne—Dom Perignon or Krug, a magnum—and when it came, I'd bend over a little, show them some cleavage, work the cork out slowly, stroke the neck of the bottle, then pour for everyone, making sure I spilled some. Propose a toast, drink a glass myself, whoops, this bottle is gone, let's have another.

"It was all so obvious. The men were like little boys, they were actually easier than little boys, so eager to spend their money and show off for me.

"My God, I was making so much money, I used to take a car service home at night. I'd get back late—my father thought I was working in Manhattan at a new nanny job—and he'd be asleep on the couch, stinking of sweat, and I knew he had made two hundred bucks, and I'd have six, eight hundred stuffed in my bra . . . but I drew a line, and I never crossed it. The other girls, they would get to know the customers, and then they'd say, *Oh, I'm short on my rent this month,* or *There is this dress I really want,* or *I really need to go to Miami and work on my tan.* You see, they were becoming whores, but it was so subtle, they fooled themselves into thinking that they liked these men. But not me, I never played that game."

Ranjit squints out into the water. His arm is aching like hell, and he wishes he could take another Percocet, but he dare not break the mood. What he needs to know is so close now, within reach.

"And Shabana? What was her connection to the club?"

Leela wipes sweat off the soft curve of her cheek. "So I had been at the club for four, five months, when I saw Mohan one night, waiting inside the club, by the dressing rooms. I figured he had a girlfriend here, that's how he knew so much about the place. I had always wanted to call and thank him for the job, but I was sort of ashamed, you know? Anyway, I went over and gave him a kiss, we started talking, and he seemed very stressed. He was smoking, which he never used to do, and staring at the dressing room door.

"And out came Shabana. I was stunned. She came out of the *dressing room.*"

"She was working at the Ghungroo?" Ranjit's pulse quickens.

"Yeah. I was shocked. Shabana was a *movie star,* she lived at the Dakota, and here she was, working at the club."

"Well, an ex–movie star. You never saw her at the club before?"

"No. But I was working the floor. She would have been in the sky-booths, it's a different world up there . . . oh, you haven't been inside the atrium, have you?"

"Only in one of the dressing rooms, I think. It had lockers."

"Oh, those are for the staff, not the girls. We have nicer dressing rooms at the top. Anyway, how the club works is, the new girls get the floor. They've gutted the building, there is an atrium four, five stories high, and they have these sky-booths up there, where the high rollers sit. That's where Shabana would have been working. Those girls are the top earners, they have their own dressing rooms, and they only work when there are VIPs visiting."

"What kind of VIPs did she work for?"

"One of the girls who worked in the sky-booths told me that when the businessmen came from Mumbai, the club called Shabana in for the evening. Those guys got a huge kick from drinking with a movie star.

"Then, a month later, Patel called me into his office. As usual, he was sitting there staring into his laptop—I swear, he's surgically attached to that thing—and he didn't say anything. I thought I was about to be fired, but then he closed the damn computer and said I had been doing a good job, I had proved to be trustworthy, *blah, blah, blah.*

"He promoted me to the sky-booths, and I began to see Shabana up there with the guys from Mumbai. They were supposed to be successful businessmen, but they wore polyester suits, cheap shoes, and they were rough. They got hammered in an hour—no champagne for them, they were drinking straight Scotch, Johnnie Walker Red Label— and then they would ask Shabana to perform for them . . ."

"What do you mean, perform?"

"You know, recite lines from her movies. Act out a scene. She'd smile and say, *No, no,* but this one young guy, he was very slick—later on I found out it was Lateef—he was very, very insistent. He had Patel talk to her, and after that, she did whatever Lateef wanted. He would ask her to dance to some Hindi film music, then throw money at her, shout at her. I don't understand Hindi, but even I could tell he was humiliating her, calling her names . . ."

The glare from the bay is beginning to give Ranjit a headache. "I don't understand. Why was Shabana working there? Did she need the money?"

Leela's sunglasses slip down her nose, and she stares at him out of her bloodshot, damaged eye. "Patel owns her apartment at the Dakota. It's his. You didn't know that?"

The dozens of statues of Ganesh lining the shelves of Shabana's apartment. Of course: Jay Patel and his obsession with the gods.

Leela continues. "Patel was very upset about the way Lateef treated

Shabana, but he put up with it. He was scared of the guy." Despite the deserted beach, her voice falls to a whisper, and she moves a little closer. "The girls are always saying, this guy is a mobster, that guy is a mobster, it gives them a thrill. But Lateef, he's the real thing. He's very well dressed, but he's used to treating people a certain way, like, like . . . servants." She chooses the word carefully, "There are rumors that his uncle is a huge mobster. He lives in Dubai, but he runs Mumbai from there."

"Don Hajji Mustafa?"

"How did you know?"

"Just a lucky guess."

Okay, so Don Hajji Mustafa's nephew has come to Manhattan, and is bossing Patel around. *But what the hell does all this have to do with Shabana's death?* Leela is still tiptoeing around the heart of the story; he has to provoke a reaction from her, a surge of anger that will carry her to the truth.

"The cops are sure Mohan killed Shabana," he says. "Why? Was he jealous?"

"No, no, he didn't kill her. You don't understand. He loved her."

"Bullshit. I was with Mohan in Shabana's apartment the night she was killed, I left some time before it happened. Mohan was drunk, and he said he was going to sleep over at her place. Maybe Shabana came home unexpectedly and found him there, they got into a fight and—"

"No, no—"

"They argued, he lost his temper, he picked up the statue, he hit her once. She went down. After that first blow, he found it easier, so he just kept on going . . ."

"Stop. That's not what happened . . ."

"So tell me what happened."

Ranjit waits, the hot sun beating down on his neck. When she speaks, her voice is faint.

"I don't know exactly. But Shabana knew something, and Patel killed her for it. They think that Mohan knows whatever she knew. That's why they want to find him."

"What did Shabana know? Something about Patel's business?"

"She had a dressing room next to mine . . ." Leela's voice cracks with tiredness, with the exhaustion that comes after revealing a long-hidden secret. ". . . I used to see her getting ready to go to the sky-booths. The rest of us wore cocktail dresses, but Lateef wanted her to wear a sari. Sometimes I'd help her get the drape right.

"She got quieter and quieter. I think she was taking some pills—antidepressants, maybe. She was definitely using coke, a lot of it, I could see the red around her nostrils. And she used more and more makeup, too: Lateef was taking her back to his hotel, and he likes to beat girls . . . you're right, that's how he gets his kicks.

"About a week before Shabana died, I was helping her with her sari. She was pretty high, she started rambling, saying *I can't take it anymore, I have to get out*. She said that Lateef and his crew talked freely around her, that she had found out what he was doing in New York. Patel had started some kind of operation, something big, and it was making lots of money, and now the Mumbai people wanted in. That's why Don Hajji Mustafa sent Lateef over, to keep an eye on things."

Ranjit thinks of the shipments that arrived at Nataraj Imports, growing in size and value, and the "special" boxes that Patel told him to set aside.

"Shabana said—she said this over and over again—*I have evidence about what they are doing. I'll nail those bastards. I'll go to the cops. I'm a star, I'll be a star again, as soon as I get out of here.* I thought she was just raving, you know? But a week later, she was dead. That's all I know, Ranjit. And now I really have to get back."

She gets to her feet. When Ranjit struggles to rise, one-handed, she offers him a hand and pulls him up, much stronger than she looks.

They walk along the hot sand, toward the tiny yellow cab parked by the bridge.

"Did Shabana say what kind of evidence she found?"

"No, she was pretty high when she told me, she was rambling, hard to understand."

"Now that Shabana's dead, they think that Mohan has this evidence? Or knows where it is?"

Leela shrugs. Her head is held higher now, made lighter by the confession.

"Can you find out more from the other girls at work? Ask them if Shabana blabbed to them?" He swallows hard. "Do you have to keep seeing Lateef?"

"I'll see what I can find out. And don't worry, I can handle him."

They walk in silence past the spot where the couple had been pouring saffron milk into the ocean.

"Does it work?" He gestures out at Jamaica Bay. "The offerings?"

"You have to believe in it. I know this is not the real Ganges, but all the oceans and rivers of the world are connected, aren't they? Water is water." Her glasses have slipped down her nose and he sees her bruised face again. "You're a Sikh, right? What do you believe in?"

"Us? We don't believe in sacrifices, or pilgrimages." He waves a hand at the trash littering the beach. "We believe in right action, in living the right way."

"Right action?" Leela laughs. "You sound so superior. So that's how you ended up divorced, living alone in New York?"

He stops in his tracks and his face turns red.

"Hey, I'm sorry, that was mean."

"It's . . . it's okay, you're right. I'm not the best example of how to live."

She puts a small hand on his shoulder. "You're a good man, okay? I felt it the first time I met you."

To his surprise, she stands on tiptoe and kisses him. It is the briefest of kisses, like the brush of a butterfly's wing, but he feels the wet softness of her lips.

Stunned, he turns toward her, but she just skips ahead to the cab, reaching it before he does.

Ali has pushed the driver's seat back and is fast asleep, his baggy Hawaiian shirt drenched with sweat. Ranjit shakes his shoulder, and he wakes with a grunt.

They drive back to Richmond Hill, and Leela asks to be dropped off three blocks from her house.

"Leela . . . those men. The ones I ran into Friday night. What if I have to return here?"

She laughs, a low, musical laugh. "Those boys? They really don't like you—you broke the big guy's nose. But they're friends of mine, I'll talk to them. You won't have a problem."

Ali's face is still bloated with sleep when the cab stops on 107th Avenue.

Leela is halfway out of the cab when she turns to Ranjit.

"I said that I could handle Lateef, but I don't know for how long. It's getting worse and worse. Whatever you're going to do, please hurry."

Before he can answer, she is out of the cab and walking briskly down the deserted street.

Ali turns onto Liberty Avenue and they drive under a giant billboard that stretches across the elevated station, advertising cheap flights to Guyana. It is decorated with the outline of waves, and a cluster of palm trees, outlined in brown. Ranjit thinks of what he's just promised Leela, and feels again the sickness in the pit of his stomach, mixed in with the throbbing pain in his arm.

Taking another Percocet from his pocket, he dry-swallows it.

"So that was the girl who ran away from you." Ali purses his lips and lets out a low whistle. "I have to hand it to you, *Sardar,* you have a way with women. What did she tell you?"

"Not enough."

"What do you mean, *not enough*? You were on that beach for an hour. What exactly were you doing?"

"You have a one-track mind, Ali." Ranjit leans back and waits for the Percocet to kick in. "She said that Shabana used to work at the club, she overheard the mobsters talking about some operation. Apparently she threatened to call the cops . . . so Patel had her killed."

"Fuck." Ali slams on his brakes as a long-nosed Buick cuts in front of him. "Watch where you're going, asshole!" He glances over at

Ranjit, a frown creasing his wide forehead. "You're sure that Patel killed the actress, not the doorman? Do you believe her?"

Ranjit thinks of Leela's soft lips on his. "Yes, I do."

"How can you trust her? You don't even know her."

"I have a gut feeling about her."

"Gut feeling? To hell with your gut feelings. If she's right, Patel is too dangerous to mess with. You need to run as far away as you can—"

"We're going to Twenty-ninth and Broadway. Best way is the Van Wyck to the L.I.E."

"I know how to get there . . . wait a minute, Twenty-ninth and Broadway, that's your night job, right? Nataraj Imports?"

"Patel has been getting shipments from India for a year, and there are these boxes he told me to set aside. I'm going to find out what is in them."

"You're crazy. People like Patel don't play around. Why don't I just take you to the Bronx Zoo? You can put your head into the lion's mouth—"

Ignoring Ali, Ranjit pulls a creased business card from his wallet and clumsily dials the number on it.

Detective Case's cool voice answers almost immediately. "Ranjit Singh. What a pleasant surprise. What can I do for you?"

He remembers her cropped gray hair, hawklike nose, and icy gray eyes. Her name is definitely an Anglicization of something Eastern European, Cassowitz or Cassinski.

"I have some information about my previous employer, Nataraj Imports. I thought you would be interested in it."

"Jay Patel?" Her voice doesn't change inflection, but there is a slight pause, and he wishes he could see her face. "Why don't you come by the precinct?"

"I don't think that's the best idea. Patel is very well informed about what happens at your precinct."

A definite pause now. "How interesting. What exactly do you mean?"

"As soon as I was arrested, Patel knew. He knew that you interrogated me. How about meeting in Chinatown instead? Pham's Pho, it's on Baxter Street. I'll see you there, in the back room, at four o'clock?"

"This better be good. I hope you're not wasting our time, Mr. Singh." Case sighs and hangs up.

Ali is driving aggressively down the highway, speeding up and changing lanes, the cab jerking forward, then slowing down.

"Are you mad or what? You want to go to Patel's, then meet the cops?" Ali peers into Ranjit's face, then looks back at the road. "This Leela, she really got to you, right? What did she do, play the damsel in distress?"

Ranjit thinks of Leela's angry fists corkscrewing into the sand. "No, that's not it at all."

"She *is* playing you, my friend. Girls like that, girls who work in clubs, they manipulate men for a living. They seduce men, and if that fails, they'll come at you and rip your face to shreds. How do you think she's survived so long? If she was helpless, this city would have eaten her up and spit her out."

"And you know all this how? As a married man with three daughters, you're an expert on club girls?"

"I've been driving a cab here for eight years. I know."

Ranjit doesn't want to argue with his friend. The Percocet has kicked in, and the sudden absence of pain is making him light and buoyant.

"Ali, I can handle this, I have a plan. Look, I'm sorry, I know that all this upsets you. Just drop me off at Nataraj, and you can split, okay?"

"*Oh*. So you refuse to take my advice and now you call me a *coward*. But that's all okay, because you have *a plan*. You're delusional, you know. You're not a captain in the army anymore, you have no troops. You're a fucking *taxi driver*."

"That's the second time today that someone has pointed that out to me."

"Fine." Ali throws up his hands, and the cab swerves for an instant.

"Don't call me when Patel's goons break your other arm. This time, though, they probably won't bother with it: you'll go straight into the river."

Ali points downward—they are crossing the Queensboro Bridge over the East River, and the water, far below, is brown and sluggish.

Ranjit hears the truth in Ali's words, but he doesn't care. The pain in his arm is gone, and he feels a strange elation: he is so close to cracking this thing wide open.

Chapter Twenty

MUMBAI, SEPTEMBER 2001

The daylight was fading when Shabana emerged from her gym on Nariman Point, wearing a tracksuit and no makeup, her hair pulled back into a ponytail. In the four years since Sanjeev disappeared, the pollution had worsened, making the sunsets spectacular, and she paused to look up at the orange-streaked sky. Her bodyguard moved quickly to her side, and waited till she was inside the chauffeur-driven Nissan Pajero, then sat up front, next to the chauffeur.

The car drove along the curve of Marine Drive, the sea to their left, roaring up and splattering against the sea wall. Shabana tried to lower the tinted window, but found it locked.

"Windows down. I need air." Her voice was curt.

"Madam." The bodyguard twisted in his seat. "Not safe here. Very crowded."

"I don't care." Her gym had been freezing, and she needed to feel the warm sea air. "Put the damn windows down."

With a sigh, the bodyguard lowered the back windows halfway, and Shabana breathed in the briny air.

In the four years since the kidnapping, she'd had a series of bodyguards, but this lumbering, long-haired man was the worst. His feet smelled, and he was violent, brutally pushing aside persistent auto-graph seekers. She'd complained to the Don, but he just reminded her patiently that she was his "prized jewel," and needed to be protected.

Traffic was heavy, and the car jerked to a stop halfway down Marine Drive. Shabana settled back in her seat and rubbed her thighs, which ached after her vigorous two-hour workout. At thirty-four, she easily put on weight, and had to compete with twenty-two-year-old actresses with lean, perfect bodies. After coming back under the Don's protec-tion, she had cancelled the remake of *Pakeezah,* and now only acted in frothy romantic films.

During the months after her kidnapping, she was convinced that Ruksana had conspired with the Don to get rid of her lover. Instigating her kidnapping and blaming it on Sanjeev would have been a typical Don Hajji Mustafa move: it brought her back into the fold, and gave the Don an excuse to go to war with the Hammer.

But Shabana had no evidence to support her accusations, and the Don was so kind and patient with her that she had gradually come to believe his version of the truth, and they resumed their old relationship. Now she took two sleeping pills each night, washed down with vodka, but Sanjeev still appeared in her dreams, and stared at her pleadingly from under his dark brows. Most mornings she woke up crying, and had to mask her puffy eyes with makeup.

Now, to distract herself, Shabana watched the crowds on Marine Drive. People walked along its long curve, sat on the seawall, and walked on the filthy beach, snacking at the food stalls and drinking coconut water. Religious devotees waded thigh-deep into the ocean and prayed to the setting sun, their palms crossed together. No matter what disas-ters befell Mumbai—the stock exchange bombings, bloody religious riots, labor strikes—its citizens always returned to this life-giving strip, to breathe in the ocean air and dream of a better future.

Just looking out of the window made Shabana feel better. Forget-ting her aching body, she let the orange orb of the setting sun fill her vision.

She was so lost in the spectacle that it took her a while to recognize the familiar low rumble.

Turning her head, she looked across the car and out the opposite window. A Royal Enfield motorcycle had slowed to a halt in the next lane, its rider's face masked by a black helmet with a smoked visor. There were so many of these bikes in the city that at first she ignored it, but then the rider gunned his engine and moved closer, and Shabana gasped.

The rider wore a padded black leather jacket with a red stripe across its chest: the same jacket that Sanjeev had worn, down to the tear on its elbow, mended with black duct tape.

She waved cautiously at the rider, and when he raised two fingers to his brow in salute—one of Sanjeev's characteristic gestures—she could hardly breathe. It was as though she had been punched in her stomach.

The motorcycle pulled away slowly, and began weaving through the lanes of traffic, headed toward a parking area by the beach. *Sanjeev wanted to meet her there, away from the car, away from the bodyguard!*

Shabana glanced at her bodyguard, who was slumped in the front seat, his eyes closed. Up ahead, she saw the black top of Sanjeev's helmet enter the parking lot and come to a halt.

Jerking open the car door, she jumped out onto the footpath and took off like a bullet.

"Madam Shabana! What the fuck . . ." Behind her a door opened.

Shabana was a blur, her sneakers pounding on the concrete, heading for the parking lot. The bodyguard thundered behind her and she heard the *Oof* of someone being elbowed in the stomach.

She dodged through the crowd, found the cracks between bodies, gained distance. She saw the parking lot, saw Sanjeev take off his helmet and walk onto the beach, heading for the food stalls. *Aha, he was heading for the safety of the most crowded part.*

Her feet crunched across the parking lot and onto the filthy brown sand, and she slowed to a walk, gasping for air. My God, here Sanjeev was, after four years, and she was all sweaty, clad in her tracksuit. But he wouldn't care, and she could already feel the stubble on his cheek as he kissed her.

Sanjeev moved behind a *bhelpuri* stand and stood looking out at the sky, streaked now with shreds of orange and mauve.

"Sanjeev. It's you." She clasped him from behind, feeling the leather jacket against her cheek. "I knew you'd return. But quickly, my bodyguard, he works for the Don—"

"Aare. Aaap kya bol rahey hai?" What are you talking about?

The man turned and pushed her away roughly. He had Sanjeev's build, but a feminine face, with long-lashed eyes and a small mouth.

She stepped back in shock. It was not Sanjeev, yet the jacket . . . she recognized the tear in the elbow, the broken zipper on the left-hand pocket.

"You . . . why are you wearing Sanjeev's jacket?"

"Who is Sanjeev? This is mine." The man gripped his lapels in a gesture of ownership.

"Madam Shabana!" The bodyguard ran up, red-faced and gasping. "You cannot do this, you cannot leave the car—"

The man wearing Sanjeev's jacket shrugged and began to walk away.

Shabana turned to the bodyguard. "Stop him. He's wearing a stolen jacket."

The bodyguard looked disbelievingly at the man, who started walking faster.

"Stop him, now! I'll tell the Don you disobeyed."

The Don's name was a tonic. The bodyguard sprinted forward and grabbed the man's arm.

"Oi! Let me go! You crazy *chutiya!"* The man struggled to get away.

Shabana walked up. "Where did you get that jacket?"

"You crazy bitch, it's mine . . ."

"He's lying." She gestured to the bodyguard. "Hit him."

The bodyguard's fist came up, once, right in the man's mouth, and he staggered back, blood pouring from a split lip.

Shabana advanced toward him like a wide-eyed demon. "Where did you get the jacket? Tell me, or he will break your face."

"Crazy bitch! Help! Anyone, help!"

"Hit him again. Hard."

The man screamed with the second blow and spat out a froth of blood and teeth.

"I bought it at Chor Bazaar! There's a man there who sells second-hand clothes! *Meere Ma ke kassam!*" I swear on my mother!

"Madam Shabana. We have to go, right now."

A crowd was beginning to form around them: bodybuilders with oiled torsos, a group of old men, and grinning street urchins.

"Take the jacket. Give him some money."

The bodyguard pulled the jacket off the man, then threw two five-hundred-rupee notes onto the sand. "Keep your mouth, shut, *samjhe?*" Understand?

Holding Shabana's elbow, the bodyguard pulled her away. Clutching the jacket, she allowed herself to be led to the waiting car, which was now right by the beach.

When they were safely inside, the bodyguard turned to Shabana while massaging his right hand. "Madam? When did that man steal your jacket?"

"Shut up. And if you say anything about this to anyone, I'll have you fired."

The bodyguard turned red and looked straight ahead.

Chor Bazaar? Why would Sanjeev have sold his jacket at the thieves' market? Was he on the run? Did he need money?

Shabana looked at the jacket on the seat next to her, still warm from the man's body. She felt its elbow, its collar, like a blind man trying to recognize a face. The more she looked at it, the less sure she felt that this was Sanjeev's jacket.

They headed down Marine Drive, and she stared out of the window, feeling confused and wretched.

They drove past a television showroom, and she saw a crowd of people peering through its plate glass window, transfixed by the wall of television sets. The same image was being played on all the screens: a plane flying into a tall building, which burst into flames. No doubt it was some new Hollywood movie.

Shabana picked up the jacket and pressed her nose into the leather, inhaling deeply, searching for any trace of Sanjeev. All she could smell was sour, unfamiliar sweat.

Chapter Twenty-One

Standing down the street from Nataraj Imports, Ranjit watches Ali's yellow cab vanish into the distance. He knows that Ali is right, that taking on Jay Patel single-handed is crazy. The smart thing would be to jump bail and get the hell out of the country. So why is he doing this?

Leela had asked him, *What do you believe in?* and he couldn't answer her question.

He is still a Sikh, yes, but after Anna's death, he has not practiced his faith. Even his memories of the past are no longer a haven. For two long years driving a cab here, he has lost more of his sense of self, till he was all but erased.

Now he has been pushed, and to his surprise, he has pushed back. He is shocked to find his core intact, a stubborn, blind, animal resistance to the larger forces that are trying to manipulate him. *I may not be a captain,* he thinks, *but I'm not just a fucking cabdriver. They messed with the wrong man.*

He walks down Twenty-ninth Street, past tall Africans who have set up folding tables and sell knockoff Louis Vuitton handbags and straw fedoras. He passes small shops selling fake flowers—bright yellow daisies, chromatic gerberas, white lilies. The shopkeepers stand in their doorways with the expression of shopkeepers everywhere, arms crossed, brows creased faintly with worry.

The bright blue sign of Nataraj Imports is dead ahead, the god Shiva dancing his dance of destruction and renewal. The last time Ranjit had seen it, it seemed like a promise of change. Now it looks like a warning.

It is just past one, and he knows that Kikiben works all weekend. She brings a tall tiffin box of food from home and eats a full Indian meal while reading her film magazines. Most likely, she will be alone: the deliveries only arrive in the evenings.

Walking up the stairs to the thick metal door, he presses the buzzer and says his name, and Kikiben's voice crackles instantly through the speaker.

"Ranjit. What happened to you?"

"Broke my arm." He raises his sling to the snout of the camera. "Can't really work."

There is a pause. "Patel Sahib said not to let you in. He said that you're not welcome here anymore."

"Okay, no problem. I was just in the neighborhood and wanted to say hello. Actually, I had some ulterior motives . . ." He smiles up at the camera. "You wouldn't have some extra *rotis* in your lunchbox, would you? I'm pretty hungry, and you make the best *rotis*."

There is a pause. "Of course I have some extra. Patel is just being silly. I'm going to buzz you in, okay?"

The outer door opens, and then the inner one, and Kikiben motions him inside. She seems tinier than ever, almost disappearing within her baggy T-shirt and dark pants. It is as though all her energy has gone into her hair, her long gray plait hanging all the way to her waist.

He steps in, smelling the familiar cloying scent of hair, and Kikiben stares at him.

"How did you break your arm? You look pale. You've lost weight. Are you taking care of yourself?"

"I fell down. It was pretty stupid. The cast should be off in a few weeks."

"Good." Kiki regards him with her head cocked to one side, looking more birdlike than ever. "I want you to come back here. These two men who do the security now, they're real twits. They show up in jackets, both of them, like peas in a pod. And they treat me as though I'm a stupid old woman."

He feels a chill. "Dark jackets? Cowboy boots? Always looking bored, yawn a lot?"

"That's them. You know them?"

"Not really. I saw them at another job . . . So, are you sure you have enough food? I should warn you, I'm very hungry."

"*Hanh, hanh.* Plenty of food." She smiles, and her plain, lined face looks girlish.

She bounds up the stairs to the second floor, and he follows. A new shipment must have just come in, because glossy packets of hair are piled up against one wall of the small room. Some of it has been acid-stripped and re-dyed blond and reddish brown. He looks at the price tags and whistles.

"Up to sixteen hundred now? This must be some good stuff."

"New supplier. Very fine hair, extra-virgin. Never cut, never permed, never dyed. I don't know where Patel finds it. The last few shipments we had from India weren't this good . . ." Kikiben undoes the clasp of her tiffin carrier and unstacks the round metal boxes. Using one of the round covers as a plate, she heaps it with food. "Is this enough for you?"

She has piled up small round *rotis,* yellow *daal,* okra *saabzi,* and even added some cut, salted cucumbers and a heap of spiced yogurt. It should be delicious, but Kikiben is a terrible cook: the *rotis* are blackened and hard, and all the vegetables have been fried to a crisp.

"It looks fantastic," he lies. They both sit cross-legged on the green linoleum floor, and he begins to eat with his fingers, the tough *roti* crackling under his teeth.

"Patel says I shouldn't eat in here. Says that the smell of food gets into the hair. But he's not here, is he." She giggles. "Eat more, Ranjit, there is plenty."

"How is Patel these days?"

"You know . . . he does all that yoga-*shoga,* standing on his head, all that nonsense, but it's not working. He's so grumpy. He doesn't like the new security guys. If you just stood around, like they do, he'd bite your head off. These two boys, he lets them be. Maybe he's getting old."

Well, those men are working for Lateef, Ranjit thinks. *Patel seems to have no control over them, and obviously he doesn't trust them. If he did, he wouldn't have secretly hired me to look for Mohan.* Praying to the Guru that the boxes are still in Patel's office, he tries to eat some more of the burned, over-spiced food. As soon as he is finished, he can make an excuse to go upstairs and check out the office.

But Kiki is toying with her food, clearly in the mood to talk. "Ranjit, what a tragedy, no? Shabana Shah being killed? And wasn't she in your cab the day before?"

"Yes, it's terrible. She was so nice. Gave me a huge tip."

"*Hanh?* Really? And how did she seem?" Kiki's eyes glisten, and her mouth is open as she waits for all the juicy details.

"Well, she went shopping at Prada, bought leopard-skin-patterned heels, and a dress with sequins on it. She showed them to me. She seemed . . ." He thinks of Shabana in his cab, chewing on her plump lower lip as she gazed out of the window. ". . . I don't know, a little lost. And she looked different from the movies. Not older, just different."

"They always do, don't they? How? Was she trying to hide? You know, dark glasses, baseball cap?"

"Nothing like that. She seemed pleased to be recognized, even said she would sign an autograph. She was wearing a lot of makeup, maybe that was it, or her hair was longer. Halfway down her back—"

Kikiben leans forward. "I shouldn't tell you this . . . Patel said not to tell anyone, but what the hell, it's you, right, and she was in your cab. That's not her real hair." She giggles when he frowns in confusion. "Shabana's a *customer* of ours. I mean, *was* a customer. I know all the movie stars who buy their hair from us—but I didn't realize she was one of ours."

"Are you sure?" He thinks of Shabana's mane of thick, blue-black hair. "It looked real—"

"I'm *sure*. Four packets of extra-thick, silky, delivered every three weeks." Her voice drops to a whisper. "She was having the hair delivered to her sister's place. Clearly, she didn't want anyone to *know*."

"Wait. Shabana has a sister? Here?"

"Yes. The name on the address was Ruksana Shah. I looked her up on the Internet, but I couldn't find anything. Nothing written about her in *Filmfare*, or *Stardust*, either, or else I would have read it. So I called this friend of mine in Mumbai. She said there are rumors that there is something wrong with Shabana's sister. She's horribly disfigured, her face was burned in a fire or something. Shabana never allows her to be photographed."

Do the cops know about Ruksana Shah? Mohan hadn't said anything, and the papers hadn't mentioned her at all. Would Ruksana know anything about what really happened?

"Really, Kikiben, you know everything. What else have you found out about this mysterious sister?"

"Nothing more."

Ranjit pauses. "Is it . . . common to have these, what do you call it, extensions?"

"Oh yes. It's not just the black and Hispanic women, you know. White women are getting extensions, too. Half the city has Indian hair on their heads." Kikiben smiles, and her small eyes twinkle. "You know the worst part about working here? I see fake hair everywhere. I'll walk to the train, look at the women on the platform, and think, *That's a weave, she has extensions, that one's tracks are showing.*

"There's just not enough supply, though. The prices are going to go up, up, but people will still pay for it. Once you have fake hair on your head, you just can't go back to your natural. You know how black people call hair straightener 'creamy crack'? Well, this is worse. This is like injecting heroin straight into your veins. Shabana was paying five thousand a month, just for her hair."

Ranjit looks furtively at his watch, but Kikiben is in mid-flow now, and cannot be stopped.

"Can you imagine it? Poor Shabana. I saw this program about her, on Zee TV last night, a three-hour retrospective, and I cried. Poor thing, you know what she was doing in New York? Came here to shoot a movie, it was supposed to be her comeback. They say she sank all her money into it, all her personal money, and then that fool Brad Dunn—he was supposed to be the male lead—he backed out at the last minute, made some stupid action movie instead. He was on the television program too, saying that Shabana's death was *A great loss to Indian cinema*. I felt like slapping him."

"Yes, sad, sad." Ranjit covers his uneaten vegetables with the remaining *roti*. There is an hour to go before meeting the cops, and he has to get moving. "Kikiben, that was delicious. You put cumin in the potatoes, yes? I thought so . . . I'll just go and wash my fingers. Okay if I use the upstairs bathroom? The first-floor one is always backing up."

Kiki nods, all Patel's warnings forgotten in the flood of emotion she feels for the dead Shabana.

As Kiki clears up the various boxes of food, Ranjit takes the stairs up to the third floor, the wood creaking under his feet. He turns on the light in the small bathroom and an exhaust fan clatters into life, loud enough to mask his footsteps. He walks quickly to Patel's office, his heart beating faster.

The small room is exactly as he remembered it, and smells of stale incense. The scarred wooden desk is in the same place, the calendar of Ganesh stares down at him, and along the opposite wall are the cardboard boxes, the neat stacks grown to twenty or thirty boxes. Picking one up—it is surprisingly light—he examines it, seeing the red stamp in the shape of a house. He turns the box over and, using the teeth of his house keys, he slits open the black packing tape on the bottom.

Inside, there is only a packet of raw, undyed hair. He opens it and holds in his hand a thick plait, almost a foot long, the hair amazingly lustrous and soft as silk. The hair seems to be alive; for a second he thinks of the Indian woman it must have belonged to, and imagines her with a shaved head, walking the streets in some small village.

There is nothing else in the box.

Damn it. He peers into the corners of the box, shakes it, runs his hand over the corrugated cardboard, but there is no place to hide anything else. He holds up the hair to the light to see if there is something woven into it, then smells it, inhaling only its musky sweetness.

Nothing here. He opens up another box at random, but there is only another long skein of blue-black hair, its edges sheared off roughly. *Whatever was in here has been taken out, but how?* The original packing tape on all the boxes hasn't been disturbed.

Over the clattering of the bathroom fan he hears Kikiben moving around, and knows that he's running out of time. He finds a roll of clear packing tape in Patel's desk and tapes the bottom of both boxes shut. With any luck, whoever unpacks the boxes won't notice the different tape.

Returning to the bathroom, he washes his hands loudly, then heads down the stairs. Now he'll have to meet the cops empty-handed, without any evidence of what Patel is smuggling in. He curses his own arrogance, his certainty that there would be contraband in these boxes.

He reaches the middle of the stairs when he sees Kiki standing at the bottom, looking up at him anxiously, like a frightened sparrow.

"Ranjit." Her voice is a little shriller than usual. "I need to ask you something. Don't get angry, okay?"

Has she seen him going into the office? If she has, she'll feel compelled to tell Patel . . . He tries to keep his voice steady. "What is it?"

"Please don't mind me asking this, *hanh?* One of my nieces just came from India. Now I know you're a Sikh, and she's Gujarati, but she's an open-minded, modern girl, with traditional values. She's come here to study computer programming, and she's a good cook. If you like my cooking, you'll love hers. And I thought, maybe, if you are not too busy . . ."

He smiles in relief. "You want me to meet her? Sure, no problem.

Maybe next week?" *By then he might either be in jail, or dead, but Kiki doesn't need to know that.*

"Thank you, thank you! I'll call her just now and tell her, her name is Rohini, but she goes by Ro, these modern girls, you know—"

"I'm sure she's very nice. Kikiben, the food was delicious, I feel better already."

He smiles at her, feeling guilty at having abused her generosity.

Walking through the doors, he steps into the hubbub of Twenty-ninth Street, and the smile on his face fades as he remembers the promise he made to Leela. For her sake, and his, he's going to have to bluff his way through this meeting with Case and Rodriguez.

Chapter Twenty-Two

The N train to Canal Street is running slow, and by the time he makes his way through Chinatown he is fifteen minutes late.

How much do the cops know? The key to surviving this meeting is to give them something new, something that will earn him points till he can find out what the hell Patel is up to.

Stopping outside Pham's Pho, he examines his reflection in the glass storefront—arm in a sling, wrinkled half-sleeve blue shirt, jeans, flip-flops, topknot hidden under his MIKE'S TOW baseball cap. Not exactly a look that inspires confidence.

Straightening out the collar of his shirt, he steps into the broth-scented interior. Even this early, the place is filled with single Vietnamese men slurping up big bowls of soup before heading out to work the evening shift.

Pham comes out of the kitchen holding a bowl of soup, his face flushed from the steam, and scowls when he sees Ranjit.

"Two police waiting in the back room for you. No good."

"What's the matter, you never have cops come in for some soup? You're right next to the Tombs, for God sake."

"Back room is private." Pham rubs his index finger and thumb together.

"It's okay. This is part of Thompson's business."

"Lawyer Thompson will pay?" Pham's face brightens.

"Absolutely." Ranjit parts the red-beaded curtain, and steps through into the back room, the strings of beads clattering behind him

The cops are sitting at the same table he'd occupied with Thompson. Case has her arms folded over her chest, and she glances down at a slim metallic watch on her wrist.

"You're fucking late." It is Rodriguez who speaks, putting down a half-eaten *banh mi* sandwich, slivers of carrots falling onto his plate. He's wearing his tan summer suit, more wrinkled now than it was three days ago. His hairstyle hasn't received the attention it needs, and his quiff of hair falls limply onto his forehead.

"Enjoying the sandwich?" Ranjit pulls out a chair and sits.

Case is immaculately dressed, the gold buttons on her blue blazer shining, her crimson lipstick freshly applied. But she, too, looks tired; the crow's-feet at the corners of her eyes are more pronounced, and there is a smudge of lipstick on her front teeth. Ranjit knows then that they must be under a lot of pressure to solve the case.

"Talk. And it better be good." Rodriguez pushes his plate away and glares sullenly.

"Wait a minute. What happened to your arm?" Case's voice is composed.

"I fell."

"Really?"

Ranjit sees the beginning of their good-cop, bad-cop routine, and needs to cut through it, fast. Playing by their rules is going to take too damn long.

"Actually, this is all your fault."

"How so?" Case arches a thin eyebrow.

"I was in the alley behind Ghungroo Friday night when you two drove through. It caught the attention of Patel's goons. You were gone by the time they showed up, but they caught me, and broke my arm. The doctor says I'm going to need a fair amount of physiotherapy."

They are both suddenly alert. Rodriguez looks at Case, and when she speaks there is a slight quickening in her voice.

"And what were you doing in that alley?"

"Patel hired me to find Mohan. The trail led to Ghungroo."

"He what?"

"Hired me to find Mohan, and bring him back. He said he would pay me fifty grand if I succeed. He even gave me this. I'm going to take it out slowly, okay? Don't shoot me."

Ranjit reaches into the waistband of his jeans, pulls out the Glock by its barrel, and places it gently on the table.

"Fuck you." Rodriguez's right hand crosses under his jacket and comes out holding an identical gun. "You pull a gun on two police officers? Are you crazy? We're taking you in, and this time—"

"It's not loaded. And I have a license for it." Ranjit's voice is mild.

Case's long-fingered hand picks up the Glock and slips out the magazine. "It's empty."

"I say we take him in. Fuck this bullshit. Pull a gun on me—"

Rodriguez's hands are trembling, his gun still pointed across the table. He's way too excitable to be a cop, Ranjit thinks. Or else he's just bad under pressure.

"Relax, Rodriguez." Case puts Ranjit's gun back on the table and leans back. "Let's cut through the crap, okay? What do you know?"

"Me?" Ranjit settles back in his chair and feels the ache in his arm start up. "My guess is that you were investigating Patel before Shabana was killed. He probably flew under your radar for years, but you guys noticed him when Lateef showed up. Because Lateef is Don Hajji Mustafa's nephew, and Don Hajji Mustafa is one of the biggest gangsters in Mumbai, and he's in the middle of a gang war." Ranjit smiles humorlessly. "Must be hard for the NYPD, huh? You just got rid of the Mafia, and now there are the Chinese, the Vietnamese, the Koreans, and the Russians. The last thing you need is a bunch of slum dogs from Mumbai showing up here on tourist visas. You with me so far?"

Case stares steadily at him.

"Of course you are. You guys knew that Lateef was here overseeing something big. You knew that Shabana was broke, that she was working for Patel as a hostess at the club.

"Now here's the big news. Shabana overheard some stuff that the boys from Mumbai were talking about. She was about to come to you guys with some evidence she found, and Patel had her killed. Mohan must have figured that he was next on the list, and he took off."

Rodriguez reholstered his weapon, but his voice still bristles with anger. "And how do you know all this? You have this evidence, or are you going to sit there and tell us fairy stories?"

"You guys have been investigating Patel for months, you still don't know what he and Lateef are up to, do you?"

"And you fucking know? You're going to tell us?"

From the look on Rodriguez's face, Ranjit knows he was right. *The cops have no clue.*

"Yes, I do. I have an informant inside the club. But I need some assurances first."

Case steps in smoothly, knowing that Rodriguez has just revealed their ignorance.

"So, Mr. Singh, what is it that you want?"

"Thought you were never going to ask. I want the charges dropped against me, of course. And there is a hostess at the club helping me. Her mother and son are illegal, and Patel knows that, he uses that information to control her. I want guarantees that they will get papers."

"That's all?" The crow's-feet around Case's eyes deepen as she smiles. "You just want us to fix a grand jury trial and circumvent federal immigration regulations?"

"Or you can just send me in front of the grand jury. Worst case, I'll get three years as an accessory, and be deported. By that time, the boys from Mumbai will be all set up here, and they'll be a permanent headache."

There is a silence. The pain in Ranjit's arm intensifies as the painkiller wears off, the torn tissues and nerves screaming out in protest.

"The machinery of justice doesn't stop on a dime, you know." Her voice is still calm, but slower, tinged with relief, and he knows he's convinced her. "It all takes time. There are no firm guarantees. But if you can deliver, we might be able to work something out."

"I'll get you enough information to nail Patel. Meanwhile, you guys stay away from Ghungroo. If Patel gets spooked—"

Rodriguez scowls. "Screw this. No deals. He's bullshitting. He doesn't know anything, he's making all this up. He's a fucking cab-driver."

Third time today, and Ranjit is getting tired of it.

"Okay. You guys do this alone. No one is going to talk to you. For example—the cabbie who knifed the other guy, Afzal Mian? That was in your jurisdiction, yes, Rodriguez? Caught him yet?"

"We'll get him. You don't need to worry about it."

"Afzal is at his aunt's house. It's above Chen's Noodles in Flushing."

"Bullshit. I'm calling it in. You just wait here." Rodriguez gets to his feet and stalks out of the room, the bead curtain tinkling as he pushes through it.

"Is he always like this? Must be hard to work with."

Case leans back and looks at Ranjit through her gray-green eyes. "You're pretty good at this. Had some training?"

"What?" Ranjit imagines Rodriguez getting on his radio, the squad cars tearing through the streets of Flushing, cops banging on the door of a frightened, middle-aged Pakistani woman's home. *What if Afzal decided to move to some other relative's house?*

"You've been trained at interrogation. You were watching his face."

"I don't know what you're talking about."

She sighs and looks past him at the bead curtain, still shimmering with Rodriguez's sudden departure. "I've seen your file. You were a captain in the Indian Army. How did you end up driving a cab here?"

"Shit happens. There are doctors, engineers, computer programmers driving cabs. What's so special about me?"

"We're not racist, Mr. Singh. Just overworked. All the resources in this city are going towards preventing another terrorist attack. Organized crime is getting a free pass, and we can't have that, can we?"

"Next you're going to tell me that some of your best friends are Sikhs. Or else you like Indian food."

"Can't stand Indian food, actually. The spiciest I can go is horseradish on my pastrami sandwich." She smiles, a real smile this time, and her eyes twinkle. "Ah, here he is."

Rodriguez comes back through the curtains. "We had a patrol car just around the corner. You lucked out, the guy was there. Though his auntie or mother or whatever tried to throw a pot of boiling water at the officers. We had to take her in, too."

Fuck. Ranjit closes his eyes for an instant, imagining the poor woman making rice just as the cops burst in.

Case stands up, a gesture of dismissal. "Okay, Mr. Singh. You have three days. After that, the deal is off. I need evidence to nail Patel, not rumors, you understand? Hard evidence."

Ranjit nods and stands up to leave.

"One more thing. You said that Patel knows what's happening inside our precinct. I want to know about that too."

Rodriguez's eyes narrow. *Did Case see that look?* Ranjit can't tell, her face is impassive.

"I'll see what I can do."

He heads out of Pham's and walks quickly across the road, through the usual mess of people standing around outside the Tombs. There are police cars pulled up on the sidewalk, relatives with tear-stained faces milling about, even a newly released prisoner, carrying his belongings in a see-through plastic bag.

Afzal Mian and his aunt will soon make their way here. He will be charged with attempted homicide, and she with assaulting a police officer. Ranjit thinks of the night he spent in the bowels of the Tombs, and shudders. He just did what he had to do, but he doesn't like it, doesn't like it at all.

Walking up toward Canal Street, he wonders if Case and Rodriguez are going to follow him, and decides they are. Yes, there is a Crown Vic with three tall antennas, pulling out behind him.

He has to head to Little Guyana and talk to Leela again. If he leads the cops to her, they can just put the squeeze on her and cut him completely out of the picture. He can't have that.

How is he going to get all the way to Queens with a tail? He sees a yellow cab ahead of him disgorge some rumpled Chinese passengers. He runs up to it, and peers in at the driver, recognizing a tired-looking Bangladeshi man in a rumpled long-sleeved shirt, buttoned at the wrists despite the heat. *Rashid? Riyaz? What the hell is the man's name?*

"*Salaam Aleikum.* Remember me? Ranjit Singh from Karachi Kabob?"

"*Waalekum as salaam. Hanh, hanh.* I remember you, Ranjit *bhai.* But where is your taxi?"

Ranjit gets in, and smiles. "I'm in a bit of a situation. I need to go to the taxi waiting line at JFK airport," he says.

"What? The waiting line? But then I will be stuck there for hours . . ." The Bangladeshi cabbie stares at him in confusion.

"Here." Ranjit forks out three of the twenty-dollar bills that Patel gave him.

"Okay, *bhai.*"

The taxi rockets down Canal Street, and Ranjit settles back in the cab and closes his eyes. Just let the cops try and follow him now. His arm is aching unbearably, and he takes his third Percocet of the day, ignoring the warning that the doctor had given him.

Forty minutes later, the cab winds its way into the huge taxi waiting area at JFK, and Ranjit's tail has been lost in the labyrinthine service roads leading to the airport. He thanks the cabbie and walks away—Riyaz, that's the man's name, he remembers, too late.

There are rows of stationary cabs here, most of them empty, though here and there a cabbie is fast asleep, or talking on his cell phone. A man with a rolling suitcase wanders between them, selling kernels of roasted corn.

Some cabbies have started a cricket game in the empty part of the lot, using a trash can as a wicket. Voices chatter and shout in Arabic, Punjabi, Creole, Russian, and some African dialect that Ranjit does not recognize. Passing the restaurant in the middle of the lot, he sees the Muslim cabbies praying on a strip of empty concrete behind it.

The painkiller is making him exhausted, and he stops by the stinking toilets, thinking that he'll wash his face, but they are broken as usual, the stall doors now replaced by black plastic sheets, urine sloshing all over the floor. Walking on, he finally reaches the front of the line, and when the next cab gets called to a terminal, he hitches a ride.

Reaching the concrete wings of the old TWA terminal, he stands in the passenger line, and gets into another cab, telling the cabbie to go to Richmond Hill. The painkiller has kicked in, and his arm is numb, but he is now feeling light-headed and very nauseous. He should have read about the side effects before he took three of the damn things.

The backyard of Leela's house is empty except for a rusty lawn chair, sunk into the earth under the tall tree. There is a blue-and-yellow child's ball lying in the grass, and as he looks at it, it splits into two images, then re-forms.

Blinking rapidly, he walks to the front of the house and rings the doorbell. It is still chiming when the door jerks open and Leela appears, barefoot, wearing a faded pink robe. Her curly hair is hidden by a tight net, and her face is made up.

"Sorry to just show up like this. I have to talk to you about Shabana—" He sways against the doorframe, and reaches out his good hand to steady himself.

"Ranjit, I'm about to go to work—"

Darkness dims the edges of his vision. "I'm sorry." His voice slurs. "Just a few minutes. That's all." He sways again, and this time his shoulder slams into the doorframe.

"Are you drunk? What the hell?" She looks up at him, her eyes wide with alarm. They are green again, and the bruise under her eye has been skillfully covered with makeup.

"Not drunk. My arm. The painkillers . . ." He tries to explain, bracing himself against the doorframe.

"Leela."

They both look down the dark corridor and Leela's mother appears, still wearing her faded red pantsuit. He sees the resemblance between them, and realizes that the old lady was once an attractive woman.

"Leela. The man is sick. He is going to fall down, he better come in."

"I'm fine, thank you, madam." Ranjit swallows hard, and feels the sweat soaking his back.

He suddenly notices everything: the toenails on Leela's feet glistening red, the roots of the old lady's gray hair showing below the black.

He swallows again. "Sorry to bother you, I—"

Before he can finish the sentence, the doorframe seems to give way. He pitches forward into darkness, but this time, arms catch him before he hits the floor.

Chapter Twenty-Three

DUBAI, 2005

Eight years had passed since Sanjeev vanished.

Shabana stared out of the window as the Emirates flight descended toward Dubai, flying low across the blue-green Arabian Ocean. With a sudden roar the plane crossed the coastline, and the city appeared underneath. The Dubai Creek coiled through it, separating old from new: on one side were the crowded alleyways and bazaars of the old *souk*, but the other side was an abstract grid, its long, straight roads lined by skyscrapers that shone like gold in the harsh desert light. And somewhere down there, where the grid faded out into the blank desert, lived Don Hajji Mustafa, in the tenth year of his exile.

Because the Don could not travel, the world came to him: Indian government ministers, supplicants, and businessmen of all stripes drove straight from Dubai airport to meet him, clutching slim, locked briefcases. Once a year, the Don grew tired of business and threw a party for all the Bollywood movie stars, who flew into Dubai for the weekend; it was a pilgrimage to show loyalty to the Don, and those who ignored it did so at their own peril.

This year the Don had requested that Shabana arrive a day early.

As a black Mercedes whisked her into the desert, she gazed at the endless sand dunes and wondered why he had sent for her. Did he still doubt her loyalty? In the years since Sanjeev disappeared, she had listened to everything he said, and acted only in films that he approved.

Maybe the Don had gotten wind of her search for Sanjeev. Ever since that day on the beach in Mumbai, Shabana had looked for him. She had hired a series of highly paid private detectives who had sworn not to talk, but the Don had eyes and ears everywhere . . .

As the road through the desert became a rutted dirt track, she sat up straighter and braced herself for her audience with the Don. She checked her appearance in a small hand mirror: barely any makeup and a simple cotton *salwar kameez*. The Don liked her to look like the young, uncomplicated girl she portrayed in her films.

The car crunched over gravel and arrived at what must be an oasis, because the Don's sprawling, marble-floored villa was surrounded by date palms, immaculate lawns, and flowering pink bougainvillea.

Shabana was shown into a sunken living room. She stood there for an instant, transfixed by a peacock on the lawn outside: it flared its tail in alarm, creating a fan of iridescent turquoise feathers.

"Stupid birds. Always panicking."

Shabana started. The Don was sitting at the end of a long white leather sofa, his white *kurta-pajama* blending with it. As she moved closer, she was shocked to see how old he looked. Now pushing seventy-five, his hair was still dyed dark black, and his eyes burned as fiercely as ever, but he seemed thinner, and the skin under his chin hung in wattles.

"Stupid birds," the Don repeated. "Some fool gave them to me as a present. Said they were from a maharajah's palace in Rajasthan." He turned his burning gaze on Shabana. "You look as beautiful as ever. Your sister is taking good care of you, *hanh*?"

"Yes, she is." The truth was that Ruksana was more insufferable than ever, but Shabana smiled sweetly. "Uncle, you seem tired. Do you need help with your party tomorrow night?"

"The party?" The Don frowned. "Oh yes, the party. That is all taken care of." He waved dismissively. "Every *chootiya* movie star from Mumbai will come, because they are afraid of me. They will eat my food, drink my liquor, then go back to Mumbai and bad-mouth me." He shook his head. "How things have changed. When I started out, I was the hero. *Me.* The government, *hah,* what did they care about the common man? People came to me to get things done. But now . . . after nine-eleven, they call me a terrorist. Can you believe that?"

He waved his hands. "Terrorist? Me? I am a *businessman.* So I do *business* with people. Afghans. Iraqis. Libyans. So what?"

"Yes, Uncle."

The Don walked to the glass door and rapped his knuckles sharply against it. "This glass might as well be metal bars. Being stuck in this house is like being in jail." He stared out at the perfect green lawn. "What is there, in this godforsaken Dubai? Air-conditioning. Silence. Peacocks. Yes, fucking peacocks."

Shabana had never heard the Don complain, never seen him acknowledge his exile, and she remained silent.

"I miss Mumbai," the Don said slowly. "I want to go back and eat *biriyani* at Azeem's restaurant. I want to smell the sewage and petrol fumes. I want to walk on the dirty sand of Chowpatty Beach and eat *bhelpuri* in a newspaper plate."

So he hadn't heard of her search for Sanjeev. *Don Hajji Mustafa, the Don of Dons, was simply homesick for Mumbai.* Shabana was shocked.

"Well, Uncle, I'm sure you'll go back one day," she said consolingly.

"One day? *Pah.* I could die here, in this dump. I'm not waiting for *one day.* I'm going back home soon. It's all a matter of public relations."

"Public relations?" Shabana frowned.

Was the Don delusional? The Indian government was still investigating him for unpaid taxes. If he set foot in Mumbai, he'd be arrested right away; leave aside the fact that the Hammer had sworn to cut him to pieces if he returned.

"Yes, I've been away too long." The Don peered out at his pristine garden. "People in India no longer know who I am. The government I can handle—do you know how many high-ranking ministers come to see me?—but it's the man in the street who must see me as a hero." The Don abruptly changed the subject. "So. You are going to the one-day cricket match in Sharjah tomorrow, before the party?" Shabana nodded, and he continued. "Good. Good. Well, enjoy yourself."

He kissed her on both cheeks, and she felt his old man's breath, scented with decay.

Knowing she was being dismissed, Shabana salaamed prettily and left.

As the black Mercedes zoomed back through the desert, she watched the sun set. The fading light caught the glass towers on the horizon, and they glittered like a mirage.

It was strange to think of the Don as a homesick old man. For so long she had thought of him as superhuman, a master strategist who played chess with other people's lives. Was his performance just now another one of his elaborate ploys? *What the hell was he up to?*

The cricket match he had asked about was an international event, and all the Bollywood stars would attend, creating a bigger attraction than the cricket. Columnists and film journalists swarmed the stadium, taking endless pictures, trying to divine the future of Bollywood: who sat with whom, and which stars weren't talking to each other. The Don, of course, wouldn't come. He never appeared in public, and he hadn't been photographed since the 1970s.

When Shabana reached her hotel it was dark, and she sat on the edge of the bed in the plush, empty suite. Seeing the Don always brought back memories of Sanjeev, and she wondered, for the millionth time, what had happened to her lover. Even if his body turned up, it would be something; not knowing was so much worse.

Her cell phone rang. It was Ruksana, who had remained in Mumbai to arrange the logistics for Shabana's next film.

"Hey. Are you okay?"

"I'm fine, why?" Shabana crouched in front of the hotel bar and reached for a miniature bottle of vodka.

"Seeing the Don always' upsets you, that's why. No pulling out your hair, okay?"

"Leave me alone, Ruki."

"And no booze with your sleeping pills. There will be photographers at the cricket match tomorrow. You can't look like a harridan."

"Good-bye, Ruki."

Taking her sleeping pills, she lay down on the over-plush bed, and fought the urge to pull out her hair. Instead, she drank two small bottles of vodka, and fell into the darkness of chemical sleep.

The next day, Shabana's wardrobe consultant dressed her to the nines, and when she walked into the Sharjah cricket stadium an audible gasp went through the crowd. Her long, thick hair fell in lustrous curls down her back, and she wore a form-fitting mauve blouse with billowing, see-through sleeves, flared white designer pants, and six-inch white stilettos.

She took her place in the box full of movie stars. Next to her was Julie Chaddha, an up-and-coming twenty-five-year-old starlet with a sensuous baby face and a sideline making exercise videos. Julie fluttered her eyelashes, and waved one toned arm at Shabana.

"Shabana! You've lost weight!"

At thirty-eight, Shabana knew that this compliment meant the opposite, but she gritted her teeth and air-kissed Julie.

Just then there was a sudden hush in the crowd. Both Julie and Shabana turned to look: was it Ameer Uddin, the hottest actor in Bollywood, with his muscles and mesh shirts, or the sexpot Naseem Begum?

It was neither. An unidentified man made his way down the slope of the stadium, surrounded by four bodyguards. He was clad in a lightweight sky-blue linen suit and an open-necked white shirt, and his eyes were masked by wraparound sunglasses. Reaching the box, he walked down the aisle toward Shabana, and she gasped in surprise.

The man in the blue suit was Don Hajji Mustafa, making his first public appearance in over thirty years.

Julie Chaddha hurriedly gave up her seat. The Don sat down and draped one tailored arm around Shabana's shoulders; she could smell his strong aftershave, and her confusion was compounded by the urge to sneeze.

The photographers who crowded below the box looked stunned, and lowered their cameras. An unauthorized photograph of the Don was as good as a death sentence.

The Don smiled stiffly, his face creasing, as though he had forgotten how to smile. He waved at a young photographer who stood below them. "*Aare*, what are you waiting for? You want to take a snap? Go ahead."

The young man slowly raised his camera, then hesitated.

"Come on, come on." The Don gestured impatiently.

The photographer knelt and framed a picture of the Don and Shabana. He clicked, and that sound released the others, who raised their cameras and began to photograph frantically.

"You see," the Don whispered into Shabana's ear. "Let them see me. Public relations."

Public relations. Shabana understood then what the Don was up to. He thought that being photographed alongside Bollywood's hottest stars would impress the Indian public, change his image in their minds. *My God, was the Don that out of touch?*

Shabana saw the movie stars on either side of her cringe slightly, but none of them dared to leave. Instead, they put on fixed smiles and looked away from the cameras. Flashes went off, blinding Shabana, but she could not move; the Don's arm was firmly around her shoulder.

The photographers shouted, *Don, over here! Look this way!* Shabana smiled till her face hurt, and prayed for the ordeal to be over.

Chapter Twenty-Four

Something yellow floats above Ranjit's head. He squints up and sees a disc dangling above his face. It makes no sense.

He is lying on a narrow bed, his feet hanging off the edge. Somewhere far away there is the sound of voices, one loud, the other calm and matter-of-fact.

The disc resolves itself into a paper cutout of the sun. It is at the center of a mobile, encircled by other paper planets, each hung with white sewing thread from a cross of thin bamboo sticks. There must be a breeze blowing, because the fragile construction shivers and the planets begin to revolve slowly.

"It's the solar system."

Leela's little boy stands at Ranjit's elbow. The child's plump cheeks puff out, and he blows upward, making the planets revolve faster. "Mercury, Venus, Earth, Mars, Jupiter, Neptune, Pluto."

Is that the correct order? Ranjit remembers helping Shanti with a school project, cutting and sticking pictures of planets onto a poster. He tries to sit up but falls back onto the thin pillow.

The boy stares at him with solemn eyes. "You're sleeping in my bed." It is a statement, not a complaint.

"I'm sorry. What's your name?"

"Dev. And it's okay, you can sleep here, Mom-Mom says you're sick."

"You're a smart kid, to know all that."

"Mom-Mom says I'm smart, but Leela's always angry at me." Dev blows again, and the planets revolve faster.

Watching them, Ranjit feels dizzy and he closes his eyes.

The voices continue their argument somewhere out there, interrupted by the sound of a car honking. There is the sound of footsteps, and a car driving off.

He must get up, he's ashamed to be lying in Leela's son's bed. Then he feels Dev's pudgy, warm hand on his shoulder.

"You're sick. It's okay, mister. Go to sleep."

The weight of the boy's hand pushes him back down into sleep, and willingly, gratefully, he feels the world ebb away.

He awakes, and for a frightening moment he doesn't know where he is. Then it all comes back to him: the endless day, the pills, passing out on Leela's doorstep.

A streetlight shines faintly through a window and illuminates the small room: there is a dresser against the far wall, and next to it is a stack of translucent toy boxes, filled with ghostly furry animals, skeletal Transformers, and piles of dull Lego bricks. There is nothing on the walls and no rugs. It is so quiet that it's hard to believe he's still in New York.

He remembers Dev standing over him, but the child is gone, and the mobile hangs motionless. His watch has stopped, and it's hard to tell what time it is, but he knows he has slept for a long time, at least seven or eight hours. At least the pain in his arm has been reduced to a dull throb.

From somewhere comes the sound of a television. Getting out of bed, he realizes that his shoes and socks are gone. He looks for them in the darkness, then gives up and walks barefoot down a long, windowless hallway that runs the length of the house. Passing a bedroom, the door ajar, he sees Dev fast asleep in the middle of a double bed, his face illuminated by the blue glow of a nightlight. He is sprawled out, arms and legs thrown far apart, and Ranjit remembers that Shanti used to sleep like this, sometimes turning a hundred and eighty degrees during the night. Only children sleep with such abandon; adults hunch into their pillows, or curl into tight fetal balls.

This bedroom houses a small shrine in the corner, just a few framed pictures of Hindu gods and goddesses, a wilting hibiscus flower, and sticks of half-burned incense. The room probably belongs to the old lady, and the next bedroom is definitely Leela's: her open closet reveals a row of skimpy cocktail dresses, and the dresser is littered with scraps of blond hair. Entering her room, he picks up an empty plastic bag and sees that it contained a "27-Piece Glue-on Weave," whatever that is.

He follows the sound of the television, hearing the swell of familiar music, followed by Hindi dialogue. A man is talking:

"I came back for you, but you are gone, my love. Oh, I wish I could turn back the clock and make years disappear."

It is the last scene in *Laila Aur Paul*, Shabana's hit remake of *Romeo and Juliet*. Ranjit had seen it, all those years ago, in India. In the film, Paul has returned to Mumbai to find Laila lying cold and waxen. He doesn't know that she is faking her death so she can wake later and be with him.

"I wanted to be worthy of you. I wanted your father to accept me. I have been away, working in Dubai, and I am a rich man now, but you are dead. Let me join you, in your cold, lonely place." There is the sound of a gunshot and a body hitting the ground.

Ranjit walks down the final length of the corridor and enters the living room. The television—a large flat screen—is very loud, and as he enters the room, the old lady sitting on the plastic-covered couch seems unsurprised to see him.

"I'm sorry about fainting like that. Please forgive me—"

"*Shhh.* This is the best part. Sit down." The old lady pats the seat next to her, her eyes fixed on the screen. "Leela has gone to work, but she wants to talk to you. She'll be back in a few hours."

There are no other chairs in the dark room. Ranjit sits next to the old lady, the plastic crackling under his thighs, and wonders how much she knows about Leela's job at the club. The old lady is absorbed in the film, and he follows her gaze: on the screen, Shabana's supposedly lifeless body stirs and sits up.

Shabana was in her twenties then, her cheeks still rounded with youth, and wears a chaste white sari. The man lying dead on the floor sports a high, glossy pompadour and wears a wide-lapeled suit. They are both on the open veranda of a village house, surrounded by fields.

Shabana's slim neck bows and her blue-black hair cascades to her shoulders as she bends over Paul's dead body.

"Oh, my love. What have you gone and done? I wanted them to think I was dead, so that I could join you. Now you are gone, and I must drink the real poison."

Shabana picks up a glass of colorless liquid and drinks. The camera zooms out, and the house shrinks to a rectangle surrounded by bright yellow mustard fields. There is a slow pan to the hills beyond, and a stone Ganesh temple fills the screen. The elephant god in the alcove is smiling gently, and the camera moves closer and closer, till his carved face fills the screen. The beat of a lone *tabla* begins, joined by the slow wail of a harmonium, and the credits roll.

The old lady sighs and her eyes are moist as she turns off the television. "Such a good film. They don't make these kind of films anymore. The old ones are the best ones."

Ranjit tries to stand, but the plastic sticks to his thighs. "I owe you an explanation. You see, the painkillers for my arm—"

"These?" An orange plastic pill bottle is clutched in her hand. "How many of them you take during the day? Two? Three?"

"I think three."

"One more of these, you in a coma. Where did you get them? I've never seen such a high dose of oxycodone. I used to be a nurse, I know all about it, I've seen many, many patients overdose. You did a real chupid thing. And you know what is more chupid? You're carrying a gun." She reaches down between the cushions and takes out the Glock.

"Found it in your pants when you passed out. What you doing with this?"

He looks at the gun and clears his throat. "I have a license for that. I'm a security guard."

"A gun, but no bullets? What kind of security guard are you?" He reaches out his hand for it, but she shakes her head and puts the Glock on the table. "I don't want guns in this house, not with the child here. I'll keep this away for you. Now. Leela and I had a long, long talk about you. You going to help her get away from this Patel?"

He remembers the muffled conversation he overheard. How much has Leela told her?

The old lady's dark eyes do not leave his face. "My girl, she's putting a lot of trust upon you. I know what Leela does. I'm not chupid. She works at the club. Everybody here knows that. My girl, she throws around her money . . ." The old lady frowns. "She says she's doing this for us, but I don't think so. She's doing it for herself. And now see what is happening to her? See her face. She's being beaten."

The old lady's steady gaze unsettles him.

"I'll do my best to get her out of there."

She stares at him with her dark eyes, her eyebrows perfect arcs above them. "Let me look at you. I can read faces. I can tell who can be trusted, who is a liar."

He feels her hot breath on his face. Suddenly feeling dizzy, he slumps back into the sofa.

"What's the matter?" She scrutinizes his face. "You're still pale. I bet you took the oxycontin on an empty stomach. When was the last time you ate?"

Ranjit thinks back on the greasy vegetables and hard *rotis* that Kikiben had offered him; he'd barely had a few mouthfuls. "Not for a while."

The old lady stands up. "So come. Eat some food."

"I couldn't possibly—"

"Don't be chupid, boy. You going to just starve? Pass out again?"

She rolls off the couch in a practiced gesture and walks through a door into the kitchen. He follows her, blinking as she flips on a bare bulb overhead.

By the window, overlooking the backyard, is a small round table covered with a yellowed plastic tablecloth. Against the back wall is a small four-burner gas stove with blackened pots on it, an avocado-colored refrigerator, and one single shelf, crowded with bottles and jars of spices. The old lady takes a chipped plate, piles it high with food from the stove, and gestures at the table.

Ranjit sits and the old lady places a plate in front of him, piled with a rich chicken and potato curry, and a stack of flaky *dhal puri* bread. The food is still hot, and he wonders if she just cooked it.

"Don't let it get cold. Eat, man."

"Thank you, Mrs. Rampersad. I'm Ranjit Singh, by the way."

"Mrs.? They only call me that at the bank." She laughs, showing pink gums, and her thin eyebrows arch with hilarity. "Name is Roop-mattie, but everyone calls me Auntie. And I know who you are."

The delicious *dhal puri* is stuffed with yellow lentils, and he uses it to scoop up the rich gravy of the chicken curry, redolent with Indian spices mixed with thyme. He hasn't had such a good meal since the leftovers in Shabana's apartment.

This kitchen reminds him of his mother's kitchen in Chandigarh, and he remembers her squatting over her two-burner stove, producing delicious meals with her few blackened pots. In fact, this place, with its barely furnished rooms, reminds him of his mother's house. A house in India is not filled with things, is not a display of personal tastes and preferences; it is a stage for life to happen, filled with cooking smells and children and visiting relatives.

"This food is great, Auntie."

"I made it. Leela, she can't even make a piece of toast. Here, you eat some more."

Before he can protest, Auntie has taken his plate and refilled it. Though he is getting full, the aroma makes his mouth water, and he eats on.

Auntie nods, as though continuing a conversation she is having in her head. "Yes, that man Patel, he is the devil. But Leela, she's got it all wrong. I don't want to stay here. I want to go back to Guyana. Let them deport us. I don't care, as long as I get back home."

He puts his spoon down. "You *want* to be deported? I don't understand . . ."

Auntie rests her elbows on the table, and clasps her hands together as though praying.

"I told you, I can tell from a person's face if he can be trusted or not. It is a *gift*. In Georgetown, all the ladies would come to me, tell me their troubles, ask me what to do. I would say: *Show me your husband's face, I'll tell you if he is cheating. Show me your daughter's face, I'll tell you if she is lying.*

"And I was always, always right. Back home, old people, they have respect. Here—if you are old, you are useless, like, like . . ." She points to a worn sponge lying next to the sink. ". . . some old useless thing. No one listens to old people here. Especially Leela. You have a child, Ranjit?"

"A daughter, she's thirteen. She lives with her mother, in India."

"Daughters bring sorrow. Sons bring joy." Auntie's voice is matter-of-fact. "Leela, she was always difficult, and after her father left to come here, I could not control her at all."

She separates her hands and lays them, palms down, on the edge of the table.

"And when she got pregnant—she was eighteen, studying nursing, like me—she was as stubborn as a goat, she would not tell me who the father was. But I did find out: he was a respectable man, a Brahmin. And he was much older, his daughters were Leela's age. Can you imagine the shame? And Leela insisted on having the child, because she thought that the man would come around. Of course, he didn't. Just shut himself up in his nice house with high walls, sent over an envelope of money. Leela went into a deep, deep depression; she couldn't take care of Dev. So when my husband, he got papers for Leela to come to America and study nursing, I said, *Go, you go. Leave the child with me. I will raise him.* I sent her away, I thought it was for the best."

Ranjit clears his throat. "Your husband was here, in New York, right? He drove a cab?"

"Yes. He was here, in this very house. But he didn't know about his grandchild. I . . . we . . . could not tell him, it was so shameful. How did I know my husband was going to die?" She entwines her hands again. "How was I supposed to know Leela would end up all alone here?"

"We make the best decisions we can, Auntie. We can't always see the future."

"Maybe." She shakes her head. "Maybe. Leela was all alone here. She started pining for her boy. She wanted to get papers for us, but it would take years, and by then he would be all grown. So she went to that devil, Patel. Someone came to my door in Georgetown; he said, *Pack your bags, Auntie, you're going to America.*

"I thought we would fly to New York, like everyone else, but you know where they took us? Canada. We stayed in motels. We were freezing—snow outside, the whole world white—and always moving, in a van with some other Guyanese, real low-class folks. Then one morning, suddenly, the men driving us, they were all relaxed, and I knew we were in America. They dropped us to a motel in some place called Buffalo.

"Leela was there. She had on a big coat, hat, boots, and all. She saw Dev, she held out her arms to him, but he started crying. He ran away from her, he came right back to me."

The old lady blinks back tears. There must be a clock somewhere in the house, because he becomes aware of a regular ticking.

"You need to give it time, Auntie. This is a new place, it's hard at first."

"It's been over a year." She looks calmly at him. "The child still calls her Leela. He calls me Mom-Mom. As far as he is concerned, I am his mother, and that makes Leela very angry. So you see, Ranjit, everything she has done, it's for nothing. She is ruining her life, and ours. For what? You tell me, for what?"

He thinks of Shanti, far away in India. The only contact he's had

with her has been hour-long conversations on Skype, conversations colored by the distance. *What will it be like to live with a headstrong thirteen-year-old girl, with all the frictions of everyday life?*

"You see what this Patel is doing to Leela? Every night, she comes back from the club bruised and battered. Help me, please, Ranjit. I want to make sure she is all right, then I'm going to take Dev and go home."

As if on cue there is a soft wail from down the corridor. Auntie half turns and listens, and the wail is followed by mumbled words.

"The child has nightmares. I must go to him."

She trots down the hallway, and he soon hears the murmur of her voice, followed by a *pat-pat-pat* as she puts the boy back to sleep. She sings softly to him, a tune that he suddenly recognizes.

Makhan roti chini, neeni baba neeni
Makhan roti ho gaya, mera baba so gaya . . .

She sings the lullaby in a soft, quavering voice: Butter, bread, sugar. Sleep, child, sleep. The butter and bread is finished. My child has fallen back to sleep . . .

He remembers lying in the darkness, his mother's hand stroking his head, hearing her sing that same lullaby. Shorn of meaning, the words were comforting and rhythmic.

Auntie sings the lullaby again, and her voice grows fainter.

Ranjit washes his plate with the frayed sponge, trying to be quiet. He can't find a dish towel, so he leaves it by the side of the sink. Walking down the hallway, he peers into Auntie's bedroom, lit by the eerie blue nightlight, and sees her lying curled around Dev, one arm thrown across him. They are both asleep, and the boy's eyelashes flutter as he dreams.

Ranjit's watch has stopped, and he wishes that he knew the time: he can hear the ticking of the clock somewhere, but can't see one. *Ah, the television.* Surely there are news stations on.

He returns to the parlor and picks up his pills from the table, but his gun is gone. Turning on the huge television, he mutes the sound

and flips through the channels. An overweight woman on a cooking show smiles as she watches a hunk of butter simmer in a pan; a man in a toupee gestures at a shining car; a basketball player flies through the air and dunks a ball.

He flips some more, past the image of a familiar head, bald and blocky. Flipping back, he sees Senator Neals—dressed in a crisp white shirt and a dark suit—standing at a podium, in the midst of a speech. The crawl below him says, "Massachusetts Senator ending fact-finding trip to China." Fumbling with the remote, Ranjit turns up the volume.

Neals speaks without notes, his football-player's frame towering above the anxious-looking Chinese officials who surround him.

". . . this stop at the Shenzen Free Trade Zone concludes our visit. We are grateful to the Chinese Labor Ministry for opening up their manufacturing facilities to us. While we realize that China has to compete in a global economy, it cannot be at the cost of human rights. We have been assured that the use of prison labor, while widespread, will be ended and . . ."

Ranjit studies the screen. The Senator looks good; he has lost some of the bulk he gained after Anna died, and the bags under his eyes have gone. His shaved head hides his age, and his bass voice is deep and authoritative.

The picture shifts to a female news anchor. "China has come under fire in recent months for their use of prison labor. Prisoners with no rights have been forced to make everything from baseball bats to children's toys, items sold to an unsuspecting American public. Senator Neals, the head of the International Trade Subcommittee, will soon issue a report that will have a major impact on U.S.-China relations. Now, in sports . . ."

Ranjit turns off the television. *Did the Senator get his phone message, or was it lost somewhere in the chain of aides and assistants?* It seems as though Neals will be back in the United States by the end of the week, but by then it will be too late.

With the television off, the house is silent again. Ranjit guesses it must be two or three in the morning; Leela should be back soon. That is, if she isn't in a hotel room with Lateef. Ranjit's fists clench at the thought of the smug, sadistic young man with his beringed fingers.

From down the hall, he can hear Dev mumbling in his sleep. It has been so long since he has been in a house with a sleeping woman and child that he savors the feeling. He also knows that they are now his responsibility; he sinks back into the couch, closes his eyes, and prays:

> *The company I keep is wretched and low, and I am anxious day*
>   *and night*
> *My actions are crooked, and I am of lowly birth.*
> *O Lord, master of the earth, life of the soul, please do not forget*
>   *me!*
> *I am your humble servant, take away my pains, and bless me*
> *I shall not leave your feet, even though my body may perish . . .*

When he opens his eyes, the shadows around him are dark and unmoving.

The sound of a car door slamming wakes him from a half doze. Getting to his feet, he walks into the corridor, just in time to see Leela enter, her keys in her hands. He is hidden in the darkness, and she does not see him as she bends to remove her white high heels. She is wearing a short turquoise dress that clings to her hips, and her platinum-blond weave is like a gleaming helmet, one long swoop of hair pasted across her forehead.

"Leela. Hey."

She looks up sharply, a high-heeled shoe in her hand, then slumps against the wall. "Shit. You scared me. You're still here."

"Your mother said you wanted to talk to me." Coming closer, he smells the sharp tang of alcohol. "Are you okay? Lateef?"

"He didn't come to the club. My lucky night, huh? But that fucker Patel wouldn't let me work the sky-booths, he said my eye . . . said I should have stayed home. How does it look, Ranjit? Bad?"

She pushes off the wall, still wearing one shoe, and almost falls.

He catches her by her elbow. "Hey, hey, steady." The edges of her slim nostrils are pink; she is pretty high as well as drunk.

"You're always grabbing on to me. If you have a crush on me, just say so."

Stung, he lets go of her. "Look, I'm sorry that I fainted, I—"

"It's okay." Leaning against him, she bends and slips off her other shoe. "My mother likes it when people are sick. She used to be a nurse. She wanted me to be a nurse, too. I started off studying to be a nurse, but now I'm a whore." Her voice gets louder.

"Hey, don't talk like that."

"How do you want me to talk? This is how I talk, okay?"

Still holding her elbow, he guides her into the parlor and she sinks down onto the plastic-covered couch, her dress riding up her muscular thighs. He stands in the doorway and averts his gaze.

"Mama says you are going to be my savior. Did she tell you my whole sad story? She likes to do that." Leela smiles up crookedly.

"She gave me some dinner. She's been very kind."

"She says you're a good man. If I wasn't a whore, she says I might have a chance with you."

"Don't say that. It's no point beating up on yourself."

"But . . ." In the darkness her eyes are green as a cat's. ". . . really, I must be a whore. You want to see how much money I made tonight? With my eye like this?" She reaches into her small white purse, and hundred-dollar bills spill onto the floor. "Hey, if it walks like a duck, quacks like a duck, then it must be a duck."

The self-loathing in her voice is corrosive. He gathers up the money and hands it to her.

She ignores the money and holds on to his arm. "You know what I read in books? Whores don't kiss. They do everything, but they won't kiss you. That's bullshit, you know? We kiss. Sure, we kiss. Buy enough bottles, I'll kiss you."

"Shhh." He reaches out and hugs her awkwardly with his good arm. "Shhh."

She leans into him, and he feels her warm lips press into his neck. "Leela, please, no."

But she is kissing his neck. Her hand fumbles at the buttons of his shirt, then her palm slides through, warm and sticky, and lies flat on his chest.

"What is it? You think I'm a whore, is that it?" she whispers into his ear, her hand still in his shirt.

"No, it's nothing like that. I like you, but—"

She leans in and kisses him on the mouth and he tastes alcohol and sweetness.

"More. Please, more." Her voice is choked and so full of hunger that he is frightened. She takes his hand and presses it to her own warm chest, and he feels her nipple stiffen under the silk. If he is going to stop, this is the point.

"It's all going to end soon." She speaks urgently. "And I don't want to be alone. It's all going to end. Kiss me."

The words make sense in the way that Roopmattie's lullaby made sense: nonsense words that morph into need, into hot desire, undermining his defenses.

He kisses her back.

Her mouth mashes into his, her tongue darts into his mouth, her saliva is sweet.

When they part for breath, she slides off the couch and pulls him up. They walk together down the dark corridor, past her sleeping mother and child, to the boy's room at the rear of the house. She closes the door, and he slumps onto the narrow bed.

Still standing, she unzips her turquoise dress and pulls it off, then her bra. The underwiring has left red lines under her full breasts, and there are other red marks high up on her arms, which he now realizes are rope burns.

"You think I'm too fat? The other girls are so skinny . . ."

"You're perfect. Come here."

Pulling her to him, he kisses the marked flesh on her arms, then her chest.

He is conscious of her mother and son sleeping feet away, but more than that, he is conscious of her heavy, warm breasts brushing his face, her hands pressing into the back of his head.

Then she unbuckles his jeans, and feels for him, holds him. He moves till he is sitting against the wall, and she climbs onto his lap.

When he holds her head, she twists it away. "Careful," she whispers. "My hair. I just did it today."

One-handed, he is not much use. She guides him in, and holds his shoulders and pushes into him. The movement is both familiar and strange, each of them searching for the other's rhythm; they find it, and go on and on. Just when he cannot last anymore, she closes her eyes tightly, breathes hard through her open mouth, shudders and gasps. He stops for a moment, but she urges him on, and they buck back and forth, and soon he is spent, too.

Exhausted, they sit in the darkness, still joined, but separate again. Over the top of her immaculate blond hair he can see the mobile of the solar system, trembling gently.

Her lips tickle his ear. "I hate this house. She thinks everything will be soiled, that's why she puts plastic on the couch. She'd cover me with plastic too, if she could."

She climbs off him and walks away. He lies down on the thin pillow and listens to the ticking of the hidden clock.

He hears water splashing in a toilet, then silence. Still naked, she comes back, slides in next to him, and instantly falls asleep.

Five minutes pass, then ten. Covering her with a sheet, he gets out of the bed and pulls his jeans over his sticky thighs. He picks up her turquoise dress, her pink lacy underwear and scalloped bra, and puts them all on the dresser.

When he leaves, she is deep asleep, the planets trembling above her. What is their correct order? *Mercury, Venus, Earth, Mars . . .*

He goes into the living room and settles as best he can onto the couch, the plastic crackling under him. Her scent is on his fingertips, her smell of alcohol and perfume trapped in his beard. Lying in the hot room, images of her face and plump body fragment in his mind.

This is the first woman he has touched in over a year. After the encounter with the yoga woman, he swore he wouldn't do such a thing again, but he has, and Leela was so hammered that she probably won't even remember this tomorrow.

He tries to imagine the next morning, the next few days, even his future when all this is over, but it is a blank. All he can hear is the ticking of the clock, hidden somewhere in this house.

Chapter Twenty-Five

When Ranjit wakes the next morning, he is soaked in sweat, and his cheek is stuck to the plastic of the couch. He sits up, listening: the room is stifling hot, and from outside comes the raspy buzzing of cicadas.

He feels a sickening guilt when he remembers last night, and delays leaving the parlor. It is shabbier in the bright daylight: the watery yellow walls are scuffed at the bottom, and, under the plastic covering, the couch is a faded purple. Only the television set retains its sleek contours.

"Ranjit? You up?" From the kitchen there is the *click-click* of the gas stove being lit. Leela's voice is flat and matter-of-fact. "You up?"

Steeling himself, he walks into the kitchen and sees Leela, her back to him, spooning tea into a blue porcelain teapot. She is wearing a red T-shirt, and cutoff jean shorts, so short that they reveal half-moons of flesh. She tugs her shorts down as she turns to him; her hair is still platinum blond but her eyes are hazel again.

"I heard you waking up, so I put the kettle on. You want some tea?"

She has had just a few hours' sleep, but her eyes are clear and her face is smooth and fresh. How strange to know the softness of her skin, the taste of her mouth, but not to know what she is thinking.

"Tea would be great." He pauses, noticing a graphic of Che Guevara on her T-shirt, bearded and wearing a beret. "Nice T-shirt. You're a fan of his?"

"Who?" She looks down at her shirt. "This is a real guy?"

"Che? Yes, he's dead. He fought with Castro in Cuba, and after the revolution . . . Never mind." He pauses. "About last night—"

He waits for her to look blank, or to say that she was drunk and high, and excuse herself.

Just then a kettle on the stove begins to whistle and Leela pours the boiling water into the teapot. Ranjit waits, conscious of his cheeks burning. She puts the teapot and an empty mug in front of him.

"Last night was great. Let it steep for about four minutes," she says.

He sits back in his chair, relieved. She toasts bread in a ridged cast-iron pan, then butters it, and adds grains of sugar, and he thanks her for it.

"This isn't a real breakfast. My mom would make bake and saltfish, but this is the best I can do." She sits across from him, watching him. "How did you manage to sleep on the couch? Dev woke me at seven thirty, and I looked in on you. You were dead to the world."

"That's one of my good qualities. I can sleep anywhere." He pours them both cups of tea from the teapot, and she sips hers, the steam swirling into her face.

"Hmm."

"This tea is really good." He gestures to his plate. "Last night your mother said that you couldn't cook."

"Oh, I can make toast, but that's it. The tea, I get it from this guy in Jackson Heights, it's a second-flush Darjeeling."

"It's okay. I don't need you to cook for me, I'm a pretty good cook."

She rears back in mock surprise. "Really? I don't know that many men who cook. You're just *full* of good qualities."

"I'm also good at passing out on people's front steps."

She laughs, a deep belly laugh, and he knows then that they have crossed over into another place.

Hearing laughter from outside, he glances out of the window. Auntie wears a faded blue housedress and stands barefoot amidst the crab-grass, watering the sunflowers. Dev whoops as he dances in and out of the spray of water. Even from here, the affection between them is palpable.

"She knows." Leela gestures at her mother. "She won't say any-thing, but she knows. She can see it on my face. Let alone yours."

She turns from the window and looks directly at him, and her unasked question is clear.

"I talked to the cops yesterday," he says, still chewing the toast. "They want Patel badly, they're willing to cut a deal. They'll protect all of you, but to close the deal, I need evidence. Hard evidence."

She frowns. "Evidence? Like what? A brick of heroin?" She drinks the last of her tea, and puts the cup down.

"You're sure Patel is bringing in drugs?"

She shrugs her slim shoulders. "What else could it be? He isn't bringing over immigrants in shipping containers. That's not his style. He likes things neat and tidy."

"Okay, so say it's drugs. How is he smuggling them in? I thought he was using Nataraj Imports, hiding them in the boxes of hair, but I was wrong. Do you have any idea, any idea at all, what Shabana found out?"

She looks out of the window: Dev, soaking wet now, is hugging Auntie.

"He's never like that with me," she says absently, then looks back at him. "Look, Shabana was coked out of her mind. People say shit when they're high." He can see a flicker of fear in her eyes. "Maybe she didn't have any hard evidence, maybe she was just mouthing off, and she got herself killed for nothing."

"I don't think so." Ranjit finishes his tea and pours himself a sec-ond cup. "Shabana was a smart woman, she survived in the Mumbai film industry for very long. These kinds of people weren't new to her. From what Kikiben told me—"

"Who?"

"This woman I worked with at Nataraj, she knows everything about Bollywood. She said that back in the day, most films were financed by the Mumbai mob. Movie stars were involved with the mob all the time. No, I don't think Shabana was bluffing. She knew something, I can feel it in my gut . . . What do you know about Lateef?"

At the mention of his name, Leela unconsciously touches her eye with her fingertips.

"He's—at first he's an attractive guy, he's clean cut, he's polite. But soon you realize that he behaves like a spoiled kid. The others— they seem sort of disgusted with him, but they put up with him. I've seen men like him before. Their fathers are powerful, rich, but they aren't like their fathers, they're weak, and they know it. It makes them nasty . . ."

Ranjit pours Leela another cup of tea, and she absently nods her thanks.

". . . there was a boy like Lateef in Guyana. His uncle was the minister of something, he would just drive through the streets in his Mercedes, pick up girls, get them drunk, rape them. One girl in my neighborhood mocked him in front of a crowd of people, she said that he had a small penis. They found her dead in a rubbish heap, two weeks later. He had raped her and poured acid on her face. And I don't know why. He was a handsome boy, he was rich, he could have dated any girl he wanted."

The two men at the club had talked about Lateef as though he was a spoiled, willful child. As the Don's nephew, he is clearly used to getting what he wants; even Patel is scared of him.

"Leela." Ranjit reaches forward and puts his hand over hers. "I know you're frightened, but . . . I was doing some thinking last night. I'm pretty sure that whatever evidence Shabana had is still out there. If Mohan had it, he would have used it to buy his freedom, he's smart like that. So my guess is that it's still hidden somewhere. It's not at her apartment—Patel would have looked there—but where else could it be? You said Shabana had a dressing room at the club."

Leela nods. "After she died, they gave it to me, but it's a pigsty, shit everywhere, broken bottles of perfume, dried-up makeup. I haven't had the time to clean it out, so I just use my old one. What are we looking for, anyway?"

"I don't know. It would be something that stands out, something not part of the larger pattern . . . Are you going to work tonight?"

"Mondays are my night off. Sometimes they call me if someone important is throwing a private party, but otherwise, no."

He squeezes her hand. "I need to search that dressing room tonight. Can you make some excuse to go back there, and take me in with you?"

Leela stares at Auntie out in the backyard, and frown lines appear on her smooth forehead.

"What did my mother say to you last night? She never talks directly to me, it's like I have to read her mind. She's ashamed of me, right?"

"Not ashamed. She feels guilty for having sent you here alone." He does not mention that Auntie wants to take Dev and return to Guyana. "She's worried about what Lateef is doing to you."

"That's not true. She hates me."

Ranjit looks out of the window, but the old lady and the boy have disappeared from view.

"Your mother hates this country, not you. Look . . . back home, she was an elder, she was respected. Here, she's an old woman cooped up in this house."

"You have the answers to everything, don't you?" Leela's face hardens and she moves her hand from under his.

"No. I don't have any of the answers. I came to this country with my wife and daughter—" He thinks of working in the Indian store in Boston, then taking Shanti and Preetam to live on Martha's Vineyard. "—and my wife, she could never adjust. She was miserable, depressed, and I didn't know how to deal with it. Instead of understanding what she was going through, I resented her—"

"Is that why you got divorced?"

"Yes. No. Other stuff happened . . . but that's not my point. My point is that it's hard for your mother, and hard for you, because you feel you're responsible for her happiness. That's a very heavy burden. Just be patient with her, and patient with Dev. It's not his fault that he's closer to her than you. He's a kid, and Auntie's the only security he's ever known."

Leela blinks angrily. "Is the lecture over?"

"I didn't mean to lecture you. I don't know much, but one of the things I've learned is that anger obscures things."

Leela closes her eyes and is motionless. Out in the backyard, he hears the rhythmic chirping of the cicadas.

She opens her eyes and nods at him. "Okay, I'll call the club, and say that I left my pocketbook behind. We can go around eight. I'll let you in the back, but you must be quick."

"Ten minutes, tops."

"What if we don't find anything?"

"One step at a time. And there is one more thing . . ." Her face becomes wary again. "I haven't washed my hair in a while . . ."

She leans in and sniffs. "You do smell, a bit."

". . . and I need help combing it out. I can't do it with one hand."

Just then Dev rushes into the room. Auntie stops at the threshold and looks from her daughter to Ranjit: they are sitting at opposite ends of the table but their bodies are aligned toward each other. Even a stranger would know that they are involved.

After he washes his hair—his left arm wrapped in a plastic bag—he wears some clean clothes that Leela has brought him, a dark checked shirt with a frayed collar and blue polyester pants. Just from the look on her face, he knows that they were her father's.

He sits on the edge of Leela's bed, his wet hair hanging halfway down his back, and she kneels behind him, combing it out. Her comb catches in the snarls, but she doesn't complain. She just tugs and pulls, and soon the comb slides smoothly through his hair.

"You have such great hair." She laughs. "All this long hair, on a man. If I had hair like this, I wouldn't have to use a glue-on weave."

"I like you without it."

"Without it? I would look just like every other girl. No man in the club would be interested in me."

She dries his hair with a small pink hair dryer and then ties it into a topknot. He thanks her, and she nods and leaves the room, returning a few minutes later with Dev.

"We're going to the supermarket, can you watch him? Shouldn't be gone for more than half an hour."

Auntie and Leela gather cloth shopping bags and leave, and Dev takes Ranjit's hand and pulls him outside into the backyard. Today the boy wears the collar of his red polo shirt flipped up, and with his pudgy knees and round cheeks, resembles a large teddy bear. He wants to play catch, but Ranjit explains that his arm is broken, and the boy looks up with concern.

"Who broke your arm? Is it always going to be broken?"

"It will get better soon. How about I tell you a story instead?"

This must be a foreign concept, but he agrees, shrugging his shoulders just like Leela. Ranjit sits on the metal chair in the cool shade of the huge tree, and Dev climbs into his lap and looks up expectantly.

It has been a long time since Ranjit has held a child, and a long time since he told Shanti a story. Thinking about her, he feels guilty: she's sent him two text messages and wanted to talk, but he just texted back that he was too busy driving.

"So." Dev tugs at his sleeve. "Are you going to tell me a story or not?"

"Yes, yes, of course. You know the one about the monkeys and the hat seller? No?"

The boy shakes his large head, and Ranjit begins, remembering as he goes along.

He tells a story about a hat seller in India, a *topi-wallah*, who went from village to village selling his hats. One afternoon, exhausted, he lowered the load of hats from his head and fell asleep under the shade of a giant banyan tree. He slept for a long time, and woke to find that all his hats were gone.

A tribe of monkeys, up in the tree, had taken all his hats, and were wearing them: red hats, yellow hats, pink hats, purple hats. The *topi-wallah* begged the monkeys to return his hats, but they just bared their teeth at him and imitated his pleading. Angered, he threw stones at the monkeys, who threw twigs and branches down at him. The *topi-wallah* was defeated, but then he realized that the monkeys would imitate whatever he did.

"So you know what he did?"

Dev's eyes widen. "What? Tell me, what?"

"He took the hat from his own head and flung it to the ground. Imitating him, the monkeys took the hats from their heads, and flung them down, too. Laughing, the *topi-wallah* gathered up all his hats and left, saying that he would never sleep under that tree again."

Dev giggles excitedly. "He was clever. The monkeys were stupid."

"Sometimes clever people do stupid things." *Like, get involved with a woman half his age. Like, go back tonight to a place where he was almost killed.*

Dev sees the shadow cross Ranjit's face, and his own eyes narrow in alarm. Constantly responding to the moods of two warring women has made him very sensitive.

Ranjit smiles and holds the boy tighter. "Have you heard the one about the crocodile and the monkey?"

Dev shakes his head, and Ranjit begins another story, talking loudly to be heard above the buzzing of the cicadas.

All day the heat builds, till the air is crackling with a strange electricity.

That night, after Dev is put to bed, Leela calls a car service, and by the time it arrives, the night sky has clouded over. A wind gusts through the streets and it begins to drizzle.

They run toward the waiting car, and by the time Leela gets into the car, her short black cocktail dress is soaked, and the wet fabric outlines

her breasts. The driver—a hawk-nosed man with a bushy beard—stares at her, then at Ranjit's shabby clothes, before looking away.

Leela notices the man's gaze and turns to Ranjit. Her eyes are sea-green again. "I have to dress up. My night off is when I go to other clubs, dance, meet prospective clients, put their numbers into my phone. Then, when I'm working, I text them and invite them to the club. If I was wearing anything else, the guys at Ghungroo would think it's odd . . ."

As they drive through Richmond Hill, a jagged flash of lightning splits the sky, illuminating the steel structure of the elevated subway, and it stretches away into the gusting rain like some mythical beast.

Leela moves closer to him and shivers. "I hope Lateef doesn't show up. He comes in at odd times and asks for me. If I'm not there, he throws a tantrum. Here . . ." She opens her small square handbag, and slides out the Glock. Using her bag to shield it from the cabbie's gaze, she hands it to him.

"Didn't your mother tell you, it's empty? The guys at the club took the bullets—"

"Here you go." She presses a heavy metal rectangle into his palm. "Glock 17, right? This will work?"

Ducking down, he slots in the magazine, and it fits. He looks at her wordlessly.

"I got it from those guys down the street when I went shopping. Apparently the Glock 17 is quite a common model."

"Good thinking, thanks."

He slides the gun into the waistband of his too-big pants and tightens the belt another notch. It presses into his skin, but it doesn't make him feel better. If he pulls it out, he'll have to use it, and that's the last thing he wants.

Leela's arms are crossed, and he sees from her stiff back that she is very scared. He wants to reach out and touch her, but he is conscious of the cabbie watching them in the rearview mirror.

"Don't worry, nothing's going to happen. In and out of there in ten minutes."

"Ten minutes, you promise?"

"Just ten minutes," he echoes. A part of him notices how badly the cabbie is driving, taking corners too wide, speeding up needlessly. Sloppy, stupid driving that will surely attract the attention of the cops.

"Hey, brother," Ranjit says respectfully, "could you slow down? We're in no hurry."

The bearded driver glances at the two of them in the mirror. "You don't tell me how to drive, and I won't tell you how to run your business, okay?"

Ranjit stiffens. "And what business would that be?"

The driver snorts. "Okay, since you asked. A pimp and his girl heading into Manhattan to start work. She's not that hot, you're not going to need that gun."

"You stupid fuck . . ." Ranjit leans forward, but Leela puts a restraining hand on his arm.

Her eyes are glittering with anger as she leans forward. "Drive the way we tell you to drive. Otherwise I'll give your name and hack number to some of my friends in Little Guyana, and sometime in the next few days, your face will be bashed in. Understand?"

The driver's face turns red. "I didn't mean any disrespect, I—"

"Shut up and drive."

The cabbie slows down, and for the rest of the trip he doesn't say a word.

Ranjit is shocked by her response, but then he remembers what Ali had said: no pushover would have survived for so long in the brutal world of the nightclub.

It is raining harder as they come out of the Midtown Tunnel into Manhattan. The cabbie speeds down Thirty-seventh Street, sending up a spray of water that soaks the pedestrians waiting on the corner.

Chapter Twenty-Six

As soon as Leela lets Ranjit through the back door of Ghungroo, he shivers. He is soaked through, and the air-conditioning is freezing, but it is not just that: the air inside the club smells thin and used up, just like the air inside the Tombs.

The hallway is dark, and he hurries to keep up with Leela. They pass the room where the men beat him—he recognizes the dirty carpeting and dented lockers—and then climb up an enclosed concrete stairway. When they emerge, they are on a metal catwalk suspended high in the air. Leela hurries onward, but he stops and gapes.

Nothing about the exterior of Ghungroo prepared him for this: five or six floors of the interior have been gutted, creating a tall, vertical atrium. A network of beams crisscrosses the space at many levels, supporting what looks like a fleet of flying saucers. These are actually circular seating pods, upholstered in deep red leather, linked to each other by skywalks made out of perforated metal. Far down below is a frosted glass dance floor, flanked by two red semicircular bars glittering dully with tiers of bottles.

Right now the whole vast space is empty, but Ranjit can imagine the club when it is full: the VIPs lounging in the red circular pods, suspended in space, gazing down loftily at the dance floor, while others stand on the skywalks, the whole atrium like a vertical hive of conversation and laugher and music.

"Ranjit. Come on. Come on." Leela gestures frantically to him from the far end of the catwalk.

He follows her through a door that takes them back into the interior of the building. Gone is the red leather seating and shiny metal; this is clearly a service area of concrete-block walls and worn carpeting.

Leela unlocks a shabby white door, and they enter a darkened room. Locking the door, she clicks on the overhead light.

"It's a fucking mess, isn't it?"

Shabana's dressing room has a plastic-topped dressing table along one wall, its large mirror surrounded by lightbulbs, most of which have burned out. A worn swivel chair has been pushed aside, and behind it is an open closet, hung with red, orange, and yellow silk saris. The small room is a mess, and Ranjit experiences a sudden sense of déjà vu: tissues blotted with lipstick are scattered across the floor, along with splayed Indian film magazines. There is a thick layer of dust on the mirror, and the dressing table is cluttered with dried-out tubes of mascara, a silver hairbrush clotted with long black hair, and a packet of human hair. He picks up the glossy skein of hair, and holds it, marveling at how alive it is.

Leela's voice is urgent. "What are we looking for? Ten minutes, remember?"

"Let me look around."

He picks up a small, silver-framed photograph from the dressing table and a young Shabana peers up at him. She wears a white *salwar kameez,* and must be fifteen or sixteen, her hair pulled back with a hairband and her brows thick and unplucked. He turns over the frame, but there is nothing stuck on the back.

Pulling open a drawer in the dressing table, he finds only more bottles of nail polish and sponge-tipped makeup applicators. In another drawer is a plastic pillbox, half full; he glances at the label and sees Halcion, a sleep medication, prescribed in Ruksana's name, and dispensed by a pharmacy on the Upper East Side. There is also a key ring with a Mickey Mouse logo, holding what look like apartment and mailbox keys. He sets the pills and keys aside.

The other drawers are empty, so he looks in the closet, unfolding the saris to see if there is anything in their folds, and even putting his hand into the toes of the shoes lined up below them. *Nothing.*

Leela is half turned to the door, her ears straining to hear. "Are we done? Anything? Shit, you didn't find anything?"

"Just a second. Please."

He looks back at the room, recognizing Shabana's mess from the Dakota. What was it about her psyche that made her feel at home when surrounded by dust and filth?

He stares hard, trying to look at the room through her eyes. Everything here is impersonal: the walls are blank, there are no vases, no postcards stuck in the frame of the mirror, no photographs, other than the one of herself in the white *salwar kameez.* He remembers that she had a similar photograph at the Dakota—why is this image so important to her? Does it symbolize something, a time of innocence perhaps?

Walking over, he sees that the silver picture frame is old and heavy. The back is secured with a series of metal tabs that hold a piece of cardboard in place, and he undoes these, and slides away the stiff square of cardboard. Nothing behind it, except for the photograph. *Damn it.*

There are footsteps outside in the corridor, and Leela turns to him, raising a finger to her lips.

"Leela? Hey, Leela, are you in there?" It is the bored tone of one of the dark-jacketed men. "Can I talk to you for a minute?"

Leela turns a pale, questioning face to Ranjit.

His voice is a whisper. "Go and see what he wants. If you don't come back in a few minutes, I can find my way out of here. There are just the two security guys, right?"

"I think so. Are you sure?"

He nods, and she opens the door a crack and slips out.

He hears her speak, using a tone that he hadn't heard before, light and flirtatious, and hears the man laugh. Forcing his attention back to the room, he surveys the mess, conscious of the rapid beating of his heart.

He closes his eyes, and opens them again, and that is when he sees it: the cardboard backing from the frame is lying on the dressing table, and even from here he can see a marking, a red graphic of a house: the same stamp he saw on the boxes at Nataraj.

". . . okay, okay, fine. Just give me a few minutes. I got to fix myself up, you know?"

Leela enters the room, slams the door shut, and leans heavily against it. The footsteps outside retreat down the corridor.

"Lateef is coming. He'll be here in a few minutes." Leela is sweating and he can smell the fear on her, acrid and hormonal. "He wants me to have a drink with him. Which means he'll get drunk, then take me back to the hotel." She looks wildly around the room. "Did you find anything? What's that in your hand?"

"It could be something . . . I don't know." He grabs an empty plastic bag lying on the floor and fills it with the square of cardboard, the keys, pills, and the skein of human hair.

"You don't *know*? All this for *nothing*? Last time Lateef slapped me around, and this time it's going to be worse, he wants me to wear one of Shabana's saris. He liked to beat her with a *belt*."

"You don't have to do this. Let's get the hell out of here."

"No. I can't make Lateef angry . . . he'll . . . my mother, Dev . . . no."

He grips her shoulder. "Lateef leaves in a livery car, right, without his bodyguards?" He can see the panic glazing her eyes. "Did you see the driver? Was it an old Indian guy, gray hair?"

"I think so. There's a dark partition, it's hard to see—"

"Where does he take you?"

"The Maritime Hotel, in Chelsea." Her eyes are far away, already anticipating what will happen to her.

"Listen to me. I'll figure a way to get you out of there. Just get Lateef away from the club. You have your cell phone? I'll text you. Put it on vibrate."

She nods her head blindly. "Okay. You have to leave now. Go back down the stairs, out the back door."

"Leela." He grips her shoulder tightly and forces her to look at him. "You're not alone in this."

He slips out of the dressing room and down the empty corridor. Reaching the catwalk that runs along the atrium, he stays against the wall, praying that he will remain unseen. The bright floodlights have been replaced by dim, recessed lighting, and the circular red sky-booths float in the gloom. From down below comes the throb of house music, murmured voices, and the clinking of glasses.

Ranjit moves quickly along the atrium, reaching the safety of the concrete staircase. He hurries down it, runs down the first-floor corridor, and opens the door into the back alley. It is still raining, a steady thin drizzle, and the moist night air feels like nectar.

He gets to Thirty-seventh Street just in time to see a black limo at the end of the block: there is no mistaking Tiwari's nervous driving as he seesaws the car into a parking space. Ranjit hangs back for a few minutes, pulls out his cell phone, and sends a text message to Leela. It seems like an eternity before she sends back a single word: OK.

Walking quickly, Ranjit heads down the block. For the first time in all these confused days and nights, he knows exactly what he has to do.

A group of hipsters in straw fedoras have taken over the counter of the diner. Anil Tiwari sits alone in a red leatherette booth, eating from a plate piled high with pancakes and links of sausages, drenched with maple syrup. He takes a sip from a tall takeout container of coffee, then uses his knife and fork with a surgeon's accuracy.

As Ranjit enters the diner, Tiwari is chewing rapidly, his Adam's apple bobbing up and down. His shabby blazer hangs off his thin shoulders, and the collar of his white shirt is so loose that the knot of his tie hangs low on his chest.

"Anil Sahib. So this is your regular spot, *hanh*? I see you're still a fan of the lumberjack breakfast."

Tiwari is so startled that he almost chokes on his mouthful of sausage. Without waiting for an invitation, Ranjit sits down and orders a cup of black tea from the sullen waitress.

"I see that you are staring at my arm." Ranjit smiles again. "The damndest thing happened. I was taking a shortcut through an alley near here—right after we met—and these two guys beat me sense-less."

Tiwari glances at Ranjit's cast, then looks away. "This bloody city." He purses his thin, bloodless lips. "It's a nightmare. A living, breathing nightmare."

"The funny thing is . . ." Ranjit's voice is conversational. ". . . those guys, they broke my arm, but they didn't take my wallet or anything. Strange, *hanh*?"

"People here are going crazy. They take out their anger on us for-eigners."

"But here's the funniest thing of all. The guys who beat me: they were Indian. You're not eating, Anil Sahib?"

Tiwari sits with his knife and fork clutched in his hands.

"Actually . . ." Tiwari makes a flapping gesture at the street outside. "It's nice to talk, but I have to go. My client will be ready to move soon. I better eat in my car." He gestures to the waitress. "Madam, can I have this in a box?"

"That?" She looks down at Tiwari's heaped plate and sniffs. "You said it was for here. If you want it in a box, ask for it in a box."

She slides the whole sticky mess into a Styrofoam box, and Tiwari pays, then gets up and puts on his peaked chauffeur's hat.

"Nice to see you, Ranjit. Sorry about your arm." Tiwari heads to-ward the door, clutching his box of food, but his tall container of cof-fee sits on the table.

Ranjit reaches for it, opens it, and tips in four white tablets. He waits till Tiwari is out the door, then knocks loudly on the plate glass, gets Tiwari's attention, and points to the coffee. Face reddening, the man returns, swoops up his coffee, and hurries away down the street, gulping it down.

That's it, Tiwari, drink your coffee, drink it all. Ranjit settles into the booth, takes a sip of his vile, tannic tea, and looks out at the dark street. High up inside Ghungroo, Lateef is busy getting drunk with Leela at his side, swaddled in a silk sari. If Ranjit's plan is going to work, Lateef has to remain inside the club for at least half an hour.

Ranjit feels calm now. This is how it was before going into combat: he was nervous beforehand, but when it really started he was always cool, able to take in the whole situation and make split-second decisions. It is good to know that this old self still exists.

The minutes tick past. The hipsters at the counter let out ironic cries of joy when the waitress brings them their greasy meatloaf and fries. Ranjit looks out into the darkness and waits.

Thirty minutes later, Tiwari's Lincoln Continental is still parked at the curb, its metallic black paint wet with rain. Ranjit raps on the driver's window, but there is no answer. He cannot see through the tinted glass, but when he tugs at the door, it clicks open.

The keys are in the ignition, and Tiwari is slumped over in his seat, his face ashen, his arms hanging down limply. He must have been still eating when he passed out: the box of pancakes and sausages has over-turned in his lap, and a stream of syrup runs down his left leg, puddling on the floor.

Please let him be alive. The dosage label on Shabana's bottle of sleeping pills had said not to exceed one pill a night; Ranjit had quadru-pled the dose. He tugs at Tiwari's shoulder and the man's head lolls back, but a thin stream of air comes out of his pinched nostrils.

Reaching into Tiwari's jacket, Ranjit fumbles around, then finds the man's cell phone: there are no calls in the last thirty minutes. Thank the Guru for that. Most of the calls to Tiwari's phone are from the same Manhattan number: it has to be Lateef, calling for pickups.

Ranjit pushes Tiwari backward and tugs off his blazer, and then takes the peaked cap from his head. It rains harder, and the street re-mains deserted. When he hauls Tiwari out of the cab, the man feels as light and hollow as a bird.

•   •   •

Ten minutes later, just as Ranjit finishes cleaning up the sticky mess from the driver's seat, Tiwari's cell phone rings. It is the same Manhattan number.

Lateef's arrogant voice says, "Five minutes. In the back," and hangs up.

Taking the sling off his right arm, Ranjit slips on Tiwari's blazer and jams the chauffeur's cap onto his head. With his broad build and beard, there is no way that he can pass as Tiwari, but as long as Leela does her part, all Lateef will see is the silhouette of a driver in a peaked cap.

He pushes a button and the smoked glass partition slides up, separating him from the passenger seats. The Glock sags in the right-hand pocket of his blazer. Murmuring a prayer under his breath, he starts the car, and its headlights sweep through the darkness.

Everything now depends on the next few minutes.

Chapter Twenty-Seven

SYDNEY, AUSTRALIA, 2008

The lights dimmed, signaling the end of the show.

The audience applauded thunderously as Shabana walked offstage at the Allphones Arena in Sydney. At forty-one years old, these three-hour variety shows exhausted her, and she was shiny with sweat, her legs trembling. She had just performed in front of an expatriate Indian audience, reprising monologues from her old films and lip-synching songs, all while wearing a see-through outfit made entirely of lace.

Just before the performance she had done two lines of coke, and now she was coming down from it, and felt cold and clammy. Hurrying to the dressing room, she changed into a sweatsuit and removed her thick stage makeup with cold cream, trying to avoid looking at her reflection.

Though her figure was still lithe, the face in the mirror bore only a faint resemblance to the one that had graced the screen. Her cheeks were puffy, her eyes heavy-lidded, her lips turned down at the corners.

"What the *hell* is wrong with you?" Ruksana walked in, her voice bristling with irritation. "You missed *two* cues, and mixed up the lines of the *Laila Aur Paul* dialogue."

Shabana winced. "Leave me alone. Nobody noticed. Most of these fools don't even speak Hindi."

"You're pushing it." Ruksana peered at her sister's face. "Your nostrils are all red. I don't care what you do, but wait till after the show, okay? And we still have to go to the party at Manuraj Pandey's."

"Why? Why do I always have to go to these damn things?"

"Because." Ruksana leaned in. "These rich Indian expats sponsor these shows for you. Thanks to them, we're making money again. You want to be broke? Have you forgotten what it was like when our father died?"

"I remember." Shabana wiped off her remaining makeup and threw the crimson-stained cotton ball into the trash. "Now leave me alone."

Half an hour later she had changed into a lime-green silk sari and once again resembled her screen image. In the car on the way to the party, she realized that she'd had no film roles for almost three years now. The only acting she did was to impersonate herself in variety shows for expatriate Indian audiences in Sharjah, Johannesburg, Fiji, Guyana, and Singapore.

Her film career had come to an end after that fateful trip to Dubai. When she returned to Mumbai, she saw a photograph of herself on the front page of *The Times of India*. The Don's arm was tight around her shoulders, crushing her mauve blouse, and above the image, in big letters, the headline said: SHABANA SHAH: THE DUBAI DON'S MOLL?

The other movie stars in that photograph had all issued statements distancing themselves from the Don, leaving Shabana in the spotlight. And then an aggressive young journalist, buoyed by public opinion, had decided it would be a good career move to investigate further.

After digging through the real estate records, he held a press conference where he revealed that Shabana's Bandra apartment had been bought by one of the Don's shell companies. The journalist questioned the financing of her films, the timing of her trips to Dubai, and especially her investments in mob-controlled real estate. He hinted that Shabana's frothy, romantic films were financed by money that the Don made from drugs, extortion, and murder.

The phone rang late one night and Shabana heard the Don's raspy voice.

"Don't worry, *beti*," he said. "I will take care of this *maderchod* reporter. He has a wife, two kids—and a boyfriend. Everything will be back to normal very soon."

And indeed, a few days later, the young reporter was on television, his thick glasses glinting in the glare of the spotlights as he shame-facedly retracted his statements, saying that he had been misled by com-plex changes in the tax code. Two days later, he was found dead of an overdose of sleeping pills.

The Don's move was so brazen that no one was fooled. Rumors flew that he had lost control, that clumsier, stupider underlings were running things now. In any case, the young reporter had died in vain: in the new India of blogs and Web sites, there were simply too many voices to be silenced.

An anonymous source posted two decades of Shabana's tax returns online, showing her entanglement with the Don's shell companies, and challenged the government to act. Desperate to protect higher-up min-isters, the tax department levied huge fines on Shabana, and confis-cated all her property.

This just added oxygen to the red-hot scandal, and the rumors began to flow: *Shabana had been the Don's mistress since she was thir-teen. She had a love child by him, kept hidden in her apartment.* Journal-ists kept a watch on everything Shabana did, and photographed her as she ran into her house, her face shielded by a raised forearm.

Shabana's advertising gigs dried up, as the Swiss watchmakers and designer brands scrambled to disassociate themselves. She completed the two romantic comedies she was filming, but when they were screened, the audiences jeered and shouted out, *Don ke raandi*, the Don's whore.

The film world suddenly concluded that Shabana was too old and too fat for the roles she had been playing for years, and Julie Chad-dha, with her defined abs and pretty, vacant face, was given the parts that usually went to Shabana.

Retreating to her Bandra apartment, Shabana stayed hidden from view. The Don remained in Dubai, and expressed his rage through a renewed gang war: if he couldn't take back his city by love, he would do it with surgical killings and car bombs that would remind *Mumbaikers* who was in charge.

Two years went by, then three. Ruksana said that they were going to run out of money soon, and concocted a tour of expatriate Indian communities. The shows were awful—attended by large, unruly crowds who sometimes clambered onstage—and afterward, Ruksana insisted that Shabana attend dinner parties at the homes of local Indian bigwigs.

Tonight the party was at a vast penthouse apartment on Bridge Street, overlooking Sydney Harbor.

"Miss Shah! You are gracing us with your presence! Welcome!" Manuraj Pandey greeted her as she stepped out of the elevator, bowing as much as his plump stomach would allow him. He had made his money importing plumbing fixtures, and now was puffed up with importance.

As was her practice, Ruksana melted away into a corner. Shabana stood alone in the middle of the room, and when someone put a gin and tonic in her hands, she gulped it down gratefully.

The other Indian guests remained clustered in a corner: the men were too frightened to talk to Shabana, and their wives, sweating in heavy silk saris, shot her looks of envy. Shabana looked around warily, hoping there was no microphone; sometimes these parties were charity events, and the host would raffle off fifteen-minute blocks of her time, when the purchasers would ask her to sing their favorite songs.

Tonight, though, there was no microphone, and plenty of booze. As soon as her glass was empty, it was replaced with another. She turned around to thank the bearer of the glass, and saw a tall young man in a black suit, wearing his white shirt disco-style, its wide collar splayed over his lapels. He had wide, gym-built shoulders, and his hair was cut short and gelled straight back, but his face was pitted with old acne scars.

"Miss Shah. What a pleasure to meet you again."

Again? The man looked like a Bollywood type, and Shabana recoiled a little.

"You don't remember me, do you?" The man's handsome face became petulant.

"Yes, yes, of course I do—" Shabana half turned toward Ruksana, but her sister had vanished. "It's just that I'm so bad with names."

"How about lips?" The man smiled, showing expensive white teeth.

"Lips?" Shabana felt confused, then something about the man clicked. The sulky face, the acne tracks on his cheeks that no amount of dermabrasion would erase: she remembered the hot tent outside Mumbai, and the acne-spotted boy who had pressed his sour lips into hers. Involuntarily, she reached up and wiped her mouth with the back of her wrist.

"Now you remember, *hanh?* I'm Lateef. Lateef Mustafa. The Don's nephew."

"Yes." Shabana stood very still. "So . . . what are you doing in Sydney?"

"Oh, just a holiday." Lateef smiled. "My uncle says it's not healthy for me to remain in Mumbai right now. But I'm heading to America soon, on business."

"Very interesting." Shabana looked for a means of escape, but Ruksana had stepped out onto the wide terrace outside and was gazing at the view of Sydney Harbor.

"Looking for your sister?" Lateef shook his head. "She's a tough negotiator, that one. She really cut a good deal for you. You won't have to earn your living like this anymore. Must be humiliating for you."

"What are you talking about?"

"Ask her yourself." Lateef stepped back, his polished kidskin loafers making a slithering noise. "Well, we'll be seeing a lot of each other soon." Blowing her an air kiss, he stepped away.

Shabana stormed out to the terrace.

"Look at that view," Ruksana said, gesturing at the white concrete sails of the Opera House and the arched fretwork of the Harbor Bridge.

Shabana grabbed her sister's elbow and spun her around.

"That was Lateef. *That fucker Lateef.* What did he mean, you just cut a deal with him? What deal?" Shabana's nails dug into the flesh of her sister's arm.

"*Oww*, let go of me. So, I made a deal. Just listen—"

"You think I'm your puppet? What else have you signed me up for?"

"Shut up and listen. Lateef is in the movie business now. He's producing a movie set in America, and he needs a star. It's an older role, a Muslim woman who lives in New York. They say her husband is a terrorist, he gets arrested, sent to Guantanamo, and she has to go to court to save him . . . a serious role, a real role."

Shabana let go of her sister's arm. "Are you sure? That creep Lateef is a producer?"

Ruksana massaged her arm. "He was just a kid back then, but he's all grown up now. He's taken over the movie financing business from the Don. He says that there is a huge Indian audience abroad, so he's going to make the film in English. This Hollywood actor, Brad Dunn, he's going to act in it. He's the FBI agent who falls in love with the Muslim woman while investigating her."

A real role, in a real film, starring alongside Brad Dunn. Shabana felt her chest constrict, felt the desire she'd stifled for so long. She could already see the part: a woman distraught, her husband gone missing, not knowing what had happened to him. Then the sadness welled up inside her, and she turned to hide the tears in her eyes.

"Crying? I thought you would be happy?"

"I am happy." Tears blurred Shabana's vision. "Thank you."

"See?" Ruksana waved into the darkness of Sydney Harbor. "I told you I'd find you a way back. Next stop, America."

bitch home. If she's messed up, you take her to the doctor. You remember where it is?"

He nods. *"Hanh."*

"And give her this." Flicking three hundred-dollar bills through the window, the man saunters back to the loading dock.

Lateef emerges from the door, sees that it is raining, and skips down the steps. Ranjit can see him clearly: gym fit and broad shouldered, wearing khaki pants and a pink shirt, his handsome face pitted with old acne scars. He walks with an arrogant stride, his head held high, and his lips turn down with disgust as the rain spatters him. Leela pauses on the stairs behind him, struggling to free the edge of her long silk sari, caught under her high heels.

Reaching the car, Lateef pauses and thrusts his hands into his pockets, conditioned by many years of being served. *The chauffeur always opens the door.* That is the unwritten rule of limos, but if Ranjit has to get out of the car, it will all be over.

Leela is still on the steps, tugging at the cloth trapped under her feet. Lateef's crisp pink shirt is getting wet, and he looks toward the limo, his face furrowing in irritation.

Just as he turns to yell to his men, Leela straightens up, lifts the bottom of her wet sari in both hands, clatters down the steps to the limo, and yanks open the back door. She climbs in, and Lateef follows her.

That was close. Ranjit waits with his hands on the steering wheel, hearing Leela gasp as she settles into her seat. Her sari is soaked through, and the air-conditioning must feel freezing.

Lateef chuckles. "Feeling cold? Your nipples are hard." His voice is loud and insouciant, and a little sloppy, too, the words slurred by alcohol. "Tiwari. Make the air conditioning colder."

"Lateef, don't be mean . . ." Leela tries to maintain her carefree tone.

"Aaare, I'll soon warm you up. Tiwari, what are you waiting for? The hotel, fool. *Jaldi, jaldi."* Quick, quick.

Nodding, Ranjit puts the car into gear and backs out of the alley. The smoked glass partition blurs their outlines, but he sees Lateef

Chapter Twenty-Eight

Lateef had asked to be picked up in the alley behind Ghunghroo in five minutes; Ranjit is perhaps a minute or so early. He brings the limo parallel to the service entrance and waits. The overhead light cuts a swath through the darkness, illuminating slanting needles of rain. The only sound is water pattering on concrete.

Another minute passes, and another, and his body tenses. Just then the service door bursts open and the two men in dark jackets emerge. One of them lopes down the steps toward the car, his hands casually thrust into his pockets, ignoring the heavy rain.

Have they been tipped off? Ranjit plucks the Glock from his pocket and slides it under his thigh.

The man walks around to the driver's side window and raps on the glass. "Tiwari. Hey, Tiwari."

No choice. Ranjit powers the window down an inch and keeps his face turned away, knowing that only his peaked cap will be visible.

"Yes?"

The man tries to peer in, rain spattering his head and running into his eyes. "Tiwari, listen. You wait tonight outside the hotel, drive the reaching over to drape an arm around Leela's shoulders. He must squeeze her breast hard, because she gasps again, this time in pain.

"Let's wait till we get to the hotel, okay? I'm all wet—"

"Don't talk." He seems to be pressing her head into his lap. "You know what I like. Do it."

There is the sound of a zipper being undone, a yelp, then a wet, half-strangled sound.

Ranjit wants to pull over, yank the man out of the car, and beat him senseless with the butt of the Glock. Instead, gritting his teeth, he drives fast, ignoring the burning pain in his left arm as he takes a sharp turn onto Ninth Avenue.

The disused parking garage is on Forty-third Street, a colorful bill-board on it announcing the luxury apartment building that will soon replace it. Ranjit sees that the attendant's booth is dark and prays that the entrance still works. Slowing to a crawl, he bumps the long arm of the barrier with his cab, and watches as it slowly lifts.

Does Lateef suspect anything? There is only his moaning from the back of the cab, and the ragged, choked sound of Leela's breathing. It makes Ranjit sick.

Well, he will feel something now. Ranjit accelerates up the spiral ramp into the garage, tires squealing as the car curves up, floor after floor. There is a shout of anger from the back as Lateef is thrown from side to side.

"Tiwari! What the hell are you doing, you *chutiya?*"

The limo takes the final turn and emerges onto the darkened top floor, its headlights sweeping across rows of flaking concrete pillars. There are no cars up here, just faded stripes on the concrete, and piles of fast-food boxes where cabs have parked, mixed with the white, half-filled bulbs of used condoms.

Ranjit slams the car to a stop, tumbles out, cracks open the passenger door, and slams the muzzle of the Glock into Lateef's fore-head.

"Get off her. Get out of the car."

Lateef sits motionless, his fly open, the long tails of his pink shirt spread around his hairy thighs. Leela pulls herself off him, retches, and wipes her mouth with the back of her hand.

"Well, well, well." Lateef looks up. His hair is carefully tousled and moussed and he wears a stylish two-day beard to hide the deep acne scars on his cheeks. "It's Patel's pet *Sardarji* again. My men told me about you. Couldn't you have waited another minute? I was almost there."

A red fog fills Ranjit's vision and his finger is tightening on the trigger when a voice says, "Ranjit, no, wait."

He realizes that Leela is looking up at him, her mouth bruised. A line of blood trickles down the corner of her mouth from where she has bitten herself.

Lateef stands against a concrete pillar in the dark, dripping garage, illuminated by the blue tungsten car headlights. He has buttoned his pants, but a pink triangle of fabric peeks through his open fly.

Ranjit is by the car, the Glock raised, and Leela stands next to him, pressing the *pallu* of her sari against her cut lip.

"*Sardarji,* last time my people broke your arm." Lateef sneers. "This time I'm going to have your balls on a platter."

"Shut up."

"That old fool Patel thinks you're working for him." Lateef's voice swells with anger as he leans insouciantly against the column. "I knew all along that the Hammer was your real boss. What does that *mader-chod* want, *hanh*? He's not getting anything. This is not Mumbai, this is my fucking town."

"I said, shut up."

"What are you going to do, you stupid *Sardarji*? Shoot me? My uncle will fill the streets of Mumbai with blood."

"Tell me why you people killed Shabana."

Lateef squints as he tries to see into the glare of the headlights. "*I killed Shabana?* Why would I kill her? She was a lousy lay, yes, okay. But you don't kill people for that. By the way, your little whore girlfriend is much better than her."

It would be so satisfying to reverse the Glock and beat this bastard senseless, but Ranjit controls his rage.

"Shabana had evidence of what you guys are up to here. She was about to go to the cops, so you had her killed. You or Patel, same thing. What are you bringing into New York? I've seen the boxes at Nataraj Imports, the ones with the red stamps."

Lateef's face hardens. "You know what, *Sardarji*? I'm not fucking talking to you, okay? The Hammer is getting desperate if he thinks one single guy can scare me. You want to shoot me, go ahead. *Fuck you*."

Lateef stares into the glare of the headlights, his eyes hot with anger. Ranjit has seen men like this: Lateef desperately wants to prove how tough he is, and inflicting violence on him will only make him more stubborn.

There is no time for this bullshit.

Out of the corner of his eye, Ranjit sees a dark shadow scuttle across the concrete and remembers what Tiwari had said, that first night in the diner. *It's worth a try.*

He hands the car keys to Leela. "Look in the trunk. I need some rope."

She nods, and walks to the back of the car. Lateef strains to see them, held back only by the Glock pointed at him.

"So you're going to tie me up now? Why don't you have the whore do it? At least it'll be more pleasant that way. And I have to warn you. My bodyguards are going to check in with the hotel . . . about now. If I haven't arrived, they'll come looking for me. Sorry, *Sardarji*, you're out of time."

"There's no rope, but look at this." Leela holds up a big roll of black electrician's tape.

"That will do."

Ranjit steps to one side, keeping Lateef in his sights. "Sit down and put your arms back, around the column. If you move, I'll shoot you in the right toe, okay? Not fatal, just a lot of blood, and you'll have a hard time balancing for the rest of your life. Deal?"

Fear flickers across the man's face, but he quickly sneers. "Fuck you

and fuck your whore. Tying me up isn't going to make any difference."
But he complies, and sits with his back to the column.

"Leela, tape his hands behind him." Ranjit keeps the gun steady.

She walks behind Lateef, and there is the rip of tape coming off
the roll, the sharp intake of Lateef's breath as she yanks his hands behind the column and binds his wrists together. In the darkness, with
her sari unraveling around her, her platinum blond hair gleaming, she
looks like an avenging angel.

As Leela heads back to the car, Lateef leans forward, tugging hard,
but he cannot move. The garage roof is leaking, and he blinks as water
drips onto his head. "Fuck you. What are you going to do to me?"

"Nothing."

Ranjit sticks the Glock into his waistband, and pulls open the front
door of the limo. From the floor he picks up Tiwari's half-eaten box of
pancakes, syrup leaking out of it. Walking over to Lateef, he opens the
box, takes out a pancake slick with syrup, and slips it into the man's
shirt.

"Hey! What the fuck? Are you mad?"

Ranjit methodically pours the remaining syrup from the box all
over Lateef's chest and lap. Stepping back, he surveys his handiwork:
Lateef's pink shirt and tan pants are coated in syrup, and he squirms as
the pancake slides down his chest, coming to rest over his belly.

"This is your town, right?" Ranjit moves close enough to smell the
sweet, synthetic maple syrup. "So you must know the figures. Eight
million people, and they say there are four rats per person, so that's . . .
thirty-two million rats . . ."

"Rats? Who gives a shit about rats?"

". . . and the garbage strike is bringing them out. I read in *The
Times* that they're getting into mortuaries and eating cadavers. You
know what else I read?" He watches the color fade from Lateef's face.
"There was this baby, left alone in a housing project in the Bronx? It
had food on its face? By the time its mother came back, an hour later,
the rats had eaten half her face."

"This bullshit isn't going to work with me—"

Ranjit shrugs. "Suit yourself. I've seen ones up here as big as my arm. Come on, Leela."

"Fuck you."

Ranjit and Leela get back into the limo. He turns off the headlights and it is suddenly pitch black. He thinks of what happened in the backseat, minutes ago, and feels sick.

"I'm so sorry. I didn't think he would try anything in the car . . ."

He can't see her face in the darkness, but her voice, when it comes, is hollow.

"So now you've seen what they make me do. You think I'm a whore."

"No, no, don't talk like that." He pulls her head against his shoulder, and feels the feathery texture of her blond weave.

"Bastard." She frees herself and peers through the windshield. "I want him to pay. Are there really rats up here?"

"I wasn't lying. I've seen huge ones."

She strains forward to see better, her clenched fists pushing down into the leather seat. He remembers her on the beach, digging her fists into the sand, and feels again the anger stored up inside her.

Soon their eyes adjust to the darkness. Behind Lateef is a view of Midtown, a million lights shining through the slanting rain. The man is just sitting there, he's even smiling. This isn't going to work. Ranjit will have to beat the information out of him.

Leela nudges him. "Look," she says softly. "That far corner. See it?"

He follows her pointing finger: one flickering shadow is joined by another, and he catches a glimpse of long, hairless tails.

Lateef must have been looking the other way. His sudden scream cuts through the darkness, and his feet slap frantically against the concrete deck.

"Fuck you! *Aaah,* get them off me!"

Ranjit is about to flip on the headlights but Leela's hand closes around his wrist.

"Wait."

The shouting grows louder, turns into a howl of anguish.

"Leela—"

"Wait."

"*Aaaah,* no, no, no . . ." The man's scream ends in a sobbing wail.

"Okay, now."

Ranjit leans forward and the blue tungsten headlights cut through the darkness. Lateef's head is flung back, his open mouth like a pink cave. Two shadows streak down his chest and make for the wall.

"*Maderchod. Maderchod.* I'll kill you. I'll . . . I'll . . ." Tears are streaming down his pitted cheeks.

Leela is the first to get out. The blue light shines on the silk of her sari and catches the side of her emotionless face. Her voice is flat. "We can turn the headlights off again."

"Fuck you, *bitch.*"

She snaps her fingers and Ranjit kills the light.

"No. No. Okay, okay . . ."

Ranjit turns on the headlights again, and this time Lateef doesn't even lift his head. He sags forward, breathing hard, and there is a rip in his pink shirt, just over his stomach. When he looks up his eyes are liquid with terror.

Ranjit leans against the car as he speaks, no longer bothering with the gun.

"So. Let's try this again. You guys had Shabana killed. Why?"

"No, *yaar,* no." Lateef shakes his head. "You're not listening. We didn't kill Shabana. She did blab about going to the cops, but that bitch, she was high most the time. No one took her seriously."

"So who killed her? The tooth fairy? Don't say Mohan, because I won't believe you."

Lateef hesitates. "Patel, it was his idea."

"His idea to kill her?"

"No, no. He didn't kill her, he's soft on her. He sent her sister over to talk to her. The sister has always been . . . more reasonable."

"Ruksana? What does she have to do with this?"

"I'm just telling you what Patel told *me.* He sent the sister around one night to talk to Shabana, to warn her to keep her mouth shut. Next thing we know, Shabana's dead. Ruksana identified the body, bullshit-ted the cops, then fucking vanished."

"Shabana's own sister killed her?"

"Yes. You don't believe me? Those two bitches hated each other's guts. The sister, Ruksana, her face, the left side, there's something wrong. That's why she wears that pancake makeup, and she blames Shabana for it. Ruksana killed her, *yaar*. Why else would she run?"

Leela rolls her eyes. "Liar. Should we turn out the headlights again?"

"No. No. *Listen to me*." Lateef's voice is pleading now, and his pit-ted face glistens with sweat. "Look, I'm not trying to protect Patel, okay? I hate that *chutiya*. My uncle sent me from Mumbai to manage this business, but Patel, he thinks I'm, I'm a *lafanga*, a no-good, he won't tell me anything. Fuck him. I'm going to take care of him soon."

Lateef's face is sullen with resentment. He really does hate Patel.

"So what are you doing in New York?"

Lateef regains some of his original bluster. "My uncle wanted me to get out of Mumbai. Too much killing going on there, and I'm what they call a 'high-value' target, because I'm like his son, see? So he sent me to New York. We bankrolled Patel's hair business, and he's doing really well now, his income stream is . . . huge. He says it's all legit, all from hair. Bullshit. You don't earn that much by selling weaves—"

"So what business is Patel really in?"

Lateef glares at him. "I'm *trying* to tell you, *yaar*. Patel insists that he's making all the money from hair, but I don't believe him. He's got to be bringing in other stuff too, but he won't tell me what. But listen, listen, I've got it all figured out, okay? I have this guy inside customs, he's going to delay Patel's next shipment, and take a look inside the boxes. Smart, *hanh*?"

Lateef's pitted face creases into a smile. "Once I find out, then it's good-bye Patel. Fuck him. I can run Nataraj Imports with one hand tied behind my back. I'll show my uncle what I can do . . ." Lateef stops and tries to look amiable. "Okay, listen, *Sardarji*, I don't know what your game is, okay? But soon I'm going to be running this show, and I can use a tough guy like you. Whatever the Hammer is paying you, I'll double it. I mean, clearly, you're a smart guy . . . this thing with the rats, very smart, very smart . . ." His voice fizzles out, and he keeps smiling, but his eyes are worried.

"Let me see if I understand." Ranjit counts on his right hand. "One, Shabana's sister killed her. Two, Patel is getting rich, and says it's off the hair, but you don't believe him. Three, you don't know what he's actually bringing in, but you're going to take over his operation in New York."

"Yes." The queasy smile stays on Lateef's face.

"Okay, thank you for nothing."

"Hey, I answered your questions, now let me go—"

Ranjit gestures to his phone. "Don't worry, I'll call Patel and tell him where you are."

"Hey. *Hey.*" Tears of rage fall down Lateef's face as Ranjit and Leela get into the car. "*Maderchod, bahinchod.* I'll cut your balls off, I'll . . . hey, don't leave me, you fuck—"

Ranjit backs the Lincoln up and the headlights sweep across the column, illuminating Lateef's twisted face. His shouts die away as the car curves down the ramp, each turn of the wheel sending a shiver of pain down Ranjit's broken arm.

Chapter Twenty-Nine

They emerge from the garage and speed down Forty-third Street. The tall, concrete hulk of the garage recedes behind them, hidden by the rain.

Ranjit looks over at Leela. "You think Lateef was telling the truth?"

"He's lying. I *know* that they killed Shabana. He's covering his ass for sure. And Patel's going to go crazy when he finds what we just did. He'll just pick up the phone and call immigration. My mother and Dev—" She sees Ranjit wincing. "Hey, are you okay?"

"Don't worry about Patel, I'll call him and work it out. Can you drive us back to your place? My arm is killing me . . ."

She nods, and Ranjit brings the limo to a halt at a deserted bus stop on Second Avenue. They exchange seats, and to his surprise, she drives swiftly and confidently, cutting off other cars. When he fumbles with his phone, she gestures to him to put it away.

"Wait. Lateef has to pay for what he did to me."

"Leela. It's been five minutes, and those rats have rabies—"

"Not yet."

The limo speeds down Second Avenue. Ranjit leans back in the passenger's seat, looking out at the city. Even in the pouring rain, there are solitary dog walkers out, accompanied by their small, inbred dogs. He hears the wail of sirens, hears the slosh of water flowing into the gutters.

"Okay, that's enough. If we wait any longer, there's not going to be too much of Lateef left."

"Let the bastard suffer."

"Leela, for God's sake . . ."

"No. Not yet."

She turns onto FDR Drive, merging into the swiftly flowing traffic.

Normally this is Ranjit's favorite highway in New York, curving alongside the East River. He likes the red neon cursive of the Pepsi-Cola sign across the river, he likes the speed, the feeling of possessing, in one sweep, this entire swathe of the city. But right now, all he can think of is Lateef, tied to the pillar. The rats will be quicker this time, knowing exactly where their food is; they are intelligent animals, after all.

"Leela, please, it's been almost fifteen minutes." Fifteen minutes of sheer terror, fifteen minutes that will haunt Lateef's dreams.

"You don't care about what he did to me? *Hanh*? All you men are the same. Pigs."

He stares at her in amazement, realizing that years and years of humiliation are stored up inside her. And because he has witnessed this latest humiliation, he is now complicit in what happened, he has become one of her tormentors.

"Leela, this is not about you. I need Lateef alive, I'm calling Patel."

Dialing Patel's number, he remembers that the man goes to bed early, nine or nine thirty, an odd time for a nightclub owner.

The phone rings for a long time before there is a gruff "Hello?"

"Patel Sahib. It's Ranjit Singh."

"It's late, Ranjit. You know better than to call me at this time. This better be important."

Ranjit can hear the *clack-clack-clack* of Patel typing away on his laptop.

"It is late, yes, sir." He pauses, then plunges in. "Your friend, Lateef, he's on the top floor of a garage at 211 East Forty-third Street, tied to a column. I recommend you send someone over there right away. There are a lot of rats around, he could get bitten."

"*Hai Ram.* Wait."

Ranjit hears the *beep-beep-beep* of Patel dialing another number on a landline, and then a rushed conversation in Hindi.

When Patel returns, his voice is breathless. "You did well, Ranjit. That boy is under my charge. What happened? Who did this?"

"Well . . . I did."

There is a stunned silence. "Are you *crazy*? Do you know who this boy is? He is *Don Hajji Mustafa's* nephew. You have just signed your own death warrant."

Ranjit presses the phone to his ear and chooses his words carefully. "Sir, Lateef was molesting a woman who works in your club. I had to step in."

"For this you tied him up in a garage? And then you call me? I am talking to a corpse. You are a dead man, definitely dead—"

"You know what Lateef does to the girls at your club. He was doing the same thing to Shabana before she died. You know and you don't care. But more important is what Lateef told me about Nataraj Imports."

There is a suppressed grunt of anger. "Nataraj? Keep talking."

"Sir, Lateef is convinced that all your money from the hair business isn't legitimate. He thinks you're using the hair shipments to bring in something else, but you won't tell him what. You won't even tell him who supplies the hair—"

"So what? This is not news to me."

"So Lateef is planning to delay your next shipment in customs—he has a contact there—and examine it. He's going to find out what you're bringing in, and how. And after that, he'll kill you. He'll take over your whole operation."

There is silence again. "And he told you this why?"

"He is afraid of rats. Very afraid." Ranjit pauses and clears his throat. "Sir, I'm offering you this information in good faith. You take care of

Lateef, get him off my back, and I'll find Mohan for you. I'm very close."

There is dead silence. Ranjit can hear Patel's bare feet slap against the floor as he paces up and down his motel room in New Jersey.

They are now crossing the East River, and a subway train clatters by, its tracks going down the center of the Williamsburg Bridge. Ranjit stares blindly at the lit train windows, conscious that his life hangs in the balance, and in that moment, New York—the dark river below, the train speeding by, the red taillights of the traffic—seems unbearably precious.

Patel's voice is exasperated. "You have some nerve, *Sardarji*."

"Sir, do we have a deal?" Ranjit holds his breath.

"Let me explain the situation to you. Don Hajji Mustafa has six daughters. *Six.* This boy is his heir. The Don is an old friend, but he's blind when it comes to Lateef, he thinks that the sun shines out this boy's arse. I'll try to reach the Don, explain that this was all a mistake, but . . . he's not the easiest man to contact right now, he has his own problems. So I cannot guarantee anything. You will have no trouble from me, but Lateef . . . I cannot control him. The best thing you can do is bring Mohan to me, and fast. I pay you, and you vanish, understand?"

"Crystal clear, sir. And one more thing. In the alley behind your club, behind the Dumpster. Lateef's chauffeur, Tiwari, he's sleeping off some sedatives. It's raining, and I'm concerned he'll get pneumonia. I put some cardboard cartons over him, but . . ."

"You're pushing it, *Sardarji*." The line goes dead.

Ranjit leans back into his seat, the phone still in his hand.

Leela turns to look at him. "Patel agreed? He isn't angry? My mother and Dev . .

"He won't do anything right now. He still needs me to find Mohan."

"But later . . . ?"

"One thing at a time." Ranjit opens his eyes as they speed down Atlantic Avenue into Brooklyn.

They hit some traffic and Leela screeches to a stop.

"*One thing at a time.* You like to say that, don't you? How can you be so relaxed? That bastard Lateef is going to come after us now . . ."

"Patel will slow him down. It's in his interest that I find Mohan."

"That lying bastard Lateef, trying to blame the murder on Ruksana. You know what Shabana told me? He beat her so badly that she wet herself. He did that to her, to a grown woman." Her hands clench the steering wheel. "I hope the rats did some real damage.

The traffic starts to move again, and Leela speeds up, weaving through the cars.

Ranjit imagines Lateef still lying in the garage in the darkness: the feeling of claws scuttling over his skin, the wiry brush of whiskers, then the sudden, ferocious burrowing of teeth into flesh and bone.

Ranjit had only intended to frighten the man, not to torture him. As an army captain, Ranjit has seen plenty of violence, but always for a tactical purpose. Violence for its own sake is pointless, and ultimately degrades its perpetrators. But Leela is in no mood to hear this right now, so he keeps his mouth shut and lets her drive.

He breaks the silence when they're close to Richmond Hill. "We have to ditch this car. They'll be looking for it. Pull over near the next subway stop, we'll leave the keys in the ignition, it'll be gone in ten minutes."

"I have a better idea. Plus, I don't feel like walking right now."

"What?"

"Wait and see. Just make sure the gun is out of sight, and behave friendly, okay? My friends do not have the best impression of you."

Half an hour later they walk the last block toward Leela's house. At one A.M., the neighborhood is silent and dark, and the only sound is their footsteps.

A few minutes earlier they dropped the limo off just around the corner. Leela's "friends" were out, the big man—his nose taped—and his smaller, weasel-faced buddy, talking and sipping from a bottle of rum. They reached for their guns when Ranjit emerged from the car, still wearing Tiwari's blazer, but Leela calmed them down, and their eyes lit up when she handed over the car keys. The big man slid into the front and cooed over the leather seats, but then cursed loudly when his hands came away sticky with syrup.

Sticky or not, the men promised Leela that the car would vanish into the chop shops behind Shea Stadium. By the next afternoon, it would exist only as a collection of parts. They offered to share the money with Leela, but she smiled sweetly and declined; instead, she asked them to keep an eye out for Lateef and his two thugs.

"More Indians? What is it with you and the Indians?" the small, weasel-faced man asked, and both men agreed that Indians from India were bad news: they were snobbish, treated the Guyanese like black people, and had no sense of rhythm.

The car was driven away, and Leela and Ranjit walked the few blocks to her house.

Now Ranjit speaks, his voice low as they walk up to Leela's front door. "Can you trust those guys? They seem like jokers."

"They stopped you before, didn't they?" Leela turns her key in the door, and they step into the darkened house.

He recognizes its smell now, of cooking and tea and old incense, and he realizes how familiar it has already become. Walking down the corridor, they see Auntie snoring gently in her bed, with Dev splayed out next to her.

Leela hurries into the bathroom and he waits in the living room, hearing the slither of her sari coming off, then the splash and gurgle of water as she rinses out her mouth, again and again.

He slumps back on the couch, wishing he could take a Percocet, but he's sworn not to. Besides, he needs to be clear-headed and assess the situation: there are only two days left till the grand jury trial, and he has no lawyer, and no evidence to show the cops. And despite what he told Leela, as soon as Lateef recovers, he will come after them, full strength.

"Ranjit. What are you doing?"

Leela stands at the door to the living room. She is barelegged, wearing a long, shapeless T-shirt down to her knees.

"Nothing. Just sitting." Without the extra height of her heels, she looks small and helpless, but now he knows the fury she is capable of.

"You need to get some sleep, Ranjit."

"I'll be okay on the couch. You go ahead."

"Come with me. Look, I'm sorry about what I said in the car. I didn't mean it, okay?"

She pulls him to his feet and leads him to her bedroom. Her yellow and orange sari lies in a crumpled ball in the corner.

Getting into bed, she gestures to him. "Hold me. Please."

He lies facing her and reaches across her with his broken arm, the plaster rough against her soft skin. "Leela, tomorrow, first thing, you take Auntie and Dev and go somewhere else for a few days. Can you get out of the city?"

Leela stiffens. "Yes. One of my mother's cousins lives in Ossining. You think that Lateef . . . ?"

"It's better not to take a chance."

She shivers and burrows her face into his chest. "Closer. Hold me closer."

He pulls her tighter, smelling the mint of her mouthwash and the tired, raw odor of her body. Her body has the tension of a strung bow, but he holds her close, and soon her shoulders slump and her body sinks down into the mattress.

Asleep, she looks as peaceful as a child, with her long eyelashes and small mouth relaxed into a half smile. He wants to forget the awfulness of tonight, to erase it from his memory. Leela must have led such a lonely and frightened life; no wonder she went to Jamaica Bay to pray, to make offerings to the dirty water.

He lies awake next to her, his brain ticking over. Despite what Leela thinks, Lateef seemed to be telling the truth—he'd spoken while still in the thrall of fear, without enough time to make up an alternate version of the events.

Is it possible that Shabana was killed by her sister? Lateef said that

Ruksana has fled, gone back to India. Is it a coincidence that Mohan has vanished, too? Has Ranjit been looking at all this wrong? He feels the ground crumbling under his feet.

He floats in and out of sleep, half listening for footsteps outside, for the creak of a window being opened. There is only the sound of cicadas, and he is almost asleep when he hears something.

He is instantly awake, and tries to disentangle himself from Leela, but she clings to him, and precious seconds pass. He pulls free, is turning, when he feels a hand on the back of his neck.

He jerks around, his heart hammering.

"Leela." Dev is standing there, eyes half closed, holding his striped pajamas up with both hands.

"Hey," Ranjit whispers. "Your mama is sleeping, okay? What do you need?"

Dev's face contorts and he is about to cry.

"You need to go to the bathroom?"

Dev nods. Getting carefully out of bed, Ranjit scoops up the child—he is heavy, solidly built for a four-year-old—and takes him into Leela's bathroom. Pulling Dev's pajamas down, Ranjit plonks him on the toilet, and holds him till he hears the tinkling in the bowl. Picking Dev up, he heads in the direction of Auntie's room, but the child whimpers and clings to him.

Walking to the living room, Ranjit sinks down onto the hot, plastic-covered couch, and Dev sighs and falls deeply asleep in his arms. Ranjit hears the child's breathing, feels his sweaty head against his own arm, and remembers that at this age, Shanti used to have nightmares and cry out in her sleep; he would spend hours sitting with her in his lap.

In a few minutes he'll deposit Dev back into bed with Auntie, but the minutes pass, and Ranjit does not move. He stays on the couch with Dev heavy in his lap, and the child sleeps on without stirring.

Chapter Thirty

NEW YORK, 2011

Outside the windows of the Dakota, New York City shimmered with heat. Shabana did not want to leave her apartment, but Maria, the cleaning woman, was coming at noon, and the sight of the short, buxom woman cleaning up—the kitchen sink was piled high with crusted dishes, the bedroom was strewn with dirty clothes—made Shabana feel ashamed.

She preferred to leave, and to return four hours later, when the shining, immaculate apartment would always fill her with a sense of hope. Every week she would wander through the clean rooms, vowing that this time would be different: she wouldn't take so many sleeping pills, and she wouldn't pluck out her hair. But as the dirty dishes piled up, as she stripped off her clothes and crawled, like an animal, into bed, the apartment would lose its luster. Once again, she would sink into a deep depression.

Not this week. She would go out now, despite the heat, and walk through the park for an hour. She desperately needed to lose weight: all the alcohol and takeout had thickened her waist and made her breasts balloon. Slipping on a white T-shirt and jeans, she put on one of her flower-shaped gold earrings, but couldn't find the other. They were the only things she had inherited from her mother—all the rest of Nusrat's jewelry had been sold—and she felt panicked.

Shabana scrabbled through piles of crumpled tissues on her dresser, crouched and looked underneath, but found nothing, except tangled balls of her hair. Maria would be arriving any minute, so she gave up and left her ears bare.

Scribbling a note for Maria about the lost earring, Shabana rode the elevator down and walked past the doorman, not acknowledging his wave. After years of being waited on, she did not even notice servants anymore.

Someone had—yet again—left a bouquet of roses at the entrance to the Dakota, at the exact spot where John Lennon had been shot. The roses, browning in the heat, darkened Shabana's mood further, and she hurried across the road. Lennon, dead, had vanished into his own myth; Shabana was alive, but felt distinctly like a ghost. For the past three months—ever since her comeback film fell through—she had been holed up at the Dakota, talking to no one, and avoiding Ruki's hectoring phone calls.

Shabana walked briskly into Central Park, passing the lake and the Great Lawn, all the way up to the reservoir. She started a loop around it, but the flat surface of the water glinted like a mirror, hurting her eyes. To make things worse, runners thundered past her every few minutes, leaving the sour odor of their bodies.

She decided to head back in the direction of the Great Lawn, and by the time she got there she was hot and sweaty. She found a patch of shade at the edge of the giant oval, and sat cross-legged. The grass here had been eroded by hundreds of bodies, so that the earth showed through, and it reminded her of the Hanging Gardens in Mumbai.

She remembered a scorching day, so hot that she had to be careful when she mounted Sanjeev's motorbike, lest its fuel tank burn her thighs. They'd driven to the Hanging Gardens, and, finding the benches full, had sat under an old, shady tree. Other lovers had been there before them, and carved remembrances into the tree trunk, hearts and names in English and Marathi.

"That's so silly." Shabana had pointed to the tree. "Nobody will see their names."

Sanjeev had taken out his worn Swiss Army knife, flicked open a blade, and deftly carved into the bark "Sanjeev loves Shabana," the letters outlined in oozing sap.

"Nobody will see it, but we'll know it's there," he had said quietly, and she'd felt a sudden surge of love for this half boy, half man.

Now, sitting in Central Park, Shabana wondered if the tree bark had grown back, obliterating their names. And that memory of Sanjeev led to others, which threatened to engulf her, and she decided to head back home to the Dakota.

Home. The apartment belonged to Jayram Patel—well, he called himself Jay Patel now—but he'd said that she could stay as long as she liked. Ruki kept berating her, telling her that she had to move to her own place, had to find more work, but she liked having the big, echoing apartment all to herself. Besides, the Dakota was full of people like her, people who had been famous once; just last week she'd taken the elevator down with an aging movie star from the seventies, and there had been an unspoken, sympathetic understanding between the two women.

As soon as Shabana opened the apartment door she heard the whine of a vacuum cleaner.

"Maria! It's me. Did you find my earring? Hello?"

Walking down the corridor to the living room, she stopped in the doorway. Maria was vacuuming the living room rug, her dark hair twisted up, her too-short blouse showing a slice of plump midriff. And standing next to her was a slim Hispanic man with long, greasy hair, his torso bare, so thin that his ribs showed. He hurriedly put down the dust rag he was holding and pulled on a faded black T-shirt.

"I'm sorry, madam." Maria switched off the vacuum. "I didn't know you would be coming back so soon. This is my friend, he is helping me clean."

Ignoring the man, Shabana addressed Maria. "Did you find an earring? A gold one? I left you a note on the dining table."

"Gold?" Maria furrowed her high forehead. "Madam, I don't know about any gold. I did not take anything—"

"*Oof*, you didn't see my note? Flower shaped, with a pearl in the center?"

"Miss Shah." The man stepped forward. His voice was shockingly deep. "I saw something in the kitchen sink. Let me take a look."

Without waiting for her reply, he walked toward the kitchen with a loose-limbed stride, and she followed him. He pointed into the newly cleaned stainless steel sink, and she caught a glimpse of something shiny, caught inside the drain.

She tried to reach in, but her fingers wouldn't fit through the metal sink guard. "Can you get it out for me?"

"Got a screwdriver?"

"There might be one, but I don't know—this is not my apartment, you see—"

"It's okay." Pulling out a slim knife from a drawer, he inserted its tip into one of the screws that held the guard in place. With a few twirls, he undid it, then the others, working precisely, lining up the screws on the counter.

Shabana started to reach into the sink, but he motioned her back. "Let me do it. It could fall in."

She watched as he lowered two long fingers into the drain and gently pulled out her mother's earring, coated in black muck. He rinsed it off before placing it in the palm of her hand.

"Thank you. Here, let me give you something—" Shabana reached for her handbag and pulled out a twenty.

The man's face turned red. "*Nahi, nahi, madam. Paise ke zaroorat nahi.*" No, no, madam. There is no need for money.

Shabana was stunned. "You're Indian? But I thought that—"

"*Aare*, everybody thinks I'm Puerto Rican. I'm Mohan Kumar, from Punjab."

His English was fluent. She noticed that he had intelligent

brown eyes, and a chiseled face with a dimpled chin. "Oh. I'm Sha-bana—"

Mohan bowed slightly. "I know who you are, madam. *Aaap bahut mashoor actress hai.*" You are a famous actress.

Maria appeared in the doorway and was watching them, her eyes darting from Mohan's face to Shabana's. Now she stepped between them.

"Mohan, we have to finish cleaning. And madam." She addressed Shabana sullenly. "I have done the laundry, but there is a pile of clothes I cannot wash. Silk needs to be dry-cleaned."

"Oh." Shabana had been throwing her dirty *kameez* and crumpled saris into a corner. "Can you take them to the dry cleaner's for me?"

"We are too busy, madam." Maria smiled mirthlessly. "Come, Mohan."

"Wait." Mohan smiled accommodatingly. "Miss Shah, I'd be happy to take them to the cleaner's for you. I know a good Indian place in Jackson Heights, they'll do it in a day."

He followed Shabana to her bedroom and waited as she scooped up the silk clothes and put them into a plastic shopping bag. They smelled strongly of her perfume, and she felt very self-conscious handing them over, but he took the clothes without comment, bowed again, and promised he would return the next evening.

Shabana remained in her bedroom as Maria and Mohan continued cleaning. She opened her door a crack and heard Maria's angry whispers, followed by Mohan's mild replies.

After they left, the apartment was silent and gleaming. Shabana walked through it, her hand trailing along the wooden wainscoting, feeling a strange excitement.

Don't be silly, she thought to herself. *Mohan is your cleaning lady's boyfriend. Ruki would die laughing if she found out.*

But a part of her didn't care. She thought about Mohan's deft fingers unscrewing the drain guard, the look of concentration on his boyish face, the way he gently rinsed off her earring before handing it back to her.

Maybe she *was* being very silly, but a part of her was also planning ahead: she had kept a few crumpled saris back, and would ask him to dry-clean those as well. So she would see him at least twice this week, and with any luck, alone.

That evening Shabana ate a small salad for dinner, carefully rinsed off her plate, and put it in the dishwasher. And as she sat in the dark apartment, hardly listening to the voices on television, she did not feel the urge to pluck her hair.

Her mind was racing ahead, thinking of what she would wear when she saw Mohan again, and what she would say. She decided on a pink *salwar kameez,* and she would sit by the living room window, where the light was good. She would have some *samosas* delivered, and some *jalebis*—the man looked like he could use some food.

She no longer felt like the old, unseen, shameful Shabana. Quietly, without even realizing it, she began to play a different role.

III

THE WOMAN IN RED

The one who only performs hollow religious rituals
Is like the unwanted bride decorating her body.
Her husband, the Lord, does not come to her bed,
And day after day she grows miserable.
She does not attain the mansion of his presence.
She does not find the door to his house.

—Guru Granth Sahib, Siree Raag

Chapter Thirty-One

The next morning, Ranjit wakes to complete silence, a ray of sunlight falling across his face. He is somehow back in Leela's bed. Squinting into the light, he remembers how she had come to him during the night, taken Dev from his arms, and led him back here. They'd slept all night with the child between them.

Now they are gone. Leela's pillow lies on the floor, and the sheet on her side is crumpled and half pulled off the mattress. He listens hard for her voice, for Auntie's low, incessant grumbling, for Dev's laughter, but all he can hear is the ticking of the clock somewhere deep in the house. Reaching under his pillow, he grips the plastic handle of the Glock and slides it out.

Holding the gun flat against his leg, he walks barefoot down the corridor, peering into the empty rooms, the ticking of the clock growing no louder or softer, just muffled and consistent. Trying to squelch his rising panic, he walks into the kitchen and touches the knuckles of his gun hand to the blue teapot sitting on the table: stone cold.

There is a sound from the backyard. Raising the gun, he steps through the screen door: the long rectangle of prickly grass is empty, and the huge tree at the end casts a short shadow. The sunflowers in the flower bed nod their round, battered heads, and bees buzz about the faded blue hydrangeas.

He hears a slither and turns, the gun coming up automatically.

Leela walks around the side of the house, her head turned, dragging a heavy coil of garden hose behind her. When she sees him, she gasps and drops the hose.

Slipping the gun into his waistband, he raises his hands in apology. "Sorry. Where are Auntie and Dev?"

"Jesus, you scared the crap out of me."

Her blond weave is gone, and her own black, curly hair peeks out from under her sweat-stained brown bandanna. She's wearing a faded T-shirt with John Lennon on it, her cutoff jean shorts, and has a smear of mud on her cheek.

She wipes sweat off her face, making a bigger smear. "You told me to send them away, remember?"

"That's right. And I told you to go, too."

Without answering, she walks past him, dragging the hose. Turning on a faucet, she methodically waters the flower bed, the water swirling over the dry soil for a moment before sinking down into it. He smells the familiar, comforting odor of wet earth.

"Why don't you get ready?" She speaks with her back to him. "I've put some fresh clothes on Dev's bed."

She seems completely absorbed in her task, so he does as he is told and goes back inside.

On the bed are a faded blue denim shirt and a worn pair of khakis. He showers and puts them on, and Leela's father's clothes so worn that they feel like wearing someone else's skin. When he walks back into the kitchen, she looks up from making tea, and her eyes widen. She does not say anything, but when she walks past him to get bread, her hand gently brushes the fabric of his shirt.

The two of them stand at the kitchen table, having cleared away the remains of their breakfast—tea again, and sugar toast. Now they both stare at the items that Ranjit had taken from Shabana's dressing room:

the photograph of her in the white *salwar kameez,* the square of cardboard with the red stamp on it, the key ring, the bottle of sleeping pills, and the long skein of glistening black hair.

Leela reaches out and fingers the blue-black hair. "This is really good quality, must be premium-quality Remi—that's virgin Indian hair, never cut, never dyed. The girls at the club are always bitching about how expensive it is."

She picks up the Mickey Mouse key ring and her voice rises. "Hey, these two are keys to the Dakota, I recognize them. They're these old-fashioned keys, with lots of teeth, they can't be copied." She splays out the keys, and looks at the other three. "And these look like apartment keys, too. Look: big one for an outer door, smaller one for the apartment door, and this one looks like a mailbox key. They're not for the Dakota, though."

He leans in. "But why would Shabana have keys for another apartment . . ." They both nod, struck by the same thought. "Ruksana's apartment. Right. Of course, she'd have keys to her sister's place. Kikiben said that she had her hair delivered there."

"So, she had keys to two apartments. So what?" Leela runs her fingers meditatively across the deeply serrated edges of the Dakota keys.

"Shabana could have left the evidence at her sister's place." He looks up. "We have to check it out."

Leela brings an old Dell laptop from her room, and they look online, but there is no listing for a Ruksana Shah, though there are eighty-seven R. Shahs in the New York area.

"We don't have time for this." Ranjit reaches for his cell phone. "I'll call Kikiben, she knows where the hair was sent."

The number barely rings twice before it is answered. "Nataraj Imports. Fine quality hair, expedited shipping."

"Kikiben, it's Ranjit, I—"

"Ranjit." The pleasure in her voice is unmistakable. He imagines her in that tiny office, alone day after day. "So I talked to my niece Rohini, and it's all set, what do you say to next Saturday, *hanh*? She's a little shy, there is this place in Jackson Heights, of course I'll keep out of the way. You can meet her there at eleven, and—"

"That sounds lovely, Kikiben." He feels guilty even saying it. "And there is one other thing. I was telling a friend about Shabana and her sister—it's such an interesting story, isn't it—and I told him that Shabana's sister lived on the Upper West Side, but he kept insisting that she lives in Queens."

Kikiben lets out a birdlike cackle. "You're both wrong. The sister lives on the Upper East Side. Oh." Her voice drops to a whisper. "Ranjit, I have to go, Patel is here with that horrible man, Lateef, and he's in a bad mood. Call me later, okay?"

There is the sound of loud, angry voices in the background, and then Kikiben hangs up.

He turns to Leela. "Ruksana lives on the Upper East Side, but I couldn't get the address."

"I heard everything, that woman is so loud." Leela's slim nostrils flare. "Who are you meeting? Her niece? You never told me anything about—"

Ranjit isn't paying attention. He picks up the bottle of sleeping pills, turns it around and peers at the label. The prescription is made out to Shabana Shah, but the address is 1011 Lexington Avenue, Apartment 2R: that's on the Upper East Side of Manhattan.

"Hah. How stupid of me. The address is right on the bottle of medicine." He shows the label to Leela, who just stares angrily at him.

"This niece is Indian? Must be a doctor? Computer programmer? Nice woman, cooks curries and all that?"

"Leela, please. I had to sweet-talk the old lady. She really wanted me to meet her niece, so I agreed. It doesn't mean anything." He reaches out to touch her shoulder, but she moves away.

"Ranjit, don't lie to me, okay? You can't just come in here and . . . and . . . Dev is getting used to you."

"Leela, you have nothing to worry about. Now can we go? Please?"

"I . . . I have to change."

"And there is some mud on your cheek, too."

"I know. I don't need you to tell me that."

She stalks down the corridor, and he hears the bathroom door slam shut, followed by the shower being wrenched on. He gathers up all the stuff from the dining table, slides it back into the plastic bag, and waits for Leela to get ready.

The subway is running slow, and it takes an hour and a half to get to the Upper East Side. Emerging into the hot afternoon, it is as though they have traveled to a foreign country: the only black and brown faces here are the doormen in their uniforms. They walk past a florist's shop window displaying a fan of yellow orchids, a store selling handmade luggage, and another specializing in Louis XIV furniture.

"Wow, look at these prices. This is a pretty fancy part of town," Leela says in a soft voice.

He is relieved to hear her speak; all the way here she averted her face and stared into space. She wears a white T-shirt and jeans, her hair is covered with a clean white bandanna, and her eyes are hidden behind her plastic sunglasses; she is completely unrecognizable as Lenore, the club hostess.

"Ranjit, what will we do if Ruksana has a doorman? We can't just walk in."

"We'll figure it out."

"That's really your mantra, isn't it?" She smiles and slips her hand into his, her previous anger at him seemingly evaporated.

They stop outside Ruksana's apartment building, a fancy-looking brick edifice with Art Deco striations, and Ranjit's heart sinks: just the kind of place that will have a front desk and a doorman. But peering into the lobby, they see just a low-ceilinged room with a wall of mailboxes, and no one in sight.

Shabana's key turns easily in the front door, and they take the elevator up to the second floor. The original building must have been chopped up into smaller apartments, because the doors here are very close together.

Ranjit's guess proves correct. Unlocking the door to 2R, they walk into a minuscule, dark living room the size of a ship's cabin, its one window facing a blank brick wall.

Flicking on a light, he sees mango-yellow walls and a blue foldout futon couch with two pillows and a neatly folded cotton blanket. Off to one side is a galley kitchen, the face of the small refrigerator covered with neat rows of takeout menus. There are no photographs, no decorations, and everything is very neat; unlike her sister, Ruksana lives like a monk.

Ranjit finds the room sterile, but Leela seems entranced.

"Wow. It's so simple and clean. I've always wanted to live alone in an apartment like this." She points to a red enamel-and-chrome machine that sits on the kitchen counter. "She even has an Italian single-serve coffee machine. Those are expensive. And look, cacti." On the windowsill is a row of tiny potted cacti, all growing crooked toward the light.

Ranjit wonders why Ruksana sleeps in her living room. He heads down a short corridor, smelling something sharp in the air, and enters a much larger, sunny room that should be the bedroom. It has no furniture, the floor is covered with a paint-spattered tarp, and in the center sits an empty wooden easel. Along the walls are stacked more painted canvases, three and four deep.

Walking closer, he kneels and examines the paintings. They seem abstract, in luminescent whites and deep reds, interspersed with faint outlines in pencil.

"It's them." Leela stands in the doorway, her arms folded across her chest.

"What do you mean?" Puzzled, he steps back, and then he sees it.

Out of the fields of color two figures emerge, a red and a white one. He makes out oval faces, long necks, and long sweeps of hair.

"I see it now." He points to a painting where the two figures are clearer. "All the paintings are of the two sisters. Ruksana's been painting the same thing over and over, it's obsessive."

"There's a closet here."

Leela walks past him, moves a stack of canvases, and pulls open the accordion door. Inside are cans full of paintbrushes, neatly stacked palettes, and tubes of oil paint. Finding a shoebox in the corner, she squats and rifles through it.

"Hey, look at this." She waves a photograph at him. It is old and faded, the same photograph he'd seen in Shabana's bedroom, then at the club: she is a teenager, standing against a brick wall, but this time she wears a red *salwar kameez,* not a white one.

"That's the same picture Shabana had at the club." He gestures around the studio. "Search this room, see if you can find anything, okay? I'll take the other rooms."

He heads back, and starts with the kitchen. The cabinets are mostly empty, and unlined, so there is no place to hide anything. The fridge is empty except for a carton of soy milk—sour now—and a plastic carton of seaweed salad from a Korean deli, now rotten and brown. Her freezer has only ice cubes. The inside of her oven is pristine.

The living room is bare except for the futon, which he pulls off the wooden frame, then replaces. There is nothing hidden in these monastic, cell-like rooms.

He is about to go back to Leela when his phone rings. It is Kikiben, no doubt excited about Ranjit's date with her niece, and he lets it go to voice mail, but it immediately rings again. *Damn it, she's so persistent.* Standing by the living room window, he answers.

"Ranjit? Ranjit, listen." All the excitement has gone from Kikiben's voice. "I'm sorry, so sorry."

Ranjit stares out of the window at the blank brick wall outside. "Sorry about what?"

"Lateef. He must have been looking through the security tapes, he saw that you had come here to visit me. He started shouting at me, asking me why you had come here, how often we were in contact. I got frightened, I told him that you had just called, you wanted to know Ruksana's address. *Baba re,* he started abusing me, calling me an old cow—"

"Is Lateef still there?"

"No, no, he left quickly, he shouted at his men, they jumped into a car and . . . I think they're going to Ruksana's apartment. Ranjit? You're not there, are you?"

"No, no, of course not. Thank you, Kikiben."

Rushing into the back room, he finds Leela is still crouched over the shoebox of photographs.

"Talking to your girlfriend again? Meanwhile, look at what I found—"

She waves a photograph at him, but he brushes it aside, and yanks her to her feet.

"We have to leave, now, Lateef's men are coming here—"

"What? How did they find out?"

"Never mind. Let's go."

The two of them run out of the apartment, pulling the door shut, and Leela heads toward the elevator, but he pulls her in the other direction.

"There must be another way out. Always two exits, it's the fire code."

Running down the corridor, they pass endless apartment doors, till they finally reach a metal fire door. Ignoring the EMERGENCY EXIT ONLY sign, Ranjit pushes it open and they stumble down a short set of metal stairs to an asphalt parking lot below, crowded with cars parked nose to tail.

Emerging out on Lexington Avenue, they find themselves a hundred feet south of the building entry.

"There's no one here." Leela struggles to keep up with him, taking two strides to his one. "You freaked me out. What the hell happened?"

"Lateef was at Nataraj Imports, he found out that Kiki had been talking to me, and she told him that I'd been asking about Ruksana's address. I couldn't take a chance."

They have gone two blocks down the avenue when a black Lincoln goes past in the other direction. Inside are the two men in dark jackets, bored expressions on their faces. The driver is chewing bubble gum, and a large pink bubble blossoms from his mouth. When he sees them, the car swerves, and the bubble bursts.

Ranjit looks frantically down the street. Only tiny businesses and boutiques, no big department stores to duck into.

Tires squeal behind them as the Lincoln pulls a U-turn.

Leela points down the avenue. "There's a subway entrance at Sixty-eighth Street . . ."

Grabbing her hand, he begins to run. "Come on. Come on."

He sprints, she stumbles alongside him, and they make it another block, but the Lincoln is right behind them, drawing nearer. They reach Sixty-eighth Street, and Leela turns to the subway entrance on the corner, but Ranjit keeps moving.

"No. The trains are slow at this time. If the men catch us on the platform we'll be trapped."

"Are you sure—" Leela is so winded that she can barely speak.

He doesn't bother to answer, grasps her hand tighter, and pulls her out into moving traffic. Brakes screech, a car slams to a halt, and a man shouts, *Are you fucking crazy?* They are across one lane of traffic, then cut in front of a moving bus to reach the other side of Lexington Avenue.

Behind them, the Lincoln follows, changing lanes and positioning itself for a left-hand turn.

Ranjit and Leela run down Sixty-eighth Street, and tires squeal behind them as the Lincoln makes the left turn.

There is a sudden *woop-woop-woop* and, out of nowhere, a police cruiser appears, its red and white lights flashing. It is right behind the Lincoln, which surges forward, showing no signs of slowing down. The cruiser's siren becomes a loud wail, and an amplified voice screams, *Pull over! Right now!*

Right behind them, the Lincoln slows to a stop, the irate police cruiser behind it, bristling with lights.

"Slow down. Walk. Don't look back." Ranjit lets go of Leela's moist hand.

"How . . . how did you know . . . there was a cop at the corner? I didn't see anyone. . . ." Sweat runs down her face, and her words come out in a gasp.

He is equally winded, but tries not to show it. "There's a 'No left turn' sign at that crossing. Everyone ignores it. The cops sit in an alley back there and bust people who make that turn. I got two tickets right there."

When they reach another subway entrance, they glance back: the Lincoln is still stopped, and the cruiser sits motionless behind it, the policeman inside typing slowly on his laptop.

"The cop is pissed off, he'll take his time now. Come on, we'll take the train."

Grabbing onto Leela's hand again, Ranjit descends into the dim, piss-smelling gloom, just in time to make the downtown local.

It is packed, and as they push their way into the center of the car, Leela leans into him, mouthing something. He can't hear her above the roar and rattle, and just then his phone begins to ring. He grabs onto an overhead pole, gestures to her to wait, and presses the phone to his ear.

Ali's gruff voice is unmistakable. "Ranjit? We found the *maderchod*."

"Found who?" He strains to hear.

"That guy, *yaar*. Kishen, Mohan's cousin."

"You found him! Good."

"*Good*? After all this effort, you *bahinchud*, you say *good*? I've been busting my balls trying to track down this guy for you, and—"

"I'll name my second-born child after you, okay? Where is he?"

"Much better. Your friend, Kishen, he's working for a high-end garage in Chelsea. Tenth Avenue and Twenty-fifth Street, it's called Five Star Auto. One of our guys spotted him. Where are you? You need a ride?"

"No, I'm fine. Look, I'm on the subway, I can hardly hear you—" His phone goes dead, and he jams it into his pocket. Leela is staring at him, her face tense, something held in her hand.

"Don't worry, we're safe. That was Ali, they found Mohan's cousin."

"Ranjit, *listen* to me. This was in the shoebox in Ruksana's apartment."

She thrusts a photograph at him. It is an old Kodak print, faded over the years, and he recognizes the brick wall that forms its background, and the muddy lane. He stares at the two slim teenage girls standing against the wall, slightly apart. The straight-backed one in the

red *salwar kameez* is looking off to the side, her face in profile. The one in white is lost in her own thoughts, leaning her slim shoulders against the wall. The girls are identical.

"I don't understand." He peers at the photograph. "How is Shabana in the picture twice? Is this a trick photograph?"

Leela leans in and points. "The one in white is Shabana. The one in red, she's hiding one side of her face, that must be Ruksana."

He stares at the photograph. "But they're . . ."

". . . twins." Leela smiles triumphantly. "They are twins. Identical twins."

Ranjit stands in the rocking train, holding the photograph closer. He'd seen both photographs—the girl in white in Shabana's apartment, and the girl in red in Ruksana's apartment—and assumed they were both pictures of Shabana, in different clothes.

Now, examining the photograph closely, he sees that Shabana, in white, has thinner hair, and that Ruksana, in red, has turned away to hide her damaged cheek. But despite the differences, they are almost identical: slim and waiflike, their slender necks almost too fragile for their long, black waterfalls of hair.

Leela reaches forward and takes the photograph. "That's why Ruksana was hidden away all those years. You can't have two versions of a movie star."

Ranjit is wordless. *This changes everything.*

Two identical women: Ruksana in her dark, sad, tiny apartment, and Shabana across the park in her light-filled place at the Dakota. One a famous movie star, the other clearly obsessed with her sister, painting the two of them, over and over. It was almost as though Ruksana wanted to *be* Shabana, to inhabit her sister's life.

Now Ruksana has disappeared, and Mohan as well.

Ranjit can't ignore the most logical explanation any longer. Yes, Mohan was having an affair with Shabana, but clearly the relationship was an unequal one. Maybe Mohan tired of her and became involved with Ruksana; after all, Ruksana was just as beautiful as Shabana, but worse off, and Mohan was always a sucker for a woman in distress.

Maybe that night in the Dakota Mohan was with Ruksana when Shabana returned unexpectedly. The two sisters fought, there was some sort of struggle, and Shabana died. Why else would both Mohan and Ruksana go missing?

So Mohan *is* a murderer. Ranjit swallows hard when he thinks of what his old friend has done. Why is he always so shocked when people change? After all, Mohan always needed a woman, and Ruksana—beautiful, but damaged and deeply resentful of her famous sister—could have easily manipulated a man like him.

As the train rattles on, Ranjit stares at the dark window, seeing his own haggard reflection. Leela's head barely comes up to his shoulder, her white bandanna now darkened with sweat. She probably won't agree with his theory: she has seen Shabana humiliated at Club Ghungroo and has suffered the same fate at Lateef's hands. She desperately wants Patel and Lateef to be guilty, and he better keep his insights to himself for now.

And now Kishen, Mohan's cousin, has been found. Chelsea is close by, and with a change of trains, it will take twenty minutes to get there. If Kishen knows where Mohan is, chances are that Ruksana is with him. Ranjit can call the cops then, and maybe this whole thing will come to an end.

Ranjit sees a white-haired man reading *The New York Times,* and scans the headlines. Shabana's murder has long since disappeared from the front page, replaced by the garbage strike. There is concern that the piles of festering garbage and the attendant rats will spread medieval diseases throughout the city: the bubonic plague is mentioned.

The train begins to slow, and there is a rustle as people prepare to disembark. Ranjit squares his shoulders, looks at Leela, and nods at the door.

Chapter Thirty-Two

Five Star Auto is a small garage on the far west side of Chelsea, its business spilling out onto the street. Sleek Teslas, Porsches, and Alfa Romeos are parked on the oil-stained sidewalk, and a few harried-looking mechanics are hooking up the cars to mobile diagnostic terminals. There are other repair shops on this street, their façades covered in looping graffiti, and farther down, in what used to be garages, is the latest incarnation of New York's art scene: spartan, white-washed galleries that earn more selling one or two pieces than the garages make in a year. Like the rest of Manhattan, Chelsea has been gentrified, and the last remnants of its industrial past are being wiped out.

The mechanics at Five Star Auto work frantically, shouting to each other, oblivious of their impending obsolescence.

"Hey." Ranjit walks up and taps a black mechanic on the shoulder. "We're looking for Kishen. He works here, right?"

"We're busy. Get lost."

"Hey, look—"

"You heard me. Get out of here."

Ranjit advances on the man, but Leela pulls him back.

"Let me do it. I know Kishen." She smooths down her white ban-danna, licks her lips, and walks into the garage.

Crossing to the other side of the narrow street, he watches her. The mechanics don't stop her as she walks toward a bald man sitting at a desk at the back. Ranjit can't hear what she is saying, but the man looks up, pushes his glasses onto his head, and smiles at her.

Leela disappears deeper into the garage, and emerges a few min-utes later. The man with her—laughing, his hands thrust deeply into the pockets of his stained overalls—looks nothing like his cousin. Whereas Mohan is long-legged and elegant, Kishen is squat, with close-cropped hair and a square jaw. He seems very comfortable with Leela, chuckling as they cross the street and walk up to Ranjit.

"Oh, this is my friend, Captain Ranjit Singh. He's an old army buddy of Mohan's," Leela says, and Kishen sticks out his hand, then glances down and retracts it.

"Sorry," he says. "I'm covered in grease. Captain Singh, yeah, Mohan used to talk about you. He said you were the only guy who was nice to him at the Academy. You taught him how to box, and he won some big fight because of you. But with Mohan, it's hard to tell what's the truth, and what's bullshit. Well, Captain, what can I do for you?"

Ranjit takes an immediate liking to this blunt man. "I'll make a long story short. You and I know that Mohan's in bad trouble. He's an old friend of mine, I want to help him get out of the city. Any idea where he is?"

"This whole thing is crazy." Kishen's broad face darkens. "Mohan didn't kill anyone, he's incapable of murder, he's a wimp. Besides, he was crazy about that chick, and she was crazy about him. All the papers say she's a movie star, he's a doorman, but so what? She was just a woman, for God's sake, not a goddess." Kishen points a blunt finger toward the shop. "See that bald Russian guy at the desk? He has a Ph.D. in physics from Moscow University. A fucking Ph.D. Same thing with Shabana. Back in India, she was a superstar, a goddess, but here? She's just another frantic, middle-aged woman with no husband."

Lapsing into silence, Kishen stares angrily down at his hands. Clearly this was a long speech for him.

"Point taken." Ranjit raises his hands, palms out, in a placating gesture. "But look, Mohan's vanished, and coincidentally, so has Ruksana. Is there any possibility that the two of them . . . ?"

"Mohan and *Ruksana*?" Kishen stares from under thick brows. "You really don't know shit, right? Ruksana hated my cousin, she would have had him fired from the Dakota if she could, she kept threatening to do it. You know why? Before my cousin came around, Ruksana had total control over her sister. Shabana is clueless about real life, all she's ever done is act in movies. She can't even go out and buy a loaf of bread, okay? Ruksana took care of everything, and she loved that power. Then Mohan began to do things for Shabana, they ate together, cooked together . . ."

Ranjit thinks of how familiar Mohan was with the kitchen in the Dakota, opening cabinets and taking out cutlery.

". . . yeah, Shabana was happy for once. The two of them used to go up to Mohan's apartment in the attic, they were like two kids in a tree house. You know that wall of pictures Mohan has? All those old photographs? The two of them went through all those abandoned suitcases, found those pictures, she helped him hang them. It was like a project."

"K! *Yo!*" The bald man at the desk stands and gestures to Kishen. "*Yo*, this Tesla got to be ready! Four o'clock, and I mean four o'clock today, not tomorrow!"

Kishen waves back. Ranjit reaches out and pats the man's muscular shoulder. "Okay, sorry if I upset you, I just had to ask the question."

"You know what? Maybe that bitch Ruksana did it. She was always pushing Shabana around. I mean pushing her, physically. Shabana was the goose that laid the golden eggs, and when the eggs stopped, Ruksana was furious. At least Shabana had Mohan. What did that bitch have? Nothing."

"Okay, I get it. You sure you don't know where Mohan is? I'm the only friend he has left in this town."

Kishen's voice drops to a whisper. "If I knew, I would have helped him myself. But no, he hasn't called. He wouldn't want to involve me. That's the kind of guy he is."

Ranjit nods. "One last thing. You seem like a straight-up guy. This old Sikh in the Bronx, he says you stole some engines from his garage—"

"That guy!" Kishen laughs bitterly. "Man, you have been talking to some *weird* people." The laughter ends abruptly. "That old man is an alkie, he took the parts, sold them, blamed me in front of his wife . . . anything else you want to know, you come back, okay? You know where to find me."

Kishen turns and stalks back into the garage.

"This must be a bad time for him." Leela stares at the man's broad back. "He and Mohan are really tight . . . Well, that's that. We still don't know where Mohan is. What are we going to do now?"

Ranjit leans against the rough brick wall, listening to the whine of a mechanical screwdriver, the clanking of a winch.

"Where do we go, Ranjit? Back to my place?"

"By now, Lateef probably knows where you live. I'm sure they have my address, too . . . I've got it. Ruksana's place. They won't expect us to go back there."

"And then?"

"I don't know. I'll figure it out. Don't worry."

"When is this going to end? My mother and Dev can't stay at her cousin's place forever. They fight like cats and dogs."

Not to mention that the grand jury trial is on Thursday and today is Tuesday and he has no evidence to take to the cops.

"I'll figure it out," he says, and reaches for her hand.

Move, he tells himself. *For now, just get off the streets and hide.*

By the time they reach Ruksana's apartment, the sun is fading from the sky. They enter the dark living room, illuminated now by a slice of light that slants past the blank brick wall outside. A quick check reveals that the apartment is empty, exactly as they left it, the shoebox lying on the floor of the studio, and photographs spilling out onto the floor.

Ranjit sinks down into the futon couch, feeling the soft cotton compress under him. Leela stands by the window, dialing Auntie; he can hear it ring, but nobody answers.

"*Damn.* She refuses to learn how to use a cell phone." Leela hangs up angrily and stares at the blank brick wall outside, now glowing with golden light.

Standing on tiptoe, she presses a finger into the dry soil of a cactus. Without a word, she goes into the kitchen and returns with a glass of water.

Ranjit watches her stretch upward to water each cactus, till some liquid dribbles into the plate underneath. He thinks of her well-tended flower bed, crowded with tall sunflowers and hydrangeas, the care she lavishes on these mute things.

"Ruksana's been gone a while," Leela says, turning to him. "Her cacti are bone dry. Nice apartment, though . . ." She gestures with the empty glass in her hand. "I was saving up to get my own place, before my father died. I really wanted to live alone." She moves closer. "Wouldn't it be nice to have an apartment?"

"I've been living in one for two years." He thinks of his dim basement. "Not much room to grow flowers."

"Oh, I'd be happy with some plants. So what do you think? You, me, and Dev in a place like this?"

No mention of Auntie, or of Shanti, who will be arriving in two weeks. Leela sits down next to him on the futon and waits for a reply.

Is she just talking, imagining her way into the future, away from this dark moment, away from Lateef's men? How can he answer that he needs to live alone with Shanti and rebuild their relationship? In any case, he cannot imagine Shanti and Leela getting along: both of them are strong, impulsive, childish personalities, but the difference is that Shanti *is* a thirteen-year-old child.

"What are you thinking, Ranjit?" Her eyes are fixed on his face.

He cannot answer her honestly, and she badly needs his reassurance right now. Instead of speaking, he reaches out and hugs her, and she must misinterpret the gesture, because she reaches in to kiss him. He wants to say, *No, wait*—but it is too late. Her mouth presses into his.

The soft swell of her breasts pushes into his chest, and he remembers clearly what they did that night on Dev's bed. She must feel his body yearn toward her, because she kisses him so hard that her teeth clatter against his.

Outside, he hears the city, muffled by the brick wall: the roar of traffic, the wail of sirens, the honking of horns. He can feel the island stretching around them, north and south, the dark rectangle of Central Park close by, all of it now seething with danger. Lateef will hunt them down, he won't stop till they are dead: Ranjit can imagine the shock of bullets hammering into the back of his head, plowing into Leela's flesh.

A shout of protest rises in his throat, a realization that he has wasted two years of his life, always deferring life, real life, to some distant future. Now the future is here, as blank as that wall outside, and in this moment he wants life, he wants this warm girl squirming in his arms, her saliva sweet in his mouth.

They kiss for a long time, and when they can't stand it any longer, they don't even bother to lower the futon. She pulls away and stands in front of him, pulling off her T-shirt. He unbuttons and tugs down her jeans, pushing the worn denim over the swell of her hips, then slides his hand between her warm, smooth thighs. She stands, her head tilted back in the darkness, her breath coming faster. They stay like this till she pushes his hand away.

"I want you on top of me. I want to feel your weight," she says, gesturing for him to get up.

She sprawls on the blue futon, looking up at him with her hazel eyes. Stripping off his clothes, he presses into her soft, warm body, and she sinks deep into the old cotton. He has to prop himself on both arms, and his broken one begins to ache, but he ignores the pain. Moving slowly at first, he pushes harder into her, and she finds the rhythm, and pushes back.

It feels as though they have sunk into the futon, have sunk to the bottom of a sea of soft cotton, and they are moving upward with each thrust, till she hits her head on the wooden armrest and goes *oh*. He stops then, but she tightens her legs and whispers, *Don't stop now, not now*, and he keeps going.

He doesn't want it to end, but then it does, like tumbling off the edge of a cliff and falling into deep, still water. Exhausted, he falls onto her, then hears her whimper and realizes that he is crushing her. She slides out from under and lies facing him, wrapping one smooth leg over his, her face inches from his, her small lips relaxing into a slight smile.

He must have fallen fitfully asleep, because he surfaces at intervals to see the light fading from the blank wall outside.

It is the loud growling of his stomach that wakes him up, and he realizes that the last time he ate was tea and sugar toast that morning.

"Leela," he whispers, but she groans, pushes her face into his shoulder, and does not wake. He levers himself up, and climbs over her sleeping form.

Without turning on the light, he opens the cabinets in Ruksana's kitchen, finding a carton of artificial sweetener, tea, but nothing to eat except for a box of strange cereal made from grains. No choice. He pours out a handful and crunches it down, but it is like eating cardboard.

"What are you doing?" Leela raises herself on one elbow and rubs the sleep from her eyes.

"I'm starving. There's nothing to eat in this place. What did Ruksana survive on?"

She swings her legs down and walks over to him, smelling of warm sleep.

"Why are you eating that crap?"

"There's nothing else."

She yawns and waves a hand at the side of the refrigerator, decorated with restaurant menus. "This is New York City. You never heard of takeout?"

She orders, and thirty minutes later, clothed now, she collects the food at the door and pays the young Chinese deliveryman, tipping him well.

Ranjit and Leela don't speak, but sit on the floor by the futon, eating directly from the cartons. Leela uses her chopsticks deftly, and he uses a plastic fork, shoveling the aromatic shreds of chicken, fried eggplant, and egg noodles into his mouth. It is greasy and delicious, and he looks up to see Leela gesturing at him with her chopsticks.

"Hey," she says. "Share. Don't hog all the noodles."

They trade cartons and he starts in on the fried rice, still so hot that its fragrance fills the air.

"I heard of this game show," Leela says, "a Japanese game show. They locked this guy up, naked, in an apartment, and he had to win everything by sending in postcards to contests: food, clothes, everything. Kind of like us, huh?"

He tries to smile, but he can't quite manage it.

It is almost midnight. This time they figure out how to lower the futon couch into a bed and lie on it, their stomachs full. Having slept and eaten, Ranjit is wide awake, though Leela seems sleepy.

"I hope . . . I hope that Dev is okay," she says. "He probably misses me."

"He's a good kid." Ranjit lies on his back next to her. "Very calm. He's got a good personality." She looks at him strangely, her head propped up on one arm. "What? Did I say something wrong?"

"No." She shakes her head. "It's just that . . . you've never asked me about his father. Most of the men I meet, they want to know right away."

"It's really none of my business."

He does not want to have this conversation now; besides, Auntie already told him all about it. He needs to figure out what to do next: tomorrow is Wednesday, the last day before the ax falls.

"Well, it's okay. I'll tell you." She laughs, a silvery, artificial laugh.

Give her a few minutes, he thinks, *let her get it off her chest.* He moves closer to indicate that he is listening.

"You know, I was this nerdy girl . . ." She reaches out and places a hand on his bare chest. "I was way behind all my other friends. They all had boyfriends, they were sneaking around and having sex, talking about how wonderful it was. Like they had eaten at this fancy restaurant that I could never go to. So I was curious."

She absently plays with his chest hair.

"There was this boy who lived up the lane, a tall, gangly boy, but sweet, very sweet. He used to bicycle past my house, he always used to slow down and stare at me. The other boys would whistle at me, but this boy, all he used to do was stare." She laughs again. "So I decided that he would be the one. When my mother was out of the house, I invited him in, and he was so clumsy, it was nothing like what my friends said."

She pauses. "Well, not a lot more to tell, really. When I got pregnant, I couldn't believe it. I didn't tell the boy—anyway, he had moved to a different city. So I had the baby . . . and, well, the rest you know."

She looks at him, her hand still resting on his chest. "Stupid, right? But I was a kid, he was a kid, it happened, so . . ." Shrugging, she moves her hand away.

He turns on his back and stares up at the ceiling. This is not what Auntie had told him. She said that Leela was involved with some rich man, old enough to be her father.

"You don't judge me, do you?" She waits in the dark for a reply. "I was so young, I didn't know any better . . ."

"No, I don't judge you. Of course not." It is lucky that she can't see the frown on his face.

"Oh, good. I've been meaning to tell you. We shouldn't have secrets between us, right?"

"Right." Out of the corner of his eyes he watches her snuggle down into the futon, using her forearm as a pillow.

"I'm so tired, I'm going to close my eyes for a minute." Her eyelids shut, and soon she has slid easily into sleep.

He watches her calm, sleeping face, and thinks of how easily she has lied to him. Is this what she thinks he wants to hear?

He has now slept with her twice, has eaten with her, stayed with her family, but each time he thinks he knows her, another side emerges. She plays so many roles: Lenore at the club, Leela at home. Is she creating another role for his benefit, that of the young, innocent girl?

The calming effect of the sex has worn off, and he feels completely disoriented. There is only one day left, and he has no idea what to do, and who to trust. A scrap of prayer drifts into his mind:

During the second watch of the night,
You are intoxicated with the wine of youth and beauty.
Day and night, you are engrossed in sexual desire,
The Lord's Name is not within your heart, but other tastes seem
*   sweeter . . .*
In falsehood, you are caught in the cycle of birth and death.

One thing is clear to him—he is lost in the darkness now because of his own weakness, his own desires. If he survives this, he must change his life.

With Leela sleeping next to him, he stares out at the dark brick wall, thinking through all the explanations for Shabana's death:

Patel and the cops said that Mohan did it.

Leela is convinced that Patel killed Shabana.

Lateef and now Kishen say that it was the obsessive Ruksana.

Maybe Mohan and Ruksana were in it together.

What is he to believe?

One thing is for sure: the doorman, the actress, and her sister have emerged as a triangle, tied together by love, obligation, and hate: the truth lies within that configuration.

Is there any stone he has left unturned? This apartment, for instance: have they searched it thoroughly?

Rising slowly from the futon, he walks to Ruksana's studio, turns on a floor lamp, and flips through a stack of canvases, seeing the two sisters, in red and white, painted obsessively, over and over. He examines the backs of the paintings for anything written or taped there, but there is nothing.

Sifting through the box of photographs, he sees familiar images of Shabana alone in a white salwaar kameez, and Ruksana in a red one. Then one photograph of the girls with their parents: a plump, long-haired woman and a tall, sallow man with a thick mustache, his hand on Shabana's shoulder, while Ruksana stands close to her mother. The group poses in an enclosed courtyard with peeling plaster walls, an overflowing garbage can in one corner.

The two identical sisters, growing up poor in Mumbai, Shabana clearly her father's favorite, Ruksana allied with the mother. Well, maybe that explains the animosity between the twins. Ranjit stares and stares, but the photographs reveal little else.

Putting the photographs away, he searches the closet, careful not to make a noise, and finds some paint-splattered shirts and more painting supplies. Then he remembers the bathroom along the corridor: neither of them had looked in there . . .

Heading to the small, yellow tiled bathroom, he opens the small cabinet below the sink. It is full of cleaning supplies and a pair of rubber gloves; unlike her sister, Ruksana clearly liked her apartment spotless.

That leaves the mirrored cabinet above the sink. Yanking it open, he sees a pair of glasses, a toothbrush, and an old silver-handled hairbrush. Nothing here. He is about to close the cabinet when he pauses: Shabana had an identical brush on her dressing table. Picking it up, he tries to figure out why this one seems different—the curlicues on the handle are the same, as are the stiff white bristles. Then it comes to him: Shabana's brush was clogged with long strands of black hair, which she hadn't bothered to clean out. Ruksana's brush is immaculate.

Oh. He stands there, stunned by a sudden flash of intuition.

Mohan killed Shabana. Patel killed Shabana. Ruksana killed Shabana. Both Mohan and Ruksana killed Shabana.

There is another possibility. *Why hadn't he thought of it before?*

But he has to be sure, completely sure, before making a move. Pulling out his phone, he dials a number from a card in his wallet.

Detective Case picks up on the second ring. "Yes?" Her voice is awake and alert.

"This is Ranjit Singh."

"What do you have for us, Mr. Singh? I'd given up on hearing from you."

"You're up very late. What's the matter, this investigation giving you a lot of trouble?" She doesn't take the bait. "Look, I need some information. About Shabana's corpse."

"Mr. Singh, you promised us some evidence, but I haven't seen anything. I'm not talking to you."

"Look, you haven't made much progress on this investigation. I know it, and you know it. And I'm very close to finding out what happened." Silence on Case's end, broken only by the sound of her measured breathing. "Right now you don't have Mohan, you don't have Patel, all you have is me, and you know, deep down, that I didn't do it. So, do you really want to solve this? Or just put me in jail and get me deported?" She does not reply. "Who identified Shabana's body? Her sister, Ruksana?"

There is a pause. "Yes. She was very cooperative. I don't see how any of this—"

"Thank you. And one last question: I need to know if Shabana's corpse had her natural hair."

"You know damn well that the autopsy report is confidential and I can't—"

"Please. One-word answer. Yes or no."

Another long pause, then a sigh. "Wait." A rustling of paper, and then Case answers him.

"Thank you. I'll be in touch."

He hangs up, walks into the living room, and shakes Leela awake.

She sits up with a jerk, her fists digging into the soft futon. "Lateef, he's *here*?"

"No, not that."

"Then what?" She blinks hard. "What the hell is going on, Ranjit?"

"I think . . ." he mumbles. "I think I know what happened. I know where Mohan is."

"How? How do you know?"

"No time to explain. I might be too late, as it is. Let's go."

She stares open-mouthed at him as he reaches across her for his crumpled shirt.

Chapter Thirty-Three

Leela and Ranjit stand across the street from the looming hulk of the Dakota. At nearly two A.M., its windows are dark, though a few dim lights burn here and there: insomniacs maybe, or the very ill.

Ranjit points to the tarnished brass keys hanging from Shabana's key ring. "Are you sure these are for the Dakota?"

Leela nods. "The larger one is for an outside door. The smaller one is for the apartment."

"Okay. There is a twenty-four-hour coffee shop on the corner. Wait there for me. If I'm not back in . . . half an hour, call the NYPD." He hands her a crumpled business card. "Tell Detective Case to get here fast, and come up to the attic."

She squints at the card, then stuffs it into her pocket. "Tell me what's going on. Why are you treating me like I'm stupid? I'm the one who found the photograph. You think Ruksana is in there with Mohan, don't you? And you think they did it?"

"It's just a hunch."

"*Patel* is the one who killed Shabana. Why won't you believe me?"

"Just give me half an hour, please."

Leela turns on her heel and heads toward the far-off lights of the coffee shop. He walks in the other direction, feeling the hard poke of the Glock in his waistband.

Entering the dark alley behind the Dakota, Ranjit slots the brass key into the back door, and there is a satisfying click as the cylinders engage. He pushes the door open and walks down the long, dark corridor, emerging into the courtyard.

The planting beds have been recently fertilized, and it smells like the countryside here, of rich, dark soil. The fountain has been turned off, and without the splash of water it is eerily silent. He listens to the wind rustle through the trees, and remembers that first evening here with Mohan, when he wished that he could live in a place like this. Now its beauty seems like a sinister cover-up.

He stays frozen in the shadows, and under the plaster his broken arm begins to throb. *What if he's wrong?* For the past week, he has refused to panic and taken it one step at a time. Now there are no longer any steps left. *This is the end of the line.*

Crossing the courtyard in a few strides, he enters the dark staircase in the corner, a faint light filtering down from far above. He gropes his way upward, and soon his heart is hammering and he is out of breath. He smiles grimly, remembering his plans to exercise; if he ends up in jail, there will be plenty of time for that.

He is gasping for breath by the time he reaches the top floor and sees the source of the light: a single low-wattage bulb in the hallway. Gripping the handle of the Glock, he walks silently down the corridor, passing the open door of a plywood storage cubicle: inside it the frayed rattan chairs and overturned couch lie untouched, coated with a thick layer of dust.

He stands by Mohan's apartment door and listens intently, but the only sound is his own labored breathing. One of the smaller keys fits, and the door swings open.

The three tall, curved windows at the far end of the room let in light from the street below, and he can see clearly. The cops must have searched the room because the bed and armchair have been pushed against the wall, and the rugs rolled up, showing lighter patches of wood floor. The kitchen cabinets in the small alcove have been emptied out, and the refrigerator door is open. Nothing here at all: just a silent room, its inhabitant long gone.

So he was wrong. Now what?

He walks through the room again, but no trace of Mohan remains. Nothing except the rows of framed photographs on the wall: the sepia portraits of servants who once worked here, long-forgotten men and women in their stiff white collars and shabby morning coats. What impulse had led Mohan to rummage through the boxes and trunks and rescue these photographs? Had these stern-faced men and women kept him company?

He stares at the photographs, and the sepia ghosts stare back at him. Suddenly exhausted, he sinks down on Mohan's bed, feeling the horsehair mattress creak under him. Its striped cotton cover is badly stained, and many of the buttons holding the tufting in place are missing.

Mohan has surrounded himself with old, battered objects. Surely it is not just an aesthetic preference—the furniture is too big for this room—and sitting in the darkness Ranjit remembers his friend's pride in the Dakota. Mohan clearly identifies with the old building, and all this—the photographs and the furniture—are an attempt to rescue the past from the oblivion of the storage rooms.

What had Kishen said about his cousin? That even though Shabana had a big, fancy apartment, she liked to come up to Mohan's nest in the attic. He said they spent hours hanging these pictures.

Staring at the photographs, Ranjit remembers that evening up here with Mohan. *This place is so huge,* Mohan had said, *it's been reconfigured so many times, no one really knows every nook and cranny. Except for me.*

Walking into the hallway, he peers into the dark storage room, seeing only a jumble of chair legs. There is no room to hide in this cubicle, but what about the other ones? If only he had a flashlight, he could search the attic.

Then he remembers what to do. Up on the Siachen Glacier, he would always sit in the darkness before going out on night missions; with his well-adjusted eyes, he could easily navigate the dark outcroppings and deep crevasses.

Reaching up, he pulls his sleeve over his palm, and unscrews the hot lightbulb. The hallway suddenly goes dark and he stands, blinded, the bulb in his hand. He forces himself to be patient, and waits for his vision to adjust.

Sure enough, as the seconds tick by he begins to see: the corridor takes on sharper outlines, and the lighter-colored plywood doors emerge from the darkness. He walks along the corridor and checks the doors, the first few of them secured with hasps and padlocks. One hasp comes off in his hand, the screws loosened, and he yanks it open, but the room is filled to the ceiling with moldy cardboard boxes.

The next few cubicle doors are locked solid, but then another screeches open. He peers into the narrow space, seeing rows of old Singer sewing machines on waist-high trundles, some with spools of dull thread still inserted.

There is a clear pathway at the edge of the room, and he follows it to the outer wall, to a closed window, translucent with dust. Turning to the side wall, he runs his fingers along the smooth plywood, searching for the outline of a door, but finds nothing. Staring into the darkness, he surveys the room, and that is when he sees it.

If he had a flashlight, its bright light would have bounced off the windowpanes and shone into his eyes, but in the dark, it is clearly visible: there are handprints in the thick dust at the bottom of the windowpane, as if someone has recently pushed it upward. And Ranjit hasn't touched the window.

This is it. This has to be it. Gripping the bottom of the window, he prepares to heave it upward, knowing that these old wooden frames are often swollen tight with moisture.

The window glides up silently and the cool night air rushes in. Touching the rope pulley within the window frame, he feels fresh oil.

Why would Mohan bother to fix this particular window? Leaning out cautiously, he sees a stone ledge that runs along the face of the building, perhaps eighteen inches wide. He sticks his head farther out, and sees, about a hundred feet away, the faint glow of light from a window.

There is someone up here, after all.

If this was ten years ago, and if his arm was not broken, he would have walked that hundred feet of ledge in minutes. In the army, heights never bothered him: the higher he went on the glacier, the happier he was.

This ledge, though, is slick with mold and its edge is crumbling in places. He inches along it, his back against the face of the building, his arms spread out on either side like a tightrope walker. He feels his feet slip on the stone, feels the heavy plaster cast on his right arm throw off his balance.

Far below him a car speeds down Central Park West, its headlights making twin cones of light across the road. If he falls, there is nothing to hold on to: the joints between the yellow brick are too narrow to offer even a finger-hold. And three-quarters of the way, a decorative curl of stone divides the ledge; to cross it, he will have to reach a leg across and straddle it.

He closes his eyes. At first the fear intensifies, but he waits it out, and soon he is conscious only of the rough brick at his back and the stone ledge under his feet. The tension leaves his shoulders, and he moves sideways, his legs falling into a rhythm:

Extend left foot out.

Pause and stabilize.

Bring the right foot closer in.

Repeat.

Behind his closed eyes, the Siachen Glacier creeps in. At nineteen thousand feet, the tops of the mountains often disappeared into the clouds, and climbing into their fleecy white was like climbing into oblivion. One time he had pushed through the clouds and emerged above them, finding himself isolated on a rocky ridgeline, looking down onto a sea of white clouds. It was as though he had reached heaven, and the sun blazing down—hotter and brighter than he had ever experienced—felt like the breath of God.

His foot slams against an obstruction, and he knows he has reached the decorative curl of stone. Lifting his foot over it, he stands for a moment, regains his balance, then swings the other leg across. *Not that far to go now.*

He hears the faint mumble of voices. Each second slows down and turns into a knife-edged eternity.

He opens his eyes and the voices grow louder. The stripe of light on the stone ledge is a few feet away now.

He sidles up to the lit window. It is open, its bottom sash pushed up, but the yellowed window shade is pulled down, leaving an inch of light.

This is the tricky part. As he moves into the window, the murmur of voices stops abruptly. Arching his back, he steps backward through the opening, the plastic shade scraping across his back.

He lands with a thud on a wooden floor and spins around, pulling the Glock from his waistband and aiming into the narrow space.

It is more of a slot than a room, with plywood walls on both sides, and stinks of body odor and sweat and instant ramen noodles. Along one wall are plastic jugs of water, bright wrappers from packaged food, and a battered metal laptop computer. Along the other wall, on an unrolled sleeping bag, lie a naked man and woman. The man raises himself in alarm on one elbow, and the woman cowers behind him, her face hidden.

"Hello, Mohan," Ranjit says, keeping the gun raised. "You want to put on some clothes?"

The woman lying behind Mohan raises her head and Ranjit sees the familiar high forehead and long neck. She has the figure of a temple carving from Khajuraho—heavy, firm breasts and a narrow waist—but without any makeup, she has worry lines engraved into her forehead, and crow's-feet at the edges of her eyes. Her thick, shoulder-length fall of hair is gone, replaced by a thinning ponytail. He realizes with a shock that she isn't in her thirties; more like mid-forties.

"Hello, Shabana," Ranjit says, lowering his gun. "Nice to finally meet you."

Shabana and Mohan scramble for their clothes. He tugs on a pair of jeans, she wraps herself in Mohan's lemon-yellow shirt, dirty and crushed now, and they both stare at Ranjit. The silence is broken only by the fluttering of the window shade.

Ranjit tries to control the anger in his voice. "Maybe you two should tell me why you killed Ruksana—" He gestures with his head. "—and pretended it was her."

Mohan stands with his arms limp at his sides. He has lost so much weight that his ribs are visible, and his long, handsome face is gaunt, darkened by a week's growth of beard.

"How the hell . . . how did you find us?"

"Your cousin, Kishen. He said that Shabana liked to come up here. And I remembered you saying that you knew your way around the attic." Ranjit gestures with the gun in his hand. "This is a good hiding place. You let Shabana in from the corridor, locked it from the outside, and then climbed back here along the ledge, yes? A good tactical move to hole up here and wait for the fuss to die down. So you learned something at the Military Academy, after all."

"I can explain everything—"

"Shut up. I'm doing the talking." Ranjit's voice quivers with anger as he points at two black rolling suitcases in the corner. "Going somewhere? I sincerely hope not, because you know whose fingerprints were on that statue of Ganesh? Mine. They arrested me, and I'm facing a grand jury tomorrow. So, my friend, before I turn you in to the cops, please *explain* to me why you killed Ruksana, and framed me."

Mohan gulps. His Adam's apple bobs up and down, but no words come.

"Come on, damn it." Ranjit's voice rises to a shout. "*Explain to me* why you flushed my life down the toilet."

"*Bhai*, no, I didn't mean for you to be involved in this—"

"It's all my fault." Shabana pulls the bright yellow shirt tight around her. "I'm the one who is responsible. You should be angry at me, not him."

Even clad in the dirty yellow shirt, she is every inch an actress; it is the way she holds herself, Ranjit realizes, her head high, her eyes downcast, both regal and vulnerable at the same time. Despite himself, he feels the same flutter of emotion he'd felt in the cab that day. But Shabana's cheeks are smooth, without any makeup, and the woman in his cab had worn a lot of foundation.

"You . . . you weren't in my taxi, were you? That was Ruksana."

Shabana sighs and pushes a stray strand of hair from her eyes. "My sister liked to pretend she was me. She used to wear my clothes, go shopping with my credit card, sign autographs. It made her feel better, I suppose."

Ranjit remembers the woman in his cab, how she had offered to sign an autograph. So it was Ruksana who had made him feel like a lovesick teenager, and he feels a sudden swell of sadness that she is dead.

"She had something wrong with her face, yes?" Ranjit gestures to his own cheeks. "Otherwise you two are identical?"

"Yes."

"Also, Ruksana had her own hair, but you have a weave, with hair supplied by Nataraj Imports."

Shabana involuntarily reaches up and touches her thin ponytail. "How do you know about that?"

"I worked there, for Jay Patel."

"You work for *Patel?*" Shabana reaches out and grabs Mohan's arm and her face contorts with pain. "He's working for that bastard. He's going to kill us."

Mohan steps forward, his arm extended, palm out. "Ranjit, please, listen to me. If only you knew what Lateef—" He turns wildly to Shabana. "Show him. Show Ranjit what that bastard did to you."

Before Ranjit can stop her, she opens her yellow shirt and tugs it off.

She half turns away, her eyes closed tightly. Her stomach and breasts are untouched, but the skin on her back is crisscrossed with long diagonal red scars, interspersed with pinkish white spots of burnt skin.

"Put . . . put your shirt back on." She doesn't seem to hear Ranjit; he sticks the gun into his waistband, picks up the lemon-yellow shirt, and drapes it over her shoulders. His voice is quiet now. "Lateef did that to you?"

"He did it." Mohan's voice shakes as he tries to button Shabana's shirt with small, ineffectual motions. "He beat her with a belt, and he burned her. Let her go, please, Ranjit. I know Patel must have offered you a lot of money, but if our friendship ever meant anything to you, in God's name—"

"Calm down. Get dressed."

Mohan finishes buttoning Shabana's shirt and then helps her into a pair of jeans, as though she is a child. Then he walks to a corner and pulls on a T-shirt.

The gun remains tucked into Ranjit's waistband. "I know all about that bastard Lateef. But why did you two kill Ruksana? She was your own sister."

Shabana leans against Mohan, and her voice is weak. "Has anyone ever tried to steal your life? Ruki wore my clothes, pretended to be me, and I let her. That I could bear. But then she crossed the line."

She wipes her eyes with balled fists, and her voice becomes stronger. "That evening, I left for the Hamptons, but I wasn't feeling well, so I decided to come back. Ruksana was already here when I got back. Patel sent her, because he'd heard that I had learned about his smuggling operation."

"Why did Patel send your own sister?"

Shabana takes a breath and continues. "Ruki is my manager. After my last film fell through, she was the one who arranged the job at the club. He trusts her." Shabana pauses and wipes a hand across her face. "Anyway, Ruki has her own key, she let herself in and found Mohan sleeping naked in my bed. I arrived a few minutes later, and Ruki was furious, she called me a slut, she started screaming and yelling . . ."

Ranjit glances at Mohan's reddened face and knows it is true. "So for that you killed her?"

"No, it's not just that." She blinks back tears. "Any man I ever was involved with, Ruki scared them away. But that evening, Mohan just stood there, naked, and laughed at her. She had no hold over him—he wasn't an actor, he wasn't rich, he wasn't worried about his career—he just loved me. He is the one good thing I have, and Ruki couldn't stand it. And then she told me something . . . something that drove me crazy."

Shabana looks at Mohan before continuing. "Many years ago, I was in love with a man, and we made a life together, a life that didn't include my sister. One day, I was kidnapped, held for money. After I was released, I was told that my boyfriend—his name was Sanjeev—had engineered the whole thing. And then he vanished. They never found his body, nothing.

"That evening at the Dakota, Ruki told me what really happened. She and Don Hajji Mustafa planned the kidnapping, and they blamed Sanjeev. He didn't vanish. *Ruki had him killed*. She laughed and told me that Don Hajji Mustafa's men beat Sanjeev to death, buried him in the foundation of a new skyscraper. Ruki said that if I continued seeing Mohan, the same thing would happen to him."

She covers her face with her hands and her voice is muffled. "I went crazy . . . I screamed at Ruki, I pushed her, and it was an accident, she fell, she hit her head on a corner of the table . . . I tried to wake her up, but . . ."

Mohan speaks calmly now, his arms crossed across his thin chest. "The rest was my idea. The bitch was dead, that was an accident, it couldn't be undone. But if people thought it was Shabana who was lying on the floor, she would be free from Patel, from Lateef, from the club. We could run away, we could be together. I mean, the two sisters are identical, and their voices are the same, the way they look . . ."

"Except for the scars on her cheek." Ranjit imagines Ruksana lying dead on the parquet floor, her thick black hair billowing around her like a shroud. "So her face had to be erased."

"I thought, we'll make it look like someone broke in and killed Shabana. We dressed Ruki's body in Shabana's white dress, then I took the statue, I was the one who . . ." Mohan's shoulders slump. "God help me, I forced myself to do it, but there was so much blood. There was the blood, and it made a lot of noise . . . I panicked. I thought a neighbor had heard us . . . so we came up here and hid."

There is silence again.

"And afterwards . . ." Ranjit addresses Shabana, speaking slowly, thinking it through. ". . . you pretended to be Ruksana. You went to the police station and identified your sister's body as your own, right? It must have been the easiest role to play, all you needed was some thick makeup on your cheeks. Then you came back here to be with Mohan, and waited till it was safe to run away together."

Shabana looks down at the floor.

"What now, Ranjit?" Mohan's voice is soft and powerless.

"Shabana, tell me what you know about Patel's operation. I found the piece of cardboard you hid at the club. I know it's from a box of hair. What does that red symbol mean?"

Her voice resigned, she tells him about the red stamp on the boxes. She tells him that she'd overheard the businessmen at the club, and then slowly pieced together the details of Patel's smuggling operation. Knowing that Patel loved old movies, she had figured out that the password to his laptop was "Pakeezah," and one night she had sneaked into his office at the club and copied his e-mail correspondence. Then she approached Patel and told him that unless he made Lateef stop, she would go to the cops. Patel had offered her assurances, but in the end, he had been powerless to intervene.

"So the red stamp was the key, yes? The evidence, it is hidden?"

"No, I have it here." Shabana digs through one of the suitcases and hands him a flash drive. She says that some of it is in Chinese, but other documents are in English, that there are names here, and dates, and dollar amounts, a clear picture of Patel's entire operation.

Shabana steps back and hangs her head and he knows that she

has assigned her fate to him; she no longer has the energy left to fight.

"What now?" Mohan repeats. "Are you going to call Patel?"

"Your bags. Where were you going?"

Mohan gestures helplessly at the old laptop lying in the corner. "I contacted this guy on a merchant ship, he owes me big time. He can get us to Venezuela, it sails in a few hours. Is there any way . . . Ranjit, any way you can keep Patel out of this?"

"You don't need to worry about Patel." Ranjit looks at his watch: thirty-four minutes have passed since he entered the Dakota. "But you will have to tell your story to the cops. A friend of mine waiting outside has called them, they'll be here any minute."

Shabana cries out, and Mohan hugs her tighter, desperately trying to comfort her.

"Let her go, Ranjit. I'll stay here, I'll take the blame."

"No." Shabana shakes her head violently. "I'm staying with you. I'm not going. Even if we have ten minutes more together, it's worth it."

Mohan's arms circle her shoulders, and she clutches at him desperately, kissing him. They are both crying, looking more like frightened children than murderers.

The cops will be here any minute, and Mohan and Shabana will be arrested and separated, they will see each other only at their trial, and spend the rest of their lives apart.

Ranjit stares at his friend, and then at Shabana. They have been up here for a week, in this baking heat, they are filthy and exhausted, and yet he feels a current between them of what can only be described as love.

He thinks about his own failed attempts: his ex-wife, Preetam, now lost forever; his affair with Anna; his two nights with Leela that will never go anywhere. And here are these two, having found each other after long, tormented lives. It is terrible that Ruksana is dead, but putting them in jail isn't going to bring their whole sad story to a close. He reaches a decision.

"Is there another way down from the attic?"

"What?" Mohan looks confused.

"Another staircase?"

"Yes, the southwest staircase, you have to get to it through a storage room. Nobody uses it, but why—"

"You still have a few minutes. The cops will take the main staircase. Take Shabana, use the southwest stair, and get out of here."

"Really?" Mohan asks. "Oh, thank you, Captain, thank you, I—"

"Leave your suitcases behind. And before you go, hit me hard, knock me out. Remember the boxing competition, that right cross I taught you?" Ranjit turns his face toward Mohan.

"Thank you, my friend, thank you—"

"No time for all that. Hit me."

There are tears in Mohan's eyes as he steps closer and raises his fist.

Ranjit hears Shabana gasp and sees her glistening eyes and smooth cheeks and feels a sharp sadness that he will never see her again and the world explodes into stars and it all goes black.

He is back on the Siachen Glacier and it is dark and he is alone, slogging through the deep snow. All he can see behind him are his own footprints, and all he can hear is the howling of the wind.

His hands and feet begin to turn numb. He walks on in an exhausted stupor, his head lowered. He knows that if he stops for even a second he will freeze to death.

The wind fills his ears with its eerie howl. Soon he begins to hear the voices that are contained within it, whispers and burbles and cries, and he knows that the dead are talking to him.

Ruksana's melodious voice tells him that Shabana stole her life. Anna, lying dying in his lap, looks up at him and smiles a bloodstained smile and asks for forgiveness. His dead from the botched mission on the glacier: Sergeant Khandelkar's calm, authoritative voice tells him to keep walking. Private Dewan, killed at nineteen, sings one of his awful rock songs.

They are all waiting for him, somewhere up on the glacier.

Ranjit trudges on, his legs sinking knee-deep into the soft snow, and the voices grow louder.

A light shines in his face, so close that he can feel the heat of the bulb.

"Is this him? This the guy, what's his name, Mo-han?"

"No." Case sounds irritated. "That's Singh, the guy we picked up last week. Is he unconscious?"

There is a chuckle. "Looks like someone clocked him good. Hey, Mr. Singh, wake up. Wake up."

A sour-smelling hand slaps his face, and he opens his eyes, staring into the blinding eye of a flashlight. Beyond it is the silhouette of Case, and more cops in uniforms. The small attic space echoes with the crackle of radios.

He drags himself up on both elbows and sits against the plywood wall, shielding his eyes with one hand. Rough hands pat him down, and pluck the gun from his waistband.

"Detective Case, this fucker is armed."

The flashlight moves away, and Case hikes up the gray trousers of her pantsuit and squats down in front of him. "My, my. First someone breaks your arm, then someone knocks you out. Quite a rat's nest you've uncovered here. So the doorman, Mohan, he was hiding up here all this time, with the sister, Ruksana?"

"He hit me. Mohan hit me." Ranjit tries to focus his eyes.

"Where did they go? Airport? Train station?"

"I don't know. Mohan's with Shabana."

"Are you concussed? *Shabana* is dead, remember?"

"Ruksana is the dead one. Shabana is alive. You got it all wrong." Case's blouse is gaping open, and he glimpses the white outline of a utilitarian bra. "I figured it out when you told me about the corpse. Shabana had a weave, but Ruksana had all her own hair. Apart from that, the sisters are identical twins. You didn't know that, did you?"

Case's mouth falls open. "It can't be."

"The two sisters fought, Ruksana fell, hit her head, it was an accident. To cover it up, Mohan bashed in the corpse's face, made it look like a murder. Look in those suitcases—you'll find his clothes stained with Ruksana's blood." He waits for the information to sink in. "The person who identified the body was Shabana, pretending to be her sister. It was an easy role to play—all she had to do was wear a lot of makeup and glasses. She's an *actress,* for God's sake."

Case scowls up at the uniformed cop with the flashlight. "You getting this? Put out an APB for them both."

Ranjit blinks painfully. "Where is Rodriguez? I thought you two went everywhere together."

"Never mind him. Rodriguez has his own problems." Case looks away briefly, and Ranjit knows then that Rodriguez was Patel's informant. "So the actress and the doorman, they were in it together? What about Patel? Where does he fit in?"

"I was mistaken about him. After Shabana's latest movie was canceled, he gave her a job at his club. That's the only connection."

Case's mouth is a straight line under the hawklike nose. "Bullshit. So what is the Mumbai mob doing over here?"

"Security. Patel's making millions from the hair trade. He needs the muscle to guard his shipments." Ranjit waits to see how his lie will play out. "It was a simple murder case. Except you guys got it all wrong."

Case presses her lips together in a bitter smile. "Even if we did, you, Mr. Singh, will keep your mouth shut, understood?"

"Of course. What about the grand jury?"

"The grand jury?" Case tilts her pointed chin downward and frowns. "We'll have to lay out this case all over again." She swallows hard. "I'll talk to my boss, who will have to talk to the Chief. You're off the hook for now . . . but your story better match up when we find the actress and her boyfriend."

She gets to her feet. "We'll find them, don't worry. We'll watch every train, every bus, every flight out of here. They are trapped."

So Case doesn't know about Mohan's past working on cruise ships.

"I'm sure you will." Ranjit stays slumped on the floor. The

uniformed cops have been joined by men in civilian clothes who are examining each inch of the room. The attention has palpably shifted from Ranjit to the missing movie star and her lover.

"You need to see a doctor? No? You can leave, then. And, oh, your girlfriend? She's the one who called us, right? She's waiting for you outside. Seems pretty anxious."

Ranjit staggers to his feet, and a young, hatless cop escorts him down the stairs and through the courtyard to the open front gate. He glances back, knowing that he will never again set foot in the Dakota.

Perhaps in deference to the building's famous inhabitants, the three police cruisers parked by the entrance do not have their lights flashing, but cops mill around them, radios crackling.

Leela is standing farther back, but he instantly spots her. She stares fixedly at him as he draws closer.

"I found Mohan." He smiles reassuringly. "And Shabana is alive. It's Ruksana who's dead. The two of them were hiding up there. Mohan hit me, then they took off. Thank God you called the cops . . . Leela?"

She doesn't seem to be listening, and is looking past him, fascinated perhaps by the cops in their bulky bulletproof vests and shotguns.

"Did you hear me?" He sees that the tendons in her neck are strained. "What is wrong?"

"Lateef." She gestures at the phone gripped in her hand. "He called."

"Called you? What did he want?"

"He said"—she blinks hard—"my mother and Dev are back home. She must have fought with her cousin, gone back home without telling me. Lateef said that his men are at my house. He said they will kill my mother and Dev, if, if you don't . . ." They stand inches apart, and he can feel her jerky breathing. ". . . if you don't . . ."

"Are Auntie and Dev hurt? What does he want me to do?"

He tries to put his hands on her shoulders, but she moves impatiently aside, as though he is interrupting her train of thought.

"Lateef wants you to go to Patel's motel in Jersey. Right now. If you do that, he'll let my family go. But, Ranjit, if you go to Jersey, they will kill you, for sure." She speaks in a rush. "Listen, you have your gun, right? There are just two of Lateef's men at my house. Can't you . . . couldn't you . . . just do something?"

He feels for his gun in his waistband, then remembers being frisked.

"The cops took my gun. But in any case, it's too dangerous. If Lateef's men even *think* anyone is coming, they will . . . No. Better that I go to Jersey."

"Lateef, he will kill you." Her voice rises. "It's just two men at my house. I could call those boys from the neighborhood, we could try to—"

He grabs her arm tightly. "Listen to me. Even if we succeed now, Lateef won't give up. He'll try again, and again, and one day he'll kill us all. That's how these people are. I have to go there and get him off our backs."

"*Ouch*. You're hurting me."

He looks down to see his fingers digging into her flesh, and lets his arm drop to his side. "There is something I need you to do, right now." He pulls out the flash drive from his pocket. "Take this, the packet of hair, and the box with the red stamp on it. Put it all in an envelope, write a note and say . . ." He lays out her task, and tells her to stay in Ruksana's apartment till he calls her.

"Are you sure this is going to work? What if Patel doesn't believe you—"

"One step at a time. *One step at a time.*"

Leela stares wordlessly at him, and he can see that her overwhelming fear has been replaced by her wish to believe him.

"You better be right this time, Ranjit."

Turning abruptly, she walks away, and he watches her for an instant, then takes out his cell phone and calls Ali. It goes unanswered, so he calls again.

A hoarse voice answers. "Ranjit. You know what damn time it is? Four twelve A.M. On my one day off. This better be good, you camel-fucker."

"I need your help, my friend. I need your courage."

"You need my car, is what you're saying."

"I'm in front of the Dakota, and I have to go to Jersey to see Patel. If I don't come back, I need you to take care of something for me. I'll tell you everything on the way over there."

"What do you mean, *if you don't come back?*"

"Can you pick me up?"

He hears the bed creak, and the swish of Ali putting on his slippers.

"Of course. I'll be there in thirty minutes." The line goes dead.

Ranjit walks away from the police cars toward the benches on Central Park West. It is still pitch dark, but he can hear the rustling of the birds in the trees above him. As the sky lightens, they will wake and fly into the park. They will live to see the new day, but will he?

Chapter Thirty-Four

As they drive off the George Washington Bridge into New Jersey, Ranjit turns to Ali. His friend must have dressed in a hurry, because the buttons of his pink-flowered Hawaiian shirt are done up wrong.

"Do you remember everything I told you? You wait for me outside the motel. If I don't come out, go with Leela to Queens. She knows some tough guys in her neighborhood. Get her mother and the kid away from Lateef's men."

Ali swallows hard and his chins wobble. "How the hell am I supposed to do that? I'm a cabdriver, Ranjit. Back home I was an *accountant*."

They drive on through the darkness. The jagged cliffs of New Jersey close in on both sides, and soon the Patel Motel appears: its orange neon sign is lit up, but as usual, it says NO VACANCY and the large parking lot is empty.

"Shit, I don't like it." Ali's pudgy hands tighten on the steering wheel. "It's like a ghost town." He is sweating heavily now.

The taxi pulls into the lot and Ranjit reaches over and touches his friend's shoulder.

"It's okay, Ali. You've done enough for me. You don't have to wait here, just head back to Manhattan. If I don't call you in an hour, help Leela, okay?"

"I'm not a coward, Ranjit, it's just that . . . with my wife and daughters and all . . ."

Ranjit climbs out of the cab and watches it drive away. As its tail-lights disappear, he knows that he is now completely alone. He thinks of Dev and Auntie sitting terrified in their house, and feels a burn of anger. No matter what happens in here tonight, Jay Patel is in for a surprise.

He takes a few steps toward the dark building, and stops when he hears a soft cough.

"Ranjit. Over here."

It is Jay Patel, leaning against one of the posts of the huge neon sign. Curling tubes of neon make up the letters PATEL MOTEL and an orange glow washes over Patel's bald head and tints his white clothes. He shuffles forward in his bazaar-trader's sloppy walk, his worn leather sandals slapping against the asphalt.

"Patel Sahib." Ranjit keeps his voice level. "You wanted to see me?"

"Come over here. Closer."

Patel grunts as he stoops to pat Ranjit down, his hands quick and efficient. "Where is the gun I gave you?"

"I didn't think I would need it. Why?"

Patel steps back and rubs his face with one thin hand. "Look, Ranjit. I can't hold him back any longer." He tilts his head toward the darkened building. "He sent his men to Leela's house. I'm sorry."

Ranjit knows then that Lateef is inside the building.

"You brought this on yourself." Patel's voice is weary. "Now you will have to pay. If it is any consolation, he has promised me he'll let the old lady and the kid go. And I'll make sure that Leela is looked after."

Patel has just handed him a death sentence. Ranjit feels the shock travel through him.

"*You'll* take care of Leela?" Ranjit stares coldly at the man. "The same way you took care of Shabana?"

"Now listen, that was—" Patel's mouth opens and closes, searching for the right words. "—unfortunate. I told Shabana to get out of the movies, but she insisted on investing all her money into Lateef's film. *Insisted,* against my best advice. But I tried to help her, I let her stay in my apartment, gave her a job at the club. She was a fine lady, a very fine lady."

"What an impressive speech. But you don't have to use the past tense." Patel looks uncomprehending. "Shabana is alive, you know. I found her a few hours ago, holed up at the Dakota with Mohan. *Ruksana* is the one who's dead. The evening you sent Ruksana over to talk to Shabana, they had an argument. Shabana pushed her, and she ended up hitting her head. You were wrong all this time, along with the cops."

"No, that is not possible. I saw Ruksana outside the police station, the day after the murder. She'd gone there to identify the body . . ."

"That was Shabana, pretending to be her sister."

"Hai Ram." Patel's eyes widen in shock. "So Shabana is alive? Really? You're telling me the truth?"

Traffic speeds by on the highway, punctuating the darkness with the red stutter of brake lights.

"Oh yes, she's very much alive. You don't need to worry about her, she's leaving town with Mohan. You'll never see her again. Before she left, she showed me her scars. Your friend Lateef, he beat her with his belt buckle. He also liked to put out cigarettes on her back. Oh, you certainly *helped* her. You helped her a lot—"

"Patel! Is he here?"

A tall figure appears in a darkened doorway, and Ranjit knows that it is Lateef. He also knows that the gun in Lateef's hand is pointed at his stomach.

"I am sorry, Ranjit." Patel's whisper is almost drowned out by the roar of the highway. "Better luck in your next reincarnation."

All three men stand in the darkened motel room, amongst the rugs and silk pillows and the brass floor lamps, which throw cones of light upward onto the walls. Ranjit is inside the room, and Lateef leans against the door, blocking the exit, a long-barreled gun in his fist, its grip wrapped in duct tape. Patel is to the side, leaning over a stereo system in a glass-fronted cabinet; he mutes the volume and the throb of *tablas* dies away, their beat held now by the pulsing blue lights of an old-fashioned amplifier.

"You know what I'm going to do with this *maderchod?*" Lateef's voice is heavy with pleasure, and he addresses no one in particular. His hair has been freshly cut and gelled, but there is a thickening underneath the fabric of his blue silk shirt: bandages, Ranjit guesses, covering the rat bites.

"I'm going to take him back to the garage, along with the whore, her mother, and the kid. I'll strip the kid, put peanut butter all over him. They can listen to the rats chew on him."

"Lateef, no." Patel's voice is weak. "You *promised* me."

"I did? Yes, you're right. This isn't Mumbai, this is New York. So tell you what—just a bullet in Ranjit's stomach, then. Should take him, what, six, eight hours to die? We can just shoot the others in the back of the head."

Lateef coughs, and it must hurt, because he doubles over slightly. He is sweating way too much—some kind of medication, probably—and the pockmarks on his forehead and chin glisten with moisture.

Ranjit keeps his voice calm and conversational. "You're a buffoon. A real dunderhead. Thick as a coconut."

"One shot in the groin, then." Lateef raises his gun. "Patel, turn on your stupid music. Loud."

"A smart person would have asked me what I found out. Like, for example, what's inside those boxes of hair."

"Bullshit. You know nothing." Lateef's pitted forehead creases into a frown.

"Of course I know what's inside them. Do you?"

"Talk, before I put a bullet in your crotch."

"You want me to talk?" Ranjit glances over at Patel, who is opening the glass doors of the stereo cabinet. "I'm happy to. Patel makes all that money by bringing in high-quality human hair, and he gets it for cheap."

"So you don't know anything—"

"Let me finish. We all know—" Ranjit glances at Patel again, who is frozen, his hand resting on a round dial. "—that the market for hair is going to top a billion dollars this year. Demand is growing, but supply, that's a problem. Eastern European hair, that's no good, it's colored, processed, too thin. Indian hair from temples was a great discovery, but they auction it now, and the prices are going up. So where can Patel get a steady, cheap supply of good hair? Not Europe, not India."

Ranjit repeats all the information he learned from Shabana. Lateef is listening, his mouth slightly open, while Patel's face is creased in misery.

"Patel figured out a new source. A country where there are prison camps full of women with thick heads of hair. A government that controls everything, that is willing to sell to him at a rock-bottom price."

"Stop making a fucking speech. Get to the point."

"Patel is buying hair directly from prison camps in southern China. He's having it shipped to his processing plants in Algeria, then sending it here disguised as Indian hair. All good, except that the Algerians are cheap. They reused the boxes, which have the Chinese trading agency stamp on them, a red house. So right now Patel is selling hair that is grown on the heads of prisoners, people who are being sheared like sheep. He's violating all the human rights agreements between China and the USA, he's essentially a smuggler."

There is a silence. Lateef smiles widely, nodding in satisfaction. "*China*. Patel, you sly dog. That's what you've been hiding from me, *hanh*? You think you're so clever. From now on, you work for me, understood, you old—"

Patel reaches into the stereo cabinet and twists the volume dial. The sound of *tablas* rumbles faster and faster, reaching a crescendo.

"You old fool. Turn it down and—"

Patel's hand comes up as a thunderclap of *tablas* fills the room.

Lateef staggers backward and raises his eyebrows in surprise. He drops his gun, touches the dark stain over his left pocket and starts to say something, but his legs buckle, and he falls slowly to his knees.

He keels forward, and his forehead touches the floor as though he is praying.

Ranjit smells the gunpowder before he sees the gun in Patel's hand, a small, lady's-handbag kind of gun that must have been stashed inside the stereo cabinet, useless at long range, but good enough from five feet away.

Ranjit crouches and touches Lateef's neck: there is still a pulse, but then the man lets out a shuddering breath, and the pulse stops.

The *tablas* are overlaid by a slow, plaintive *bhajan* invoking the Nataraj.

You, who drank the poison of the ocean, causing his throat to turn blue. Come, you who free us from troubles. You wear the world as your hair, you bear the Ganges, you are the ruler of the world . . .

"Is he dead?" Patel steps forward, raises his foot, and pushes Lateef over, and the man slumps onto his side, his eyes open. A foul stench fills the air: he must have emptied his bowels as he died.

Ranjit stands, staring at the neat hole in Lateef's chest. Hard to believe that such a small wound could have done this.

"Look at what you made me do." Patel's face is gray as he turns off the stereo. He lowers the gun, steps back and gulps for air. "Couldn't you keep your mouth shut, *Sardarji*? Look at this mess. The Don is going to go crazy when he finds out his nephew is dead. I will have to throw in my lot with the Hammer now, and he'll want a big chunk of my profits. Your little story has cost me millions."

Ranjit manages to find his voice. "So . . . Shabana was right. You're buying hair from the heads of Chinese political prisoners."

Jay Patel shakes his head in irritation. "Of course I'm dealing with the fucking Chinese." He gestures with his gun as he talks. "Where else could I get that quality of hair for such a low price? Look, Ranjit, I'm a businessman, okay? It's just demand and supply, I don't let politics get in the way. This kind of clean business is the future. Something that fools like him—" He gestures at Lateef's slumped body. "—refuse to understand. They're always thinking prostitution, drugs, extortion. No, no, no. The future is hair, illegal information storage, organs. Low risk, high profit. And when I have enough capital, I'll go legit. I'll invest in technology, like everyone else."

As Patel warms to his subject, he seems to forget the gun in his hand. "Look, this is the American way, you have to start somewhere. John D. Rockefeller and Standard Oil. Do you know that Rockefeller used criminal tactics to monopolize the oil business? Andrew Carnegie and his mines: he was building marble libraries all over the country while his miners were dying from drinking contaminated water."

Patel seems to remember the gun again. "And you, *Sardarji*. I thought you were a pragmatist. Now look at the stinking mess you created." He raises the pistol and points it at Ranjit's forehead. "I'm sorry about this. It's not personal. But I can't have you running around this town telling stories. You understand that, right?"

"Wait—"

"*Shush.* You're making it worse." Patel squints along the barrel of his gun.

Ranjit steps backward, but there is nowhere to go. "Wait. There is an envelope."

"Envelope? What envelope?"

"An envelope containing all the details of your operation. It's not with me or with Leela, I gave it to someone you don't know. If I'm not back in Manhattan in an hour, that envelope gets mailed to my friend, Senator Neals. You remember my old employer, right?"

"Why the hell would a senator care about the hair trade?"

"You don't watch television? He's on the Senate trade subcommittee. He just got back from China, he was examining labor conditions over there. He'd love to expose a multimillion-dollar illegal trade with the Chinese. You've got people inside the NYPD, but do you think you'll survive a federal investigation?"

Patel squints. "You're lying. There is no envelope."

Ranjit's back is to the wall. "You were right to be worried. Shabana figured out your computer password. She copied all your e-mails onto a flash drive. That drive is inside the envelope."

"Bullshit. She's not capable of such a thing. You say that she hacked into my computer. In that case, what's my password?"

She had mentioned the name of some movie. *Pyara? Aawara?* What the hell did she say?

"I thought you were bluffing. Better luck in your next reincarnation." Patel's finger tenses on the trigger.

"Pakeezah. The password was Pakeezah."

The gun in Patel's fist does not waver.

So this is how it ends. In this room, on the edge of a highway in New Jersey. Ranjit notices the elaborate patterns in the Persian rugs. Strange to think that in a few moments the rug will be there, but he won't.

"Okay." Patel abruptly lowers the gun. "Okay."

Ranjit slumps back against the wall, and the plaster feels cool through his soaked shirt.

"But you destroy that flash drive, *Sardarji*, and keep your mouth tightly shut. If I hear a peep out of you, the faintest rumor, I'll find you, and that whore of yours. I'm not a man of violence, but I will make an example of you." Patel looks disgustedly at Lateef's body and kicks at his expensive calfskin loafer. "And you know nothing about what happened here. I'll call Lateef's men and tell them to get out of Leela's house. With their boss gone, they'll knuckle under."

"One more thing." Ranjit clears his throat. "You promised me fifty thousand dollars. I want it now. And Leela doesn't work for you anymore."

"Fifty thousand dollars?" Patel laughs, throwing his head back. "Really, *Sardarji*, you astound me. You know that Leela makes a thousand on a good night? Fifty thousand, she'll spend it in six months. And then what? You think she'll stay with you when the money runs out?"

"You don't need to worry about all that. Just give me the money."

"Okay, okay. It is in the next room." Still chuckling, Patel pockets the gun and walks past him into the back room.

What the hell is he up to? Ranjit moves quickly, unplugs a heavy brass lamp, and flattens himself against the wall, the base of the lamp raised and ready to strike. Through the thin wall, he hears the latches of a suitcase being clicked open, then a rustling sound. When Patel emerges from the back room, he carries a white plastic bag.

"Going to hit me over the head with that thing?" Patel's face creases with amusement as he hands over the bag. "Don't worry, I'm a man of my word. It's all there."

Lowering the lamp, Ranjit looks in to the bag and sees the neatly banded stacks of hundred-dollar bills.

"I never would have pegged you for a romantic, *Sardarji*. I wish you the best of luck with Leela, but remember—"

Ranjit drops the lamp, steps over Lateef's stiff legs, and heads for the door.

"—remember, if it walks like a duck, if it quacks like a duck, chances are that it *is* a duck."

Leela had said exactly the same thing. Had she heard the expression from Patel? Ranjit walks out of the room, and slams the door behind him.

Will Patel come after him? His back tenses as he walks away.

There is the sudden screech of tires and he jumps back as Ali's cab barrels into the parking lot and slams to a stop. And following Ali are four, then six, then eight yellow cabs. They speed into the parking lot, their doors fly open, and the drivers emerge, armed with baseball bats and tire irons and sticks.

"*Sardarji!*"

"We heard a shot—"

"We'll thrash the son of a bitch who fired at you—"

Amongst the crowd of ragged, sweating men is Sridhar Murugap-pan's bespectacled face, and many other regulars from Karachi Kabob. They are clearly frightened, but their faces are determined, their eyes angry slits.

Ali rolls out of his cab and looks around wildly. "Ranjit, I called the guys, we were just about to go into the motel and get you—"

Ranjit feels a surge of love for these men, who would have risked their lives for him. "I'm fine, guys." He spreads out his arms to show that he is intact. "Thanks for coming here, but really, I'm fine."

"But . . ." Sridhar Murugappan bobs his head at the motel. ". . . there was definitely a shot. Should we call the police?"

"No. Trust me, it's okay. I'll explain later, guys. We need to get out of here."

Ranjit slides into Ali's cab and his friend takes off, driving like a madman toward the George Washington Bridge. The other cabs drive alongside and behind, boxing in the cab, protecting it.

Ranjit calls Leela, and she picks up on the first ring.

"It's done. You can head home now. Lateef's men will be gone by the time you arrive. I'll see you there."

"Are . . . you . . . sure?" She is hyperventilating so badly she can barely talk.

"Yes. I'll be there in a bit."

He leans back into his seat, and the shock of Lateef's death replays in his mind: in the split second before Lateef hit the floor, he had known that he was dying, and that knowledge had puzzled him. Men like Lateef never believe in their own mortality, not even at the very end: he had gone out as he lived, in a fog of confusion . . .

"Hey, are you okay? Ranjit?" Ali's bulldog face is bright red, and it looks as though he is about to have a heart attack.

Ranjit reaches over and gently pats his friend's shoulder. "You came back for me. Thank you."

Ali manages a smile, though his big face is pale and shiny with sweat. "No big deal. I parked on the shoulder and called the other guys. We were driving over when I heard the shot, I thought you were dead, for sure."

Ranjit looks at the dark waters of the Hudson below. "It wasn't fired at me."

"Then who? What the hell happened?"

"Forget about it. Forget everything about tonight."

"Okay." Ali rubs nervously at his cheek. "So you worked it out with Patel? What is in the bag?"

"Patel is off my back. And let's just say . . ." Ranjit smiles a thin smile. ". . . that we'll be able to get your mirror fixed, and I'll still be able to buy the guys some *biriyani*." Ali's forehead is still creased in worry. "And I need to ask you a last favor. Can you keep this money for me? In that safe deposit box where you keep the jewelry for your daughters' weddings?"

"Of course, of course. Now listen, Ranjit . . ." Ali steers deftly through traffic, heading for the Cross Bronx Parkway. Blinking their headlights, the other cabs head for other exits, and Ranjit raises a hand in salute.

Ali continues, "You should leave town. Get out, fast. I have a relative who runs a motel in El Centro, and—"

"Shanti's coming. And Leela is here, with her son and mother. Where am I going to go?"

"Leela." Ali sighs. "*Leela.* I told you, that girl is trouble . . ."

"Don't start now, Ali, not now. Please."

"Okay, okay."

It is no longer dark now, and the sky is beginning to turn rosy pink.

A dirty white garbage truck lumbers past, the taciturn garbagemen sitting in the front with cups of coffee in their hands, and Ranjit realizes that the garbage strike is over.

He takes in a deep breath: the terrible stench of the garbage is gone. The air coming off the East River smells pure, like nectar.

The sun has risen by the time they reach Leela's street. It is deserted, and there is no one about except for a few crows that fly cawing through the sky. Ranjit sits in the cab with Ali, watching, but there are no signs of life in the faded yellow house.

Asking Ali to wait, he walks around to the backyard and vaults the chain-link fence, which jangles slightly. The huge tree in the backyard is a dark outline, and Ranjit sees the large, battered heads of the sunflowers, laden now with dew.

He makes his way around the house, peering in through the windows, but it is too dark to see. The front door moves when he pushes it open with one foot and he enters the house, listening intently.

There is a low burbling coming from the kitchen, unrestrained and anguished. Something has gone very wrong, and he feels the hair on his arms stand up.

He moves like a wraith down the empty corridor and pauses by the kitchen door, steeling himself for the worst: Dev's lifeless body, Auntie slumped in a corner with a hole in her forehead, perhaps both. And Leela—why the hell did he tell her to come back here alone?

"Leela! Auntie! Are you okay?"

The crying continues, in fact grows louder.

He grits his teeth and walks into the dark kitchen.

The three of them are huddled in a corner: Leela is in the center, with one arm around Auntie's shoulders, the other clutching Dev tightly. All three are alive, crying steadily, snot and tears dribbling down their reddened, creased faces. Leela must hear him, but doesn't even look up.

"What the hell happened? Is anyone hurt?"

Leela shakes her head no. She reaches over and kisses the top of her mother's head, and then her son's.

"The men were here. Bad men." Dev spits out the words between sobs. His small chest heaves, and he doesn't bother to wipe the tears from his round cheeks.

Ranjit crouches in front of Dev and tries to pick him up, but he clings on to Leela.

"Leela," he says, "I want Leela," and she takes him into her lap.

Helpless, Ranjit squats on the floor in front of the three of them, his arms limp at his sides. The two women and the child cling desperately to each other, all barriers suddenly gone.

It feels like a long time before Leela allows herself to be helped up.

"Lateef's two men," she says, "they sat across from my mother, they told her all the things they would do to her, and Dev, he heard it all. When I got here, he was hysterical."

"It's over. I swear, I talked to Patel, and he said—"

"How can you believe him?" Her face is smudged with crying.

"He can come in here anytime and do anything to us. All that man does is lie."

"He paid me fifty thousand. Half of it is yours." Wordlessly, Ranjit puts the plastic bag onto the table.

Leela shakes the bricks of banknotes onto the kitchen table, then laughs helplessly. "Money? What good is money if we're all dead? This guarantees nothing."

Leaving the money in a pile, she takes Dev and Auntie into her bedroom.

As the sun rises into the sky, the three of them fall sleep, huddled together. Ranjit calls Ali, who is still waiting in the car, and tells him to go home. Then Ranjit crawls alone into the bed in Dev's room, looking up at the still mobile of the solar system, the planets above him trembling as he breathes out.

He tries to remember their correct order—is it Mercury, Venus, Earth, and then Mars?—and is still trying as he falls deeply asleep.

Chapter Thirty-Five

Two weeks later, the light has changed.

Sitting in Ali's taxi on the way to JFK Airport to pick up Shanti, Ranjit notices that the harsh glare is gone from the sky. The softer light of September burnishes the rows of brick houses, shines through the trees, and silvers the sagging electrical wires.

The cast is still on his arm, but Ranjit is back to driving a cab now, and he feels the change in his customers. The summer tourists are thinning out, and the Hamptons tans on the investment bankers are fading. As the days shorten and fall creeps in, the city will close into itself, and its inhabitants will return to their hidden, fevered pursuits.

"Hey, Ranjit." Ali's voice cuts into his reverie. Despite the cooler weather, Ali is sticking to his Hawaiian shirts: today he wears a blue one emblazoned with white flowers. "Looks like they got away. You think that they made it?"

By *they*, Ali means Mohan and Shabana. He reads the newspapers carefully and obsessively watches all the news programs. Each day when he meets Ranjit at Uptown Taxi, he says, *No news of them today*.

Ranjit thinks of the two lovers clinging to each other in the gloom of the attic. He hopes that they are finally at peace, wherever they are. "Yeah, I hope they made it."

Ali floors the accelerator and they fly down the Van Wyck. "What are you going to do now, Ranjit *bhai*? Keep driving a cab here?"

"What else am I going to do? I've put a deposit down on that apartment in Queens, Shanti will have her own bedroom."

"How are things going with Leela?" Ali's small eyes squint shrewdly. "You looked pretty upset when I picked you up. Have you two been arguing again?"

Ranjit is silent. He was heading out to the airport alone, but at the last moment he felt nervous and asked Ali to accompany him. Auntie and Dev waved as they drove off, but Leela stormed back into the house with a furious look on her face.

"Not really arguing." Ranjit is lying: they had been up half the night, going over the same thing again and again. "She doesn't understand why I want to live alone in the new apartment with Shanti. She thinks I'm leaving her, but all I need is some time to sort things out. How the hell can I take Shanti to stay in Leela's house? It's a mess. Dev cries all the time, and the old lady is clearly traumatized.

"Leela's terrified. She keeps talking about going back to Guyana with Auntie and Dev. That's crazy, right? What kind of a life will she have over there?"

"You know what I think?" Ali has grown a wispy gray beard, and he strokes it as he drives.

"I know you don't like her. You've made that pretty clear."

"No, this time I agree with Leela. You know too much about Patel's operation. That man is like a snake. He's hiding in his hole right now, but one day he will strike. The brakes on your cab will fail, or else you'll mysteriously fall down some stairs and break your neck."

Ranjit does not answer. He remembers the puzzled look on Lateef's face as he fell, dead before he hit the floor. Patel's face was impassive as he turned the gun on Ranjit. *I'm sorry about this,* Patel had said. *It's not personal.*

"I get your point, Ali. But where the hell do I go? Guyana?"

"That's where Leela's *from, yaar*. She feels safe there. Why don't you get that?" The taxi speeds up as Ali grows more agitated. "You need to get over this damsel-in-distress crap. Leela's tough, she'll survive. Just admit to yourself that it's over."

Ranjit stares at the weedy-looking gingko trees that line the side streets, their leaves beginning to yellow, as though the trees are exhausted and ready to shed their loads.

His voice is hoarse when he replies. "I have a thirteen-year-old girl now. Where the hell am I going to run?"

"You don't have to go to Guyana, but you have to go *somewhere*. I told you, I have this cousin in El Centro, she needs someone to run her motel, it would be perfect for you."

"Where the hell is El Centro?"

"Southern California, it's on the border, a farming town, lettuce, melons, stuff like that. It has a huge Sikh community, and a *gurdwara*. You would be safe there."

Ranjit remembers that last night in Ruksana's apartment, and the vow he made to change his life. He tries to imagine himself running a motel, surrounded by fields, visiting the *gurdwara* each day, praying and meditating and returning to a self he has lost in the madness of New York City.

"I'll think about it, okay? Hey, you think this is a good present for Shanti?" Ranjit gestures to the package in the backseat. Inside is an electric pink hoodie from a Japanese store that just opened on Fifth Avenue. Leela said that any thirteen-year-old girl would love it.

"Why are you so nervous? Shanti will be excited to see you. Girls are easy. Now boys, at that age, they're like dogs, sniffing around."

"Easy for you to say. You've got three daughters, you see them every day. I haven't seen her for so long . . ."

They enter JFK Airport and soon the international terminal comes into sight, its swooping metal roof shining in the afternoon light.

"We're half an hour early. Look at this fucking mess." Ali gestures at the cars clogging up the arrivals area, their inhabitants struggling with battered suitcases. "You go inside and get her, I'll circle. I'm not paying for goddamn parking. And remember—this is strange for Shanti, too. Take it easy."

Ranjit leans against a column by the arrivals area, sipping from a paper cup. He went to a fancy chain coffee shop and spent some of Patel's money on a cup of *chai*, but it still tastes watery.

Ahead of him automated doors open and close, letting out dribbles of Taiwanese who greet their relatives with tears and silent hugs. The flight from India should have just landed, but it will take Shanti time to clear immigration and customs. He imagines her as she used to be, her waist-long hair pulled back in a ponytail, wearing a sweatshirt and jeans. What is she thinking right now, as she stands in the long line, waiting to have her passport stamped?

The doors open and close soundlessly, and he catches glimpses of the baggage belts, and beyond that, the glassed-in booths of U.S. Immigration.

He looks around him, seeing no other Indians, just bored livery drivers in dark jackets holding up their cardboard signs. Maybe he should have made a sign, so that he doesn't miss her?

Just then a white-bearded Sikh man in a crushed pink turban pushes a laden trolley slowly out of the doors, his wife limping behind him. They have the heavy-lidded look of the deeply jet-lagged.

"Uncle," Ranjit says, using the honorific. "Is this the flight from India?"

"What?" The old Sikh stops abruptly, and one of his suitcases slides off the trolley. "No, no, we're coming from Dubai."

"Let me help you with that." Ranjit slips under the barrier and, one-handed, hauls the suitcase back onto the trolley. Seeing the panic on the old man's face, he smiles reassuringly. "Is someone meeting you here?"

"No. My daughter wanted to come, but she has to work. We're supposed to take a taxi to . . ." The old man consults a crumpled piece of paper. ". . . someplace called West-chest-er. Do you know it?"

Ranjit glances at the address: a long way from JFK, and the helpless old couple are just the kind of people who will get ripped off by a crooked cabbie. He looks at the digital clock on the wall; he probably has a few minutes before Shanti appears.

"Uncle, let me help you to a taxi, okay? Shall I push the cart for you?"

The old lady gives her husband a sharp look. "She said, don't trust anyone. She said, don't talk to strange people."

"Don't be stupid." The old Sikh gestures to Ranjit. "Can't you see that he's one of us?"

Ranjit escorts the couple out to the taxi stand, and finds them a Pakistani cabbie whom he knows. The cabbie swears to take the shortest route, and the old couple drives off, still looking terrified. *Oh well, at least they'll get to their daughter's house in one piece.*

Returning to his post by the pillar, Ranjit sees a flood of Indian passengers emerging, so many that the automatic door remains wide open. They stream past him, still clutching their passports, and he catches the smell of home, of polyester clothes and coconut hair oil. Craning his neck, he looks for a girl with long hair, but sees only more adults.

Damn it, what is taking Shanti so long? She has a green card supplied by Senator Neals, and should have cleared immigration with no problems.

The stream of Indians slows. The door remains closed for longer periods of time and he feels a sickness in his stomach. *Has she missed a connecting flight? Has something bad happened?*

He turns to look around, and the unmistakable olive-green of an Indian Army duffel bag catches his attention. It is lying on the floor, secured by the foot of a young woman almost his height. Her back is to him, and he stares at her skinny black jeans and tight black T-shirt, at her black hair cut as short as a boy's.

"Shanti?" He walks toward her as though he is in a dream. "Is that you? You cut your hair?"

"Papaji?" She turns, an iPod clutched in her hand, and yanks her

big headphones off. He sees her heart-shaped face and large brown eyes, so much like Preetam's, but the eyebrows are his, as is the strong curve of her mouth.

Her eyes widen when she sees his cast. "*Papaji*, what happened to your arm?"

All he can think about is the pink hoodie he's bought her. "It's going to be too small," he says. "You're so tall."

"What are you talking about?"

Then she is in his arms, hugging him hard, and he hugs back. He feels moisture on his face and thinks she is crying, then realizes that the tears are his.

"New York City, princess." Ali, who has a taste for the theatrical, has taken the Brooklyn-Queens Expressway, so that the skyline of the city appears on the horizon, shimmering in the afternoon light.

Shanti is in the front seat next to Ali, and she leans forward with excitement. "Wow, it's just like I imagined it. Are we going there?"

"Hey, Ranjit," Ali addresses the backseat. "We can't take your daughter straight to Jackson Heights, she'll think she never left India. What do you want to see, princess? Empire State Building? Statue of Liberty?"

Shanti screws up her nose and thinks. Ranjit can't get over how unfazed she is by the journey, how crisp and fresh she looks.

"I want to go to Central Park and eat a hot dog, like in the movies. Can we, *Papaji*?"

Ali smiles. "How about it, *Papaji*?"

She wants to go to Central Park. *That is fate.*

He manages a smile. "Sure. There is something I need to do there, anyway."

They park the cab by the Metropolitan Museum, and buy hot dogs from a vendor there, getting extra mustard and mayo. They walk into Central Park, find a shady bench, and Ali and Shanti chat away happily. *Well, Ali does have three daughters, he's had plenty of practice.*

Shanti proclaims that her hot dog is delicious, and after she's done, she leans her head against Ranjit's shoulder and smiles up at him. Her big headphones curl around her neck; apparently she leaves them there all day.

"I can't believe I'm finally back in America. I love it here."

"It's like a dream for me, too, *beti*. Now, I told you on the phone that my apartment is very small, but we're going to move soon, and—"

"I don't care, *Papaji*. I'm here, that's the important thing."

"You're not missing home? Your mother? Surely she will miss you?"

She shrugs. "Mama doesn't care. All she cares about is Mr. Big and his bullshit."

Two young men in tight T-shirts smile at Shanti as they stroll by, and Ranjit feels a sudden apprehension; she's just thirteen years old, but already a woman.

Shanti springs up. "Let's walk. I want to see the park. Look, it's huge. What do you need to do here?"

"See a friend."

"You have a friend *here*?"

"Princess, your father has all sorts of friends." Ali chuckles and his chins wobble with hilarity. "You wait and see."

"Ah, shut up, Ali."

The three of them walk slowly along the edge of the Sheep Meadow, and Ranjit keeps a lookout for the nannies, but does not see them. When they are close to the John Lennon memorial, he mumbles that he will be right back, and walks ahead.

Hector sits on his bench by the memorial, as though he hasn't moved all summer. His jean jacket is dirtier and crustier than before, and every inch of it is covered with brightly colored pins. He tosses his scraggly hair out of his eyes and his eyes crinkle as Ranjit walks toward him.

"Bad boy. I thought you were never coming back."

"Hello, Hector. Do you still have it?"

"Do I still have it?" Hector's head bobs back in exaggerated surprise. "Of course I still have it. I'm safer than a bank." Bending down, he rummages in a bulging backpack and produces a thick manila envelope. He waves airily at Ranjit. "No charge, this one is on Hector. I'm not even going to ask you what's in it."

"You wouldn't believe it, even if I told you. Thank you, Hector. And stay out of trouble, okay?"

Ranjit walks back to Shanti and Ali, who have appeared at the edge of the memorial, and are staring curiously at him. When he reaches them, Shanti peers at the manila envelope.

"What's that?"

"Oh, something that my friend was holding for me."

Ranjit tucks the envelope under his arm. It is dirtier now, but still sealed securely with packing tape, stamped and addressed to Senator Neals at his Washington, D.C., address. Inside is the piece of cardboard with the Chinese markings on it, the packet of hair he found in Ruksana's apartment with the same stamp, and the flash drive Shabana gave him. As instructed, Leela had added a note explaining the connection between Nataraj Imports and the prison camps in China. She had deposited it with Hector early that morning, two weeks ago. That envelope was Ranjit's only insurance when he walked into Patel's motel in New Jersey.

The packet is heavy in his hand. He thinks of the glossy black skein of hair inside, and of a Chinese woman halfway across the world, her head shaved clean. He remembers what Shabana had told him: that Patel bought the hair of young women prisoners, women who were given extra rations and allowed hair oil so that a healthy crop could be harvested from their heads.

If he destroys this packet, all the evidence against Patel will disappear. Ranjit can carry on living in New York, and hope that Patel keeps his word. The hair will continue to arrive in those cardboard boxes, Patel will get richer, and the women who supply the hair will be forgotten, and rot behind barbed wire.

Shanti walks ahead now, chattering with Ali, and they emerge out onto Central Park West. The Dakota looms ahead, and a new doorman in a blue suit stands in front of the copper sentry box.

Ranjit looks up at the hundreds of glittering windows but cannot make out which ones belong to Shabana's apartment. By now, it will have been professionally cleaned, all traces of Ruksana's death scrubbed away. In a few years, the murder will be just another faded scandal in the history of the building.

"Are you mailing that package? Want me to do it for you?" Shanti points to a squat blue mailbox at the curb.

Ranjit stares at the mailbox. *Yes, Ali is right.* Sooner or later, Patel will come after him, and now there is so much to lose.

"Hey." Shanti smiles quizzically at him. "Want me to mail that?"

"No, thanks, *beti*. I'll do it myself."

He walks over to the mailbox, pulls open the slot, and the envelope slides inside, the slot closing with a clang. *There is no turning back now.*

Seeing the look on Ranjit's face, Ali steps forward. "Ranjit, are you okay? You look pale. Arm hurting?"

He forces himself to smile. "No, no, I'm fine. Let's head home. Shanti must be tired after the long flight."

They walk back through the park, and Shanti chatters on, but he is not listening. Soon the packet will reach Senator Neals, and the feds will start their investigation. When Patel is indicted, he will know exactly who has ratted him out. There will be no place to hide in this city.

The three of them walk through the dying light of the evening. Shanti holds Ranjit's arm, and laughs excitedly as they walk through the Sheep Meadow. The vast green lawn is crowded with shirtless boys tossing Frisbees, which rise up and skim the sky.

Soon, all this will end. But nothing has happened yet. Right now Ranjit sees Shanti's flushed, excited face, the emerald green grass of Central Park, the tall buildings beyond shimmering with reflected light.

It has the look of something that once was, but now exists only in memory.

Acknowledgments

While a work of fiction, this novel is grounded in reality, and several sources proved invaluable. Anupama Chopra's *King of Bollywood* described links between the film world and the Mafia, and several scenes in this novel are based on real-life incidents in her book. Amy Braunschweiger's *Taxi Confidential* gave me insights into the surreal world of the New York cabdriver. Lisa Taddeo's 2010 article in *New York* magazine sparked my interest in the nightclub "bottle girl" culture. Two articles alerted me to the shady underside of the human hair trade: Britta Sandberg's 2008 investigative reporting in *Der Spiegel Online*, and Aina Hunter's 2006 piece in *The Village Voice*.

One of the pleasures of writing a book is that it sparks new friendships and deepens old ones. A big thank-you to all these folks:

In New York: Charlene Allen, who knew where my plot was going even when I didn't. Maija Makinen and Laura Chavez Silverman, whose literary insights always kept me on track. Katia Lief, for her support over many years. James Monroe at Monroe Partners, for a magnificent Web site, and for coming up with the title for this book. The super-smart Tara Sarath, for her hard work as a publicist. My agent,

Stephanie Abou, for her wise counsel. My editor, Hilary Teeman, for her unwavering guidance.

In D.C.: My writing group, who know when "It's not working yet": a huge thank-you to Angle Kim, Beth Thompson Stafford, Karla Araujo, and Nicole Idar, for reading my stuff while you were writing your own books.

I owe a particularly big debt to Stewart Moss and Sunil Freeman at the Bethesda Writer's Center, and my students there, who taught me a lot about writing: Vickie Fang, Gary Frank, Terri Huck, Eileen Iciek, Rollie Lal, John Lubetkin, Lynne McKelvey, Jeannine Mjoseth, Terry O'Connor, Joe Oppenheimer, Pasky Pascual, Sally Rainey, Tracy Warren, Farzana "Doc" Walcott.

My friends, who always asked, "How's the book going?": Tom, Nikki, and Luca Guglielmo; Reshma, Tim, Asha, and Naiya Gardner; Jayati and G. Datta, Amba Datta and Dan Fowler; a big *namaste* to Darshan-ji Krishna; Attiya Ahmad for visits to the zoo; Amy Reichert for wise council. Susan Coll and Gary Krist: let's keep the lunches going.

The Soho Coffee Shop sustained me in all weathers; thank you to Sami Antoine for many omelets and many conversations, and to Fran Levine and Helene Bloom for creating such a warm, accepting place. I'm particularly grateful to the Politics and Prose Bookstore, which provided refuge on many cold winter days.

In cyberspace: the talented Chaiti Sen for her incisive comments on endless drafts. Emily Russin for many conversations about writing and life.

My family: My father, Ameer, who read the first book and said, "Everything seems to be in order," and my mother, Naseem, whose fiery spirit never ages. My brother, Karim, and my sister, Naira, who kept tabs on me from cars, hotel rooms, and airports all over the world. Douglas and Carolyn Nash, who have been there every step of the way, and are the key part of team Nash/Ahmad. Let's head to Bennie's in Englewood when this is all over. My son, Amar, who, during the course of my writing these two books, has become a fine young man with a wicked sense of humor. And this one is for Jennifer Christine Nash, who has been with me, literally and figuratively, to the ends of the earth. Wherever she is, I am at home. From where to where, babes.